IMPOSSIBLE *dreams*

BY

MYKLE-KANE

ATLANTA, GEORGIA 2007

Table of Contents

CHAPTER 1

The Morning

The alarm clock chimed at 7 a.m. in the morning and the sound of Yolanda Adams' Open My Heart filled the room. Nikko lazily rolled over to the other side of the bed to turn off the alarm. As he agonizingly opened his eyes, he noticed his 3-year-old Golden retriever Sasha looking intently at him in his face and wagging her tail in anticipation of her morning walk. Nikko awkwardly gained his composure while mentally arranging all the day's events he must endure on this wonderful September morning. Nikko realized that he couldn't forget a single detail, as he pulled his favorite jogging clothing from the walk-in closet and put them on.

He understood that today's events must be organized to perfection. He printed the final details for his daily activities from his computer: the Alpha Kappa Alpha fashion show brunch at noon, the fundraiser drag show at 3 p. m., and at 7 p.m , an evening of pleasure to celebrate his six-year relationship with Lake Cameron; his lover, companion and friend. He smiled as he wondered where he would find the time and the energy to endure all of the day's activities. As Sasha pulled him downstairs, he smelled the mocha aroma of his favorite coffee. It alerted his senses as he took a detour to the kitchen instead of the front door, Nikko was surprised to see one red rose lying on the kitchen table alongside a poem handwritten on powder blue stationary in calligraphy; it was from Lake. Nikko reminisced about the first time he seen this 6'5" African god, Cameron Lake, with his dark complexion, chiseled long face, bald head, thick eyebrows, light colored brown eyes, and a smile that could melt the glacier from the movie Titanic. Lake possessed the body of an NBA power forward: tall and lean, yet massive and strong. Noticing Lake because of his height, Nikko assumed he was another gorgeous model from the fashion show with a typical model attitude: superficial with an attitude from Hell, a quality Nikko hated, especially since he had to deal with models on a constant basis. Whether he's producing a show, overseeing a magazine ad or commercial, he always assumed models were all the same, male or female; they were all bitches from hell on a never-ending quest to bring evil to every single being on Earth. Because of his profession, Nikko made a habit of never staring at a gorgeous face or body. Nikko thought if you've seen one gorgeous body you've seen them all: big tits, little tits, big dicks, little dicks. They all are self-righteous or self serving people who make lots of money. Lake approached Nikko. He noticed that this model was wearing a security uniform.

"What a strange get-up to be wearing to a fashion show," Nikko thought. "Why not wear Prada, Gucci or Fubu, but a security uniform? I've seen it all." Nikko smiled.

"Mr. Grey, I'm Cameron Lake from Rush Securities. We have the garments from Phipps Plaza. Where would you like them to be placed?" Cameron asked with authority but without the attitude. Nikko looked shocked but stayed calm.

"You can put the garments in dressing room 12A. I will have the dressers follow you and take account of all the pieces," he said. "Hey, Chris, could you follow Mr. Lake and have the dressers take account of all the garments that Phipps sent over?"

Nikko mumbled as Cameron walked away. "Damn, damn and more damn."

Nikko fell back into reality when the phone rang. He answered, "Hello!"

"What's popping'? Girl, you know we're getting ready to start this softball game and we do need your help," said Zarius, or Z, in which he is affectionately called, as he yelled in his most feminine voice.

"I know, but you guys know my schedule. I had to let something go today, especially with this show you guys coerced me into dressing up in a drag tonight dressing up to look like my twin sister. This is crazy, but I promised I'd do it," Nikko replied.

Z interrupted, "girl, you will be all right, and I don't know where that damn cousin of mine is, fucking waiter in the sky. He knows we need his cock strong ass to beat them damn cock sucking girls on the other team. I gotta get that boy a real job at the hospital!"

"Zarius, have you talked to Tré?" Nikko asked.

"He said his flight was landing at 7:05 a.m., and he would be here for the line up, punk-ass fucker. Girl I need a drink. I'm nervous as HELL. Girl, if we beat these fuckers you know we have the series in the bag, and it's off to motherfucking New York for the Gay World Series, where the dicks are bigger and the throats are deeper. Yes ma'am," Z screams.

Nikko asked Z what the starting line-up was.

"Girl I don't know. You know them bitches don't tell me anything," Z responded. "I know I'll play either left field or left-center. I'm the fastest and the prettiest, and I'm leading off since your ass ain't here." Nikko, realizing the time, said "Z, I have to go. Sasha is looking at me like I'm crazy. Call me on my cell after the first game. I'll be out of here by 8:45 a.m. The AKA show starts at noon and I have to have the final line-up, make up and hair, plus the fittings with all the models done."

"Okay girl," Z replied. Where's your fine husband, Atlanta's finest?"

"He's at work protecting the innocent," Nikko replied. "You know today's our anniversary and he has planned a wonderful evening for us with a catered dinner, and I don't know what else, but you probably already know. You don't miss a thing."

Z laughed. "Girl, I know! I own the gazette. I not only own the paper, I'm the head reporter. Call me the real Monica Pearson," he said.

Nikko grinned. "Bye man! Call me later," he told Z.

Z whispered, "okay, there's that late ass Tré and Ms. Fag Hag herself, Ms. Malia. Smooches."

Nikko realized he only had less than an hour to get dressed for three different events and he had no time to spare. He only had time to walk Sasha, take a long hot shower, and pull the last minute details for both shows. Nikko, realizing he hadn't read the poem from Lake, decided to tuck it into his sports jacket's inside pocket for safe keeping. He had to admit that he was a little nervous. Even though he had produced more than 100 fashion shows, this is the only one that would feature his supermodel sister and also launch her new perfume. His twin sister had spent years on this perfume. When Revlon offered her $5 million to endorse this new product, she became the only African-American female supermodel to have her own perfume. He got goose bumps just thinking about it; they would be launching one of the biggest market campaigns in less than 45 days! Being a freelance photographer with a marketing degree had finally paid off.

After packing the last minute garments for the fashion show, he was off to the races. As the garage door opened, he heard Sasha barking as he locked her in the downstairs bathroom. She hated that, but Lake would be home at noon to let her out.

It's a warm Sunday morning and as Nikko began the drive from their Stone Mountain home to the city, he decided to let the top down on his dream car, a white '93 Mazda RX-7 convertible. He had this car for almost thirteen years. He also had the new 2006 Lincoln Navigator SUV his sister had bought him. He had helped her in the early days in her career and now she was not only a super model but a established businesswoman.

He again started to replay mentally the overview of the fashion show, hoping Victoria had all the models ready to begin the final run down of the last two scenes. Nikko was also excited to see his famous sister and the fabulous gowns she would be wearing for her sorority's fashion show finale. He also hoped she didn't forget to bring the Gianni Versace nightgown for him to wear for the drag show.

CHAPTER 2

The Afternoon

As Nikko pulled up to the Grand Hyatt Hotel, he had a funny feeling that something wasn't quite right. As the bellhop assisted him with the programs and the printout of the format of the show, he realized his hunch was right on target. Once again, nothing was done. The models were all socializing, Victoria was no where in sight, the sound and light techs were doing their job. Of course the caterer was no where around, and the clothes were missing.

"I'LL BE DAMNED! WHAT THE HELL IS GOING ON? LOOKS LIKE A FUCKING ZOO!" Nikko thought. Nikko was always mild mannered with a reserved attitude, losing his temper only when events didn't go according to his plans. He started yelling at everyone within earshot. "Where is Victoria Rivers?" Nikko said.

One of the models shouted, "She went out the side door to smoke a cigarette!" Screaming at the top of his lungs, Nikko shouted, "ALL MODELS ON STAGE! WE HAVE TWO SCENES TO FINALIZE AND THE HAIR AND MAKE UP PEOPLE WILL BE HERE IN 30 MINUTES!" Everyone began stomping on stage, so Nikko felt it was time for the supermodel speech. After giving the speech, Victoria stepped in shamefully, but still the bitch from hell.

She tried apologizing. "Everything was so hectic I had to take a break," she said.

Nikko continued shouting "we'll talk about this later. Right now, I need you to call and find the garments and the caterer and, locate the hair and make-up people. They should've been here over an hour ago. All the names and numbers are in the information I gave you yesterday." Nikko had Katie, his administrative assistant, to run down the last two scenes with the models since she knew the show backwards and forwards. Now Nikko had exactly 15 minutes to sneak away and call the three loves in his life, including his twin sister, Nikki; his niece, Kennedy, and the other love of his life, Cameron Lake. First, he called Nikki on her cell because she should've been there to rehearse. She answered on the first ring.

"Good morning big brother," Nikki said. She often referred to him as "big brother" because he was three minutes older. "I'm running late. I had to wait for Tevona to come pick up Kennedy. She's taking her to the zoo this morning and shopping for you and Lake's anniversary present." She knew by saying this would make Nikko melt and not yell at her so badly. She always knew what to say to soften him up, just utter the name Kennedy and he would just turn into play dough.

"Okay, you're off the hook but hurry up. I'm pulling out my hair and I need my twin's touch to keep me calm and collected," Nikko said.

"What?" she exclaimed.

"Sorry that just slipped. Hurry up; I'll see you when you get here. Love you, Precious," Nikko radiated.

"Love you too, bro," Nikki replied.

Just as he was about to call Lake, his cell phone rang and he scrambled to retrieve it from his Coach duffel bag. He answered the cell phone as the person on the other end screamed. "Girl, what took you so long to answer the damn phone? Girl, we beat the shit out of them bitches 20 to 5 in the seventh and Tré's cock strong ass hit two motherfucking homers," Z said. "She needs some, BAD. I got three hits. That stupid-ass umpire called me out on one of them, because I guess I didn't slide. You know a genie in the bottle doesn't slide. I can't slide and have a miscarriage. You know I'm 10 months pregnant. I shouldn't be out here playing no damn ball anyway I should be in my Lamas class doing some heavy breathing and learning how to push this baby out my (pussy)."

"Please slow down," Nikko whispered. But Z kept talking.

"Girl, we are on our way to the Gay World Series, The Divas are going to Canada to rule, but I gotta go. You know the show starts at 3, bitch. Don't be late, and tell Precious I want to wear some of that new perfume y'all launching. I need to spray some between my legs. I ran out of (FDS???). Nikko, do not be late. You are the opening act, and remember, we're doing a duet to close the show, girl. So I need you to know the words. You know how you love to stumble across your words. Girl, we need to turn this shit out because the other teams are already jealous. Now I need to give them a reason why. Crazy Tré is doing Maxwell and DeAngelo. I'll give –you the lineup once you finish with your AKA shit. Girl, I told you and Precious y'all should've pledged Delta, but I won't hold that against y'all 'cause y'all still my sistas. Talk to you later girl. Don't be late, or I'll drug your (pussy) up with some Morphine. Love ya chuckles" And with that, Z hung up the phone.

Realizing he didn't have time to call Lake but noticed he had tucked the poem in his jacket pocket, he decided to read it instead:

Impossible Dreams

Dreams are imaginary feelings that come in the night
some good and some bad.
To wake up and feel my dream right next to me
is a sweet reality.
Baby, I don't know what I would do without you.
You are my yesterday, my present, and my future.
You lifted me up from life's miserable destruction.
I live for you and I breathe your air.
You blew life into my soul,
opened my heart and created my spirit.
This day notes our sixth year of existence.
With you I was born again.
You are the Spirit of my Existence.

I Love You, Lake

There were tears coming from Nikko's eyes as Katie was approaching him. He was in such a daze that he never even felt her when she knelt down in front of him as he sat slumped over one of the chairs in the corner of the hotel's ballroom.

"Mr. Grey, it'll be alright. The show will be a success, there's no need to cry," she whispered.

"I know Katie, I know," Nikko said, as he fell out of the trance, not realizing he was crying. Standing up and gaining his composure, he realized she had already finished the last two scenes, plus the finale. "Thanks," he said. "You are a blessing." She looked back in amazement as she walked away. Victoria was walking toward him and he could actually see a dark cloud hovering over her.

"Nikko, the make-up people are here and the caterer is setting up the food!" she yelled. Katie rushed back, yelling to Nikko.

"I found the garments and the props we'll be using. Rush Securities said they went to the downtown Hyatt instead of the Grand Hyatt," she said.

"Thanks, Katie," Nikko replied. Victoria gave Katie the evil eye; Nikko noticed this but didn't say a word. He was waiting to let Victoria have it in a professional manner.

Nicholette (Nikki) Grey, Nikko's twin sister strolled through the doors standing 5'10", with a size four frame, her long sandy brown wavy hair bouncing off her back. She wore a burnt orange backless linen vest with tie-up straps, matching Capri jeans and matching shoe boots with 5-inch heels. Everyone just stopped and stared: the caterer, the make up artists, the hair stylists, the dressers, the stage hands, and even Ms. Victoria Rivers. Nikki was simply elegant. Nikki was a definitely a diva and a fashion icon. She was Atlanta's very own country girl, now one of the world's top supermodels, coming back home to help her sorority sisters with their benefit fashion show. She was indeed a diva; her presence just demanded attention. As everyone gathered their composure, Nikki walked right up to her twin brother. "I'm sorry, big brother," Nikki said, as and gave Nikko that kiss on the forehead that was a so familiar greeting between the two siblings. Nikko gave her a smirk and then kissed her on her cheeks. That was his secret way of saying that all was forgiven.

"Now go get in the hair and make-up line. The show starts in an hour and a half, the door will be opening in a minute and I heard the people are already waiting at the door," he said. As Nikki walked away, he thought about how proud of her he was for not allowing her career or her millions to change her. She was still the sweet little girl who looked just like him and acted just like him; shy, articulate, educated and intelligent, she never compromised her ideas or wishes and wit. That's why so many people had grown to love her. Some may say she's a diva or a bitch, but to him she was just his sister.

The AKA fashion show was a huge success. It was standing room only, and at $50 a plate, which consisted only of fruit, crepes, and orange juice; it was a rip off , but for a good cause to benefit the homeless shelter, Childkind, children with AIDS and the Frank Ski Youth Foundation. The show raised more than $70,000, which was a remarkable achievement. They also surprised Nikki by honoring her with the Humanitarian Award, alongside Wanda Smith, Tara Thomas, Melissa Summer, Jamila Lockhart, Joyce Little, Monica Pearson, Brenda Woods, Karen Greer, and Lynn Russell, for achievements beyond normal expectations.

After the show, Katie instructed the dressers to finish packing all the dresses, gowns, suits and props. This was an opportune time for Nikko to speak with Ms. Rivers.

"Victoria, I need to speak to you for a moment please," he said. Nikko escorted her into a private room to discuss her behavior and how it would no longer be tolerated. "We were paid $7,500 to do this show, and if I hadn't come in when I did, the show could've been a total disaster," Nikko said. "I have to rest assured that I can count on you. I understand this show is a part time gig for both of us, but we still need to maintain a level of professionalism. You came highly recommended from my friend, Malia, but I don't think it'd be feasible for us to work together again.

"I'm giving you most of the money because I don't want any hard feelings between us or you and your boss, Ms. Mayerson. I wrote you a check for $3,000, $2,000 for Katie, and I just kept $2,500. I'll even write you a letter of recommendation if you want to do another show with someone else. I know BET is always looking for someone to host their private parties and there are always groups contacting me to do shows but I'm launching my sister's perfume line and really won't have time to pursue any of them. So I hope there are no hard feelings, and I look forward to seeing you at the kick off party for the perfume in two weeks." As Nikko walked away he could've sworn he heard her call him a "faggot bitch" under her breath.

Nikko was trying to pull Nikki away from her adoring fans and telling her, "We have to go; it's already 3:30 p.m. and the show will start at 5:00 p.m. sharp." She smiled, "I will have to do your make-up and hair."

"Yes, and don't put clown make-up on me like when we were small."

She laughed, "You know I had big plans for you, big brother." They both laughed as the valet bought their cars around. Nikki nudged Nikko.

"When are you going to drive that Lincoln Navigator Revlon bought you? I'm driving mine and you should be driving yours."

Nikko responded, "I know, but I wanted to feel the September sun on my face and capture my highlights," he replied.

"Boy you are so crazy. Shut up and follow me."

CHAPTER 3

Bring in the Drag

The club where the show would be held was in downtown Atlanta. It was less than a 10 minute drive, so Nikko decided to call his baby.

"What's up, my love?" The voice on the other end of the cell phone could make Nikko's nature rise at the drop of a dime. He had a northern accent, his voice smooth and soft, deep and sexy. He could have devoured anyone with his voice. He had done numerous voice-overs for local radio and television stations. His ancestors had to be African gods. Mix Denzel's alluring power to captivate an audience, Shemar Moore's washboard abs, Tyson Beckford's complexion, and Shannon Sharp's body, and you had Cameron Lake.

"Hi, my love. Happy anniversary. Did you get the rose and the poem?"

"Lake, please don't have me crying in the middle of traffic on this Sunday afternoon."

"Cry for what?" replied Lake.

"The poem; it was spiritually deep."

"Come on, baby. You're deep. You're my life, and I tell you that all the time."

"But to express it the way you did...I got goose bumps."

"Well, baby boy, that's only the beginning. Wait and see what I have planned for you. Just wait until you get home."

"Lake, don't be surprising me with any party!"

"I swear it's not, but tomorrow is your birthday and tonight is our anniversary. I want it to be special, so I have a surprise for you."

"What is it?"

"Baby, it's a surprise. How was the show? And how was my sister-in-law?" Lake asked, trying to change the subject.

"She was wonderful. You know she's a supermodel, so she had to give the audience what they wanted. Don't try to change the subject."

"What time is the show?" Lake asked, trying to change the subject again.

"Z, Malia and Tré are waiting for me, so I guess I'll do this thing."

"You know I'm coming to see you."

"Don't you dare!"?

"You know I'm patrolling the area, so I'm going to see my baby's debut. Stop tripping baby. You don't want me to see your performance?"

"No! I'm already embarrassed, and if I see you in the audience I will be so nervous that I may forget the words. You know I got sucked into this stupid thing, but it's all for a good cause, so I'll do it."

"By the way, did they win the game?"

"Yeah, and Z is going ballistic blowing up my cell phone every 10 minutes and talking about the show. He's driving me crazy, so I had to cut off my cell phone."

"Well, baby, your policeman has to go and make some money so he can buy that mansion his king deserves to live in."

"Stop!" "You know I'm content as long as we're together; nothing else matters."

"Love you baby. Break a leg."

"I love you, too, Lake."

"Don't forget to give my sister a kiss for me. Bye, baby boy"

"See you later Baby."

Nikko and Nikki pull up behind The Closet, a gay club located in the center of Midtown, which is known for its openly gay community. Nikko began to get nervous as he walks to the trunk to get his clothes. Sensing this, Nikki walks up behind him and wrapped her arms around him.

"Everything is going to be alright. Just go on stage and have fun," she encouraged. "Nikko just look at me if you begin to get nervous. I'll comfort you. Remember, this is the advice you always give me, so I'm giving it back to you. You have accomplished a lot in your life and now you're nervous over some little benefit show, come on big brother, you're a professional fashion photographer, you own your own marketing firm, and you're the best twin brother a twin sister could have. I love you. Never forget that. I'm just dying to see you in the silver Versace dress I have for you!"

Giving her a million dollar smile, he said "Precious, you always know what to say to get me through anything. I just love to produce the best. I'm not used to being in the forefront; I leave that up to you."

"Boy, be quiet. You've always been the wind beneath my wings, even after Momma and Daddy were murdered," she replied.

"Precious, I have you. That's the song I'm singing," Nikko muttered with tears in his eyes. "I know," Nikki replied with another radiant smile.

Zarius came storming through the door. "Girl, you better get your ass in there," he said. He was in full face and looked like a horrid version of Madame the puppet. He had a raggedy stocking cap on his head and a blonde wig in his hand.

"Hey Ms. Nikki. Girl, your sister has to open the show and we ain't got a lot of time to make her look as pretty as you and me. Did y'all bring the torch and jackhammer?" Z said. "'Cause lord knows I gotta work a miracle with this face of his. Girl, Nikki and I got all the looks and you must have been blessed with the brains, no pun intended Nikki. Come on now girl. We need to pray on your face. Nikki, could you please do your brother's face? Make him you. I may need to lay hands on you, Nikko, because, baby, we gon' need a miracle." Nikki and Nikko just looked at each other and followed Z through the side door.

Nikki cut Nikko's mustache and shaved his freshly grown 5 o'clock shadow. Nikki admired her brother. They looked exactly alike, even though they weren't identical. Their skin was a light cocoa color; they had the same chiseled face, with beautiful full eyebrows and light brown eyes accented by long eyelashes. They almost looked orange in the sunlight as they sparkled. Nikko was 6 feet even, 180lbs with a 29-inch waist and 44 inch chest. He was always a track and field athlete but could play any sport; you name it, he could play it. He had been offered track scholarships from some of the major black colleges in the southeast. People always thought he was a model after they noticed the resemblance between him and his sister, which was usually immediate. After five minutes of rouge, blush, eye shadow, lips, mascara, she presented her masterpiece to the cast for their final approval. They all stared in awe. The guys, who were in drag, said in unison, "I want to look like that." As Nikko opened his eyes, he couldn't believe it; now he looked more like Nikki than Nikki looked like herself, if that were possible. This is the same feeling he felt when he was younger; people could never tell them apart, until their mother started putting Nikki in dresses. It was a strange feeling.

"Okay, bitch. You better work! RuPaul eat your (motherfucking) heart out, there's a new diva in town and she's ready to take your crown!" Z yelled. Everyone just laughed.

"Okay queens, its show time. Here's the line-up you (bitches). Memorize it, because I'm not telling you again. Nikko, girl I need your name so they can announce you, Thomas can't say Nikko Grey is wearing Versace, so give me a girl name," Z said.

"Z, I don't have one," Nikko replied nervously.

"Ms. Thing, give me something before I give you one, and you don't want that. I'll give you Medusa, queen of Cypress Street."

Help me, somebody. Y'all know Z is crazy." Nikko gave a nervous laugh.

"How about Sasha Grey-son," yelled Nikki, as she was trying to wrap duct tape around Nikko's waist. "You have exactly 10 minutes to stuff that size nine and half in that 11-inch pump."

"You have my blessings," shouted Z, in his stockings, girdle, bra equipped with birdseed and a matching scarf to hide those broad shoulders. "We present, SASHA!"

"You look marvelous," yelled Craven, who played first base.

"Okay guys and GIRLS, we have a full house. Go and do your best. Ms. Grey, please go talk to your brother, he's asking for you." Nikki strolled into the men's bathroom across the hall, carrying her garment bag. Nikko was there putting his final touches on his makeup. "What's up?" Nikki asked.

"Nothing, I'm just ready to go out there and make a fool of myself. Here's my bracelet. I don't want to wear it out there. Give me a kiss and I'm outta here."

"Okay, baby," she said as she kissed her brother on the forehead. As Nikko hesitantly moved out the door, Nikki began to change her clothes, putting on her baggy jeans, big sweatshirt and a Brave's cap. She washed off her makeup and tucked her long, wavy hair under her cap. Now she looked more like Nikko. "What a switch," she thought. As she was snapping her brothers matching bracelet on her wrist, she remembered that she had given it to Victoria to hold. It had been snagging on her garment, so she'd asked her to hold it until the show was over and had forgotten to get it. "I must call Victoria as soon as I get home," she thought. Nikko had bought the bracelets for them when they were in college. She vowed to never take hers off, as it was one of the only pieces of jewelry she had always cherished; maybe because there were only two in the world made like it.

When the emcee introduced "Sasha", Nikko strolled on stage, the picture of a true diva, poised and graceful; simply gorgeous. He took the microphone, and before the music started he mentioned that he wanted to pay homage to Precious, Princess and also, his king. Nikko instructed the DJ not to play any music. He decided to play the piano that was rolled onto the stage at the last minute to sing Wind beneath My Wings. Everyone was waiting in anticipation, as no one besides Nikki had ever heard Nikko sing before, and she hadn't heard it in quite some time. Now she knew why he was so nervous. As he began to sing, his eyes were tightly closed. He was unbelievable. Nikko must have been practicing for months. His voice was a combination of Anita Baker and Faith Evans, and it was simply sensational. He brought the crowd to their feet. Everyone was up cheering and throwing money. They were not ready for this, not even Nikki as she sat in the back of the club and began to cry. She hadn't heard her brother sing since the death of their parents. He had vowed never to sing again after their parent's funeral. Tears started to roll down Nikko's face now because it brought back joyful memories of when he used to sing and play the piano for his mother. As he ended the last note, he said happy birthday to his sister and walked off stage. They begged for five minutes for an encore but Nikko just couldn't. He was full of tears. That song had struck his spirit so deep that he couldn't move. He ran upstairs, ready to take off that damn drag when Z caught up with him.

"What are you doing? We have a number together and don't make me ugly, Nikko," Z said as he held Nikko and let him finish crying on his shoulder. Z can be an angel sometimes; rare but true.

"I don't think I can go back out there, man," Nikko said.

"Yes you can, and you will, baby, because you have me to hold you up and to protect you. Just take a big breath, just breath, Nikko. It's all right; you needed that cry. Girl, you brought the spirit out of all those girls."

Nikko apologized, "I'm sorry, Zarius. I didn't mean to."

"Girl, shut up a wipe your eyes. We're last, so just rest. You have about 30 minutes to get yourself together. Do you want me to get Nikki up here to keep you from running out on me?" Z said.

"I'll be alright, but I know she will be up here in a minute. I feel her spirit," Nikko said. And sure enough, Nikki was walking up stairs.

"This (shit) is too spooky. Stop doing that around me. I'm going downstairs I hear my cousin doing his thing. That boy wants to be a stripper; big ass dick loves to swing in the wind. I'm outta here. Go change, Nikko. We have less than 30 minutes, so hurry your sweet ass," Z chuckled.

Nikko slowly started to take off the Versace gown that got him rave reviews and then pulls the two-piece, off the shoulder, hot pink leather Capri outfit out of the garment bag. Nikki broke the silence by saying, "You know Z is going to kick your butt if you wear that hot pink outfit. Where did you get it?"

"That's my little secret." Nikko replied.

Without another word, they started hugging each other, both realizing how much they miss their parents and how lonely they really were, even though they were celebrating their 34th birthday together. They both had accomplished so much since their parents were murdered while they both were in college. They never really had a chance to say good bye and Wind beneath My Wings was the song Nikko sang at the funeral. It was the only song he knew and felt. He thought it would be therapeutic to sing so he wouldn't end up filled with a sense of loss and despair.

After putting the finishing touches on his ensemble, he was ready and more beautiful than ever. He looked like his sister, who was looking like him. He was now ready to conquer anything, even Ms. Z. Z went on stage first, giving a monologue about how every woman is jealous of her and everybody wants her man.

"I'm tired of this (shit). The next (bitch) that comes my way, I'm going to cut the (bitch's pussy) out and use it as a choker." Then Nikko walked across the stage and tapped Z on the back and said, "May I speak to you for a moment?" They started with Brandy and Monica, Whitney Houston and Deborah Cox, Madonna and Britney Spears, and ended the song with Whitney Houston and CeCe Winans.

The show was a huge success. Z and the rest of the team were elated, knowing that they were going to New York, and that they raised more than $5,000 in less than two hours. Everyone was thrilled and couldn't stop congratulating Nikko for a job well done. Ready to jet out the side door, Nikko was home free, until Z and the rest of the team cornered him and were trying to entice him into going out in drag for a night on the town. He humbly declined because he had to go home to his king. "Well, we have a bet. We got $100 that you won't go to your car dressed in your little hot pink outfit." Nikko was ready to decline when he said, "What the heck? It's only to my car." Nikki was in the background laughing her head off; they were always getting her brother to try and do some crazy things. As they packed the rest of his accessories, Nikki suggested that Nikko come to her house first. She was trying to stall Nikko for at least an hour, knowing Lake was home trying to prepare the last minute details on the anniversary dinner for two. Nikko accepted. He was so ready to get home he had goose bumps.

Indulging in small talk, Nikko bumped into this guy that swore he was Nikki. So as not to embarrass himself by opening his mouth, he tried to motion the guy off, but the stranger persisted, saying that he knew him and demanded his autograph. Not taking no for an answer, the stranger started enforcing his demands, yelling that he was Nikki's biggest fan. Z and the rest of the team were watching from the upstairs window and started to shout obscenities at the man. "She's got a man, now leave her alone!" Nikki, not saying anything, tried to motion to Nikko to walk to the car. Finally, after a moment of stares, the stranger let Nikko go and ran across the street. Nikki grabbed Nikko's hand and walked with him to the parking lot. He looked at her and said, "Is this what you go through on a daily basis?" Nikki replied, "Welcome to stardom." She turned the cap backwards as she kissed him on the forehead. "You take my car, and I'll take yours. We don't have time to put up the top on you car. Follow me so we can get you out of that getup. You certainly can't go home looking like that. Cameron will have a fit." As he drove the 15 minutes to Nikki's house, Nikko found the need to pop in a Rachel Farrell CD, as it usually eased his mind and made his spirit soar.

As Nikki pulled up to her three story condo, she jumped out of the RX-7 like one of the new-school Charlie's Angels, while Nikko pulled into the garage, hoping no one could recognize him in his disguise. Nikki rushed to open the inside garage door, hoping the coast was clear, praying that Kennedy wasn't home or anywhere in sight. She ran up to the second story to find that Kennedy and Tevona, the baby sitter, were nowhere in sight. Sebastian, Nikki's cocker spaniel, greeted her as she opened Kennedy's bedroom door. Nikki whispered to Nikko that the coast was clear, as she laughed wildly. Sebastian, wagging his tail and barking enthusiastically, was waiting for someone, anyone, to take him for a walk. Nikki elected to take Sebastian out for a short walk while Nikko changed from his drag attire. Nikki didn't realize she was also still in drag with her sweatshirt, baggy jeans, and her cap turned around, and still looking like her brother. It had been a crazy day. She was ready to see her daughter and give her a big kiss. She could only imagine the birthday present Kennedy had made for her this year.

By the time she had reached home, the phone was ringing. Nikki yelled to her brother to let him know that she had it. It was Tevona, informing Nikki that she and Kennedy would be there in about an hour.

It was almost a quarter to nine, and she had done her job, detaining her brother long enough so Lake could prepare a wonderful night of true bliss for their anniversary. Nikko rushed from upstairs, without his make-up, lipstick, mascara, and foundation. He was Nikko again, and boy did he love that. Nikki said, "What a great transformation. Now it's my turn, and your little princess will be home in an hour, but you can't wait, Lake is waiting for you."

"I know you were detaining me. I'm not crazy," replied Nikko, "but I do want to see my princess."

"You can see her tomorrow. You know she wants to give you your birthday present in person. Now go." Nikki demanded.

"Okay I know when I'm not wanted," Nikko said.

"You're so crazy, I just need to get out of these clothes and take a quick shower before Kennedy gets home, I missed my baby and I need a hug."

"Okay, cool. Let me give you your birthday hug. You deserve it. It has been an eventful day," Nikko added.

"You're telling me," Nikki laughed.

"Happy birthday, Precious."

"Happy birthday, big brother. I love you."

"I love you more," Nikko grinned.

"Call me when you get home?" Nikki asked

"Try and stop me."

"Please take Sebastian with you, he hasn't seen his sister in a month, I know they will love to play for at least a day. I'll pick him up tomorrow when I come pick you up for lunch," Nikki suggested.

"No problem, sis. That will be great." Nikko replied. "Sasha may need some company tonight, if you catch my drift."

"Get out of here, you crazy boy. Don't forget to call me once you get home."

"And you don't forget to give Princess a kiss for me," he said as he pulled his favorite cap off this sister's head.

Nikki locked the front door behind Nikko and rushed upstairs to take a quick bath before her baby got home. As she turned on the water in the master bathroom, she noticed she still had on her brothers charm bracelet. This reminded her to call Victoria about her bracelet. She had never taken it off for any reason and felt empty without it. As Nikki reached for the phone, it rang. Nikko was calling her to let her know that he noticed that she left the garage door open.

"I should close it, but Kennedy should be here in a little while, so I'll leave it open for Tevona."

"Okay Precious," Nikko responded. "I'll call you once I get home. Love ya."

"Love ya, too," Nikki smiled.

Next, Nikko called his husband to let him know that he was on the way home. Anticipating Nikko's arrival, Lake answered the phone. "Hello, Sexy. Are you on your way?"

"Yes, my king. Can't wait to fall into your arms"

"Well, baby boy, I'm just here butt ass naked with a big, big red bow wrapped around my dick; or should I say your dick. Your anniversary present is here standing and waiting for your arrival. And don't forget, I have another big surprise for you once you get here." "Baby, I should be there in 20."

CHAPTER 4

The Unexpected

Upon hearing a sharp knock at the garage door, Nikki, still partially wet from her shower, quickly grabbed and threw on her favorite bathrobe. She had been anxiously awaiting the arrival of her daughter, Kennedy, but wasn't expecting her so soon. She rushed to the door and opened it, but it was not Kennedy or Tevona; it was the stranger that she and her brother, Nikko, had had an altercation with earlier that day. Startled to see the man standing there, she asked what he wanted. The intruder replied, "I want you and I want to know why you treated me so unfairly today?"

"Get out of here before I call the police," Nikki ordered. The man had already put his foot in the door to prevent Nikki from closing it.

"I watched your punk ass brother leave, so now we can spend some time together," the intruder retorted.

"Mister, I don't know you, so get off my property!" Nikki yelled as she tried to push her weight on the door while, at the same time, reaching for the kitchen phone. The assailant barged his way into her home, snatching the kitchen phone out of the wall before she was able to call for help. Nikki started to scream, "What do you want!" "I want you," the assailant said slyly, "I have always wanted you." "Please, mister; I'll give you anything you want. My little girl is upstairs, just please don't harm her… I will give you anything you want." Nikki was pleading now. She had to think fast, because she knew Tevona would be bringing her daughter home in a matter of minutes. Nikki backed up to the kitchen counter and grabbed a drinking glass. In an instant, blood began to pour from the man's face where Nikki had just smashed the glass against his head. She had hoped this would give her enough time to run to the front door, but the man dived and tackled her from behind just as she grabbed the front door knob. Nikki screamed to no avail as the brute flipped her over and punched her in the mouth, knocking out three of her teeth. With blood spilling from Nikki's mouth, he tore the bathrobe from her body and, with a single blow, thrust his fist up into her vagina. The pain she was experiencing led to an open-mouthed, silent scream; no words would come out.

"How do you like that? You belong to me, no one else…I've loved you, Nikki Grey, since the first time I seen you. And now you're going to love me," he whispered through clenched teeth. Seeing the floor covered with his blood, as well as hers, Nikki fainted from exhaustion and fear. She awoke minutes later from the excruciating pain that was being inflicted on and inside her body. The man was raping her uncontrollably. Nikki's life flashed before her eyes; from what was happening to her at that moment to thoughts of her daughter. Maybe, she thought to herself, if she just lay there without resisting, the man would spare Kennedy's life. Although she wanted nothing more than to beg for him to stop, no words came from her mouth. She fainted again. Subconsciously, she swore she heard the sound of a car in the distance speeding down the street. The stranger let out a beastlike groan, his body jerked, and then he lay limp on top of Nikki. In the next few seconds, it was as if he was another person. He snapped back into reality, and, realizing what he had just done, could not believe that he had just hurt the one woman whom he'd loved and lusted after for so long. He had secretly worshiped this woman from afar, to the point of obsession; finally, his obsession had consumed him. Gingerly lifting Nikki's motionless and bloody body from the floor, he proceeded to carry her upstairs to the master bedroom. He walked through Nikki's house and straight up to her bedroom without making a wrong turn, as if he had been there before. With every step he took, crimson drops of blood speckled the Berber carpet from the kitchen all the way to the foot of Nikki's lavish king-sized bed. Gently placing her body onto the bed, he pleadingly begged her to wake up so he could apologize for his actions. When she still didn't move or show any signs of life, he began to panic. He clumsily picked up the phone next to Nikki's bed and made one phone call.

A female voice answered, "Hello?"

After a moment of eerie silence, he uttered, "I think I killed her…."

A stunned voice quickly replied, "Killed who, Jamal?! What are you talking about??"

"We had a confrontation earlier and I followed her home, and then we had another argument, and it got out of hand."

"Jamal get out of there, now!"

"But I can't leave her like this! I have to call the police!"

"Police!" "Jamal get out of there, now! I will take care of everything. I promise."

CHAPTER 5

Happy Anniversary

Nikko pulled up to his two-story Tudor home, the place where he's lived for the last four years. As he unloaded the car, his phone rang, and a voice on the other end of the phone starts yapping, "Girl where are you and what are you doing, I just talked to your husband and he said you were not at home."

"Z, I just made it home, where are you?"

"Me and the girls decided to come to the Castle. You know its trade night on Sundays; every gay and bisexual is up in here trying to get their dance on from hip hop to reggae and house music, whatever your flavor is. Tired ass Tré had to get ready to fly out in the morning, and Ms. Malia said she has a early morning briefing, but I think that married man is coming into town tonight and she wanted to go douche that sour ass pussy out. She ain't fooling me; a diva knows these things. Well, girl, go and get your pussy sucked and fucked and call me tomorrow with all the details. I'm working second shift tomorrow, so come and get your birthday present from the hospital. I'll be in the ICU wing. Smooches."

That boy never let anyone get a word in edge wise, Nikko thought as he continued to unpack the car and let Sebastian out of the front seat.

Zarius strolled around the club waiting for someone to say how fabulous he was at the Host Bar, but no one ever did. They just stared in amazement. Some guys were now gathering at the other end of the bar, laughing and staring at Zarius. "What the fuck are you staring at?" yells Zarius

"You! You ugly ass bitch! Whatcha gonna do about it, fucking bitch?!" screamed one on the guys.

"You better go play with your mother's rank ass pussy and leave me alone before I cut your tongue out of your mouth and stick it up your ass for pleasure. Trust me; I'm not the fucking one." Before another word could be uttered, Zarius had pulled out his blade and was charging through the crowd. Everyone scattered except the loud mouth prankster who was going word for word. The bartender, witnessing of all this, had already summoned security. Zarius grabbed the boy's neck, trying to aim for the trachea.

"Hold it, Z. Drop that shit right now," demanded the security guard, "before I bust you in the back with this Billy Club."

Z hesitated for about a minute, looking at a tear roll down the face of his helpless and scared victim. Z let the boy up and said, "Next time, motherfucker, you won't be so damn lucky. Count your blessings for today." The music had now stopped and the owner, with the security guard, summoned Zarius outside.

"Ms. Z, why are you always starting trouble? Why can't you just let it go sometimes?"

Z didn't utter a sound. He just stared, and whispered," Are you going to call the cops? If not, I'm going home."

The owner just looked at him and said, "Z, go home and sleep it off. By the way, I heard you turned the shit out tonight. Sorry I missed it."

"Sorry you did too, with your sorry ass." Z rushed to his car knowing that he had about one hour to cruise the strip before he called it a night. He was horny as hell. He needed some dick. Whether he sucked, licked, or got fucked by it, he was determined to get at least two out of three. He wasn't going home until he was satisfied.

Nikko, along with Sebastian, opened the door to find nothing but candles lit, with the scent of vanilla filling the air and one dozen red roses at the foot of the stairs, with a note stuck inside. It read: "Your orders are to follow the rose petals upstairs and take off all your clothes. Your bath has be been drawn to your satisfaction." Floating in the tub had to be at least a hundred red rose petals, and there was a glass of champagne sitting by the tub. There was another note on the vanity.

"After soaking your body for 15 minutes, please dry and dress yourself in the clothing lying on the bed. Your next surprise awaits you downstairs."

Nikko jumped into the linen ensemble that was lying on the bed and rushed back downstairs through the living room to the outside patio, where he finds Lake in a matching outfit, accompanied by a multi-course meal and three hundred rose petals covering the outside swimming pool. There were tiki torches and soft music in the background. Nikko could only think that only his man could dream of such an enchanted evening filled with romantic ambiance.

CHAPTER 6

The Extra-Marital Affair

The phone rang as Somalia took the quiche out of the oven. She was trying to prepare a light meal for the man she loved. She looked at the caller ID and prayed that it was Drayton and not Z. She answred it on the third ring.

"What's up baby girl," the voice on the other end whispered.

" Hey baby. I thought you would be at the gate by now." Malia asked.

"No not quite, I just wanted to stop by the corner market to pick up a little package."

"Well hurry up. Your dinner's getting cold, and this cat is not going to be waiting for long."

"It's my cat and I'll take care of that little kitty as soon as I get there"

"Just hurry up, I'm missing your love," Malia sighed.

Malia sat back on the couch and waited for the married man to come and fulfill her every sexual desire. She realized she had, once again, fallen in love with a married man, and she knew she would do anything and everything to make him hers. She could have hit herself for loving every inch of his body. She has come to accept his ways; his giving heart and his compassion. Oh, chivalry was not dead, and the way he made love made her toes curl and her pussy wet just thinking about it. He always made sure her every need was taken care of. He would open doors for her, massage her back and suck her toes. He was never afraid of showing his emotions by telling her his deepest darkest secrets. They became the best of friends and lovers. Malia knew sleeping with a married lawyer had its perks. She never had to worry about being smothered or having to deal with someone who was intimidated by her six-figure salary, but the bullshit she had endured for the last six months had been unbearable. She had allowed him to leave his dirty underwear on the bedroom floor and she listened to his constant complaining about how he hated his wife and wanted a divorce. An occasional surprise with a bouquet of flowers, even one gesture of love would have been appreciated. "How could I fall in love with that tired ass motherfucker?" she thought. The phone rang, jarring her from her trance.

"Baby, let me in, I'm at the gate."

CHAPTER 7

The Loss

Tevona blew the car horn as she drove into the garage. She saw that the kitchen door was open, which seemed strange. She also thought it was odd that Sebastian was not running out to the car. Tevona instructed Kennedy to stay in the car as she cautiously walked toward the open kitchen door, calling Nikki's name. Before she could take another step, she noticed blood everywhere. She frantically ran back to the car. She called 911 on her cell as she backed out of the driveway. Kennedy, not understanding Tevona's actions, started screaming and crying for her mother.

Tevona began yelling into the phone as the operator begged her to stay calm. The operator was only able to understand the street address, but that was enough information for the operator to give the police and the ambulance. As Tevona tried to regain her composure, she called Nikko.

"Get over here quick!" screamed Tevona. "Something has happened at Nikki's house!" Before she could say another word, someone was knocking on the car window and her cell phone went dead. Nikko immediately called Nikki's house, but there was no answer. Lake saw the look on Nikko's face and knew something was dreadfully wrong. Without emotion, Nikko said, "We have to go!" and rushed back into the house. Lake was right behind him, begging to know what was going on. Nikko responded, "I'll tell you in the car." Moments later Nikko and Lake were locking the dogs in the house and jumping into the black Navigator.

Z circled the gay strip for the fifth time, flirting with all the male prostitutes and asking them how much their service would cost. Z was horny as hell, but he did not want to suck someone else's dick; he wanted to be fucked. Knowing that it would cost at least $100, he debated going through his little black book, but he finally decided that it would just be a headache. He said to himself, "Why the hell am I out here looking for dick? I'm Zarius Washington. I don't look for dick, dick looks for me." In the back of his head he heard a voice say, "But you are, Blanche. But you are." He replied loudly, "Shut up Bitch!"

Opening the door to the man of her dreams always made Somalia a little moist; with flowers and her favorite wine in hand, the man sure knew how to please. "Hey baby," Somalia purred, before accepting an intimate and passionate kiss that made her panties wet. She responded by saying, "Your dinner is getting cold; come on. Are you hungry?" Drayton stood 6'2", 190lbs and was strikingly handsome. Any woman or man would do a double take at his appearance. Wearing a blue starched shirt and blue jeans, he was a vision of sex. Drayton replied, "I'm hungry, but not for food. I have a taste for some dessert; possibly some peaches and cream." As he started towards Somalia, her nipples began pulsating. She couldn't contain herself as the man of her dreams was getting ready to eat her in her foyer and she didn't even give a damn. As she stood there in awe, he had already pulled her Vanity Fairs down and was tonguing her clit. She had managed to contain herself as he picked her up; all the while his tongue was still working and taking care of business. She wasn't even worried that her head may hit the chandelier. He carried her to the bedroom, set her on the bed and continued his probing. Lying on the bed, she began to orgasm, as he tasted deep inside her with his erect tongue. Malia grabbed the sheets, comforter, pillows and her favorite teddy bear. She was moaning and groaning with ecstasy as she rode each wave of her multiple orgasms. Tears started rolling down her face as she shuddered on the pulse and just lay there numb for about five minutes. Then she realized that Drayton had not once come up for air. He whispered to her, "Baby girl, are you all right?" As she came back to reality, "Drayton, what are you doing to me?"

Zarius has given up on his quest to find his Sunday night fuck. As he was cruising to the gas station after realizing his ES300 was low on gas, he never realized that a car was following him. "I can't believe I did not find anyone or anything to fuck me tonight. I guess I'll go home and watch Noah's Arc and The Wire. Thank the heavens for TiVo." As he started pumping his gas he noticed a green Mazda 626 pulled up right beside him on the same gas isle to start pumping gas, even though the entire gas pump was empty. A tall attractive thug got out of the car and began pumping gas, sneaking a peek at Z once in awhile. He stared right at Z and asked, "Why you are so damn mean and why do you have so much attitude?"

A shocked Zarius replied with that sharp tongue, "Who wants to know?" Z didn't realize that the man looked like the type of man who would cut, rob, and then burn a faggot in a heart beat. Knowing the butch attitude would not work, he just waited for a response and was ready to fight for this gay life. The thug replied, "Maybe you would be a little more subtle in nature if you had some good dick up in you."

"Bingo" thought Z. "Well, if you can find me some good dick, we can find out. I tried to find some tonight but I had no luck. Any referrals?"

The guy muttered, "You're looking at it. All the dick you can handle."

"Well, put your dick where my hole is or shut up. Lead the way," Z responded. "I may be horny, but I'm not a damn horny ass dizzy queen. I could get you to my house, have you fuck me real good, then you rob and kill my black ass."

The guy replied, "Well, shorty, I'm Jeremy Jamison, or JJ. Here's my drivers license," and, unzipping his pants, "here are my credentials," he said, pulling out a soft big and thick 7 inch dick with the prettiest red head Z had ever seen. His ass started to get moist, but he tried to keep his composure. "Okay, license first." Z snatched the license, grabbed his cell phone out of the car, and began dialing Nikko's number. After five rings, the answering machine came on and Z started leaving information on Nikko's cell phone: name, birth date and address. He asked JJ his phone number and also got the stranger's license plate number and gave a brief description of the guy. He ended the message by saying, "Nikko, this guy is getting ready to fuck my brains out. Call me once you get home, and if I don't call you back, have Lake run a check on the information in case I come up dead. "OK," Z said, turning to the stranger, "we took care of the small business. Now try and keep up; I'm a fast driver," yelled Z as he fastened his seat belt.

When Nikko finally got to Nikki's subdivision, there were police cars, ambulances, and news reporters everywhere. Not knowing what direction to go, Lake pulled over and headed to a recognizable policeman from his precinct. The policeman directed him to the chief of police and Nikko just started running to the house, feeling something was awfully wrong with his sister. Running past the security and policemen, Lake tried his best to keep up. Nikko was stopped by a group of policeman putting police tape around the house. Nikko is now screaming and yelling at everyone, asking what happened to his sister and niece. Lake finally caught up with him and grabbed his shoulder. "Lake!" Nikko screamed, "Why I can't go see what's wrong with Nikki?" As the tears started to roll down Nikko's face, Lake, trying to stay calm, informed Nikko that this was procedure and that he should wait there. "Let me get some clearance from the chief of police." Nikko refused to wait and ran inside the garage to the open kitchen door. He suddenly stopped in his tracks when he saw what seemed like buckets of blood on the kitchen floor and leading up to the stairs. Nikko lost it and dropped to his knees as a policeman, a forensic specialist and a detective grabbed him, forcing him to the floor and trying to put handcuffs on him until Lake managed to stop them. Nikko, not really knowing what was happening, was just crying on the floor and going into shock. He'd become powerless and numb to the puddles of blood he'd just seen on his sister's kitchen floor. Lake picked him up and led Nikko back outside. Lake tried to explain what happened. "Baby, there's been an accident. Nikki has been attacked and raped. She lost a lot of blood and the police and detectives have to do their job, by trying not to contaminate the crime scene."

"Lake, where is she?" sobbed Nikko.

"She's still upstairs, unconscious."

"What about Kennedy? Where is she?" "

"She's in one of the officer's cars," Lake murmured. "And Tevona was hysterical, so they had to sedate her," he added. "Nikko, pull yourself together. I need you, Nikko, and Precious needs you, too."

"Okay, Lake what's next? What do you want me to do?"

"Nikko, pull yourself together," Lake ordered again. "Take a deep breath, before you start hyperventilating." Lake gave Nikko a hug and whispered, "Everything is going to be alright, I promise. We'll get through this."

Officer Grant approached Nikko and Lake; he needed to ask Nikko some questions. Nikko agreed as they went to one of the squad cars. Nikko said, "I will answer all your questions, but I need to find my niece first." Officer Grant agreed. He began talking on this walkie-talkie to try to locate Kennedy. She was not in a squad car; one of the neighbors had taken her down the street and given her some ice cream and cake. When Nikko arrived, he was stunned by Kennedy's reaction.

"Uncle Nikko!" she screamed, "Something happened to our house and somebody tried to hurt mommy! Ms. Wierkoski says mommy is going to be alright but they didn't even let me see her!" Nikko tried to avoid eye contact with his Precious, with tears in his eyes. He replied, "Well, mommy has to go the doctor, so I'm taking you and Sasha and Sebastian back to my house and mommy may come get you in the morning. How does that sound? I'll make it even better; you don't have to go to school tomorrow. You, Uncle Lake, and me can stay home and watch videos and read Harry Potter. How does that sound?"

"That sounds good," Kennedy agreed. Nikko asked Ms. Wierkoski to please keep Kennedy for a second while he answered questions outside. Ms. Wierkoski agreed. Nikko ran back down the street as the tears started to roll down his face. Apologizing to Officer Grant, he said, "I'm ready, officer. What do you need to know?" Nikko tried to ignore all the lights, policeman, news reporters and neighbors in the upscale neighborhood. Officer Grant asked if there was anywhere else they could go that was a little less distracting, Nikko offered the Navigator, as it was quiet and roomy. After a series of never ending interrogation, Officer Grant apologized for the lengthy questions but explained that it was routine due to the fact Nikko was the last person Nikki called.

"However," said Officer Grant, "there was another number on the redial that went to the Hyatt hotel, and that call was right after yours. Mr. Grey, would you happen to know who your sister would be calling in that hotel?"

Nikko replied, "We had a fashion show there earlier this evening, but I don't know why she would be calling back to the hotel, unless she left something there, but we didn't spend the night there like the other models and the dressers."

"Mr. Grey, if you happen to think of anything that could be useful, please give us a call." Nikko responded, "That will be fine; my roommate is on the force so I will definitely inform you or him."

"Oh you mean Detective Lake?"

"No, I mean Officer Lake."

"Well, he probably didn't tell you he was promoted on Friday, and he will most likely be handling your sister's case. Once again, Mr. Grey thanks for your cooperation."

Z made it to College Park in no time flat. The 20-minute drive only took him 12 minutes, with JJ close on his tail. He entered the security gate, leaving his access card in the slot so JJ could follow right behind him. As he pulled up to the driveway in his apartment complex, he hoped he hadn't left any faggot shit lying around the damn apartment. He knew he had all his drag shit in the trunk and he refused to get it. He would wait until tomorrow or next year, but he didn't dare bring that shit in now. Z was fumbling for his keys as JJ walked up behind and grabbed him by the waist. He asked Z if he needed any help with putting the key in the hole. "No," replied Z. "I got this end and in a while I will have you and I still will not need any help. I want you to just lie down and let me and your 11 inches have a conversation. Would you like anything to drink?" asked Z, as he rushed into the living room to light some candles.

"Yeah, man. Whatcha got?" Z rushed to the bar and thought, "I need to work on his grammar."

"I have wine, gin, rum, a little cognac and beer in the fridge."

"I'll take a beer; don't like the hard stuff. Beer makes me perform better."

"Oh you need stimulation to get your John up?" chuckled Z.

"No, I need a depressant to keep that motherfucka down. I stay hard. He's always begging to get inside something hot and juicy." Z, being quick with the tongue replied, "I have some frozen burritos in the fridge, and I can always microwave them and stick him in one."

JJ replied, "Man, you got jokes," and before Z could respond, JJ had laid a hard, thug-like kiss on him, putting his tongue straight down Z's throat. In the midst of all this, JJ had already taken off his Timbs and Girbaud jeans, leaving him with nothing on but his wife-beater T-shirt and a fitted baseball cap on his bald head. His Johnson had already started swelling from a soft 7-inch to a pulsating eleven-inch muscle veined dick. Z almost fainted once the love vessel reached its full capacity. Z fell back on the couch and thought about Heaven. He quickly responded, "Follow me. I have just the thing for that swelling. I can get it down in no time." JJ followed Z upstairs to the bedroom with his dick in one hand and his beer in the other. Z lit some scented candles, turned on the Bose stereo with his favorite love making music, R. Kelly, Missy Elliot and Luther Campbell. He commanded JJ, "Get comfortable and I'll be right back. I need to take a shower; give me a sec." He shouted. Z started running the shower and did the douche test. Everything came out crystal clear, but he did it again, just for reassurance. He jumped in the shower, rubbed some peach gel between his legs and armpits, and he was out of the bathroom in five minutes flat. "Marion Jones has nothing on me," he thought as he opened the bathroom door, only to find JJ fast a sleep with dick still in hand. Z thought, "I guess the swelling went down by itself, but I can't go out that easily. I need that Johnson to stand at attention. I have just the thing." Z turned off the ringer on the cell phone and pager. He was in for a bumpy ride and did not need to be disturbed as he began sucking Johnson's head ever so gently, bringing him back to life.

CHAPTER 8

Reality Check

It was already 2:15 a.m. and Nikki was still in surgery. The doctors hadn't come out to tell Nikko and Lake anything. Lake tried to call Zarius, Somalia, and some other friends of Nikko's, but no one was home or answering their phones. Lake desperately needed to get in contact with Zarius because this was his hospital and he could pull some strings to find out the status of Nikki. The news reporters and police were now swarming Brady Memorial Hospital, asking questions to anyone wearing a white uniform. Nikko was now shaking and was a total wreck, not really saying anything to anyone. Lake tried to start a conversation many times but the most he could get was just an unintelligible mutter or two, not really making any sense. The doctors finally came out around 3:05am to inform Nikko and Lake the status of Nikki, "Your sister has lost a lot of blood. She has been raped and severely beaten. It seems as though she put up a fight with her attacker. She has skin under her nails and we have discovered semen inside of her as well. Also, Ms. Grey has a very rare blood type; unfortunately we don't have that type available or anything else that could be used, mainly because of the crisis that erupted in Florida a week ago, as most of our supply was shipped down there."

Before he could say another word, Nikko responded, "Nikki and I have the same blood type, so I could be a donor. Doctor, do whatever you have to do to save my sister's life. When can we get started?"

Dr. Yoncey replied, "The sooner the better. We can get started right away." The doctor escorted Nikko down the hall to start the procedure while Lake stood there. He took this opportunity to call the precinct to see if the forensic department found anything else pertaining to the rape and robbery. "This is Detective Cameron Lake. I need to speak to Lt. Allen; I need to get an update on the Nikki Grey incident that happened around 9:00 tonight."

"Hold on," ordered the dispatcher. After a long pause, a voice shouted, "This is Lt. Allen."

"Good morning, sir. This is newly appointed Detective Lake. Sir, I was trying to get updated information about what's going on with the Nikki Grey case."

"Detective Lake, I don't know all the details at this time, but it seems that you and your team will be handling this case. Sorry to say you just got promoted to detective and this will be your first case, but I'm quite sure your department will find out who did this. What time would you be reporting in for duty?"

"Sir, there's a problem," replied Lake. "I'm the roommate of Nikki Grey's twin brother. His family is like my own and Nikki's like a sister to me, so I don't think I'd be a good candidate for this job."

The lieutenant interrupted, "You're not in a beauty contest or running for office. You're trying to find the motherfucker who did this to one of Atlanta's own; that's your job and I repeat, what time are you reporting for duty?"

"Sir I'm at the hospital now and I've been here all night."

"AND?" shouted Lt. Allen.

"Sir, I will be there at 9:00 sharp." All Lake could hear was a dial tone on the other end. How was he going to be there so early? It was going on 5:00 when the doctor came to start the blood transfusion. Dr. Yoncey had a puzzled look on his face as he summoned Nikko to follow him into a private room. Accompanied by Lake, Nikko asked Dr. Yoncey if everything was alright with Nikki. The doctor replied, "She is still in critical condition but we have another problem, Mr. Grey." Nikko dropped his head, "What's wrong with Nikki? Don't we need to start the transfusion as soon as possible?"

"That's where the problem lays, Mr. Grey. We can not use your blood."

Nikko looked puzzled as he asked, "Why?"

"Unfortunately, your blood is contaminated."

"What do you mean contaminated? Tell me doctor what the hell do you mean?" shouted Nikko at the doctor.

"Mr. Grey, are you aware that you are HIV positive?"

"WHAT?" screamed Nikko and Lake at the same time.

"Well Mr. Grey we can run another blood test but this is what the results have indicated." Nikko fainted; it seemed as if his whole world collapsed at once. He could only hear Nikki singing, don't cry for me, and don't shed a tear. It was 5:45 when Nikko regained consciousness, thinking that he just had the worst nightmare in his life, knowing that once he wakes up everything will be just fine, but it wasn't a nightmare; it was reality. Lake was sitting in a chair right beside Nikko's bed. Realizing he was still in the hospital, Nikko began to cry, and Lake started pleading with Nikko to stop crying and try to reassure him that everything is going to be alright.

Nikko asked, "How could it?" Why me? Lake, our life was so perfect less then twenty-four hours ago. Lake, tell me… how could this be?"

"Baby, I have no explanation, but God will see us through. We can't allow our spirits to be broken. Nikki and Kennedy need us more than ever." Nikko stopped crying and hugged and kissed his mate.

"What would I do without you? I need you in my life so much. Lake, how could I have contracted THE virus? We get tested every six months."

"Baby, let's not talk about that right now we have to concentrate on Nikki and Kennedy," replied Lake.

Nikko looked straight into Lake's piercing black eyes. "I have never, nor will I ever cheat on you, but if anything should ever happen to me or Nikki, I want you to take care of my Kennedy. I need for you to promise me that Lake."

"I promise baby," sobbed Lake.

CHAPTER 9

Another Day and Another Dollar

The alarm sounded at 5:45 a.m. Tré popped out of bed routinely as if he was a mother-to-be. He had to be on duty in at 7:15 a.m. and he wasn't feeling a turnaround flight to New York, back to Atlanta, then a round trip to Houston, then a trip back to(fucking)New York. It was all in a days work, but he knew if he worked hard enough and long enough he would be successful with the number one airline in the country. He rushed into the bathroom to take a two minute shower; he wondered how an ex-drug dealer could have become a flight attendant. Tré loved the fact that he was able to travel and see the world. He switched the bathroom light on and the radio automatically came on. He thought listening to some music would change his mood a little. Jay Z's Hard Knock Life came on. It was Trés theme song; he hadn't made millions, but he was trying. There was a breaking story on the radio immediately following the weather report. The DJ came on to announce that Nikki Grey's house had been broken into and she had been brutally raped and that her condition at the time was critical. Tré's mouth fell open. He called Nikko's house but he didn't get an answer. He then called his cousin, Zarius' house, cell phone, and pager, but got no answer. Then he called Somalia. "Hello," she agonizingly answered.

"Malia, cut on your radio. Nikki's been raped. I can't find Nikko or Zarius!"

"Slow down, Tré. Take it easy." yelled Malia. "Have you tried calling Lake at the precinct or on his cell phone?"

"No I haven't," Tré screamed.

"Hold on, let me try to reach him on his cell." Lake picked up on the first ring. "Lake!" Somalia screamed.

"Yes, Malia?"

"Hold on. I have Tré on the other line."

Lake began explaining the entire nightmare. When he finally finished, everyone had tears in their eyes.

"What can we do?" asked Malia.

"Just pray. That's all we can do right now; pray for us, and hope everything work out for the better," Lake solemnly replied. Tré had completely forgotten that he was getting ready for work and that he was about to be late. "Lake, I have a flight to catch, but keep me posted. I'll be back sometime tonight. Don't leave me out. I'll continue to call and get updates. Yo, Lake, give Nikko and Precious kisses for me. Malia, keep a brotha posted now, don't forget. I'm out." Rushing to duty-in was going to be hell, thought Tré knowing his day was going to be fucked up even before it started. He was out of the little West End apartment in 20 minutes, hoping traffic would not be heavy so a brotha would not get written up for being late to work.

Malia said, "Lake, I know that there's something I can do. You know my prayers are with you guys. Do I need to call someone or check on Sasha?"

"No, that will be alright for now," responded Lake. "I'm going to stay here. You know this was supposed to be my first day at work as a detective, and Lt. Allen has already put me on this case, even though I told her I didn't think it would be a good idea. I need to call my supervisor and beg for today off or even a leave of absence. The road ahead is going to be a shaky one, and my Nikko needs me more than ever." Lake paused and then said, "Malia, there's something that I omitted to tell you guys; please keep this a secret. Nikko can't do a blood transfusion because the doctors found out that he's HIV positive, and that's something else we have to take into consideration."

Malia replied, "You are lying, Lake. How is he taking it? I feel so sorry for him. If there is anything I can do, don't hesitate to let me know."

"I know, Malia, I know. Well, I need to go and call off from work and check on my baby," said Lake.

"Remember I love you guys, and give Nikko a kiss for me…let me know if anything changes. Have you talked to Z?" asked Malia.

"No, not yet. I tried to reach him, but he's not responding," replied Lake.

"I will try to locate the buzzard. Call me if anything changes, please. I'm going to keep my cell phone on. I have one briefing this morning, but after that I'm free. I can reschedule if you want, just let me know." Malia continued.

"Will do," replied Lake.

Malia had totally forgotten that Drayton was right there still fast asleep; she immediately got on her knees and prayed to God.

"My dear Lord and Savior, I come to surrender my soul and ask forgiveness for my sins. I pray to you that my day will be filled with your holy spirit, and lead me to the right path. Today, Lord, I'm asking for the full strength of your holy power. Give me strength to endure and the wisdom that I so desperately need to wash the feelings for this married man from my soul. My flesh is weak for his flesh, but I know you are not done with me yet. This is the struggle that I must get through in order to appreciate your presence. My Lord and Savior I'm asking for a special blessing for my friends are in need of prayer and your blessing; I bestow your ultimate healing on them. That when they come through this nightmare they will realize that your will must be done and tomorrow all the pain they are feeling will just be a state of being and their pain will be no more. In this I pray, Amen"

CHAPTER 10

Why? Why? Why?

Somalia immediately got up and rushed into the bathroom and started running her bath water. As she knelt down to sprinkle her favorite bath beads into the hot steamy water, tears began to fall from her face into the water. She became so emotional she could not contain herself, her stomach began to turn in knots, she could not control her tears, and didn't know whether she was crying because of Drayton, Nikki, Nikko, Lake, Kennedy, or even herself. She knew she just needed to be cleansed inside and out. Somalia had suffered so many obstacles in her life when it came to men. She was a successful black woman who earned more than $300,000 a year, but she couldn't find a man of her own. "Where is my life going? What is it coming to? When will I find someone for me and how in the hell do I always get myself into this stupid shit? Good dick comes a dime a dozen, so why in the fuck do I have to find one that is always attached to another (pussy?)" she thought.

A voice came from the bedroom, "Baby, are you alright? Why didn't you wake me? I'm going to be late for my morning meeting. Do you want some breakfast, or do you want to come back to bed and let me eat my breakfast?" yelled Drayton. Malia didn't open her mouth; she just eased into her bath, her temporary sanctuary, a refreshing body of water that would cover her soul, spirit and cleanse her tears. Drayton yelled again, "Malia, are you all right?"

This time she mustered up enough energy to respond. "I'm all right baby, just taking advantage of my bath!"

"I'm going to take a quick shower in the hall bathroom and fix up a big breakfast. I have a feeling it is going to be a blessed Monday!" shouted Drayton. The tears started rolling down Malia's face once again.

Tré rushed out of the house, headphones and travel bags in hand, asking himself if he should go to work or go to the hospital and be there for Nikko, his first and only roommate. Nikko and Tré had known each other for more than 10 years. Nikko was probably the only person Tré could and would ever talk to. Hesitating to get in the car, he decided to go to work; Nikko would have wanted it that way. "I have to be strong for my (nigga)," he thought as he exited onto the freeway heading to the airport. "I can't believe some fucked up motherfucka raped Nikki. That is some fucked up shit. If I knew who that motherfucka was I would cut his fucking dick off and stuff it in his damn mouth." Tré made it to the parking lot in 10 minutes flat, leaving about 15 minutes before he had to duty-in. Before getting out of the car he started to pray: "My Heavenly Father, I come to you in prayer. I pray for forgiveness for my sins. God, your son needs a favor. My friends need a miracle or a blessing. They have gone through a lot in one day."

Tré be-bopped out of the car, hoping no one had seen him. He felt better; he felt God heard his prayers and everything was going to be all right. It was going to be a great day despite all the drama that had happened. Strolling into the employee lounge, he noticed most of the flight attendants were gathering around the TV and some were reading the morning paper. Plastered across the top of the paper was Nikki's face. The headline read "Supermodel Raped in Buckhead." The words sent chills down his body and his eyes began to fill with tears. Before anyone noticed, he dashed into the restroom, trying to regain his composure. He said to himself, "I'm a fucking man. I got to be strong for my friends. I know these motherfuckas are going to ask me some stupid-ass shit about Nikki or Nikko. I'm going to bust a punk-ass faggot in his mouth if he asks me some crazy shit." When he heard his flight number called he wiped his eyes and flew out of the lounge, trying to do a checklist before anyone can ask him a question. Once Tré managed to sneak on the plane without being noticed, he finally felt safe. He couldn't wait for his day to start so that it could end. "This is going to be a fucked up day; I can feel it," he thought to himself as he began to stock the carts with the pre-packaged breakfasts for his morning passengers.

Zarius finally woke up around 8:00 a.m. and noticed that there was an unfamiliar body sleeping next to him with an enormous morning hard on. He thought it looked like a camping tent that could sleep a family of four. He smiled. Z eased under the sheets and started sucking the 11-inch pole like there was no tomorrow. Suddenly, the owner of the love machine woke up with a smile on his face and whispered under the sheets.

"Are you alright down there?" asked Jeremy.

Z replied, "I'm handling my own," as he tried desperately to deep throat Jeremy's dick. "It's going to take some practice to make this pole disappear but I'm determined.".

"Just take your time. I'm just going to lay here until you're finished," Jeremy replied as his eyes rolled in the back of his head. Z, concentrating on the masterpiece at hand, didn't even notice the pager, cell phone or the answering machine's light blinking.

"Hey I think it's ready", shouted Z. "Are you ready for round three?" Without hesitation, Z slipped the last lubricated magnum XL condom on Jeremy's huge dick. Z relaxed as he sat on the dick. Not moving, Jeremy just lay there, looking at Z in amazement. No one had ever taken charge of his cock with such ease. He was looking at a pro in action, and it was exhilarating to find someone who knew what they were doing. Z started riding three fourths of the love muscle as he started moaning with pleasure and delight. Jeremy shouted, "Ride that shit, (nigga). Sit all the way down on that motherfucking dick." Z was holding on for dear life; he couldn't believe he had 11 inches of pole up his ass, realizing that no pussy is better than his. Z had become wet and, now having full control of the fucking, began to squeeze his muscles, sending Jeremy into total ecstasy. Jeremy grabbed the pillow and put it over his mouth. Z realized that he had Jeremy just where he wanted him. Slapping his own ass, he gave one final squeeze and Jeremy screamed with delight as he started to come. "Damn, motherfucka. What the fuck are you doing to me? Your shit is the motherfucking one!"

Z, still sitting on Jeremy's dick, secretly patted himself on the back and whispered, "My job is done." Z jumped off Jeremy's dick (and pulled off the condom), like a gymnast off the balance beam. "Would you like something to drink or some breakfast?" asked Z. Jeremy just lay there in amazement, "(Nigga), what are you made of; sponges and rubber? I have never had anyone take my dick like that; your shit is the bomb. You need to market that shit, but only if I can get it anytime I want," shouted Jeremy.

Z completely ignored Jeremy and his last comment. "How bout some French toast, turkey bacon and cheese eggs?" asked Z.

"Sounds good to me," responded Jeremy. "Hey man, I need to take a shower. I'm sweaty as hell," said Jeremy.

"Cool, no problem. I'm going to take a quick shower downstairs. The towels and washcloths are behind the door in the linen closet; breakfast should be ready in about 20 minutes," responded Z. Before running downstairs to cook breakfast and take care of his necessities, he admired Jeremy and hoped that last night was not just a fuck. He couldn't wait to call Nikko and Malia to brag about his exciting and blissful night. Also, he was dying to find out whether Lake fucked Nikko to oblivion and if he sprang the exciting news about becoming a detective. He thought he would wait until Jeremy left so he could really kick it on the phone. In the back of his head he was hoping that Jeremy was not stealing shit from his bathroom, remembering that trade boys will do that shit in a heartbeat; they will steal your cologne, watches, jewelry, anything they can sneak into their baggy ass jeans. Z was cooking the breakfast fast like he was a short order cook at IHOP. "Hey, JJ, your breakfast is ready. Stop washing your damn nuts and bring your dick down here and eat before it dies of exhaustion."

Jeremy strolled downstairs fully dressed with Timbs and jeans.

"Yo, nigga, did you enjoy yourself last night and this morning?" asked Jeremy as he approached. Z's response was stern and cold.

"Yeah, I did." Jeremy searched for something to say.

"Well, tell me about yourself. I've seen you out a couple of times, and I must say you're a bitch; cussing and raising hell all the time."

Z became more defensive. "What the hell you mean?"

Jeremy continued, "I admire a motherfucka like you; feminine but don't take no shit from nobody. I was at the club last night when you were getting ready to cut that bitch's throat. You only weigh a buck and a half but don't mind going toe to toe with a (nigga), so saying all of that, tell me about yourself."

"Shit it seems like you know every damn thing about me," uttered Z. "I'm the only fucking child so I always had to take up for myself and being only 5'8" and 'feminine,' as you say, I was determine to not let any motherfuckas take advantage of me, and I don't give a damn about anyone other then my family and friends. I've been a damn nurse for over seven years. I don't have to ask no one for shit. I love dick and more dick; can't find a cut buddy because I keep meeting these tired ass brothas, no pun intended. They want to lie, fuck, fight, beat, raise hell and leave your ass, I don't have time for that shit, I'd rather hang out with my friends and talk shit and occasionally hook up with a brotha who don't want nothing; no obligation or nothing; just some good ass."

"And that you got," Jeremy responded quickly.

"My mother is also a nurse. She lives in South Carolina with my half-brother. My father's dead, thank goodness. I also have a step sister who lives in Alabama. My mother married my step sister's tired ass father ten years after my father died. I have three nephews and seven nieces; my step sister is a prostitute and my brother is her pimp, and my stepfather is a child molester and minister; just kidding. He's in construction, with his old ass; he needs to retire. Okay, sir, is their anything else you needed to know before we jump the broom?" muttered Z. "Now, Mr. Jamison tell me about yourself. You may now begin," Z instructed.

"Well, you know my name. I have three siblings. I'm the second youngest. I moved here to the ATL over a year ago from Ohio to become a rapper and singer. I currently work with an independent record label and also worked as a bouncer at a nightclub. I'm not making six figures, but it allows me to get to know the right people. I've probably met all the celebrities, from athletes to entertainers. Most of the motherfuckas are down for the count; the men and the women, and all freaks. I could tell you some stories about the parties and the orgies." Jeremy now had Z's full attention. "But I can't."

"You can't, or you won't?" Z interrupted.

"I've only been in love with one shawty. He still lives in Ohio; he didn't like the fact that I wanted to be a rapper or the fact that I meet a lot of people. We used to get into arguments everyday about that shit. I got so fed up that I just had to leave and get away, so Atlanta was my next stop. My boys said I could make some money with all the night clubs here, so here I am."

"Do you have a girlfriend?" Z asked.

"No, not really. I was kicking it with this girl I met when I first got here, but I told her I liked boys fucking me in the ass and she ain't with that. So now she doesn't want to fuck anymore, but I still share an apartment with her until I decide to move out. I pay her rent and I come and go as I please; I ain't tapping that ass, but I do walk around the house naked as a jay bird, just for the hell of it. She couldn't take the dick anyway. I have a 6-year-old son named Jerason. His mother is a trip. I have to go through that baby momma drama. I send that (bitch) $500 smacks a month, but she still wants me to send an extra $500. She's crazy as hell, but I send it because she threatens me all the time, that if I don't send her that fucking money I can't see my son. Starting next month I'm going to send her $1,000. I never knew my father, so I don't want my son to grow up hating me because he doesn't know me. I never knew my father, that bastard, and I really don't care if I never know him. I wouldn't know my punk ass dad if he was to come suck my dick. He ran off with the fucking Avon lady when I was three and my little sister was just six weeks old. My mother struggled to support four rug rats; it was hard, but she did it. She is probably the only woman I will truly love. I dropped out of school just to help her support my bitch ass sister to go to med school. I felt that, being the only boy, it was something I had to do. I slung rocks, powder, meth and ecstasy, whatever it took to help my mother so she wouldn't have to clean white people's houses. After getting caught and spending a year in jail at the age of 17, I quit the shit, but I made $66,000. My mother didn't have to work as hard, but her stupid ass gave most of it to my sister for school and the rest to the church. I was so fucking mad, I could have cut my sister's neck off. She didn't even care, selfish bitch. Now she looks at me like I'm the bad seed of the family. Being in jail for a year helped me become a man. I grew up fast as hell; you learn some shit in prison. What makes it so bad is that I never had a chance to spend any of the fucking money. I gave most of it to my mom and about $7,000 to my no good ass baby's mommy. I made my mom buy that damn car outside and begged her to give me $5,000 so I won't be begging for a hand out." Z stopped him dead in his tracks.

"Hey, sing for me! You said you can sing, so put your money where your mouth is."

"I'm not going to sing for your punk ass. What's in it for me?" asked Jeremy.

"I'll let you fuck me right here on the stairs while I stand on my hands," Z blurted out. "Damn, (nigga)! Who can pass that shit up? What would you like to hear?"

Z busted out, "My Funny Valentine."

"Look here, (nigga), don't tell nobody this shit. I'm just doing this shit because your shit is the bomb and I don't want to sing in your ass next time I eat it, so this is a sample of what to expect when I have your ass on that pillow and that pussy starts wetting itself.

"My funny valentine/ sweet comic valentine/ You make me smile with my heart/ Your looks are laughable, unphotographable/ Yet you're my favorite work of art / Is your figure less the great?/ Is your mouth a little weak?/ When you open it to speak, are you baby are you smart?/ Don't change your hair for me/ Not if you care for me/ Stay with me, Valentine./ Stay, each day is Valentine's Day. Stayyyyyyyyyyyyyyy"

Z was speechless, he did not believe that Jeremy could sing. He thought he was lying, but instead he made Z wet in his robe. With his dick hard as hell, Z pounced onto Jeremy like a lion onto their prey, calling for Jeremy to give him some. Jeremy was ready to oblige without hesitation.

Lake hesitantly opened the door to the hospital room as Nikko was slowly getting up. He said he was ready to go see his sister and needed to call Princess. Lake looked at Nikko in amazement and worried about the possibility that Nikko would have a nervous break down, knowing that Nikko was the strongest out of everyone. They had never been through anything this traumatic. Nikko's eyes were blood shot and he could barely speak, but his determination was there. "Baby, let me call the doctor and see if it's all right to visit her. You know she is still in ICU," Lake responded slowly. Before another word was mentioned, Nikko was out the door and down the hall, pushing the elevator button to the fourth floor. "Nikko!" Lake shouted. "Wait up, baby," he said, reaching for Nikko's hand; the people in the hallway just looked in astonishment. They rushed out the elevator to the intensive care unit. Immediately Nikko and Lake noticed the overcrowded hallway of the ICU. Without hesitation they ran pass the nurses station and started toward the private room where his sister was now resting. Before the couple could enter the room, the hospital security asked who they were and if they had permission from the doctor to enter the room since the hospital wasn't allowing visitors for Ms. Grey.

By this time, Nikko was about to break. Lake intervened and cautioned the security guard that he was a detective and Nikko was Ms. Grey's brother. "I apologize," uttered the security guard, "but I was under strict orders not to let anyone enter the room. They're still prepping Ms. Grey and are trying to make her as comfortable as possible."

Nikko shouted, "Get out my fucking way, now!" The security guard just stood there in a frightened trance, too scared to respond. Nikko pushed him out of the way and slammed the door open. He stood there for a moment in total shock, seeing his sister hooked up to IV's with all types of needles and machines everywhere. Her face still had dried bloodstains, her hair was stringy, her left eye was swollen and the right one was permanently closed. The tears just started rolling down both twins' faces at the first glance of each other. Nikko could only mutter, "Hey, Precious." and his lips started to tremble. Nikki just stared into space, trying unsuccessfully to speak. Nikko and Nikki began communicating without saying a word. Nikki stared deep into Nikko's eyes, and he responded, "Princess is fine. She's staying over at Ms. Weirsoski's house. It's going to be alright, Precious. I will call the agency and we can delay the perfume campaign. Lake is going to find out who did this to us. I'll take care everything, don't worry. I just want you to get better. We have a big fashion show next month, so get all your rest.

Happy birthday to you, too and I love you, too, Precious." Lake was in the distance watching in amazement. Nikko stood up and rushed out of the room; Lake was two steps behind as Nikko got on the elevator, walked out of the hospital, got in the Navigator, and dialed a number on his cell phone. "Hello, Ms Weirsoski. This is Nikko. I'm coming to pick up Kennedy. I do want to thank you for taking care of her for my sister and me. She's in ICU. The only thing I can ask for right now is prayer. I should be there in 30 minutes." Totally ignoring Lake, Nikko tried to call Kennedy's school and talk to the principal, but he was unavailable. He informed the assistant that Kennedy would not be in school. "This is her uncle. Her mother is in the hospital. Any type of communication will be coming directly from me until further notice. Please have Mr. Brasington to call me, as soon as possible." Nikko was getting ready to make another call when he realized that Sasha and Sebastian were in the back seat. As he acknowledged them, he finally acknowledged Lake as well. "Baby, sorry about what happened in the hospital, but I was about to explode. Everything is hitting me at once," apologized Nikko, and kissed Lake on the cheek while he was driving. "And congratulations, Mr. Detective," he said as he smiled at Lake. "Thank you, baby," responded Lake. "Baby, I must tell you that I will be working on Nikki's case. It will be my first assignment and I won't let you down."

"I know you won't," interjected Nikko.

"Malia and Tré called, and they are aware of everything. I haven't talked to Zarius; no one seems to be able to find him. Nikki's publicist, manager, and agency called, and they want to talk to you about her status and also the marketing campaign. Baby the reporters and police are going to have a field day with Nikki's case. I will try my best to keep things calm, but everyone knows about this case and it's not even 10 o'clock yet.

"So what is our next step, baby? I know we need to keep our private life private, but what is most important is that we must keep Kennedy from the paparazzi and the local press."

"I understand, Lake. I just don't know what I'm going to do, I feel like I'm suffocating. I can't breathe."

"Baby, don't worry. I'll breathe for the both of us," replied Lake. The car suddenly became quiet; only the music from the CD player filled the space with the incredible voice of India Arie. "The time is right, I'm gonna pack my bags and take that journey down the road, cause over the mountain I see the bright sunshine I want to live inside the glow, I want to go a place where I hear nothing and everything that exist I want to I....the walls are closing in on me....please understand that's it's not that I don't care, but this walls are closing in on me, I love you more than I love life inside, but I need to find a place I can breathe."

Nikko was now in deep thought; his heart began to cry once again. Moments later, he heard Lake calling his name. "Baby, wake up. We're here," said Lake. Nikko became nervous once again, approaching his niece. He really didn't know how to face her or what to say to her when she asked about her mother. Before he could get out of the car, Kennedy ran up to Nikko and she jumped into his arms, almost knocking him down. Kennedy squeezed Nikko so hard he could hardly breathe, but he needed that; he needed her touch and he felt whole again as if life was flowing into him from her. "Uncle Nikko, where's my mommy?" Before he could respond, Sasha and Sebastian were at Nikko's feet begging to be loved by Kennedy as if they knew the drama that took place; they also needed tender loving care from the littlest angel. "Princess, I need to talk to you about Mommy. Do you want to go home with me and Uncle Lake?" uttered Nikko. "Uncle Nikko, I'm ready to go home and see Mommy. They didn't let me last night. Tevona saw something last night and it scared her and she started crying. She wouldn't let me in the house, and when I asked her about mommy she just started crying," Kennedy said. Holding back the tears, Nikko knelt down and told Princess the only lie he could think of. "Mommy had to take a sudden trip for a job. I'm going to reach her today so she can talk to both of us. How does that sound?" he asked, trying to sound convincing. "She wanted me to take you to my house. I believe you have enough clothes at my house, and guess what we have to celebrate? Today is me and mommy's birthday, so we have to have cake and ice cream and maybe Uncle Lake will go and buy me a present," Nikko chuckled. "But Uncle Nikko, I already have your birthday present at my house. Can't we walk down the street and get it?" Kennedy replied.

"Well, not yet, Princess. Tevona said there were mice in the house last night and that's why the police and firemen where down there last night. We need to stay away for a little while. Is that cool?" Nikko asked Kennedy, as if to get permission for the lie he was telling her. Lake interrupted, "Princess, how 'bout we let the people find the mice then we can go get Uncle Nikko's present later?"

"Okay," Kennedy agreed. Kennedy grabbed Lake's hand and started toward the Navigator. Nikko thanked Ms. Weirsoski once again and headed for the back seat of the SUV. He couldn't wait to get back home to start making all the phone calls that were needed for his sister: the publicist, managers, agencies, Revlon, attorneys, hospital and all the friends and fans. This is someway to start a fucking birthday, he thought as he rested his eyes and soul for a much needed nap.

CHAPTER 11

One Day at a Time

Somalia Mayerson had not yet made partner in her large corporate law firm in downtown Atlanta, but she was determined. She tried her best to handle the best and biggest cases she could sink her teeth into. She was one of the pivotal factors in the class action suit against Coca-Cola. She had always wanted to be a lawyer and fight for the right of the underdogs. Her wit and relentless attitude got her noticed even before grad school. She was sought after by hundreds of law firms from east to west, north to south, even in Canada and as far as South Africa. But her dream was to stay close to her hometown of Valdosta, Ga., a small town south of Atlanta where her elderly parents still lived. Malia was the fourth child out of six bright and wonderful children. All well disciplined and professional, determined to be the best in the world, focused on nothing but success and happiness. Somalia was 5'10", 125, her hair was jet black cut in a short feather-spike, and with an oval shaped face she was very attractive, her skin was like dark chocolate caramel. Her eyes were piercing brown, but looked as though they were made of glass. She was articulate and well versed in any subject under the sun. She could even give Johnny Cochran a run for his money; however she was never opinionated about anything. Somalia thought everyone should be happy and free living life to the fullest most of the time she would tell people she works in a law firm as a file clerk, because she didn't like hang-ups or titles and really wanted people to judge her spirit rather than judging her profession. She loved sports, basketball, football, baseball, soccer, tennis, golf, volleyball, kayaking, and track and field; whenever it was mind against matter she was all for it. She played basketball, and volleyball until she went to grad school, but then knew she would have to concentrate on a long-term profession rather than her physical attributes. Malia received several full four-year scholarships to attend a couple of high profile universities, but she decided to attend Spelman College as that's where her mother, aunt and sister attended. Her father majored in Chemical Engineering at Georgia Tech; her brothers followed the same footsteps. Samuel Mayerson, her father was one of the first black engineers to graduate from Georgia Tech. His motivation was instilled in Somalia wherever she went, she was determined to a make a difference even as a little girl.

Ms. Mayerson, "there have been several messages from Mr. Gordon; he wanted to let you know he will be running about 30 minutes late. The meeting with his former employer is scheduled for 10:30 a.m. Do I need to call the lawyer representing his former employer and inform them of his current status?" asked the temp clerk who was filling in for Malia's permanent secretary. "That won't be necessary Alex; I'll take care of it," replied Malia. Mr. Gordon was the code name that Drayton gave himself for Malia, so whenever he called or she needed him the sharks in the office would not know. Drayton wanted to take Malia out for lunch, but every offer he made her she humbly declined, as if she was preoccupied with work. He didn't know what to think. He made several suggestions for them to spend time together, and then she finally told him of the situation with Nikko and his family. Drayton was amazed being she didn't mention anything at the house or even at breakfast, she seemed distant. Drayton could never understand the relationship Malia had with these gay guys being her best friends. He could accept Nikko, Lake and Tré, because they were men and not obvious. He often wondered why they wouldn't try to hit on her, as fine as she was, but he could not understand the flamboyancy of Zarius and how he paraded around like he was the last of the Queen of the Zombies tribe. He loves to flirt with whomever and doesn't care about who see him. I only tolerated his behavior, because of Malia, but I wish I could throw him in prison with a bunch of dykes, they would eat him alive, Drayton thought.

Nikko jumped out of the car trying to ignore the reporters and the rest of people gathering around his Stone Mountain home. He became very frustrated, not wanting to be questioned or for Kennedy to witness all this. It was all so unbearable. The phone was ringing off the hook as they entered the house. Completely ignoring the reporters at the front door, Lake took action. "I am one of the detectives handling this case. A meeting will be held today at six o' clock at the Dekalb County Headquarters. Until that time, can I please ask everyone to give Mr. Grey his privacy? He has endured a very stressful ordeal and is trying to handle the outcome. With all due respect I must ask everyone to leave the property." Kennedy was standing right behind Lake, as well as the two cockers, barking in the background.

Nikko rushed upstairs; noticing the candles, and the rose petals, hoping this was a bad dream and tomorrow he would wake up and life would continue to live as normal. He instantly pinched himself, realizing this was very real and this is life and the reality of it all. He immediately called Katie, his administrative assistant from his marketing firm, to ask her if she could help him with the ordeal, she gracefully agreed. Now he was ready to face the nasty, ugly world and the entire slimy outcome. He started checking his messages; there were more than messages on his voice mail. Celebrities such as, Tyra, Monica, Susan Taylor, Oprah, Janet, Beyonce, and even Bill and Hillary called to give their condolesences and to find out if there was anything they could do. It made Nikko feel good, but what did it all mean? It was as if Nikki was dead or something. Chills ran up and down his spine.

Z was lying on the living room couch totally naked when he finally woke up. It was 1:45 p.m. and he was going to be late for work. Jeremy was on the sofa butt ass naked as well. Z slowly came to life to notice that hunk of a man lying less than three feet from him; he could only imagine it was going to be a great day after all. It would all be worth it if he were late for work. He nudged Jeremy as he ran upstairs to take a two-minute shower. Without saying a word, Jeremy ran behind him and jumped in the shower, explaining to Z, "you need to get use to taking a shower with me, so move over," shouted Jeremy, Z humbly obliged. "Hey I'm going to be late for work if this keeps up and if your pole keeps standing to attention," responded Z. He knelt down and gave Jeremy's one-eyed snake a kiss on the head as he eased out of the shower. Thank heavens for being a nurse, scrubs will be the wardrobe for today with a white doctor's coat to make the outfit complete, Z mumbled to himself. Jeremy was putting back on his clothes when he blurted out," So Mr. Z, when can I see you again?" Z was shocked, "let me pencil you in for next August around 8:00 p.m. Will that be fine?" asked Z. "You have a smart-ass mouth little boy, don't have me stuff your mouth with my meat, again". Z replied, "Promises, promises." "I don't get off until 11:30; let me give you a call." "That sounds like a brush off if I've ever heard one, just tell me that my dick is too damn big for you and you can't hang. Honesty is the best policy," Jeremy responded. "Meet me here at

12:15 a.m., what time did you have to be to work?" "I had to there at 9:00 this morning, but it was all worth it."

"Working for a record company allows me to come and go as I please. My real money comes from the club. I don't get off until late myself, so let me give you a call around 12:30 a.m., and then you can let me know if it's good to come over. And don't have no other motherfucking (nigga) in that ass of yours," replied Jeremy.

"Ooh ownership; there's always a price to pay when taking ownership of property," Z immediately replied. "I'll wait for your call," Z shouted, as they walked into the parking lot." Save some for me," yelled Jeremy as he got into the Mazda 626.

Z tried to gather his thoughts as he noticed his cell phone light blinking, damn messages, I bet its Nikko cussing me out because I didn't call and say happy birthday, Z thought. The tune of, I'm telling you I'm not going blasted on the radio, as he was checking his voice mail; and then there was a breaking news on the radio as he was trying to steer the ES300 and listen to the radio and listen for the messages on his cell phone. Z almost ran off the road and hit two cars. Both messages came almost at the same time, Nikki Grey; Atlanta's very own Supermodel had been raped in her home in Buckhead. Z slammed on brakes in the middle of the street, "What the Fuck?" Z screamed as he completely ignored traffic. He immediately called Nikko to asking him what was going on. Nikko tried to explain the best he could and said that he really needed him, "I feel Nikki needs you more, could you please see how she's doing. I'm trying to take care of her business, talking to her agency, manager and Revlon." Nikko explained. Zarius I'm so scared I don't know what to expect. It seems as though our world is crumbling down, and there's nothing we can do about it. The paparazzi, reporters, magazines, newspapers are coming out of the woodwork. I'm falling apart, Z please give me an update on Nikki, I promised her I would take care of all this stuff but I can't concentrate on anything but her, and Kennedy," Z became very serious and responded, "I'm on my way, anything else just let me know," he could hear car horns blowing in the distance. "I will call you with an update and don't worry Nikko I will handle everything once I get to work." Z put on his flashers and slammed on the gas.

Tré completed his first leg and was on his second. He was not in a very good mood; everyone was talking about Nikki, from the flight attendants, to the captains, to the passengers in New York, and now the passengers in Texas. Can't anyone talk about anything else? Tré thought, fucking animals,

"I'm tired of this damn shit." He mumbled, as he greeted the oncoming passengers. He noticed a muscular man staring at him as he was greeting all the passengers. He started staring because he knew he had seen him before but didn't know where. "Is he an athlete or celebrity?" Tré wondered. "Oh well. It ain't that serious." After the announcements, Tré noticed that some guys in first class were asking for autographs from the guy and then it dawned on him that's the motherfucker that plays for the most hated baseball team, Tré could have sworn that (nigga) winked at him, he couldn't believe it; maybe his mind was playing tricks on him.

Tré was elated when the 747 landed in Atlanta, he was nervous for no apparent reason. He could finally call Nikko to find out the status of Nikki and also find out did anyone here from Z. After saying his goodbyes to the passengers and wishing them well on their next flight he had time to sit down for a moment and get the update on Nikki. He called Malia, who was already at Nikko's house helping him with some legal papers and talking with Nikki's agency and her manager. "Lake had reluctantly taken Kennedy shopping for necessities until they could go back into the house. "Malia told Tre," Z finally called, and was very upset that he was not here for Nikki or Nikko. He's at the hospital now getting all the pertinent information and giving us an update on Nikki; she's still in intensive care and, Tré, it really does not look good. Nikki lost a lot of blood and the supply for her blood type is very rare." "Nikko is trying to stay strong for all of us, but I know he's going to break down if the unexpected is realized. Kennedy suspects something but they're trying their best to hide the truth from her in hopes that everything will be all right. The authorities are cooperating, and there will be a press conference at the hospital sometime today. At present, they have no leads and now they are saying it seems like two people entered the home, but they don't quite know how the other intruder participated in the crime." Tré was so engulfed with Malia that he never noticed someone was standing over him. He jumped when he saw a tall figure standing in front of him. "Sorry to bother you, man, but I think I lost my watch, and I was just wondering if you've seen it," asked the gentleman. Tré just stared and replied, "Naw, man. I haven't seen any watch, but the cleaning crew will be here in just a minute. You can wait outside for them if you'd like bruh."

"I really don't have time to wait, but if they run across it, please call me. Here's my card," he said, pushing the card in Trés face.

"Yeah man no problem, and if they find it I will give them your card and have them give you a call." Tré responded.

"I would prefer you calling. By the way, what's your name, man?"

"Tré Washington."

"My name is Lincoln Buchanan. I'm sure you have heard of me before, yo. I play for the Connecticut Razors. I'll be staying at the JW Marriott in Buckhead. The Rolex is worth over $20,000; I will give you a reward when it is recovered," Lincoln replied. Tré just stared as the player walked away.

"Cocky ass faggot motherfucker," Tré mumbled to Malia, as she just held the phone. "Sorry, Malia. Well, I have just one more leg to pull; going back to fucking New York. It's still not the same after 9/11, but they have almost finished the reconstruction. Afterwards, I'll go straight to Nikko's house. I'll probably spend the night with Lake and Nikko. I don't have to come back to work until next week."

"Hurry up," Malia whispered. "I have another call coming in. See you soon, Tré. Love ya."

"One," replied Tré.

CHAPTER 12

Give Us Strength

Reporters from every newspaper imaginable were swarming the hallways of the hospitals, police were checking ID's, and the employees were getting nervous and pissed off. "This is a hospital, not a damn circus," shouted one of the head nurses. "Z, you're in for a treat," yelled another nurse from the nurses' station. He completely ignored her and headed toward ICU. "I'll be back; need to check on my girl." He ran up four flights of stairs; Z didn't want to be stopped by anyone. He flashed his badge to the security officer as he slipped through the doors into the room where Nikki laid.

"Baby girl, what have they done to that million-dollar face of yours? I can't believe some motherfucka raped you." As Z continued to speak, the tears started flowing. Trying to hold them back, he became weak and immediately exited the room. After drying his eyes he started reading Nikki's chart; because of the shit that the rapist had done to her and the amount of blood she had lost, things didn't look good. Z was on a mission. He began searching for the doctors to find out what they were doing to help Nikki. He finally tracked them down in the lounge. He asked them what were they doing for Nikki's situation and most of the doctors replied that they were looking for blood and that, since her blood type was rare, it would be very difficult to perform a blood transfusion.

"We're making all needed arrangements to expedite her surgery. We don't have much time," responded the chief surgeon.

"Then why the fuck are you just sitting here on your motherfucking ass? I don't understand," screamed Zarius. He slammed the door and ran back to the ICU nurses' station to look at all the available blood supply throughout the surrounding area, and across the country.

"You mean to tell me that we can not find any blood around this fucking country," he yelled at everyone within earshot. Erica ran up behind him, trying to console him. "Zarius, you know the blood supply is still low after the situation with New York and Hurricane Katrina. Most of the blood supply was sent there last year. So, baby boy, things look very slim, but you know our doctors are the best in the country, and they are going to do everything they possibly can."

"Erica," Z yelled, "time is a factor. I don't know our current situation, but this patient is like a sister to me and I'm fucking helpless. I can't do a fucking thing about it. I'm going to her brother's house; maybe I can be some help there."

"Z!" Erica replied, "We need you here and so does that girl in there. She needs to feel that there's someone here that is familiar with her."

"I feel helpless," Zarius mumbled.

Back at Nikko's house the phone was ringing constantly with the media, flooding the lines with questions about Nikki's medical situation. People, Entertainment Tonight, Access Hollywood, ABC, CBS, Fox and NBC were all trying to get an exclusive. The Atlanta Journal Constitution had reporters at the door. The paparazzi were having a field day; they even had a helicopter hovering over the house.

Malia had to put an end to this she stepped outside without hesitation to order everyone off the private property at once. If everyone did not oblige, she would start litigations against everyone that she could recognize. Everyone shamefully obeyed. She confirmed that there would be a press conference and that they were in the process of organizing the time and the place. As she headed for the door, she thanked everyone for their cooperation. Nikko was so busy with his sister's lawyers that he never looked up from the table. His eyes were blood shot red and he was very weak and tired, but he tried not to let on. He was concerned about Nikki's contract with the agency, with Revlon and her other endorsements. He was responsible for the launch of her new perfume line and the commercial ads all of this was overwhelming because he knew she could be sued if her professional obligations were not met. Nikki's lawyers explained to him, her manager and publicist that everything needs to go ahead as planned. The ads and the perfume promo must go as planned nothing can change under any circumstances.

"Uncle Lake," Kennedy whispered, while they were arriving at the mall, Lake could actually hear his heart skip a beat. "What's wrong with my mother?" She stared him directly in his eyes and he knew he could not lie, He started to fidget but was helpless and he started telling Kennedy what he knew. He started off by telling her about the intruder and how her mother fought the person or persons. "Mommy is in the hospital. Your mother lost a lot of blood; the doctors are trying everything so she can come home soon. Your uncle Nikko didn't want you to know because he was concerned about your well-being and how you would react."

Kennedy stopped him. "I want to go see my mother and I want to go see her now, Uncle Lake. I must. I give my mother energy and she gives me the same. She needs my energy and my touch to make her feel better. Whenever I'm sick, her touch always makes me feel better. Please, Uncle Lake," Kennedy started pleading. "Precious, I don't know if I can do that. We have specific instructions to protect you, and your Uncle would be furious and mad as h(ell)." She stopped him as tears rolled down her face. He tried his best to ignore her demands and her tears but he couldn't he too started to cry. "Okay, baby girl, you win we have to sneak in the hospital and please don't let your uncle know? He'll kill me." Lake starts the engine and steers the car in the direction of Grady Memorial Hospital. Lake picked up the cell phone and called Z to request a huge favor. Z was relieved that he could finally help and feel important. Lake arrived at the hospital in 15 minutes. Z directed him which entrance door to come in and how to avoid being seen by personnel or security. He told him what time he needed to be in the intensive care unit and that he would distract the security guard waiting outside of Nikki's door. Kennedy slipped into her mother's hospital room without making a sound; at first she just stared at her mother's limp body lying in the bed, with tiny tubes stuck in her arms and nose. Kennedy slowly walked to the bed, approaching her mother with great caution. Then she spoke, "Mommy wake up", Nikki could barely open her eyes, but she felt her daughter's presence.

"Hey, baby girl. How did you get here?" Kennedy ignored her mother's question, "Mommy, when are you coming home? You know my play is coming up and you promised to help me make my costume," Kennedy pleaded. Nikki didn't have enough strength to console her daughter; the tears just started rolling down her face.

Nikki whispered, "Kennedy, I love you, don't forget that." Kennedy replied, "I love you." "Kennedy just put her head on her mother's chest and started to cry. Lake suddenly slipped through the doors and was in pure shock; this was the first time he had seen Nikki and his tears starting falling as he approached her. He could not imagine what she had been through or the pain she endured. Her eye was still swollen, lips cracked with dried blood, and her tooth was chipped. She was helpless and experiencing a great deal of emotional and physical pain, but she was a survivor and Lake was convinced that she would have a full recovery; especially after Nikko, Zarius, and Malia nursed her back to health with the help of celebrity divas, Naomi, Tyra, Veronica, and the rest of the crew. Today, though, the heavens were crying at the sight of their beautiful angel in pain. Just at that moment a swarm of nurses rushed in, Nikki's monitors were going hay wire. There were doctors, nurses, orderlies and security guards were all rushing in to the little room, trying to prepare Nikki for what would be the scariest point in her entire life. One nurse was yelling, "Get that little girl out of here! She doesn't belong in here!" Another nurse was pushing Lake and Kennedy out of the room. Zarius rushed in, ordering Lake to call Nikko. "Tell him to get his ass down here now!" Kennedy seeing all of this started screaming. Lake forced her down the hallway as she begged to be with her mother. Lake ran to the nurses' station and called Nikko. Malia answered the phone on the first ring.

"Hello!"

With a disturbed voice, Lake said, "Malia, this is Lake. Nikko needs to come to the hospital at once something is happening to Nikki. The doctors, nurses and even Zarius are trying to revive her. Somalia, please hurry!"

Malia rushed into the den where Nikko and Nikki's agents were meeting, Malia shouted, "Sorry, fellas. This party is over. Nikko we have to go now." Nikko saw the urgency in her eyes, and asked, "Is something wrong with my sister?" Without hesitation, Nikko and Malia were out the door, down the street, on their way towards Grady. "Malia!" Nikko asked, "Did Z call you from the hospital?"

"No," she replied. "Lake called from the hospital."

"Lake!" "What is he doing at the hospital?" Nikko shouted in desperation. He's supposed to be at the mall with Kennedy getting her some clothes. Malia, something is definitely going on with my sister. I can feel it. He closed his eyes as Donnie McLurkin sang, We Fall Down. Nikko fell into a deep meditation. He finally woke up when Malia swerved her large Mercedes into the hospital parking lot. She jumped out of the car before it came to a complete stop. Ordering Nikko to catch up, they ran up the stairs to the ICU floor. Lake spotted them and ran to Nikko to explain what was going on, but Kennedy jumped in his arms first, hollering and screaming for comfort. "Uncle Nikko! My mommy is hurting, and the doctors are trying to help her feel better," cried Kennedy. Nikko held his niece, while looking at Lake in frustration; he was trying to understand why Kennedy was in the hospital without his permission. Malia, sensing the tension, grabbed Kennedy from Nikko, encouraging her to come and get something to drink and trying to comfort her so Nikko and Lake could have a chance to talk. She reluctantly followed Malia down the corridor to the break room. Nikko, with a stern look on this face, said, "What is going on Cameron?"

"I'm sorry baby for bringing Kennedy here, but she felt she needed to see her mother." "Lake, she's a little girl who's been through a lot. We've all been through a lot. How could you do something like this, this may cause an emotional break down with her. I can't believe you did something as crazy as this." Lake just stared at Nikko without saying a word.

"Are you finished?" Lake demanded, and before Nikko could respond Lake walked away. Nikko, too tired to beg him to stay, headed for the room where his sister laid lifeless. The security guard was telling Nikko that no one but hospital personnel could enter the room it was about to get very heated when Zarius walked out and grabbed Nikko by the arm, pulling into a small supply room. Zarius stared at Nikko, with water in his eyes. "It doesn't look good, Nikko. Nikki lost a lot of blood and she fell into a coma. Her body is in complete shock. There's nothing else we can do. We have the best doctors working here in the country they specialize in trauma patients, but now it's up to Nikki! Only she can pull herself out of this, and when she does, she may be in a vegetative state." Nikko's knees buckled and he began to break. He was wondering how much more he could take mentally and emotionally. His parents were killed and his only link to them is his twin sister and now she wants to leave him too? Holding on to Zarius, he had a strange sense of energy from somewhere, and then he looked at Zarius. "What can I do?" Zarius was floored; he sensed the burst of energy and was kind of startled by the sudden change in Nikko's behavior.

"Nikko, you have to go in there and talk to Nikki and make her realize that it's up to her and only she can snap out this. You have to convince her, trigger something in her brain, so she feels she's needed, to take care of Kennedy, her modeling career. Whatever it takes, you need to say it. Time is a factor and these precious moments are of the essence. It's crucial that this is relayed to her."

"Consider it done, Zarius," responded Nikko. Without hesitation, Nikko rushed into the room with the monitors, little clear tubes pushed up her nose, needles were slowly pushing fluids in her limp body, the sound of beeps steadily going off, the enormous cold air flowing through the drafty room, the dingy white sheets cover her body, steel tools hand over the bed, and the color of gray lingers over the ceiling. He could feel his sister's spirit, as evident as ever. He knew his sister could hear his whispers. She could feel his touch, and know his thoughts, he stared directly at her and demanded her to wake up, and begged her that he, Kennedy, Lake and the world needed her to bounce back and be the person they deserve. He cried to her letting her know that he needed her to live, he couldn't live life without her. He begged her to snap out the coma that he too was sick and she had to help support him. He needed her guidance, needed her love and needed her heart to survive. Without her he would surely perish. He was laying on her stomach sobbing away, when she placed her hand on his head, in a whisper she said in a trembling voice, "Niiikkoooo, I will always love," without opening her eyes, tears rolled down her face, Nikko not understanding what just happened, begged his sister to wake up. Suddenly the monitors stop and the nurses and doctors swarmed back in the room. Nikko was horrified, walking out of the room in a trace. A nurse had to help him to a seat in the waiting room. Malia and Kennedy were already sitting in the room, not uttering a word. Finally, Kennedy approached Nikko.

"Is my mother going to die, Uncle Nikko?" Nikko grabbed her and hugged her tightly, not allowing her to see his tears, or to feel his deflated spirit. Malia interrupted with an ingenuous remark. "Come on, Princess. Why would you say that? Your mommy just needs some rest. She will be good as new in a couple of days."

"Princess, I need to stay with your mommy for a moment. Would you like for Aunt Malia to take you to the house? Remember, the dogs have not been fed, and you know it's your turn to feed Sasha. You know how she gets when she hasn't been fed," Nikko said. "Okay, Uncle Nikko, but come home soon. You look terrible; you need some rest. Don't worry about mommy; God will take care of everything, just wait and see," Kennedy confirmed. Malia grabbed Kennedy's hand, and they disappeared down the hallway. Nikko could not believe how mature she was and how fearful it would be for her to grow up without a mother. He was lost in thought when he saw Zarius coming down the hall. Nikko noticed the sadness in Zarius' eyes. Zarius was crying and said that Nikki had gone into cardiac arrest and that she'd passed on. Nikko was numb. He could barely hear Z; his words were fading out and the waiting room was turning black. He just sat there, dazed.

When Nikko came out of his trance, Zarius was driving him home. He really didn't say anything —just stared into space. "Z, could you please take me home? I need to find Precious…I mean Princess…I mean Kennedy," Nikko whispered.

"She's with Malia, Nikko. Don't you remember? Malia took her to her house. I haven't told them anything. I wanted you to be the one to tell them. I thought maybe you wanted to be alone, so I suggested they go to Malia's house for dinner. Nikko, have you talked to Lake?" Nikko had completely forgotten about his other half. It was getting dark and he had not talked to Lake for quite some time. This was very unusual in light of everything. He knew he had to apologize, but he had more pressing issues. At this very moment he needed his lover; he wanted his niece and he missed his sister. All his thoughts were dark and dismal, not knowing what to do or say. He just felt empty and lost. He was at a loss for words; he was experiencing so many emotions: anger, sadness, disgust, heartbreak, despair, depressed, sorrow, pain, disappointment, and weakness.

"Z, if you don't mind, I need to be alone for a second. I will call you if I need you." As Z drove into Nikko's driveway, he was determined not to let Nikko be alone, especially since he didn't know where Lake could be.

Nikko still staring straight ahead, said, "Z, I know you care and love me, and you really don't want me to be alone, but there are some things I need to do before dealing with the public. I need to find Malia and my baby and also Lake. I yelled at him for something and didn't give him the opportunity to explain. I really need him because there are some arrangements we need to make. I need to get started on the funeral and finalize the campaign. If you need me to do anything with identifying Nikki's body or the funeral home let me know, but if you could take the liberty and handle all the necessities pertaining to the morgue I would greatly appreciate that. Remember that I love you and I will always be indebted to you for being there for me and not betraying our love." He kissed his friend on the cheeks as he wisped out of the car. Z looked on as Nikko stumbled to his front door. Zarius' lips began to tremble as the tears started cascading down his face. He put the Lexus in reverse thinking Nikko would never love another soul in the world; he's lost one too many friends and his heart couldn't take anymore.

CHAPTER 13

Check Your Reality

Nikko stood in the middle of the foyer and screamed at the top of his lungs, begging for his sister to come back home, pleading with God that it was not right, cursing the Supreme Being for taking his sister away. He begged and pleaded that he would change his life; he would leave Lake, he would change his sexuality, he would become a priest, just return his sister, his only sister. They were fraternal twins. They shared thoughts; love and hate, good and bad times. He could not go on. "God," he screamed, "I must be with her!" He rushed into the kitchen, reached for a knife, and tried to cut his wrist. Tears were pouring out. He became blind and wanted to fall on the knife. Then, suddenly, he heard Nikki's voice; it sounded like it was coming from upstairs, or the living room, or the backyard. He yelled, "I'm coming!" She was singing, "Don't cry for me, and don't shed a tear." With knife in hand, he was looking for his sister like an insane man. He looked upstairs, downstairs, in the basement, outside, in the garage; he was calling for Nikki. He started hyperventilating and flopped down at the piano in the study. He continued to cry, and then he heard Nikki's voice again. He started to play the piano; whenever he was down or depressed he would play, play and play, until his heart was content. I've been so many places in my life and time and then he stopped and started playing Don't Cry for Me, Don't Shed a Tear, then he stopped and started playing Out Here on My Own, then he stopped and started playing, His Eyes are on the Sparrow. Nikko played and cried, cried and played; he didn't even hear Lake when he drove up or entered the house. Lake stood there for a while, just listening to Nikko sing and play. He couldn't believe his ears. Nikko's voice was very similar to Maxwell's, with a little Donnie Hathaway and Marvin Gaye mixed in. Without missing a note, Nikko yelled to Lake and said, "Nikki passed." Lake was overcome by shock. He knew his lover of six years was trying to play away his pain, his sorrow and despair, because this made him strong enough to face anything. Lake knew that he also had to be strong for Nikko and Kennedy. He immediately started thinking about Kennedy and wondering where she was. He knew he'd left the hospital angry and upset over the argument he and Nikko had, but he hoped they didn't leave Kennedy. As he was thinking this, he looked down and noticed blood on the carpet leading from the kitchen to the study. He walked up to Nikko and noticed that he was bleeding. He'd tried to cut his wrist, but punctured his forearm instead; it was still bleeding. Lake screamed at Nikko, "Baby, are you alright? You're bleeding!" Nikko was numb and hadn't realized he'd accidentally cut his forearm. With blood shot eyes, he begged for Lake's forgiveness and told him that he would always love him and that Nikki loved him too. As he stood up to approach his lover, Lake pulled away with apprehension not realizing what just happened. Nikko headed for the medicine chest.

Lake's pager started vibrating and the phone started ringing simultaneously; he ignored his pager and headed for the kitchen phone. It was Malia, informing him that Kennedy was safe and sound and they where on their way to the house. Zarius and Tré were close behind. "We should be there shortly," Malia said. Nikko came downstairs looking and feeling somewhat refreshed. Lake informed him that Malia and the crew were on their way with Kennedy in tow. Nikko had not imagined what he would tell his niece about her mother or how she would take it. The phone rang again. It was Star Magazine asking for a confirmation and begging for an exclusive. Lake pulled the phone from the wall in anger. "Damn sons-of-bitches!"

"What's wrong, Cam?"

"Everybody's calling for a fucking confirmation."

"Baby cut all the phones off. I only want to hear from family or friends, and they should have our cell numbers." Nikko insisted. Malia was pulling in the driveway and Z and Tré were nearby. Lake ran to the front door and summoned everyone to the patio. Kennedy, ignoring his commands ran straight into the house, past Lake and straight to Nikko, asking where her mother was. Nikko grabbed her. "Precious, I have some news to tell you about your mommy. Come on, baby girl. Let's go in the backyard by the pool." Sasha and Sebastian were already in the backyard. They hadn't been fed all day, but it didn't matter as they sensed something was wrong. Lake walked behind them carrying their drinks. Nikko focused his attention to Kennedy, still holding her in his lap. "Precious, you asked me about your mommy. Well, you know she was in the hospital and she wasn't feeling very good. She had an accident and God felt it was better for her to go with him so she could get better, but the bad thing about that is she won't be coming back." There was not a sound from anyone, not even the crickets were making a noise. Nikko went on to say, "The good thing about it is we'll get the chance to visit her soon in a wonderful place called Heaven; you know all the bible stories we taught you about, God and Jesus, and angels and Heaven. Well, it's a wonderful place where good people go, some to become angels and watch over us, and I think that God wanted your mommy to become an Angel. Even though she always wanted to become one later on when you were grown up, God decided that she had a lot of work to do in Heaven, and he wanted her to teach some of the angels how to model, how to wear the wings in a certain way, Kennedy. You know that good things happen to good people, and God wanted to make sure that Nikki would watch over us and protect us until you have little ones yourself. One day, you'll tell them about your wonderful mother who is a model and an angel. So now you have to stay with me and Uncle Lake and Aunt Malia, Uncle Tré and your Auntie Z, I mean your Uncle Z," he said, trying to smile as the tears continue to fall. There was a long silence, and Kennedy said, "Uncle Nikko, mommy told me that she had to go away and I had to be brave and take care of you and Uncle Lake, and don't cry for her, because she didn't want me to cry and God will take care of her. So, Uncle Nikko, stop crying. You, too, Auntie Z. I will take care of everybody because my mommy told me that I had to." Everyone was trying to wipe their tears away by laughter and joy; no one could imagine the strength this little girl had and the insight she had given them. It was silent again for the next 10 minutes.

"Uncle Nikko, I'm getting tired. I need to go to bed, but I need to feed Sasha and Sebastian first." Kennedy turned to face Nikko and said, "Uncle Nikko, mommy wants to know why you cut your arm. She wants you to take care of yourself." Now the attention was on Nikko as Kennedy entered the house. An eerie feeling covered the air. Z curiously asked, "What is she talking about?" Nikko purposely ignored Z's question. He started his conversation by telling his loved ones that he loved and adored them very much.

"Just as much as Lake and Kennedy, you are my family, but now we have a job to do. Our dear sister has departed and it's up to us to do whatever we can to protect Kennedy and lift Nikki's name.

"First of all, Z did you have a chance to take care of the proceedings with the mortuary and pronouncing her death?" Nikko asked.

"I called Wallace Funeral Home because they are the best in the business and I know they will do Nikki right. Richard promised that he'd give us his best, and wouldn't charge us because his wife and Nikki were in the same sorority."

"Lake and I have all the insurance policies, and everything else. The biggest test is that I have to continue with the perfume campaign or Nikki's estate could be sued. There's a lot of important unfinished business. Malia, that's where you come in; I would like to retain you as our lawyer or you can refer another reputable lawyer; whatever steps you feel would be necessary. Tré, I'll need your support. Things are going to be hectic for the next several days." Lake received another page, this time excusing himself to find out who kept calling. It was while dialing the number that he figured it was the number to his new job where he hadn't started to work yet. He figured it was probably his Lieutenant firing him. What else could go wrong? The voice on the other end was stern and authoritative. "We have some good news for you. You need to come down to the precinct as soon as possible. We have the assailant in custody."

"What?" screamed Lake, "What do you mean?!"

"He was trying to catch a flight out of the city when we apprehended him," Lt. Allen said. "He still had dried blood on his person and even a picture of Ms. Grey in his wallet. He's a security guard at the hotel where the fashion show was held yesterday afternoon. We searched his locker and he had loads of pictures of her; he was totally obsessed with Ms. Grey. He's giving a full statement as we speak.

"We will have him processed in a couple of hours. Do you want to come down and do an additional interrogation or leave it up to the department?"

Still in shock, Lake responded, "I will be down there shortly. Just keep him in the room until I get there, regardless of whether it takes all night." Lake was angry, relieved, upset, pissed as a motherfucker; he didn't know whether to tell Nikko and the others or how to excuse himself without letting Nikko know where he was going. Lake walked back to the patio, and said he had to leave. "There's some pressing information that came up at the office which needs my immediate attention."

Nikko looked puzzled. "Is it concerning Nikki?" Nikko asked.

"I really don't' know. They just told me to get my ass down there, quick!"

"But I need you here, with me and Kennedy."

“Uncle Nikko” Kennedy yelled from upstairs, “We have to say our prayers together before I go to bed!”

“Okay, Precious. I’ll be there in a minute,” Nikko yelled. The gang was in awe, wondering how he and Lake could be so calm after the devastation they had been through and the things yet to come.

CHAPTER 14

Family Comes First

Drayton was furious. He had called Malia all day and she had not once returned his calls. He knew she was comforting the faggots in her life, but that was no reason to put him on hold. She knew he was flying out the following morning and he desperately needed to get his rocks off one more time before going home to his lovely wife and children. He was about to leave her home when his cell phone rang.

"Drayton, where are you? I've been calling the office and the hotel all night looking for you, but you are nowhere to be found," screamed Cecilia, his wife of 10 years.

"Baby, there's a crisis that's been developing down here. Nikki Grey, the super model has been raped and murdered and we represent her agency. They are one of our biggest clients down here. One of my constituents wanted me to look at their legal affairs. Sorry, baby. I just got bogged down with the contracts and trying to figure out how my firm is going to handle this problem."

"Drayton, I've been watching the story develop, but we have a crisis here. When are you coming home? Your daughter has a hundred and one fever and she's throwing up all over the house."

"Cecilia, take her to the emergency room or call the 24-hour nurse. What is she doing now? Let me speak to my little girl," demanded Drayton.

"She's sleep right now. I gave her a children's aspirin, which seems to have done the trick."

"Then why are you calling me, Cecilia? I will be home in the morning." Drayton slammed the phone down in her ear. He shouted, "Dumb bitch!" He immediately called Malia's cell phone again and she picked up on the first ring. "Where are you, Malia? I've been here waiting at the house forever for you. I need to see you before I leave in the morning," Drayton said, anxiously. Malia stopped him right in the middle of his sentence. "Drayton I'm quite sure you know I had an emergency and I may be here all night with Nikko and Lake."

"Malia, baby, I have needs that require your attention."

Malia cut him off again. "Well, my dearest Drayton, I see you have two choices; you can handle your sexual desires tonight alone, or you can wait until you get home to your loving wife and have her give you a blow job in holy matrimony. I'm busy with my friends and the arrangement for the burial of their sister. Now, Counselor if you can't understand or accept that then you have a problem. I received all your messages; I just didn't have time to call you back. Do I make myself clear, Drayton?"

"Yes, Malia, I'll be here waiting for you if you should happen to come home before I leave. My flight is not until ten but I can change it if you like. Malia just hung up in his ear and turned off her cell phone. "Married men get on my fucking nerves," she whispered loudly in frustration to Z. "Well, girlfriend, leave them alone and come to the other side," Z quickly responded. That was the laughter they needed; everything had become so gray and morbid and Z was trying to find a way to make light of the situation. It was 12:30 a.m. now and everyone was exhausted and ready to go home, but they were fearful of leaving Nikko alone. Lake had slipped away almost two hours ago and he still hadn't called.

Z volunteered to stay the night with Nikko. He didn't have to be to work until 3 o'clock so he could leave from Nikko and Lake's house and go to work. Z asked Tré to stay at the house while he rushed home to get some toiletries. As he was pulling into the garage he noticed someone standing on his porch. Reaching for his mace in the glove compartment, he thought, "I'm not up for this shit this early in the morning. This (bitch) is tired." After realizing it was JJ he put the can of mace back in the glove compartment. "What the hell are you doing at my house at 1:00 a.m. in the morning?"

"I had a fight with my roommate, so I decided to cool off for a moment; my car led me to your house." JJ explained.

"You have a very smart fucking car," Z replied. "I'm just rushing home to get some clothes. I have to rush back to a friend's house. His sister just died, so I just can't do anything."

JJ cut him off, "I understand, man. I just wanted to get away and chill for a minute."

Z feeling his ass getting moist said, "Okay, I could chill for a minute.

Let me call my best friend and give him a lie; it will only take a minute.

"Baby boy, this is Z. I have a flat tire. I don't know what the fuck I ran over in my driveway, but I called the Lexus tow truck and they are on their way, so as soon as they get here I'll be on my way," Z said sympathetically. "Let me speak to Tré for a moment. Tré, I will be there shortly. I'm just waiting on the tow truck so they can change my tire; I just got my nails done."

"Stop lying, Z. Who are you getting ready to fuck? Nikko needs you man, and you'd rather go fuck some motherfucker than to be with your best friend? You are a whack ass motherfucker. I don't believe you. (Nigga), you know Nikko needs your punk ass right now, but I'll stay. Don't worry. Have a fucking good time." Tré was yelling under his breath, making sure Nikko did not hear the argument with Z. Not giving Z time to continue with his lies, Tré slammed the phone down. Nikko walked into the room. "So who did Z pick up tonight?" asked Nikko.

"No one, Nikko, man why would you say something like that about your best friend?" asked Tré.

Nikko replied, "Because I've known your cousin and my best friend for 10 years. Z acts hard but that's just a front. When things get tough Z can't handle it. He will break in a heartbeat. I know because I love him and to love someone you must first know his ways and love them first and if anybody got some fucked up ways it is definitely Zarius."

Tré changed the subject. "Nikko, can I ask you a serious question?" and before Nikko could agree, Tré asked, "Do you feel your sister right now? You guys were twins and I was always told about twins and their feelings and how they finish each other's sentences and all that stuff."

Nikko started explaining, "I felt my sister's pain the other night. I really didn't know what it was because that was the same time Lake and I were celebrating our anniversary and I was hoping I was just excited about being in the midst of everything Lake had done for me. I felt my sister's pain, but I couldn't do anything, or I chose to do nothing. I could have prevented her from dying. You can't imagine how I feel. I felt her when she took her last breath, but for some unknown reason, this is the way she would have wanted it. She's touching me right now. I feel her spirit and it's calm and peaceful. But it's so hard, it's unbearable, I'm trying to stay afloat, but it is devastating. Tré do you know what happened to my parents and the near breakdown Nikki and I had? We found our parents dead from a home intrusion. We were all coming back from a cruise that our parents had planned for us, celebrating their 12th wedding anniversary. They got home 30 minutes before Nikki and me. We found our parents lying in a puddle of blood, a knife was lodged in my father's back and my mother was strangled like a dog. Nikki just fainted at the sight of our parents; it was all she could bear. I have been taking care of Nikki since then. Even though we are twins, I felt I had to protect her, and in some ways she protected me. We are all we have. During that time is when I met your crazy cousin. He was at the same college, taking up nursing. He was as flamboyant then as he is now, never changing, but he helped us so much. He was our outlet. He made us laugh when we wanted to cry, he made us smile when we wanted to sink in our blanket of grief and sorrow. He knew how to comfort us in so many ways and I will be grateful for his generosity. Other than you, Malia, Lake, Kennedy and Nikki, Z is my best friend. I understand he has some strange ways, but he means well, Tré you should know; he's your cousin," Nikko said.

"That's all true, but he's so embarrassing with his flamboyant behavior. He feels that every man wants him and he always wants to fight. Z is over 30 years old and he acts like an 18 year old flaming faggot. Don't get me wrong, he's my cousin, and I love him, but I really don't like him. He's obnoxious. Nikko, man I don't mean to be venting but that cat boils my blood sometimes. Why can't he act more like us? We know what we like in bed, but we don't have to advertise our shit to the whole fucking world. Sometimes I want to break his fucking neck, that (nigga) cousin of mine. I just don't know what to say sometimes."

"Okay, Tré. You made your point. Try to accept Z for the good things. He's a damn good nurse, he knows more than any doctor I know and he could run the entire hospital if he wanted to. He truly has a good heart. Sometimes he falls short of loving himself and I believe that's why he behaves the way he does. Tré, continue to pray for him as I do for all of us everyday and night." Nikko began to sob. The phone rang again and Nikko answered it on the first ring. "Hello," he mustered up enough courage to say. It was Lake on the other end.

"How's everything going, baby boy?" asked Lake.

"As well as can be expected, Lake." Replied Nikko.

"What was the situation back at the precinct?" Nikko lazily asked.

"It was a false alarm, the call I got earlier was from another detective. They thought they had apprehended the guy that raped/murdered Nikko, but it was a homeless guy. Someone had planted a jacket on him covered with Nikki's blood. They have given him some money and some pictures of Nikki just to throw us off. Baby, I really don't want to tell you this being all we are going through. I'll be home in a minute." Lake hesitated.

"Do you want me to bring anything home? I'm on my way back," asked Lake.

"Just yourself," replied Nikko. "Tré is still here sitting with me, talking about life."

"I need help with the obituary and contacting any remaining relatives," Lake said. After hanging up with Lake, Nikko decided to call his sister's house to retrieve all her voice mail messages. It was eerie listening to Nikki's voice he yearned to feel her touch once more. The voice mail announced there were 99 calls; he didn't think a machine could hold that many messages. Tré grabbed the phone and insisted on retrieving the messages. Nikko didn't argue instead he rushed upstairs without saying a word. He felt the house begin to spin. Without a second to spare, Nikko lay on the bed and the tears began to fall. It was now three o'clock in the morning and he suddenly realized that he had to spend the rest of his life without his sister. He began to cry louder, hoping that the pillow would drown his sorrow. Nikko had cried himself to sleep and awaken when he felt a familiar hand rub his back. He didn't move. He felt safe and secure knowing that Lake had finally come home; it was something that he desperately needed and would continue to need for the rest of his life.

"Baby, just lay there; I'll get some massage oil. Let me take some stress off." Lake started undressing Nikko, until he was fully nude. Nikko just lay there, not saying a word. Lake hit the CD changer and the sounds of soft violins, the ocean hitting rocks and the birds singing filled the room. Lake started from the middle of Nikko's back, pouring the massage oil all over Nikko's back, rubbing his thumbs in the heart of Nikko's spine, massaging every muscle and feeling the nerve pulsating. Lake knew this was what Nikko needed when he was stressed and needed the touch. Lake gave Nikko thirty minutes of intense massaging leaving him fast asleep. It was five o'clock in the morning and it was quiet in the house as Lake began to fall into a deep sleep. He immediately started dreaming of an old, decrepit man lying in a hospital bed with sores all over his body; his hair had fallen out and he looked about ninety years old; lonely just looking in space. A nurse entered the hospital room and asked the man, "Mr. Lake, how are you feeling today?" Lake jumped out of his sleep screaming at the top of his lungs. Nikko woke up and Tré came running in the bedroom with Sasha and Sebastian right behind him. Upon realizing what had happened, he was totally embarrassed and drenched in sweat. He had a nightmare that was so unbearable he couldn't believe it. Nikko tried to comfort him, but he was so out of it he really didn't know exactly what was going on.

It was 6 o'clock and Malia was rolling over to find Drayton between her legs, sucking and licking up a storm. She really wanted to tell him that she didn't want to be bothered but the feeling was so good, she couldn't even utter the word "no". She just lay there for a moment, soaking up the pleasures of being discomfortable. She started to cry because she wanted to be whole again. She wanted God to bring her a whole man not a man to share; a man that gave her pleasures 24-hours a day, seven days a week. A God fearing man; one with whom she could procreate with. She wanted a child that they could raise, one she would love and keep close to her heart. She suddenly started thinking about Kennedy, and how she would cope after losing of her mother. Who would teach her about growing into a woman? Who would teach her about her first period, about little boys and their mischievous ways? Who would help her with her first prom and her real first date? Nothing is sweeter than a mother seeing her baby growing up to be an adult. Suddenly, Malia jumped up, her thighs shaking, leaving Drayton with his mouth wide open.

"What's wrong, baby?" Drayton yelled.

"Nothing, I have to do a lot of shit for Nikko!" she replied. Drayton just lay there in disgust, but didn't utter a word.

"Baby, do want me to fix you some breakfast?"

"Don't have time, sir. I'll catch something at the office," replied Malia. "Drayton, I got your suits from the dry cleaners so you will have something clean to wear back home," she yelled from the bathroom.

"Thanks, babe," Drayton replied, staring at the cathedral ceilings in the bedroom, wondering how he would tell Malia that his wife was pregnant with their third child. How would she deal with this after he'd promised her he was getting a divorce? What kind of lie would he come up with? He had already drawn up fake divorce papers and lied about how his wife refused to sign them. He can tell that Malia is losing interest and is fed up with the lies and deceit, but she hasn't asked him to get the fuck out. "I know she must be in love with me," Drayton thought. "Why else would put up with my bullshit?" There had to be an angle to why she had not yet told his wife. Drayton was confessing to himself that he truly loved Malia, but he also loved his wife despite her naïve behavior, and he would never give up his little girls for anything in the world. How could he choose? He had the best of both worlds: a black independent woman, with a good head on her shoulders, who was wealthy and knew what she wanted out of life, and on the other hand, the mother of his two children and another on the way. He hoped it was a little boy. Malia nudged him as she was going out the door. "Get up, Drayton. You are going to be late for work," she said, not realizing he had fallen back to sleep. "I'll talk to you later," she said as he kissed his forehead. Malia strolled downstairs wearing powder blue short skirt suit with a two-inch slit on the side of the skirt, draped with a crème colored blouse with 5 carat diamond earrings, and finished her ensemble with crème three-inch pumps and stockings. With her briefcase in hand and her Coach bag over her shoulder, all Drayton could see was the backside but what a backside it was; and it was all his, for the time being.

CHAPTER 15

Get your punk-ass up

Z lazily answered the phone that had fallen on the floor.

"Who the fuck is calling me this early in the damn morning," Z yelled.

"Get your sorry ass up, Z. Remember, you're supposed to be here at Nikko's. You are a sorry son of a bitch!" As Tré yelled back, Z fell back into reality.

"Oh shit, I'm sorry, cuz! I lost track of time. I just wanted to take a nap before I had to come back over."

"Forget the excuses, (nigga.) Just get your ass back over here!" Tré continued to shout. "Lake had a nightmare and woke up the entire house. Get that dick out your ass and get over here."

"I'll be right there, man, and who the fuck you think you are cussing?" The phone went dead, and Z responded, "I know that son of a bitch didn't hang up on me." JJ woke up. "Who was that, man?"

"That was my sorry ass cousin giving orders; confused motherfucker; don't know if he wants to be gay or straight."

JJ began to apologize. "Sorry for getting you in trouble. I just wanted to see you and hold you man."

"Don't be silly. I wanted to get fucked, and fucked by you, so there it is; we were both satisfied, but now I gotta go. Can I trust you to lock my door and don't try to steal nothing in my house? Remember, I know where you work and live," Z asked, sheepishly. "Sure, man. Anything you want your slave to do, Master Z," responded JJ.

"Naw, you're my sex slave, and that's Miss Z. I gotta get to the hospital and take care of my sister. She died last night and I am running behind. I'm trying my best to be strong, but the shit is killing me."

"What?" JJ shouted. "Man, your sister died last night and you wanted to fuck?! That's deep!"

"It's not my real sister; it's Nicolette Grey, the supermodel."

"Shut the fuck up. You know her? She's the bomb!" JJ exhaled.

"She was raped and badly beaten, and she passed late last night. I had to (pronounce ??) her and get all the necessary procedures taken care of. Nothing can be done without my signature. I will have to make sure everything is running fine. I hate this fucking situation; it was not supposed to be this way. We were supposed to grow old together. I don't want to talk about this anymore, I don't even feel like having sex tonight either." Z said reluctantly.

"Well, let me give u something to ease your mind. Let me run you some bath water, and give you a massage and I'm going to roll you a big fat one. That always chills me out," JJ replied.

"I don't smoke, boy. I used to do that shit, but I'm a nurse now; I don't have time for that shit."

"Relax, man. I got a lot of stuff you can take and it will never show up in your blood stream," JJ said.

Z argued, "I'm a nurse. I know how to get shit out of your blood stream." Before he could utter another word, JJ kissed him, softly and passionately, tongue all the way down Z's throat, making him weak and starting to tremble. JJ had to hold him up. They both started getting moist and the tonguing continued. Z finally pulled away.

"Let me go get undressed; that bath will do me some good," he said softly. JJ jumped up and said, "Wait right here let me pour you some wine and then I will get started on your bath, then massage. You felt a little tense and I want to help you with that, Z. Just lay on the couch." Z was weak and moist, and his head began to spin. JJ pulled Z's pants off, removed his shirt, underwear and T-shirt. Z laid there, butt ass naked in oblivion. JJ began to lick his nipples and slid his tongue down Z's chest, stomach and around his navel. Z started to moan as he begged JJ to stop, but JJ kept stroking him with his tongue, now more intensely than before. Now he was holding Z's hands as he glided towards Z's dick. He started sucking it with long strokes, making it disappear as he watched Z's eyes roll back in his head. As he put his hands over Z's mouth to smother the screams, he immediately started sucking his balls and was now tonguing Z's rectum. Z was screaming to the top of his lungs, begging for JJ to stop; that was Z's hot spot, guaranteed to make him climax on demand.

The phone started ringing at 6:25 a.m. and the drama began all over again. Kennedy jumped up at 6:30 a.m., crying for her mother. The sound startled the entire house and poor Tré didn't know whether to wind his ass or scratch his watch.

"This shit is too much for me," he said. He started toward Kennedy's bedroom when he stopped his tracks. Nikko was holding Kennedy and crying his eyes out, trying to console his niece and breaking down himself. Lake had approached them and started holding both of them, trying to be strong for the entire family, realizing that now that's all they had; just each other. Tré leaned back on the hallway wall. He suddenly turned away, realizing that he needed to walk the dogs. He thought it would be a long walk maybe 10 miles. That would give him enough time to dry his own tears.

Z blew the horn at Tré while passing him on the road he wanted to stop but was still pissed off about the shouting match they had earlier. As he stared at Tré in the rear view mirror. He mumbled "Punk-ass faggot." Z pulled into the driveway of the four bedroom Tudor house, which seemed ghostly as if there was something hovering over it. Z didn't even knock; he just strolled in, yelling for Nikko and Lake. They were sitting at the kitchen table with Kennedy eating bacon, eggs and grits.

"I have some information we need to discuss and I think we need to make some additional preparations pertaining to the f-u-n-e-r-a-l," he said, trying to throw Kennedy off the trail. Tré entered the kitchen door from the garage staring at Z while he said good morning to everyone. "I have already called Malia; she should be here shortly. Nikko, when will your aunt be arriving?" Z asked.

CHAPTER 16

Anything I Can Do?

As Tré approached the house, his cell starting ringing. It was Keisha, his son's mother. "Tré I heard about Nikki from my co-workers from the hospital. Is there anything I can do?"

"No not as this point, Keisha. How's my little man?"

"I took him to school already and now I'm headed out the door. I just wanted to give you a call to see if you needed my help. If you need anything let me know. By the way, I understand if you can't get Jr. this weekend. Love you, Big Man. I'm out!" Before Tré could utter a reply, Keisha had already hung up the phone. Tré sat on the hood of his beat up Sentra and pulled out a Black and Mild, reminiscing about how he'd (fucked) up Keisha's life, how he'd made her fall in love with him, got her pregnant and then decided not to marry her after all the bullshit he'd put her through. "And she still loves my sorry ass," he thought. Keisha was a project girl who had raised herself and her two younger brothers. She had a dead beat father who stayed in jail more that he stayed with his family, a drug-addicted mother who stayed high more than she slept. Keisha managed to work a part-time job while in high school, support her two brothers plus fight off the men, boys and bitchy ass girls in school. She managed to graduate with honors, attend a community college, plus continue to raise her little brothers and a 5-year-old son. She was a remarkable lady with long black hair, slightly slanted eyes, thick eyebrows, and perfect white teeth. Tré had to be grateful for Z; he helped Keisha get a nursing scholarship, a part time job at the hospital and he helped her find a nice apartment for her, her brothers and Jr., but when it was time to marry, Tré just got cold feet and knew that he could not put this project princess through more hell. He knew he still had crazy desires to be with a man. It was a feeling that he could not shake, no matter how much he prayed, cussed and fought his desires. He knew if he married her he would eventually leave her to satisfy his carnal appetite. Ironically, Tré hated faggots, sissies, drag queens and homos; everything he represented, he hated. He couldn't understand why, in the past, he had beaten the shit of out guys who acted like girls. Their actions provoked him to curse, spit and even cut (motherfucking faggots). He befriended Nikko because of his brotherly love. Nikko acted like a man; no one would ever have suspected he was gay. Nikko never hid his sexuality, but, if it didn't come up, it was only assumed by women who desired him as their husband or lover. When Lake first came into the picture, Tré hated him because he was straighter than straight, tall, muscular, masculine, and sexy as hell. Tré could never imagine those two in bed, fucking, sweating, fondling, sucking each other's dicks; he could only imagine who was penetrating whom. Tré had always been attracted to Nikko, even when they'd first become friends, but he never expressed it, nor would he ever. He was the type of thug trade that would never make advances at another man, regardless of how fucking sexy they were. Tré harbored these feelings for Nikko, even when Nikko gave him a place to stay when he was training for the airlines. So many times, he'd wanted to sneak into Nikko's bedroom and start making love to him, but he was never really sure if Nikko would accept that. He prayed for those feelings to leave. When Lake entered the picture, all hopes of Trés fantasy coming true ended.

Everyone in America now knew about the death of Nikki Gray, and everyone was talking about it. It was the only story on the news; it was being covered by everyone from Larry King to Dan Rather; now the paparazzi were camped out in front of Nikko and Lake's house. They knew they would eventually have to give a public interview, but they didn't know how or where they would hold the meeting. Malia arrived and she started to discuss the current situation and how to handle the press and the public. She said had passed by Nikki's little mansion and people had started leaving mementos and just standing outside the subdivision. Little girls were crying; everyone was just in shock by all that was taking place; it seemed as though there were a major disaster or a loss of a high profile celebrity every three to six months: Aaliyah, the Twin Towers collapsing, Lisa Lopes, Luther Vandross, Hurricane Katrina and now Nikki. Somalia informed them of how cruel the press could be, how they mustn't let them see them break. She was briefing Nikko for the worst and hoped for the best. "You will be asked to give information about your sister's favorite charitable foundation.

This is where they will send their donations. They are going to ask you about Kennedy and her safety and health. Also, they will ask you about the attacker and about how you're cooperating with the authorities. Nikko, you must understand, this going to be hard; probably one of the most difficult events you will have to endure, but we will be there for you every step of the way.

"Okay, first thing's first. Let's set up a time when we can talk to the media, letting them know when we want to set up a press conference, and we will do it from here on our stomping grounds. We will give only five stations access to this story. We must demand that the agencies stop leaking information out to the press and make sure there is a gag order for anyone associated with the agency. This is the ugly part of the press, the public and the law. Be as precise as possible, do not exaggerate the unknown, and do not elaborate about her life; just give details of what you know. Nikko, if you become uncomfortable, look at me and I will handle it from there. I can and will interject at anytime. I will sense your hesitation and finish the interview. Nikko, do you have any questions? If not, try to pick a suit that is conservative, but not dull or boring. You need a tie that will compliment the suit. And that goes for all of us. Do you hear me, Z? This is very important. Leave the bullshit aside; this is my job and my reputation, so we have to make sure that the media vultures do not try to box Nikko in or cause him to break. As of today, we are all family; the media may come to us, one by one. Any reply should be, 'No comment, and if you want to discuss this case, please contact my attorney,' which will be myself." Somalia gave Nikko some additional paperwork detailing the time she was going to release to the media and the parameters of the media conference. It was scheduled for 5:00 EST. This way, it would give the media a small timeframe to have their cameras and anchor people available. Malia wanted to make it short and sweet, stopping the bleeding midstream. She knew Nikko and Lake were suffering a great deal emotionally and mentally, and she didn't want to add insult to injury. She didn't want their relationship or Nikko's current health problem to leak out. She could and would handle it all. Her attitude had suddenly changed; it was almost scary how this attractive sister that they once knew could become so direct, distant, and abrasive at times. But that was her job; to protect the innocent and fuck the rest. It was a trait that came with the territory, something she had to develop in order to be a successful lawyer. They all had seen her this way before, but only on TV. Afterwards, she would come around and become the meek, little innocent sister they all knew and loved. Z was the first to say, "Girl! Do you have a split personality? How do you change from a nice, innocent little girl, to a media-eating bitch?" She completely ignored Z. "Nikko, when is the funeral? I need the time and place. Have you made any arrangements as far as the eulogy? I need all that information now; the more information the better." Everything became foggy to Nikko; he had not realized that today was his and Nikki's birthday. He had not realized that he had been up for twenty-four hours.

Victoria heard the news about Nikki from every passing passenger in the airport. She was trying to call her boss, Malia, or even the other assistants at the law firm. Everyone knew that Malia was Nikki's family lawyer, and they were also very close friends. Victoria was reading the update in the paper; USA Today had run an exclusive story on Nikki and her amazing career. They talked about the $50 million contract with Revlon, the movie deal she'd just signed with DreamWorks for the remake of Valley of the Dolls, and she'd negotiated the rights to West Side Story. She had so much going on for herself. Her line of clothing was scheduled to hit stores next year. Victoria felt so sorry for her and especially for what would happen to her daughter. She started thinking about Lake and how he would handle the death of his lover's twin sister. She would call him to give her condolences but she knew she'd want to gloat over the fact he left her for a motherfucking faggot. Even though she tried to remain friends with them both, she still had it for Lake. Their relationship was brief, but she felt hard and heavy. Lake was different; he was sensitive to her needs, but strong, he shared his most intimate secrets, yet seemed invincible. Nothing really seemed to shake him, and Victoria tried with her girlish antics to trap him. She tried lying by saying that she was pregnant, but Lake always used condoms, so she had to think of another way to catch that hunk of a man. Her plans fell through one night when Lake came to her and told her that he had a homosexual experience with a man and he felt that he could not handle being unfaithful to her. He said he had to get his head together and begged her to understand. She refused to let him go that easily; she was even more desperate, trying to convince him she was pregnant, dying, or had a rare disease. He would always come whenever she called but refused to sleep with her, no matter how much she pleaded, screamed, yelled and cussed. After two months of hell, she decided to let him go and be a faggot, but she made a promise to herself that she would get him back, fuck his whole life up, no matter how long it took, but today she would have to wear her empathetic armor to show support to the Grey family. She would first get all the dirt, then she would probably head over to Nikko's house, where she would play the best role ever, giving everyone the impression that she really cared about their pitiful asses. She began to dial Malia's number again on her cell as she thought about how much she hated Nikko, Lake, and even that bastard of a daughter, Kennedy. "Hi, Malia," Victoria said as she tried to use the most pitiful voice possible. "I wanted to give my condolences and to let you know I'm back in town. The plane departed a little late, but I'm here. Malia, everyone is talking about Nikki Grey. Is there anything I can do?"

"Well, first of all, Victoria, I need those papers on my desk by tomorrow. I need to start my briefing with that case, and I don't have a moment to lose. Also, if you're not too tired, I need for you to come over to Nikko's house in Stone Mountain. His address is in my Rolodex on the desk. I may need you to assist me in some legal jargon with the fucking press. How soon can you get here? We're scheduled to have the press conference in less than two hours," Malia said in a very authoritative tone.

"I'm on my way," Victoria said as she rushed Malia off the phone. Victoria loved her boss, but hated that her boss was Malia. Malia always kept Victoria at arms length; she would only invite her to client parties, celebrity functions and different legal affairs. Malia knew that Victoria was a good assistant, but she never mixed professional relationships with personal ones. That's one reason she was never seen with Drayton at the job. She didn't have time for idle gossip and the people who created it. Victoria knew she had a wonderful and gracious boss; she was the only assistant in the office that was making sixty thousand a year. Malia fought for her to have that; she would give her all types of presents, gifts, mementos and souvenirs every time she would go out of town. Everyone loved how Malia could be a sweet and mild-mannered attorney. Everyone admired the fact that she could turn on and off the nasty, stern attitude, how she could become condescending to anyone and belittle his or her actions. Malia had a certain type of innocence that attracted people to her. She was warm, and affectionate to everyone; a kind-hearted person who always had something good to say about everyone. She knew that all law firms had a high level of gossip: who's sleeping with whom, whose fucking, who's gay, who's a whore, who's broke, who's an alcoholic, and the list goes on. They were some powerful and rich sharks at her law firm, which was the biggest in the southeast, and they knew it. They were a bunch of pompous assholes and had the money to prove it. Malia was a civil lawyer, and she studied criminal and entertainment law. Victoria had been her administrative assistant for more than. Malia knew just how to handle Victoria; she knew she had issues but admired her for being a good administrator. She knew Victoria started a lot of shit in the reception pool, but it never contaminated her work. For the most part, Victoria was a hateful bitch; she was conniving and two-faced, and she would fuck you up in the blink of an eye, but when it came to Malia there was a hidden alliance. She knew how far to go with Malia, who could make or break you in the state of Georgia. Malia knew everyone, and everyone knew her. From politicians to doctors to celebrities, she spent a lot of valuable time in the community from volunteering with the Frank Ski Foundation, to coaching a little league girl's softball team. She had donated a lot of time and money to almost every non profit organization in Atlanta. Victoria knew that if she made one false move against Malia she would be toast and would have to flee the country.

It was show time and all the players were in place, headed by the quarterback, Malia. She had taken the liberty of informing Monica, Amanda, and Brenda of all the details of the funeral and the latest on the attacker. They all agreed to cooperate to the fullest and gave their condolences. Joyce Littel called to inform Malia that she wanted to start an emergency fund for Kennedy and wanted the permission of Nikko and Lake, since she'd had long- lasting friendships with Nikki and Kennedy. The public was now calling in to Portia's radio segment, crying, giving their condolences to the family and friends, expressing how much they loved Nikki and how she will be missed. Portia, along with other radio stations, started a big sympathy card with more than 50,000 people anxiously ready to sign.

CHAPTER 17

The Procession

It was a cool and crisp morning; there was a heavy dose of freshness in the air of this late autumn morning in September. The weather was changing, and so would Lake and Nikko's lives forever. They were about to face the inevitable: it was the day of Nikki's funeral. The alarm sounded to Yolanda Adam's voice as it always did. This time, it was "I Believe." Nikko didn't move. He was numb and exhausted and just wanted to die, but at that very second a voice came to him as it always did when he felt he had nothing to live for; "Don't cry for me don't shed a tear," but this time this voice was different it said, "BE STRONG, BE STRONG, BE AND STAY STRONG." The voice was heavier and deeper. It sounded like his father, a man to whom he had given nothing but respect. Nikko started speaking back. "I have been strong. I have been patient. I've been whatever I had to be, but I can't be anymore. I'm tired, Daddy." Lake lay silently in the bed, not moving an inch. He decided to let Nikko pray out loudly and to talk to his God alone. The voice continued, "I created you to be strong, a man of virtue and man that had faith in God, and perseverance. You can do this and you will. Me, your mother, brother and now your sister Nikki are all counting on you. Your battle is just started; you will have to raise your niece and fight your demons, mentally, and spiritually, and we will be here for you Nicholas. Always remember that." Nikko started to cry and he shouted to the ceiling. "I refuse! I want to die! I'm tired, and my body is weak and poisoned!" At that point, Lake jumped up and grabbed Nikko, begging him to wake up out of the dreadful nightmare he was having. Nikko was drenched in sweat and tears. As he was awakening, he was holding Lake tighter then ever. "Wake up, baby," Lake pleaded. "It will be alright." Nikko was slightly embarrassed, but refused to acknowledge the nightmare.

It was time for the day to begin. Grabbing his robe, Nikko called to Lake, "I need to start breakfast and get Princess up and get her ready for the funeral." As Lake was brushing his teeth and Nikko washing his face, they both smelled coffee and bacon and they knew Auntie had beaten them to the kitchen. She burst into to master suite. "I hope y'all boys are dressed, 'because an old lady is coming in," she shouted.

"Yes, Auntie, we're dressed," shrugged Lake.

"Well, come on down. Your breakfast is getting cold. I got the little one down there eating by herself. Nikko, you know the camera people been sitting outside all night. I was gonna let the dogs out and let 'em bite the shit out of them, but I didn't want a law suit, so I decided against it. But you better call that lady lawyer 'because sister is good and ready to make them MF's get off your lawn. The funeral is at 1 o'clock and I don't want them around 'cause you know the celebrities will be coming here, or to Nikki's house."

Nikko completely ignored her and rushed downstairs.

"Princess," he yelled, "you know we gotta get ready, baby. Have you finished your breakfast? We have to say bye-bye to mommy." He was trying to act as nonchalant as possible.

"But mommy's not dead, Uncle Nikko." She's just resting and she will wake up." Auntie interrupted, "Yeah, baby, she will wake up but she will wake up in Heaven, baby, and sooner or later we will all be together."

Tré and Z spent the night at Malia's house in hopes they would all be arriving at Nikko's house as a unit. Nikko felt that they were the only family he and Lake had, so they had to act that way. They had spent all night talking, first about the death of Nikki, then about Kennedy, and then the conversation veered towards life after Nikki. Z was the first to acknowledge that he would dedicate a percentage of his time helping people from the hospital; this was one of the projects Nikki was spearheading, helping people with no health insurance by finding them money for medical bills.

"I can help with aiding those agencies," Z mournfully replied. Malia changed the subject quickly. "Tré, what are you willing to sacrifice?"

"Well, Nikki was the god mother to my son, so I'm determined to spend more time with him and try and love everyone as she loved everyone. I must admit I'm very prejudiced against gays, faggots, and punks. I do hate them, but I must learn to love and accept everyone."

Z interrupted, "How in the fuck can you hate motherfucking faggots when you one, yourself?"

Malia interrupted again, knowing the shit was getting ready to hit the fan. "Tré, we all know your sexual orientation. Why you still hate other gay men, I don't understand," she said, trying to diffuse the situation between Tré and Z.

"I hate what they stand for. "Why can't a man be a man? "Stop parading around like fairies and acting like women. They have to let everyone know their fucking business."

Z interrupted again, "Tré, do you hate me? We are cousins. We grew up together, and our mothers are sisters, but I'm a faggot, a homo. I'm considered less than a man because I get fucked in the ass; and I don't go around fucking everyone on the universe to prove my manhood. I'm the one you are talking about. I feel you hate me for my lifestyle and what I represent. Tré, we are the same, and the sooner you realize that, the better. All my life I had to fight for myself and I had to fight for you. When we were small and motherfuckers tried to fight me, you would always try to fight for my honor but I always fought for myself, because I was a 'sissy'. I knew I had to fight for myself, but now, over 20 years later, I have my own flesh and blood reducing my life to nothing but a punk; a piece of wood. Tré, I just want you to open your heart and realize that we are all the same. I suck dick, I eat ass, I get fucked in the ass, I have had two or more motherfuckers fuck me at the same time, I have had the crabs, I have had STD's, but that has not stopped me from being gay. You may feel that this makes me feel less then a man, but it don't. I'm a proud, secure black man who makes over $60,000 a year. I support my mother, pay my bills; I even gave your son's mother a job. I am a good black man who happens to be gay and love it. I love getting my ass eaten, getting fucked and love the warmth of a man's body and tongue. Tré, you are bisexual, on the down low, but that don't make you better then me. Malia makes over $300,000 a year, but that don't make her better then me. If I have to be an advocate for every black gay, faggot, sissy, homo, punk, queer, anti-man, AIDS carrying motherfucker, scum of the earth, then so be it, but Tré, my dear cousin, if I ever hear you call me or any gay person out their name again, I will personally fuck you up myself."

The conversation ended when the phone rang. Malia rushed to answer it; it was Lake informing them of the last minute details and the time to arrive at the church. "Bishop Molton will be presiding over the funeral, Whitney and CeCe will be singing; also, Charlotte Church will be singing, along with Barbara. Oprah has some words she wants to say; Mayor Franklin also wanted to offer some words of encouragement and last on the program will be Bill and Camille. It will be short and sweet; the way Nikki would have wanted it. I need you guys to meet us at Nikki's house in about two hours. There will be a limo to pick you guys up, so chop chop."

Malia solemnly responded, "We will, Lake, and remember that we love you."

"We love you too," melancholically responded Lake.

Arriving at the house brought instant chills to Nikko's spine. He was not ready to face the horrible event all over again, but something wonderful and amazing lay in the midst as they approached the house: There was a huge sympathy card with more than 10,000 signatures and flowers. Balloons and teddy bears of every shape and size were smiling at the family as they arrived at the house. Lake and Katie had anticipated the arrival of the family, friends and the media. Lake wanted to make sure everything was suitable, comforting and pleasant for the family and friends to enter. Going back to the house was Nikko's idea; he wanted to face his fears, and there would be no better time to conquer those fears than now. Katie had an interior decorator redo the entire house. It was almost unrecognizable; she'd redecorated the house from top to bottom. It was simply gorgeous. No sign of the horrible rape or the home invasion was left. Kennedy immediately escaped from the limo and ran upstairs to look for her mom. Even though she knew she wasn't there, she was hoping she was as she flew up the stairs. She had just left the gravesite, but still it was too much for her to bear. She screamed her mother's name over and over again; she had slipped away so swiftly that no one could catch her. Lake immediately ran behind her as the entire family stood at the entrance in shock. Nikko was simply mortified. He didn't know what to do or say; he just knew that his heart sank into his stomach once again, and he knew he had to be strong for everyone's sake. Everyone had followed the procession from the gravesite to the 3,800 square-foot, four bedroom Tudor house. It seemed too big for Nikki and Kennedy, but today it was definitely filled to capacity. Everyone, from Whitney and Bobby, Oprah and Stedman and Vanessa and Rick, Beverly Peele and Johnson, Veronica, Nia and baby, Denzel and Paula, Will and Jada, Mayor Young, Campbell, Franklin, India and Musiq, Gladys, Patti Labelle and Austin, Barbara and a host of others came to the house to continue their condolences, even though most had to prepare to leave right after the funeral. Chaston, Kennedy's father had suddenly appeared; the security was very tight and no one really knew who he was, but Victoria, Malia's assistant, had met him once, so she had given him clearance to enter the house. Everyone was trying to gather in the little castle when Auntie summoned everyone into the backyard for a moment of silence and prayer while the caterers were anxiously waiting to serve all the celebrities. The backyard was about 5 acres with a swimming pool, tennis courts, a garden and a gazebo. Tents were provided to protect their privacy and keep the late summer heat away. Auntie wanted everyone to feel the presence of her niece's spirit; she mentioned how Nikki had always been an angel, a child of God, and how she'd gone to Heaven and would no longer have to deal with this dismal society. "She lived by peace and strived for virtue in everything she did. I want everyone to eat and remember to pray for your remaining family, Kennedy, now a motherless child and my two nephews, Nikko and Lake, for they have a great journey ahead of them. Also, pray for my extended family, Malia, Zarius and Tré, because, when we all go back to our designated homes, these three will need strength and guidance to continue to help my children."

Malia noticed that Chaston had walked in as everyone started to eat. She tried to get his attention, but he was completely ignoring her; he was busy trying to find his daughter or Nikko. She started toward him, but Z and Tré stopped her. They both ordered her to get upstairs where Nikko, Kennedy and Lake were anxiously waiting. They immediately disappeared upstairs to the master bedroom. Nikko and Kennedy were both lying in the bed, sobbing from ear to ear. The tears were unstoppable. Lake was trying to console both of them, but was having a difficult time doing so. Malia rushed over to Kennedy and started consoling her. Almost immediately, Auntie walked in and her spirituals started to flow. She sat on the end of the king size bed and began to tell the story of Nikko's late mother; about how they were twins growing up in Savannah, Georgia and how they almost lost their mother. "Our mother had a debilitating disease, something that we as little girls could not understand. We prayed a lot, we went to church almost everyday; we didn't know what else to do. But one night, as we were sleeping, we both felt the spirit of our grandmother. She came as a vision, urging us to continue to pray. She said that she would protect us, whether our mother passed or not. That night, our whole world changed. Our mother became stronger and stayed with us to live to the age of 82, but we became spiritually grounded that night. We knew that, regardless of what happens in our lives, our grandmother, Nikko, your great grandmother and Kennedy's great great grandmother lives inside of us and protects us, so I want to continue to pray for the pain to ease and for the days to get stronger. We are all we got. Kennedy, your mother is in Heaven with her mother, her father and her brother, Meeco. Their memories will make us all stronger, but we can't do it alone. We have them to strengthen our hearts; they will always be with us."

There's a knock at the door and in comes Kennedy's father, Chaston. He ran toward Kennedy as the door sprung open. "Daddy!" she cried.

"There's my baby girl," he responded. Nikko and the rest of the family stood up. Lake was the first to respond. "What are you doing here, Chaston?"

"I had to see about my little girl," Chaston immediately responded, as he hugged Kennedy. Everyone forgot all about the current situation as a cold chill covered the master bedroom. Everyone knew it was time to join the others downstairs and that this gathering would have to be rescheduled very soon. There were over 200 people in the little mansion: celebrities, bodyguards, reporters, news men, radio personalities, some selected church people, the funeral personnel, the caterers, and of course friends and family. Some people were starting to wither and others were admiring the house; the decor and all the memories that surrounded the house. It was becoming overwhelming with everyone in the small mansion, but it allowed Nikko and the rest to appreciate all the people who admired Nikki and her life.

Victoria found this to be her golden opportunity. She cornered Chaston in the foyer as he was about to leave and summoned him to follow her to the downstairs study. He thought she wanted to get his number because she'd been flirting with him since he entered the house. She told him that she was Malia's assistant and that she had some valuable information for him. Chaston's eyes grew with excitement. Victoria told him about the $5 million insurance policy and that it would only go to the person or persons who obtained custody of Kennedy. Chaston never assumed the responsibility of raising his daughter; he only saw her three times a year. Nikki had always raised her daughter alone and never asked Chaston for anything. They'd met when Chaston was playing professional football and Nikki's career was soaring, but he couldn't stay from drugs, women and injuries. They were supposed to get married before Kennedy was born and twice after. The last straw was when Chaston began to physically abuse Nikki when Kennedy was only three years old. Nikko and Lake beat the shit out of him, almost killing him. He left after that and didn't return until a year later, when he'd decided he wanted to start seeing his daughter again. His request was approved, but only with supervision through the courts. Nikki never filed charges against Chaston due to the fact that Lake could have lost his job by attacking him. They all agreed that that was behind them and that he did have a right to see his daughter. Chaston was currently working with the CFL, not making much money at all. He was just grateful he landed a job. Victoria proceeded, “I have something that may be quite valuable to you. Nikko and Lake assumed they would raise your daughter, but Nikko recently found out he is HIV positive. This could be your weapon against them. Of course, you would have to go to the courts to get custody of your daughter, but it should be an easy task. Now my boss is good, she's one of the best here in the southeast and she could be brutal, but I'll contain her. You would file for custody and give me 10 percent of the insurance money after the money goes through probate court. I believe $500,000 sand is a small fee for getting your daughter and some cold hard cash. Here's my card and my cell number. Call me if you need any legal information. As Chaston started to turn away, Victoria grabbed him, putting her arms around his shoulder, encouraging him as she kissed him, “If you need some pussy while in town, please don't hesitate to use my number, for sure.”

“I may need your assistance tonight for professional and pleasure reasons,” Chaston whispered.

“Just call me and I will definitely debrief you of your gavel,” Victoria whispered.

“That will work,” Chaston snickered as he exited the study. Kennedy had been standing at the door the entire time waiting for her father to come out of the study; he almost knocked her down as he was walking out. “Daddy,” she yelled, “you leaving so soon? I wanted you to stay a little longer, Daddy.”

“Baby girl, I will be back. I have some work to do. I can come get you tomorrow, but first we have to ask your uncle Nikko.”

“Okay, Daddy,” she responded. She ran down the hallway, yelling, “Uncle Nikko! Uncle Nikko!” She almost knocked Oprah down; she turned around and apologized, “I'm sorry Ms. Oprah. “My Daddy wants to get me tomorrow and I have to get permission from my uncle.”

She sympathetically responded, “It's alright baby. Kennedy, I haven't had a chance to talk to you, but as soon as you finish talking to your uncle please come back. I have something I want to give you, okay?”

“Okay,” Kennedy responded. Nikko heard her voice and ran toward her.

“What's wrong, Princess?”

“Uncle Nikko, can I go with Daddy tomorrow?”

Nikko didn't hesitate to respond. He immediately said, “Yes.”

CHAPTER 18

The Gathering

Malia heard her cell phone buzzing in the kitchen. "Damn. Who the hell can that be?" It was Drayton. "Yes, Drayton, I'm sorry baby. I know things are hectic over there. I just wanted to let you know that I'm still at Nikki's house, and I will cook dinner for you. Drayton, that won't be necessary. Don't know what time I'm coming home; I need to discuss some legal matters with the family."

It was getting late and most of the guests were gone; the only people remaining were the hired servants who had to restore the little mansion to normal. They were busy cleaning, wiping and washing, dusting, vacuuming, and reassembling the house back to state of normalcy. Auntie and Kennedy were resting while the rest of the family was assembled on the lanai. It was getting late and Malia wanted to advise the five some of the aftermath that was about to transpire. Nikko was not saying much; he just sat there, motionless. Malia started by saying, "We have to remain spiritually connected to our lost; it will strengthen us for things that are yet to come. I want to get the feedback about today's event. I want to go on the record and say that our days are definitely going to be difficult, but we will continue to heal and to live for the sake of Nikki and Kennedy."

Nikko interrupted her. "We need to go to the room." Lake didn't understand. Nikko repeated, "We need to go to Nikki's room." It had been blocked off to the entire public, but Nikko was persistent and looked toward Lake and requested the key. He reluctantly gave him the key and Nikko headed upstairs toward the master bedroom. The clan was right on his footsteps without uttering a sound. They knew that Nikko had to see and feel the presence of the room to keep his sanity and to restore a certain level of emotional tranquility. He unlocked the door and entered to see that the bedroom had been redecorated; the walls had been painted a deep yellow, speckled with burnt orange hues and scented with the aroma of Hawaiian Orchid. The tears started to roll again, without hesitation, from the five of them. There were no traces of blood-stained sheets or pillows and no sign of a struggle. It was simply peaceful, with flowers, plants and scented candles. The spirit of Nikki smothered the room; it was as if she was there looking over her family. The awards, trophies, pictures, paintings, water fountain, her favorite chair, the Solar Flex machine, lights and mirrors were all in tact. It was obvious that time and creativity were put into recreating a sense of peace and serenity. Nikko spoke first. "I'm pleased, Lake. I'm so happy, and I know Nikki would be happy as well." He turned on the waterfall, sat on the bed and asked Malia to finish the conversation they were having earlier. Nikko started smiling as he put his nose in the comforter and smelled his sister's scent. Malia resumed her summation of all the events they'd shared. Z and Tré had been very quiet up until this point. After Malia gave her professional and personal opinion, Z started by saying that he loved his friends; he continued, "I never really realized how important each and every one of you are to me. I took for granted your existence, never realizing that, in a blink of an eye, I could lose one of you or you could lose me. We all have grown together since our college days and your presence to me is like breathing. I'm the one who is the clown, the flamboyant center, the one who speaks his mind and doesn't give a damn what the public says about me, but today I realize that my family is in this house. Nikki will always be in my heart. I always wanted to be her. I've emulated her ever since I've known her; she was one of my idols. I will always cherish our moments, our little talks, the laughter we shared and what she meant to me. Accepting her untimely death, I will dedicate my time to one of her non-profit organizations. Losing her made me realize that I have so much talent to give to people who are less fortunate. I will volunteer what ever it takes to help whomever. I am one of the best nurses here in the state of Georgia, and I have never really tried giving back. I have helped some people, but I realize that I can help more and I will." Tré hesitated, and then cleared his throat. "I never thought life could be lived without any of you, so to have Nikki gone is like my worst nightmare, but I realized today that her presence lives on, that I feel her spirit, I still smell her scent. I know that we will survive this because that is what she would want. Her death has affected all of us and has been very devastating to the world as we know it. We take for granted day by day that we will be here tomorrow, but as we congregate in Nikki's room I now understand that God's order has been written even before we are born. Sometimes it's not the way that someone will live that life that hurts us so much but the way they leave. Nikki's exit was sudden but it's her love that will keep us strong and continue to make us stronger. I loved her for the angel she is; she earned her wings long before her death. She never said anything bad about anyone; she helped everyone. Her presence has been known throughout the world and yet she remained humble to all. She shook hands with actors, dignitaries, celebrities, legends, and still remained true to herself. If I could just receive an ounce of her humility I would be grateful. I must continue to be strong for all of us. I will be here for Kennedy and the rest of the crew." It was Lake's turn to give closure, but he knew it would be Nikko who had the last word. "I'm honored to have known Nikki. She inspired me to go for my dreams, even when I thought them impossible and unreachable. She taught me to face my fears of my love for her brother and the outside world. True love is unconditional; love doesn't have a sex, race or religious background. It is based on the soul of two people, the spirit of respect and loyalty, and the essence of communication. Nikki taught me that love is pure and to share that love with an open heart. Her life has been somewhat symbolic to me because she loved her daughter and her brother with all her heart. Nothing or no one could ever come between that; she never compromised her love for all of us. Her love was truly unconditional and I will always love her for that." Now it was Nikko's turn. "The accolades that my sister received have been immeasurable, alive or not. She has inspired the greatest singers, dancers and designers of all nationalities. She taught me to dream impossible dreams. I never dreamt of having a wonderful man of this magnitude. I could never dream of having the best friends in the world. I could never dream of the best niece any black gay man could have. I could have never imagined dreaming of a life without my sister. We shared more than a cell, or a chromosome; we shared life, we shared dreams, we shared breath, we shared pain, we shared sorrow and heart aches. Before there was life there was us inside my mother's womb. Only a twin could feel my pain. I don't know how I will manage, but I will survive. I have my life to live for her. I feel her presence. I want to captivate her impossible dreams, to continue to give life and love to those who knew her and those who didn't. I have my lover of six years, I've had my niece in my life for seven years and I have my three best friends whom I have known for a lifetime. I will survive. I just want everyone to know it is hard and it will be hard, but having our parents murdered when we were young made us stronger. We have a lot of hard days ahead of us, but that's life, and with my sister looking over us, we can only be more determined to survive.

CHAPTER 19

The Day After

Malia decided to work from home today. She had concentrated so much on Nikki that she was backed up in work. She asked Victoria to redirect all important calls to her home office number. She still had to look over insurance papers for Nikki and read through all the legal mumbo jumbo to which she was accustomed, but she really didn't want to deal with this one because of its personal nature. She had called Nikki's accountants to review Nikki's assets, how much she was worth, how much she owed, what Nikko would want to sell, and keep. After an entire day with Nikki's accountants, managers, publicist and agencies, they realized that Nikki was worth about $25 million. She indeed was a shrewd business woman, with investments, endorsement, life insurance, property ownership, and a host of CD's and money market accounts; the girl was truly well off. She was puzzled by one of the policies concerning the rearing of Kennedy; a disclosure indicated that there would be a $5 million allowance fee for anyone who assumed the responsibility of raising her daughter if something happened to her. She was still trying to figure this out when the phone rang. It was Drayton. "Hi baby. How are things going today?"

"It's going, just finished talking to Nikki's accountants and the rest of the gang. Would you like for me to have lunch catered?" Malia asked, reluctantly. "I can have them over in about 30 minutes." She decided to call Z and Tré. There was no answer from Trés house, so she decided to call Z again. He answered on the first ring. "What up girl? How are things going?"

"It's okay," Z. How did you sleep last night? I prayed a lot last night and prayed about so much. I had to pray for Nikko, Lake and Kennedy; I prayed for the strength to get Drayton out of my life, I prayed because I really want to adopt a baby. I just prayed." She looked in the mirror and asked, "Do you think I need to get my hair cut? I think it would be best for me to start fresh today. I could call over my stylist to cut it."

"Girl let me come cut your hair. You know I used to cut Nikki's hair in college. Girl, let me whack it off for you. Still got my shears, you know." Malia didn't respond. She was deep in thought, looking in the mirror and holding the phone.

"Girl, I know the first time I had long hair," Z continued. "I was in my mother's bathroom. I was about seven or eight. I took a black towel from the linen closet and wrapped it around my head and tied it as tight as possible. I secured it with a rubber band and I was ready for the stage. I was Diana Ross, putting my mother's lipstick on. I was belting out, 'I'm coming out, I want the world to know, I want to let it show,' Girl, I was shaking that towel hair like it was nobody's business." Malia still was not responding, so Z continued. "I always wanted to be Diana Ross without the Supremes, Tina Turner, and Donna Summer. I would steal my mother's high heels, and wrap a hand towel around my waist and instantly I was Tina Turner, singing' 'What's love gotta do with it, do with it'. Girl, I remember I used to perform for all my stuffed animals. I would steal my mother's makeup bag and hide in the basement and I would play old records like Billie Holliday, Sara Vaughn, and Mahalia Jackson. Eartha Kitt, Minnie Ripperton, Pearl Bailey and of course Dorothy Dandridge; just call me Carmen, (bitch). Girl, one day I got suspended from school for fighting. I didn't tell my mother or step-daddy. I hid behind the house till everyone was gone, snuck back in the house, dressed up in drag from head to toe, with my grandmother's wig, I put on my mother's too little shoes, my cousin's dress; it fit me better, my own spiked belt and my mother's patent leather purse. I was belting out Billie Holliday, God Bless the Child that Got His Own. I had put on some of my mother's Lee-Press-on-Nails, and suddenly I was interrupted by a knock at the door. It was a UPS delivery man; I answered the door in full drag. I open the door to sign for the package and one of my damn nails popped off. I was so damn mad that the delivery man was laughing, I screamed, 'That shit ain't funny!' I just told him to be gone; I had to get back to my craft. I slammed the door and went back to singing, 'mother may have, papa may have, but god blesses the child that got his own'." Malia fell out of her trance, laughing her ass off. Z was on a roll. "Girl, I was singing so hard and dancing so hard, that my step-daddy walked in. He had been there for a minute, but I didn't know it. My eyes were closed, and I was trying to stay on point; you know stage presence is very important. My daddy yelled, 'Zarius, what the hell are you doing?' I said, 'I'm auditioning for a play. It's very intense, Lonnie; it's the updated version of Yentle." Malia fell out her chair, she was laughing so hard. "I got grounded for a month," he continued. "Oohh girl let me tell you this; we had this stereo in the den sitting on the table. One Saturday, everyone went to the grocery store, so I needed to perform. I went in the linen closet, got some flat sheets, tied a rubber band around them and instantly I was Cher. I dragged that hair from room to room. I rushed and got a pair of my mother's highest heels and started back downstairs, got to the den, tripped over the damn sheet hair and fell on the stereo, broke the damn table, got grounded again." Malia hung up the phone; she could not catch her breath. She was trying to regain her composure from laughing so hard when the doorbell rang. Z never realized Malia had hung up the phone. He went on to tell her bout his Wonder Woman adventures. "Child, one Christmas my aunt had got me a three pack of underwear for a present, cheap bitch. There was a red pair; my favorite color. Girl, I used to wear them underwear everyday, take them off and at night and wash them and hang them over the shower rod. Girl, one Saturday, I was glancing at the cartoons and the Justice League came on, and there was my girl, Diana Prince. I ran upstairs, took them underwear off the shower rod, slipped them on, grabbed my mother's red knee boots, took her two gold bracelets from the dresser, grabbed my faithful towel hair, tucked my blue T-shirt in my drawers, put on my house coat, did my three turns and that house coat flew off and voila, it was 'Wonder Drag' from head to toe." The phone went dead and the only thing Z heard was, "If you would like to make a call, please hang up and try your call again." Z looked at the phone. "That ho' hung up on me. I'll be damned." He couldn't hit redial quick enough. When Malia answered, Z asked, "Girl, why you hang up on me?" She burst out laughing again as the caterer was assembling the food in the master bedroom.

"Z," she replied, still laughing, "You are soooo damn stupid. Man, come over here and help me eat this damn food Drayton had catered for lunch."

Z replied "Gimme twenty minutes."

Malia burst out laughing again. "See you in twenty minutes, man." Malia needed the laugh; she had not laughed that hard since Nikki's death. She had to brace herself for her call to the Greys.

Tré had just returned home from his morning workout and run.

He rushed into the apartment when he heard the phone ringing." Hello! Hello!" he said as the caller hung up. He immediately turned to his caller ID and saw that he had three missed messages. The first call was from Malia, the second one was from the scheduling department at work and the third was unknown. He decided to call scheduling first. "This is flight attendant 465879. I had a call, but no message. I'm not scheduled to work today; I thought I had today off," said Tré.

"You do," replied the scheduler. "Your manager wants you to give him a call. It's very important," rattled the scheduler.

"For what?" yelled Tré?

"Call and find out!" screamed the scheduler before hanging up the phone. He reluctantly called his boss, Mr. Worthington.

"This is Tré."

"Tré, you have a reward waiting for you, from Mr. Buchanan for finding his Rolex watch and returning it, and on from me for doing me a favor; I need you to pick up me four tickets for the game tonight. I'll be seated behind home plate. Tré this is off schedule, so please do not tell anyone I'm accepting tickets from a passenger. I promised my son that he could get the autographs of all the Braves players and even Bobby Cox. Please don't let me down; I definitely will look out for you in the future." Tré reluctantly obliged. "I hate that damn man; wrinkled-ass motherfucker," screamed Tré. Afterwards, he called Malia back to see what the deal was. After declining her invitation for a late lunch, he decided to face his fears and go over to the Lincoln's hotel room to pick up the tickets. As he prepared for a day of working out and meditating, he decided to pick up his son for a spiritual bonding. He called Keisha and told her he would pick Junior up from school and bring him home later. He thought his would be perfect since he had to go pick up the damn tickets. He was feeling Keisha today; maybe he would try to entice her later to give up some pussy. He knew that she would after putting the boys to sleep. He wanted to nestle his dick in her wet and soft pussy. He still loved her and would always love her. There were two other girls he fucked with when his nature would rise, but no one ever made him feel the way Keisha did. He came and went as he pleased, literally. He picked up Junior and headed to the JW Marriot to pick up the tickets. Junior enjoyed being with his dad; he loved everything about him and wanted to be just like him. They wore the same colored Timbs, the same jeans, he even talked like his dad, and Tré loved it. After walking to the hotel room Tré let junior knock on the door. Lincoln opened the door without hesitation, wearing only a towel. He was stunned at the sight of Junior and not Tré. Lincoln Buchanan immediately introduced himself and invited the duo inside. "Sorry about my attire. I was trying to take a quick shower before room service arrived. What up, little man? I'm ..."

Junior interrupted. "I know who you are. You're Lincoln Buchanan."

"How do you know that?"

"I watch sports with my uncles at home." Tré and Lincoln were both surprised. "How is the injury? My uncle says you will be out for the entire season."

"Wow, little man. How old are you?"

"I'm six. I'll be seven in four weeks."

"Sorry 'about that," Tré interrupted. "I have a talkative one."

"No problem, man. Why don't you guys stay for a little late lunch? I have more than enough."

Junior urged his father, "Daddy, can we?"

"Sure, shorty, if it's alright with Mr. Buchanan."

"Anytime, man, anytime. I ordered lobster, shrimp, and salmon. Can't go wrong with seafood." The three sat down and talked sports, cars, athletes. The adults also talked about women while Junior listened. Lincoln informed them that he was married with a six year-old little girl. Her name was Catherine and his wife was Ann Marie. He'd been married for about eight years. He kept rambling on about his life, money and sports. Finally, Tré interrupted, excusing himself and Junior. They really had to leave. They had been there for more than two hours and Junior had fallen asleep. Lincoln kept staring at Tré, undressing him with his eyes and winking from time to time. Tré kept his composure, ignoring his advances and was pissed that he was being seduced right in front of his son. "Sorry for keeping you guys from your father and son day. I just wanted some company. I've been here since the plane landed, trying to find different therapeutic techniques for this injury. But nevertheless, here's the reward for finding my watch and also the tickets I promised your supervisor. Tré, I wish you could come back later, after you drop your son off. I could use some company, you know, just to talk and chill. I don't want to be with other big-headed athletes, or reporters, or doctors. I need to be in company with an honest to goodness brother. I feel we have a lot in common." He was talking as Tré was waking Junior. As they headed toward the door, Tré thanked Lincoln for everything, took the tickets and the envelope without opening it and walked out the door. "Again, thank you for a great lunch and great conversation, and also thank you for giving my son the autographed baseball and jersey."

Chaston came to pick up Kennedy very early, giving Lake and Nikko a chance to talk and be alone for the first time in almost ten days. Lake was schedule to be at work later that evening to continue to work on Nikki's case. The forensics department compiled evidence including DNA, semen and blood samples. The detectives were getting very close to the culprit. Nikko was doing a lot better today and the breakfast in bed created by Lake was an added touch. Lake just lay there as Nikko devoured his entire meal. "Baby, what are our plans? There's Nikki's house, all her contracts, Kennedy's mental stability, and a host of other problems with have to deal with."

Nikko responded, "I've been struggling with the same problem. First thing's first: we must have a meeting with Malia, her accountant, her manager and her agency, pertaining to Nikki's assets and how we can legally adopt Kennedy. I do believe Nikki was worth well over a $100 million, but we rarely talked about her money because it was not important. I really don't know what I want to do first. Should we sell the house, the cars and the furniture, or give it to charity. I do want to auction the cars off and give the money to the non profit agencies she was affiliated with. I want to have something named after her in her honor. I guess I have to ask Malia about that. I also want to launch the campaign for Revlon, with their permission. I promise to make it the best marketing campaign ever."

"Baby, what are we going to do about your health? Don't you think we need to go to the doctor and figure out how we're going to handle this?" encouraged Lake. Nikko acknowledged his remarks and agreed. He went on to say, "This is bizarre. We have always had protected sex. We should have invested money in Magnum condoms; we would have been multi-millionaires by now. They've made a lot of money off us in the past seven years.

"Yes, we need to go to the doctor. I don't understand how I'm gotten infected and you're not, but baby I'm glad you're not. I want you to know, Lake that I have never cheated on you. It's just not in my nature. I love you unconditionally and the love that we share will never be compromised, baby and if something ever happens to me, I want you to take care of Kennedy," said Nikko.

"Don't talk like that. I don't want you to ever talk like that, Nikko. Ever," Lake shouted in retaliation. The phone rang and Lake picked it up before the second ring. "Hello!" he shouted again. It was Kennedy.

"Hello, Uncle Lake! Me and Daddy are going to lunch now. He took me shopping, to the zoo and also the movies," she shouted. "Uncle Lake," she was still shouting, "why are we shouting at each other?" Lakes started laughing, lowering his voice. "I don't know, sweetie, but let's lower our voices, okay?"

She shouted again, "Okay!"

It was around 7, when Tré dropped the junior off; the boys were in the back bedroom watching TV in the spacious three bedroom apartment. Keisha was looking sexy as hell, with nothing on but an oversized braves T-shirt, black house slippers, no makeup, and her hair was pulled back. Junior gave his father a kiss and ran to the bedroom to show his uncles his new clothes and new spider man action figure. Keisha welcomed Tré in and he humbly accepted. He kissed her on the forehead and headed to her bedroom. She watched him as he looked back, smiling. Most times she would oblige his sexual desires because the dick was good, but he came too far and in between to satisfy her completely. Tré was a superb lover; he had skills that only another could have taught him. He would take his time and massage Keisha's feet, her neck and back with her favorite oils. He sometimes would brush the hair on her head and sometimes the hair between her legs with a small tooth brush. This would drive Keisha wild, but she could never utter a sound knowing the boys were in the bedroom next door. Then he would start licking her toes, gently putting each toe in his mouth. Smacking and licking her heels, ankles, kneecaps, the backs of her knees, directly up to her thighs and then he would suddenly stop. He would then get up, go check on the boys, making sure they were fast asleep or pretending, detour to the kitchen to get a glass of ice water and return to Keisha. He would then take some of the crushed ice in his mouth and ever so gently start eating Keisha's pussy, freezing her clitoris, then melting it with his tongue, making her moan and groan, begging him to stop while coming in his mouth. Keisha's toes would curl and her eyes would roll back in her head before she shut them tightly. She would murmur something in a foreign language, call on Jesus and cuss Tré. He would not stop until he was assured she'd had at least two orgasms. But this night was different. When Tré headed to the room, she headed to the bedroom where the boys were and sat down, as if she was entertained by the show the kids were watching, after ten minutes of absence Tré asked Keisha if he could see her for a moment . "Sure, Tré," she replied.

"What's wrong, Keshia? Something's waiting for you in the bedroom."

She quickly responded, "I have company coming over in about thirty minutes." Trés eyes started to bulge out of his head. His immediate response was," Okay, I'm out." Tré flew out the door without uttering a word, not even saying good bye to his son. He got in his car and swerved to the corner of the street, barely missing an oncoming van. He was shocked and pissed off at Keisha. He started to go home and call it a night when he realized he'd left the damn tickets for his manager, knowing he had to drop them off early in the morning, "I'll be damned," he kept saying. He hesitantly called the hotel where Lincoln was staying, I hate to bother you, but I accidentally left the tickets for the game tomorrow for my manager. If you drop them down at the front desk I can swing by and pick them up."

Lincoln agreed. "Sure, no problem. I'll leave them down stairs for you." It took Tré about 15 minutes to get to the JW Marriott. He ran to the front desk and asked the attendant for the tickets. There was nothing for him. "I'll be damned," he repeated. He picked up the front desk phone and called up to room 4715. Lincoln answered on the first ring. "Oohh! Yo, my bad, I completely forgot. I'm on the toilet right now; can you come up and scoop them up?"

"I guess man; let me move my car before they tow it". Tré replied.

"Sorry again, yo." responded Lincoln. Tré just hung up the desk phone. Moments later Tré was knocking on the hotel room door. "'Bout time you get up here," shouted Lincoln as he open the door, completely naked. "Come in, man, while I get the tickets from the bedroom." Tré was mad as hell. "This punk ass motherfucker didn't know if I was coming back with my son or someone else; he just assumed I was coming here alone. Punk-ass (nigga)," he thought. Tré then said to himself, "Punk-ass faggot."

Now wrapped in a hotel robe, Lincoln came back moments later with the tickets and some more stuff for Junior. "I was just relaxing when you called. I was about to jump in the shower. I got a question for you, T. Can I call you T?"

"The name is Tré," replied Tré, ready to get the hell out of the room.

"Do you smoke?"

"Smoke what?" replied Tré?

"Trees, yo; blunts; you know, weed."

"I have, but the airlines don't play that," Tré replied sharply.

"Well, the league don't play that shit either, but I don't see nobody here but us, so let me fire up a tree, if that's alright with you man. I got a taste for a big fat blunt; what about you, Tré?

"Its cool, man; I could go for a big fat one," Tré hesitantly replied.

"Ok man, it's on. Be right back, and help yourself to the fridge or the bar, and while you're at it, how 'bout you make me a gin and juice straight up?"

" Fo' sho'." Tré did not hesitate this time. "I need a fucking drink after what Keisha did to my ass and after dealing with this motherfucker. I should make him suck my dick and come in his fucking mouth," Tré thought.

"Yo, K, man, how 'bout you come in the bedroom and bring the drinks," shouted Lincoln "Who the fuck do he think he is, giving fucking orders?

Ain't no Hazel here." Tré said to himself. Tré entered the huge bedroom suite where he found the motherfucker on the bed smoking a blunt, butt-ass naked and Pay Per-View.

"Man, excuse my appearance, but I hate wearing clothes in the room and besides, you're a fucking man; quite sure you've seen a dick and ass before. Here, (nigga); puff puff pass," he murmured. Tré took a deep toke as he held the shit in for about 15 seconds, hoping to get an immediate high. Lincoln looked on in amazement. "Damn, (nigga)! You're a fucking expert, acting like you don't like milk and cookies." Tré completely ignored him and let the weed do its job as his dick began to get hard.

CHAPTER 20

Remembering Nikki

Lake was going in early; he wanted to get a jump start on the investigation of Nikki's murder. The department had compiled a great deal of evidence and leads in hopes making an arrest. He was hoping he could contain himself if he was the one to catch the murderers. The department was working around the clock and everybody had called in with something they heard or saw. The hair samples, along with the blood and semen narrowed down the suspects, and even Nikki left clues during the intrusion. The outside surveillance camera caught one intruder on tape, but it –was not get a good picture of the face; that was the missing piece to the puzzle. The other intruder had cut the wire prior to him getting on tape. The second guy was smart as hell; they both knew the layout of the house as if they had been there before. It didn't make sense. They had to have been to the house before. What was also strange was that nothing had been taken. Lake was now in deep thought about how he first met Nikki. She had just had Kennedy a couple of months before he and Nikko started seeing each other. He had never met anyone famous before, but he tried to contained himself and was calm as possible. He remembered sweating and stuttered as he tried to introduce himself to Nikki. She and Nikko started to smirk as sweat began to pour from Lake's eyebrows. After about thirty minutes of light conversation, Lake began to relax a little and stopped stuttering. He was so fascinated by her presence, her skin, her hair, her teeth, her smile, her laughter, her smell; everything about her was soft and sweet. She was a supermodel, but she was as comfortable as the girl next door. They both were (vibing??) as if they had been siblings in another life. Lake developed an immediate fondness for Nikki.

Lake fell back into reality as the ringing of the phone broke his thoughts. It was his commander ordering him to report to the office at once. "I'm out the door," Lake said. He was about to ask what was the urgency when the commander hung up the phone in his ear. "Rude-ass motherfucker," Lake thought. "I wonder what the urgency is; it's five o'clock in the fricking morning." He was trying his best not to wake Nikko and Kennedy, but that was virtually impossible; Sasha and Sebastian was waging and barking begging to be taken for an early morning walk. Nikko jumped up from a deep sleep. "What's wrong, Lake!" screamed Nikko.

"Nothing, baby; just on my way to work; something came up at the office. Didn't want to disturb you," said Lake.

"What time is it?" Nikko asked lazily.

"It's a little past five. Go back to bed, baby. I'll call you when I get to work. By the way, what are your plans for today?" asked Lake.

"I need to finish the arrangements for Nikki's house."

"Okay, baby. Maybe I'll meet you over there later on. I know I'll be working at least 12 hours today, so maybe we can do dinner after I'm done, if that's alright with you."

"That will work, baby. I'm gonna take Kennedy to school and I almost forgot Ms. Aldridge is picking her up from school. She's spending the weekend with Amanda. She's having a weekend sleepover for 10 second graders; Mrs. Aldridge is a brave woman." Nikko laughed lazily. Nikko didn't want to tell Lake he had appointment with the Infectious Disease Clinic. He had made an appointment with one of the specialists there concerning his status. He had a million and one things to do. His marketing firm was suffering; it seemed as though work was picking up after Nikki's death; he was being pulled from modeling agencies, corporations, publishers, magazines, you name it and they were calling. Poor Katie had hired two more marketing reps and three additional promo agents. The calls kept coming and Katie kept calling. Nikko knew Katie was very instrumental in all his endeavors. He had relied on her even more due to the set back he'd experienced with Nikki. He fell back to sleep thinking about the Revlon campaign he had to finalize and how difficult it would be without his darling sister by his side.

Kennedy was shaking Nikko. "Wake up! It's 7 o'clock! I'm gonna be late for school! I already ate my breakfast and you're still not up," Kennedy was screaming. "Unkie, I need to finish packing my clothes! Remember, I'm going to Amanda's house for the weekend," Kennedy was still screaming. Nikko was drenched in sweat, his pajama bottom, top and the sheets was soaking wet. He nudged Kennedy after realizing what was going on. "Okay, baby girl. Okay," Nikko murmured. Nikko jumped up while Kennedy rushed back downstairs complaining about how she was gonna be late for school. "Gimme five, little girl, and I'll be downstairs to help you finish packing," he said as he turned on the shower laughing but very concerned about the bed sweating. When Nikko came downstairs after seven minutes, Kennedy had finished packing mixed matched outfits, threw in some more tops and bottoms and she was ready to (jet). Nikko started laughing again. They were about to leave when there was a knock at the door; it was a special delivery guy, but he wasn't from FedEx or UPS. The delivery guy introduced himself and asked : –"Is Mr. Nicholaus Grey was home? Nikko responded. Nikko signed for a bright yellow envelope and dropped it in his briefcase. "Must be some papers from Malia, but why the delivery guy?" he wondered.

Kennedy broke his thoughts. "Unkie, can you help me with my lines for the school play on Sunday when I get back?" she asked.

"Certainly; the play is in two weeks, right?" he asked.

"But Unkie, we have a dress rehearsal the Friday before the play," she explained. "What's a dress rehearsal?" she asked.

"It's when everybody dresses up in their costumes and goes over their lines so that everybody can go through the play without making any mistakes. Everybody is there: the actors, stage managers, teachers, the light people and me, if you want me there."

"Sure, I want you to be there and I know mommy will be there watching over us," she said proudly. Solemnly, Nikko agreed.

CHAPTER 21

Adjusting

Nikko got to Kennedy's school in the nick of time. He was amazed at Kennedy, at how she was adjusting to Nikki's passing better than he was; damn, better than anyone. It is so amazing how people could learn a lot from kids if only we tried to learn from them rather then teach them. He was pulling out of the school parking lot when his cell phone rang. It was Zarius. "Hey child, how are you doing today?" Zarius asked hesitantly.

"I'm fine. How's everything with you?" Nikko quickly responded.

"Okay, girl, so when are we gonna see your tired ass?" Z responded quickly. "I'm tired of this shit; we don't see you anymore and I'm 'bout to go fucking crazy. Show your face to the gang or I will find you and cut it off. I need to see you, diva; you, Lake and Kennedy, so shape you're ass up and come visit us. And I forgot; I love you. So call me when you have time." Then all Nikko heard was the dial tone. "I can't believe he hung up on me," Nikko thought. The phone rang again. "What the hell do you want now, Z?" Nikko shouted.

"Sorry, this is not Z. This is your lover," Lake snickered.

"Hey, baby, I thought you were that crazy ass Z. He called me cussing me out because we haven't been around. I tried explaining the situation but he just hung up the phone." Nikko started to chuckle and so did Lake.

"Baby, I'll meet you at the house. I have to discuss the status of investigation," explained Lake, his tone very serious. Nikko didn't want to ask what about, he just agreed to meet and talk at Nikki's house. "Baby, where are you now?" asked Lake.

"I just dropped Kennedy off and now I'm going to run some errands before I go to the house," Nikko lied, and sighed as he was doing it. Lake picked up on it but didn't want to persist. He responded quickly, "Okay, baby. See you later. I love you."

"I love you, too, replied Nikko.

The Infectious Disease Center was on the 3rd floor of Metro Atlanta Center. Dr. Vertise's office was in the center of the floor, right in front of the elevators. Nikko became very embarrassed, hoping no one would see him. Sitting inside the office was a very attractive, professional lady sitting reading Sports Illustrated, and an older lady, she looked as if she was about sixty years old, reading a bible. Nikko sat down and picked up one of the magazines that were lying on a beautiful marble coffee table. The magazines were all meticulously placed on the table. The decor was freshly done in a deep mustard-colored wall paper with burgundy molding. There were beautiful paintings of Waldo and Buccaneer. Nikko started to read one the magazine after filling out the necessary paper work, but decided to look over the papers that Malia sent over. He started to open the envelope but he noticed the papers were not from Malia's firm; they were from Dubois and Carter, Malia's competitive law firm. He began to read. "I'LL BE DAMNED," Nikko shouted. "This motherfucker is trying to get custody of my niece! What the fuck is going on??" Nikko screamed.

"Excuse me, Mr. Grey, is there a problem?" the receptionist asked. "You must contain yourself. This is a waiting room, sir." Nikko became even more frantic. Dr. Vertise came into the waiting room. "Mr. Grey, I can see you now," the doctor commanded nervously. There were tears falling from his eyes as he followed the doctor to his office. "Mr. Grey, my assistant usually talks to new patients prior to me seeing them, but it seems as though you need my immediate attention."

"I'm very sorry, sir. I usually can contain myself, but my niece's father is trying to gain sole custody of her on the grounds that I'm HIV positive."

"That's absurd," replied the doctor.

"Read it for yourself. That no good bastard. After all the motherfucking shit he put my sister through, he has the unmitigated gall to try some bullshit like this. (I will fuck his motherfucking shit up!")

"Please, Mr. Grey. Please calm down."

Nikko cut the doctor off. "You don't understand. I will kill him before I let him or the law take my niece from me," Nikko replied sharply to the doctor. The doctor quickly changed the subject.

"Mr. Grey, we must take some blood tests. We need to know your T cell count and viral load."

Nikko cut him off, "Doctor I understand all of that. My best friend is a nurse, and trust me, he preaches about safe sex, regular check ups, and how the government tried to kill all gays and blacks."

The doctor changed the subject, "Do you know how you got infected?"

"Dr. Vertise, I've been with the same man for seven years and to this day we use protection. I'm not promiscuous; I practice safe sex; always did and always will. My partner and I should have invested in Magnums and if not that my best friends supply us with free condoms and lubrication."

"Wait a fucking minute; how does that bastard know that I'm HIV positive? I just received the fucking news myself less than two weeks ago," Nikko said, referring to Chaston. "I'll be damned," Nikko screamed again.

"Please, Mr. Grey," the doctor begged as the nurse knocked on the door.

"Dr. Vertise, may I see you for a minute. Please," she begged. Nikko's stomach began to tie itself in knots, his throat became dry, and he couldn't even feel his tongue. Tears began to fill his eyes. The tears began to roll down his cheeks on to his blue oxford shirt. Nikko was furious, but had to remain calm, he was thinking of a way to kill that bastard. When the doctor returned, he informed Nikko that he was ready to start the blood test and then afterwards they could see where Nikko was mainly to start taking his medication. After they took a gallon of blood and stuck Nikko in every vein possible, the doctor instructed him to take it easy and not to worry too much. "The ground on which he wants to take sole custody of your niece is unethical and we could easily fight that in court. We will be giving you a call in a couple of days to go over your test results," said Dr. Vertise.

"We ain't gonna have to fight it, because he will be dead or wishing he had died," Nikko thought. Nikko called Malia; she would know what to do. Unfortunately, she was in a meeting, so he left her a message and emphasized to Victoria the extreme urgency. He was steaming as he hung up the phone. He just wanted to take Kennedy from school and run away far away. "I can't take this bullshit, motherfucka. I lost my sister, I got a fucking virus, and this bitch is trying to take one of the most important people in my life." He began to cry again. Not realizing he'd run a light, he jerked as a nearby car slammed on brakes only inches from Nikko's car. He just looked out into the distance, not really understanding what just happened. "You have to pull yourself together. You can make it through the rain," he told himself. He thought he heard Nikki's voice, but it was Mariah on CD, singing like a heavenly angel. Nikko finally gained composure and detoured to Nikki's house. He needed solace; he needed a place of refuge; a place of peace where he could rest and clear his head. He needed to lay in Nikki's bed.

CHAPTER 22

The Morning Pain

Tré could not believe what had happened. He wanted to vomit. Héd had sex with this man and it was off the fucking chain. He hadn't felt like this in a minute. The touching, feeling, sucking, licking, massaging, caressing, and kissing; it was something Tré so desperately needed. Lincoln finally woke from a very deep sleep. Tré was half dressed and was looking dumfounded when Lincoln caught him trying to slip out the door. "What up, partner. What's the deal? I thought we would hang out today maybe grab some lunch."

"I thought you had plans today and I got some stuff to do myself, bruh," Tré eagerly responded.

"Yo, Tre, man, I thought we had a good time together last night; the sex was off the hook. I'm digging you and thought we could just hang man, spend some more time together. If you ain't with that I can dig it," Lincoln said pitifully.

Tré interrupted. 'Man, last night and this morning was tight, but I ain't trying to feel no man right now," Tré replied.

"Well, let's hang out as boys, man, and we don't have to get down again. I just can't find any motherfucker that's a real man and like to freak. I'm on the DL and I hate faggot-ass motherfuckers. I do get my dick sucked on occasion from a faggot, but that shit ain't safe. Being married, pro player, and I got a daughter; I don't want no disease I can't get rid of." he sounded pitiful again. "But that's been few and far between. Man, you don't know how you made me feel last night, just to be held by a man. I love the hardness of a man, the muscles. I'm sorry, man, I love my wife to death, but she can't make me feel that way. All I'm trying to say, man, is don't leave. Lets spend the day together, and if you still ain't feeling it, I'll understand," Lincoln blurted. Tré reluctantly finally dropped his shoes and socks and was about to get back in the bed when his phone rang. "Yo, who dis?" he asked.

"Child, this is your cousin. Where are you, Tré?" Z yelled.

("Nigga) you know you don't ask me no fucking questions like that. What up, yo?" Tré became irritated.

"I want to have a get together for Nikko and Lake next weekend, so you need to get that day off. Next Saturday night. Don't forget, it will be at Malia's 'because she got that big ass house."

Tré interrupted. "How many people you trying to invite, Z?"

"It's gonna be quaint, just us, me, you, Malia, Lake, Nikko and our closest friends. No more than thirty. "Oh, before I forget, I need about $50 from you to go in the pot," Z said pathetically.

Tré was now shouting. ("Nigga), you having this shit! Why you need money from me?"

Z cut him off. "Don't you me, Nikko, Lake and Malia?" Oh, before I forget, you can bring a friend if you want. It's going be a mixed gathering, so I hope she is open minded. I'm bringing my new boyfriend; the one with the eleven inch dick." Tré hung up the phone.

"I know that bitch did not hang up the phone in my lovely face. That's my line, anyways," Z was shouting to himself. He adjusted his face and punched one number on his speed dial to call Malia's office. Victoria picked up on the first ring. "Ms. V, this is Ms. Z. Where's Malia?" Z asked rudely.

"She's in a conference meeting."

Z deliberately cut her off. "Interrupt it and tell her I'm on the phone. This is an emergency."

"Mr. Washington, she can not be disturbed. She is in a conference with all the partners," Victoria explained.

"Have her give me a call; tell her it's important," Z said angrily. Victoria was about to ask him something but he hung up in her ear. Victoria just listened to the dial tone and said, "Faggot bitch."

Z looked at his phone as if he heard her response, "Bitch, I heard that," he shrugged. He was so happy to be having a gathering for his friends. Z was notorious for throwing parties of all types. He would have a Janet Jackson concert party, a Whitney Houston party, a Mariah Carey, anything dealing with Whitney, Janet, Anita, Mariah, Soul Food, Sex in the City, Noah's

Ark, Grey's Anatomy, Desperate Housewives, American Idol, you name it, he had a party for it. If you sneezed, Z — we would have a party for that, and then he would have it at someone else's house, depending on how he felt. He felt parties were interesting and could be full with gay gossip. It was almost 2 o'clock in the afternoon and he hadn't heard from Nikko, Lake or Malia. Something was definitely wrong. "Bitches ain't returning my fucking phone calls." JJ had called him three times already. "Damn, I knew my pussy was good, but not to have a motherfucking (nigga) ring my phone off the hook." Z decided to wash JJ's clothes being that the motherfucker had been staying over here almost every night. He kicked the laundry basket all the way down the stairs. "That's my cardio for today," he thought. "Almost broke my damn foot." He put some more coffee on and off to the laundry dungeon he went to wash his man's clothes. "Bitch, did that come out my mouth? My man? Honey, please." As Z started separating JJ's darks from the whites, a small plastic bag fell from his Sean John jeans. "What the fuck is this? Oh, I know this motherfucker ain't doing drugs in my house." It was a clear powder. "This motherfucker is doing cocaine in my house, punk ass bitch." Z became furious. He rushed to the kitchen to pour some coffee. As he reached to grab a coffee cup from the cabinet, it fell on the floor. "I'll be damned," Z shouted. He reached up under the sink to get the dustpan and started cleaning the broken mess up when he noticed another clear bag with some small residue of powder in the corner of the bag in the garbage can. It looked like rocks. "Oh no, I know this bitch ain't smoking rocks in my house!" Z became dizzy; he fell on the living room couch gracefully. "My temp man is a dope dealer, or a dope fiend. Oh the bitch gonna get it now." After getting his composure, he called JJ on his cell phone. "Hey, baby," Z said subtly. "What time you gonna make it to my house?"

JJ replied, "'Bout 8."

"Okay, cool so what do you want for dinner? I thought we could have spaghetti and a salad," Z suggested.

"Sounds good baby," JJ replied. "Okay, J. Oh, I almost forgot, I'm having a little get together for Lake and Nikko next Saturday. Are you down for that?" Z asked.

"Of course, baby," JJ responded.

"Oh and another thing; I got a big surprise for you when you get home, and don't ask me what it is, 'cause I ain't gonna tell you. See you at 8. I'm out," Z hung up the phone. "Fucking bastard. So much for that. Let me get my plan together and put my gun in a good place, 'cause if that motherfucker tries some shit, I'll blow his fucking dick off. Just call me the real Cut- A-Dick-Off Bobbitt." The phone rang as Z was about to pour his second cup of coffee. He picked up the phone. "What!"

"Zarius Washington?" the voice asked.

"Who is this and what do you want?"

"This is Connie from Southern Pioneer Financial. This is your final warning. We need your payments on your 1998 Lexus as soon as possible."

Z abruptly cut her off in mid sentence. "You'll get it when I get it," he said before hanging up the phone. Connie called right back.

"Mr. Washington, I think we got disconnected. I just wanted to inform you that we can only take a money order or Cashier's check or Collect Pay through Western Union from you sir; no more personal checks. It needs to be in my office by 12 noon Monday, or we will start the repossession procedures. Thank you, Mr. Washington. Isn't this where you hang the phone up in my ear, sir?" she sarcastically blurted. Z just put the phone down and walked away. He could hear Connie on the phone. "Mr. Washington? Mr. Washington?" Z always got the last laugh. He went to the kitchen drawer and retrieved his faithful whistle. He came back to the phone and blew it as loud as he could in the telephone receiver. "That will show you not to be sarcastic with me," he said as he hung up the phone. "Now, where were we?" he said as he continued sorting JJ's clothes. Z was trying to decide what the theme for the party would be. "Got it, I'll call it 'The Black Chair Affair'! It will be a gathering of openness, true confessions, speaking your spirit, and putting closure on the past. I'm brilliant," he said as he started the washing machine, pouring a cup of bleach on JJ's colored clothes.

Malia's conference meeting with all partners of the law firm finally ended at 2:05 p.m. "A day of bullshit," she thought as she picked up about 15 messages from Victoria's desk. "Damn," she thought; three calls from Nikko, five calls from Z, two calls from Mr. Drayton, and the rest came from clients. "Busy, busy, busy," she thought to herself as she closed her office door behind her. Drayton was sitting on her couch when she walked in. "Good afternoon, my Nubian queen." Malia was startled at first.

"Drayton, how did you get in here? Victoria knows better than to let someone in my office when I'm not here."

"Well, Victoria took a late lunch and besides, I belong here. Baby, please sit down; I have something to tell you, and please let me finish before you say anything. You know we have been seeing each other for quite sometime, and I know it has not been easy for you, me being married and all. I haven't been a real man, at least, not the one that you deserve or need. I cried so many nights when I could not be with you, when I'm home with Eve and the kids. I don't know how I fell in love with you so quickly and so hard, but

I want to make it right. I know I've been telling you that I've been asking Eve for a divorce, that I was not happy, but she would always refuse; she kept saying that the children need both parents. Well, baby, she finally granted me a divorce. Last night I told her I was going to take the kids and move out. I told her I was going to move to Atlanta and leave her in Delaware. I will have my friend Damien draw up the papers and hopefully she won't drag it out for a long time. I'm thinking the divorce will be finalized in three to six months. The determining factor will be the assets and property. I made her sign a pre-nuptial agreement prior to us getting married, so it should be a done deal. I want to be with you, Somalia. I love you and I can't live without you another day. Please don't leave me, and say you will be with me until we can be together as one," Drayton begged. Malia just stared into space; she was speechless. Victoria knocked on the open door. "Malia, I got you some lunch. I know you must be starving," Victoria said exuberantly, not even noticing Drayton in the winged back black chair. "Oh, my apologies; I didn't know you had a visitor. Hi, Drayton. I didn't even see you there," she apologized again.

"That's alright, Victoria, he was about to leave," Malia interrupted as she stood to escort Drayton out the door. "Thank you giving me that heads up, Drayton. I will definitely look into that situation and give you my immediate summation later," Malia smirked.

"I look forward to your answer, Malia."

"Okay, no problem, talk to you soon." Victoria just stood there taking it all in. She had always suspected something was going on between Drayton and Malia. Though she didn't smell anything fishy, she would continue to sniff.

Malia began returning all her phone calls and Victoria just stood there lurking and looking for something clever to say. Without looking up, Malia said, "That will be all." Malia first called Z, who sounded furious when he answered the phone. "Bitch, where have you been? I'm going through drama and I need your legal advice. I'm kicking that no good (nigga) out of my house. If I accidentally shoot him, are you going to defend me?" Z was serious, but Malia just chuckled. "What's wrong now, Trap?" Malia asked.

"I think the motherfucker is doing drugs in my house."

"You're lying," Malia responded.

"I found some bags of cocaine in some plastic bags; I'm going to Lake and I'm telling him to pick up this fucking bitch," blurted Z.

"Well, legally speaking," Malia went into lawyer mode, "you can't shoot on those grounds alone, but you can get a restraining order after kicking him out, but I know you, Z; you will START some shit in order for him to hit you and you will run in a corner and then shoot his nuts off."

"Oh, you know me so well, bitch," replied Z.

"Z, we don't need anymore drama. Drayton just told me that his wife is getting ready to sign the papers for the divorce," Malia said pitifully.

"So, girl, what you are going to do?" Z anxiously asked.

"I don't know," Malia replied. "I don't know if I want his tired ass now. It's been over a year since I've been fucking with his punk ass, and now I think I'm fucking pregnant." "Girl, don't tell me you haven't told him," Z said.

"I haven't told him anything, I really don't want him to know. I don't want anything from him," Malia responded.

"Well, whatever you decide, I'm here for you, Ms. B," Z chuckled. "By the way, I'm having a party at your house next Friday, so could you have your cleaning lady make the house extra clean; you know how meticulous I can be; just call me anal retentive!"

"Why do you have to have a party at my house, hoe??" Malia shouted. "I'm trying to remain professional, sissy, but you bring the bitch out of me." Z, completely ignoring her, said, "I'm having it for Lake and Nikko, but more so for Nikko. He don't even call us, he rarely returns our calls, and he's become very distant."

Malia interrupted. "Z, he's still suffering from Nikki's death."

"I know, but he needs to at least try to put closure on her passing, I don't think he has acknowledged her death. I have a theme for the party, too. I'm gonna call it 'The Black Chair Party'."

"Bitch, you're crazy. I'm not going to even ask why you're calling it that. What time on Friday? I'm going to invite Drayton; duh, what the hell am I talking about, invite, it's gonna be at my damn house. Bye, sissy. I got work to do," Malia laughed.

"Bye, Queen!" Z smiled. Malia's next call was to Nikko, but he didn't answer, so she left a voice mail message. "I guess Z was right," Malia thought. Neither Lake nor Tré answered their cell phones, so she decided to eat her cold lunch and look over some new litigation files. She was deep in thought as she felt she was indeed pregnant by a married man. Her father would roll over in his grave. "He raised me to be a respectable woman, to know right from wrong. I slipped up bad, Daddy." She continued to beg for forgiveness. "I don't know how to even tell my mother that I have sex, and let's not even think about my fornication. I was taught to be virtuous. Oh, Lord, how I know I must have let you down. I feel the tears of displeasure run down your face. Forgive me, Jehovah for I have sinned; I have committed a disservice to your words. I must repent and beg for your forgiveness, to be your child again. I must do right. I want to be in your good graces again." Malia figured out what she had to do. Tears were running down her face to the crack of her lips, down her chin and landing on her files. A knock on the door stopped her prayer of forgiveness in midstream. Malia quickly wiped her face and turned her winged back chair around to face the big picture window. She summoned them to come in; it was the local delivery guy dropping off an envelope from Nikko. She couldn't imagine why Nikko would be having paperwork delivered. She dismissed the delivery guy and quickly opened the package. She couldn't believe that Chaston was suing Nikko for custody of Kennedy. She thought this was absurd and she started laughing at the thought of Chaston having the audacity to even think he could raise his daughter. "OOOH this is the stuff that I love to sink my teeth into," Malia said with exuberance.

CHAPTER 23

Dèjú Vu

It was around 7 o'clock in the evening when Nikko woke up from his much needed nap. His dreams were peaceful and serene. The shadows of the sunset were coming through the blinds of Nikki's master bedroom. At first, Nikko had to take in his surroundings as he had completely forgotten he had fallen fast asleep at his sister's house. He just lay there in her bed for minutes, hoping that she would come back just for a second to tell him that she was fine and doing well. He already knew she wouldn't come; he just wanted to imagine the impossible. He decided to get up. Knowing that Lake would be there by 8, he started to wonder why his cell phone was not ringing off the hook. He knew Malia had received his envelope, he knew Lake should have called him back to at least to check up on him, and he could not forget Z; he calls at least three times a day. "No wonder," he thought. "I left the damn phone in the kitchen." He was hoping Lake had dropped by the house and fed the dogs. Nikko could not imagine selling this house, this perfect castle, the little mansion that he and Nikki picked out over five years ago. It created so many memories that he did not want to part with. He started to walk through the house, room by room: the master bedroom, the enormous closet with all of Nikki's shoes, bags, accessories, gowns, sweaters, caps, dresses and suits. He walked into the office where there were pictures of Nikki, Kennedy, himself and Lake and awards from every modeling agency throughout the country. He started to walk down the hall to Kennedy's room, the first guest room, and then the second. He waltzed downstairs to admire how well Katie had put the house back together on such short notice. The family room, the den, the living room, the Solarium, the study with the piano, the oversized kitchen, with the island in the middle, silver refrigerator, Dutch oven, the whole house looked new. Nikki didn't spend a lot of time in the kitchen or the game room. He hesitated when it was time for him to visit Nikki's private room with all the front covers on which she was featured: Ebony, Jet, Essence, Sports Illustrated, Elle, Glamour, Harper Bizarre, People, Seventeen, Vogue, Redbook, Vanity Fair, and Code. He rushed to the basement where Nikki had just finished redecorating. There was a 20-foot projector inside a 30 seat theatre, a small dance floor built in the corner with a small bar, and a mother-in-law suite with adjourning bathroom. The weight room was equipped with mirrors and a dance bar and almost every type of workout machine possible. Nikko could never imagine what he would do with all these memories. He noticed in the corner, of all things, the wig and gown he'd worn that horrible day, still in tact. He couldn't understand why Katie had not thrown this stuff away. Nikko started to snicker at the memories of Nikki and him that day, acting like damned fools. Suddenly he heard the phone ringing. He rushed up the two flights of stairs back to the main level. He answered the cell phone on the third ring. "Hello," Nikko said, almost out of breath.

"Hey, baby! Where have you been? I've been trying to call you all day." Lake sounded worried.

"I'm alright, Lake. I fell asleep upstairs and I accidentally left the cell down here in the kitchen," Nikko replied.

"Well, baby, I will be there in about an hour. Are you still at Nikki's?" Lake hesitantly asked.

"Yeah, Lake, just trying to get some closure, and I needed this time alone to get my thoughts together, so hurry, Lake; we've got a lot of decisions to make concerning the house and all these furnishings." Nikko realized he still had the wig and gown in his hands. Still talking to Lake, he just stared at the objects. Nikko hung up the phone and rushed upstairs to play dress up. He felt the need to wear the gown and hair; he wanted to be a part of Nikki's illusion. He dashed into the master bedroom to look for a brush and some fake titties. This behavior was not like Nikko; he could never fathom the thought of dressing in drag. He'd only done so that one day that would haunt him forever. Nikko had always been a man's man: very masculine and also a gentleman. He was the kind of man who made every woman want to bear his child. Nikko possessed qualities of a fairytale prince; caring and giving, his mere presence would enthrall you. Nikko was a man of compassion; he would teach a broken winged bird to fly again. He embodied the tremendous power of love and devotion. He and Nikki were like angelic figures of peace and serenity when they were together; they never argued, or disagreed on anything. They thought as one and their hearts beat as one. Nikko decided he would play a trick on Lake and dress up in drag just to be humorous. He looked high and low for the heels he wore that night, but all he could find were Nikki's bedroom shoes. He sat down on the chaise lounge in the master bedroom and started to wonder what people did with all the stuff when their loved ones died. The clothes, shoes, pictures, toiletries, make up, the personal items; it's like throwing memories away. The jewelry, the mementos from long ago; it had to be more meaningful and heartbreaking to adjust to the loss of a loved one. Life should guarantee more and not less. Nikko remembered when his cousin was killed in a car accident and his aunt had to identify the body; she came out of the morgue looking depressed and confused. She wept as the policeman gave her my cousin belongings: her watch, wedding ring, pearl earrings and pearl necklace. "God has to give us more when we lose our hearts to the people who mean so much to us," he thought. Suddenly the door bell rang. Had he fallen out of his thoughts? He ran downstairs wondering how Lake got there so quick and how he was going to get a laugh about him dressing up in drag. He opened up the door. "How did you get here so quickly?" But it wasn't Lake; it was the man from that evening when Nikki was killed, the man from the parking lot who had mistaken him for Nikki. He lunged at Nikko. "What are you doing in Nikki's house and in Nikki's clothes?" the guy yelled, choking the hell out of Nikko. Nikko broke away and gathered his composure, punching the guy in the eye. "What the fuck do you want?" Nikko was outraged, and here he was, fighting an intruder; an intruder who was trying to kill him. The assailant came back with a nasty blow to Nikko's stomach. He fell to the floor. The intruder pulled out a knife, trying to stab Nikko in the back. Nikko hit the intruder in the nuts and snatched the knife, allowing him time to regain his composure. He ran to the kitchen and hit the panic button on the alarm, not realizing the assailant was behind him. He hit Nikko in the back of the neck with a blunt object. Nikko turned around and stabbed the intruder in the shoulder with the knife and broke the knife off in his shoulder. Nikko snatched a mallet from the counter and started hitting the assailant for the loss of his twin sister. He hit him for being diagnosed as HIV positive. He hit him for the fact that he may lose his niece. He hit him for all the shit he had endured since he'd come out. He hit for all the bullshit he'd taken since his sister's murder. He hit for every gay person and the heartache they felt in this fucked up society. Nikko felt that, if he were to kill the person who killed his sister, everything would be better. He continued to bust him in the eye, stomach and nose. As he was about to hit the Nikki's killer again someone grabbed his fist. It was Lake, begging Nikko to stop; Nikko was on the kitchen floor, covered in blood. Blood was gushing out of the intruder's shoulder. Lake grabbed Nikko and begged him again to stop. "Who is this?" Lake screamed. The man was lying on the floor in a fetal position, moaning and grunting, coughing up blood... "I don't know, but I know he killed my sister, and I want him dead," Nikko said as he exited the room. Lake looked at Nikko in dismay. He then got on the phone and called for a squad car and ambulance. Nikko, in the mean time, went upstairs and freed himself of the evening gown. He threw the wig and the bloody gown in the bathroom trash. The downstairs was in shambles. He hurriedly dressed knowing that the police would be there soon to ask questions and he wanted to look half way presentable. He completely ignored Lake and directed his attention to the officer that was asking a million questions. Nikko became even more distant in his questioning with the police. His evasiveness annoyed the police; they even asked him to come to the precinct for questioning and he refused. He abruptly stated to the officer that he wanted to end this episode; he needed to leave and go home. Lake just looked in disgust, but refused to confront Nikko at this point. The media was assembled on the street, and the neighbors had already posted their front row seats. Nikko wanted to avoid a media circus and knew that it was not going to get any better. The Sergeant came in and eventually excused Nikko, but instructed him that he would need to come by the precinct tomorrow to finish the questioning pertaining to the altercation. He went on to say that the assailant was indeed one of the people who murdered Nikki. "He had been under surveillance but we lost track of him today. We searched his home and also his place of business. There were pictures, photos, and cut outs of your sister. Unfortunately, we don't have any leads on the second murderer, but we're on it. By capturing his guy, we are close to putting an end to this case." Nikko's cell phone rang. It was Malia; she sounded disturbed when Nikko answered the phone. "What's wrong?" Malia asked.

"I tried to kill him, Malia; the man who killed my sister. I felt her spirit when he came to the door. I knew it was him, and the motherfucker had the balls to come up to the door and ask for my sister. I tried to beat the living shit out of him, but Lake stopped me. I was going to kill his ass and bury him in the backyard by the carriage house." Malia was in shock. She could not believe the murderer had come back to the house. Nikko continued, "The stupid ass cops almost had the motherfucker and he got away from them. They searched his house and found pictures, letters, memorabilia of Nikki, some of Nikki's jewelry, perfume, and the perfume that hadn't even come out yet." Nikko got a beep on his cell phone. "Hold on, Malia, it's Z."

"Why the fuck haven't you called me?" Z asked. Nikko clicked the cell phone again; now all three were on the phone. "Nikko, can you hear me?" Z didn't even realize Nikko had clicked over. Nikko was sitting in the master bathroom on the toilet with the lid down, looking into space. "Shut the fuck up and listen," he yelled at Z. "Malia, tell him what happened," Nikko ordered. Malia started telling Z the story. Afterward, both waited in silence for Nikko to continue. "What can we do?" cried Malia and Z.

"There's nothing you can do. "The damage has already been done," replied Nikko. Lake was calling Nikko from downstairs. "I gotta go. I'll call you guys when I get home, Love ya," Nikko said before abruptly hanging up the phone. Z immediately called Malia back. "Girl what the hell is going on? I know we desperately need to keep a close watch on Nikko; he may lose it." Malia got a beep. It was Tré. She asked Z to hold on while she clicked Tré on to third party, so they all would be on the phone. "What's going on, Malia? I called Nikko, but he told me to call you and hung up the phone," Tré said. Malia ran down this evening's episode to Tré while Z was busy putting the finishing touches on JJ's dinner. "I'll be damned," Tré said. He was outraged. "That fucking (nigga) is gonna fry. I wish Lake would have let Nikko kill his faggot ass. Damn, I gotta leave. I gotta flight, and I won't be back until Sunday evening. Z, Cynthia and her boyfriend will be staying at my house for the weekend. I told her she couldn't drive my car so they will have to catch a cab or the bus to get around, so she'll be begging you to pick her and her sorry (nigga) up from the bus station."

"I ain't got time," yelled Z. "I got something I gotta throw out." Malia cut them off.

"What's she coming down here for?" Malia asked.

"She says that he has to come down and pick up the rest of his shit from his roommate; the same room mate who kicked him out for not paying rent. I hate the (bitch). What are we gonna do about Nikko? He's going through so much: Nikki's passing, his health, the media, the will, and Kennedy's punk ass daddy trying to stick around, with his sorry ass." "Let's stick to the matter at hand; we need to meet Nikko at his house. There are some pressing issues that are vital to his well being. I have to discuss with him his rights because the state could very well accuse him of attempted murder. I've been very conscientious of his behavior and the direction in which he should be taken with all he has endured, especially after this episode with the accused. All this chaos could backfire on him and his custody of Kennedy."

Z interrupted. "What are you talking about, Malia? You have alluded to the fact twice that Nikko may lose custody of Kennedy. What is it that you're not telling us?"

"I cannot divulge anything at this time. I must consult with Nikko first, but I am very concerned with his well being and his mental capacity."

"Come on, Malia, Nikko is very strong, probably stronger than all of us put together, and you know that's pretty strong," Tré interrupted.

"How much can one person take?" Malia started to sob. "I just feel for him, Lake and especially Kennedy; now that's a strong little girl."

Z blurted, "If Nikko needs us, he knows to call us. What he really needs is this party; it will put closure to a lot of his distress, so who's gonna help me decorate and prepare the food?"

Malia said, "You're crazy, Z. We're concerning ourselves with one of your closest friends' situation and all you can think about is partying."

Z replied, "Yep. We all are in each other's lives for different reasons. I'm in your lives for guidance, laughter, fun, gossip, and love. This is what I'm made up of and this is what I share. Malia, you share your intelligence, your knowledge of legal matters and your subtle tenacity. You are pure and honest; you never compromise your integrity. Tré is rugged, yet firm; he gives us a good look at a real man, at how they think and act. It's like peeping at straight and bisexual men through a hole in the locker room. We can also dissect them through his eyes. It allows us to understand the definition of 'down-low'. Why do men fuck men but swear they hate faggots?" Tré didn't say anything; he didn't know whether he was being insulted or flattered. "We, together, make up a unit of love and humanity; we make up the world, good, bad and indifferent." Malia and Tré were silent for a moment while Z put the salmon in the oven. JJ would be home in less than an hour. Z smirked to himself. "You know, guys, this gay shit ain't cracked up to what it used to be. Why is it motherfuckers with big ass dicks are stupid as hell? Their fucking brains are located in their nuts and their eleven inch pipes. They do ridiculous shit; this motherfucker brought drugs into my fucking house. Can you take him to jail for that, Malia? I'm going to shoot his balls off. His shit is packed and I'm kicking him out," Z complained. His statement struck a nerve with Malia. She blurted, "How in the hell is a married man gonna insult my intelligence by asking me to marry him after he gets a divorce from his wife? Why do heterosexual men with money think they can rule, beat, hit and steal your spirit and think nothing of it? I just don't understand them; if I live to be a hundred, I will never understand them. They are dogs; they will lie and lay with anyone and us as females allow them to do just that. I wish the government would pass a law legalizing women to cut off any man's dick when he fucks up." Malia screamed, "Straight men ain't shit!"

Z added, "Gay men ain't shit!"

Tré blurted, "Bisexual men ain't shit, either!" Malia and Z looked at their phones at the same time. Tré interjected finally, "Excuse us, Z. I met this punk ass nigga; he's married, pompous as hell and more obnoxious than you, Z. He thinks he's God's gift. This motherfucker wanted me to suck his dick, and you know, Z, if I get down I get my dick sucked and I do all the fucking, but he's a cool brother once you get past the exterior. He's passionate, but he fucks over his wife. I'm not worried about that; I'm more concerned with what that makes me. I don't fuck with faggots that often, but when I do, I don't take the dick and I have never fucked with one that's married. I feel like a fucking mistress, no pun intended, Malia," Tré apologetically said.

"None taken," she replied.

Tré continued, "I'm so confused about my sexuality. I love fucking women because of the softness, the breasts, the smell of the hair; I love the way she softly moans and groans, the way she begs for more and gently digs her fingernails into my back. I love the way her pussy tastes and how I tense up when she's about to come. Damn." Malia was in shock; Tré had never opened up to them about his sexual experiences with men or women. Tré continued, "And with a man, we can vibe, smoke a blunt, talk about sports and in bed he knows how to suck dick and take dick, no hang ups. If I want my ass eaten, no hang-ups or If want to get freaky with him and stick a dildo up his ass, no hang ups. I like the hardness of his muscles, his dick rubbing against mine; me palming his muscular ass. I love smelling his masculine scent. It takes me to another place, a place where it's natural to have intercourse with a man. Laying there in sweat after the act is over, the scent of sex and humiliation starts to sink in and you realize that the flesh was stronger than the spirit of God and you become like Adam, confused and ashamed. You rush to wash your sins away with a shower or just a wash cloth; you rush out the door without even acknowledging the person you just fucked. The confusion lingers on until you can smoke a Black and Mild or until you get to a bar to grab a drink; that will settle everything. God didn't see my sins; he was busy bringing life into the world and helping life exit into the doors of death. He forgave me, so why can't the world?" Z dropped the salt and pepper shaker; Trés words were so prolific, he couldn't believe it. He knew these were feelings that Tré had kept bottled up for a long time. Hearing the noise in the background, Tré fell back into reality. He directed this insult to Z, "You see, Z, we have feelings, regardless of what a gay man may think, we have feelings. We are not all dogs, Malia. It's just a level of confusion within us that cannot be easily explained. We don't know why we fuck men and have sex with women. I can not speak for all but it's like apples and oranges; you want both because they satisfy different parts of your soul. You can't speak about it because it's a sign of weakness and humiliation, so we creep and sneak, hoping that the light will never shine, making us visible to society, to the black race and to the world, hoping that the world continues to be oblivious to our carnal sins, so we won't be judged by people who don't know us. Society don't know us but want to crucify us and hang us by our dicks in hopes we will not lust for the same sex ever again." With that, Tré hung up the phone. Z spoke first, "Hello?" Malia repeated, "Hello."

Z screamed, "Girl, you heard that. My fucking cousin is deep and real after all. I was lifted, girl, to another place."

Malia added, "I'm mortified. Damn, my African brother, I am amazed. I love him even more, now. Tré keeps so much bottled up that when he speaks we listen; and you, Z, always putting him down, always talking about his sexuality. See, we need to understand that being bisexual or on the 'DL' is a state of mind and flesh and its hard for a man to decide, not wanting to be gay, because of the consequences and the baggage it brings. Z, you're totally different; you can adjust to any situation and come back with a vengeance, but Tré is subtle; his personality is that of a thug who doesn't like drama or bullshit. He's been through a lot and now he's trying to find himself sexually and emotionally. I love him for it, whether he settles for being straight, gay or bisexual."

"Shut up, bitch!" Z shouted, "I love him, too. Damn, he's my cousin, and if he wasn't I would be trying to give him some."

"That's nasty, Z," Malia replied.

"Malia, I need to call you back; I have some last-minute preparations for tonight's events. It's gonna be nasty but tasteful; catch the news brief at 11 o'clock," Z said authoritatively.

"Z, please don't do anything you will regret. I have enough to worry about besides trying to get you off death row," Malia pleaded. Z was saved by the beep; Dani was calling on the other line. "Let me go; I need to see what kind of drama she's going through. "Tootles." Z clicked over to the next line. "What's up, girl?" Z asked.

(It seems that the last conversations leads into this Chapter.... Is this what you mean????

CHAPTER 24

Make up Lovemaking

"Nothing, really; I just got a phone call pertaining to your friend, Nikko. I heard he almost killed the guy who murdered his sister," Dani explained. Dani, short for Danielle Greene, was a paralegal at a downtown firm. She was an aspiring professional. She and Z had become friends about five years ago. Dani had very beautiful features; she had a round face, big almond shaped eyes and shoulder length hair. She was about 5' 8" and about 125lbs. She was 32 years old and remarkable; she, too, was dating a married man and really wanted to have a baby with him, but several complications made her dreams very unlikely. She often conversed with Z about fertility drugs and even an operation to make her more fertile. Z responded, "I really haven't gotten all the details, D, but I will let you know; and if you find out any dirt first, please don't hesitate to call a diva. Remember; a diva has to be the first to know." D was about to divulge more information to Z when his phone beeped again. "Baby girl, I gotta go. It's JJ. I'm kicking his punk ass out tonight. I'll call you later." Z immediately clicked over. "What up, baby boy?" asked JJ. "I'm around the corner. I'll be there in about five minutes." The house was filled with the scent of aromatherapy candles burning in every room. Z stayed in a modest condo loft with 3 bedrooms and 3 baths, a large great room, a den, dining room and a huge kitchen with a breakfast nook. There were windows everywhere. He had purchased over 15 pieces of art, including a painting of Nefertiti and Cleopatra and afro centric sculptures.

JJ entered the house all happy and chipper. He kissed Z on the cheeks as he stared at the dining room table. The food looked marvelous, like a picture from a Martha Stewart magazine. He rushed to the downstairs restroom, washed his hands and started to dig in without saying his prayers. Z just stared at him, almost having the urge to take a steak knife and pierce JJ's heart. JJ was about to reach for the salmon, when Z burst out, "Why the fuck are you bringing drugs in my house, JJ?"

JJ looked puzzled. "What are you talking about?"

"Today, when I was washing your funky ass clothes, your shit fell out of your pocket. Fucking drugs, JJ? In my house? I'm a nurse, for Christ sakes! I can't have that shit in my house, so that means you gotta go, JJ," Z shouted.

"Let me explain, baby! The powder is for sex, believe it or not. I put it on my dick so I can fuck longer. C'mon, Z; you never noticed how hard my dick is when we're fucking and how long we can go before I come? It's 'cause I put a little 'caine on my shit. I also sneak and put some on the lips of your pussy to make it numb. Now you know I don't do drugs; you must think I'm crazy, boo. I just like the way it make my dick feels when I'm inside of you, and since you make me wear fucking condoms, I can get more of a feel when we're fucking. At first, baby, I couldn't hang with your wild escapades, but now we fuck like rabbits," JJ said calmly and reassuringly. Z just looked in disappointment and jumped and said, "Eat your dinner before it gets cold."

"I hope this isn't our last meal together, baby."

Z responded, "I hope it isn't either," and walked in the kitchen. JJ followed him.

"What's wrong, Z?"

Z responded, "I hope I can trust you, because if I feel you're lying to me, I will cut your balls off, and trust, I know how to do it; I had a lot of practice."

JJ, insulted, replied, "If I ever lie to you I will give you the knife to cut off my dick …sorry, my balls."

Z reluctantly started telling JJ the latest news about Nikko and the intruder. He told him how Nikko single-handedly caught the suspect who'd killed Nikki. "The police have the assailant in custody now and Nikko will have to answer a lot of questions. He is still grieving and now he has to deal with this shit. Hopefully the media won't have a field day with this situation. Hopefully they will have enough decency to allow him to put closure on this part of his life until the trial starts, because that will be unbearable for him, Lake and especially Kennedy." JJ was in shock as he tried to stomach his food. "By the way, baby," Z continued, "you need to go shopping for some more clothes. I accidentally spilled bleach all over your clothes; my apologies. So, are you finished with the salmon? Do you want some more?" Z asked.

"If you're up to it, boo, I want some dick for dessert." Z dropped his sweat pants, grabbed the wine bottle off the table and headed to the living room; JJ followed him without saying a word.

Z dropped to his knees as he started to pull JJ's pulsating dick from his jeans. He started sucking it until it was enlarged and half way down his throat. JJ pulled his Z's shirt off and then his own. He started to push Z's head back and forth on his dick. His knees almost buckled as Z continued to suck longer and harder on JJ's dick. Z resembled a snake devouring an innocent mouse as the dick went slowly down his throat. JJ grabbed the wine from the coffee table and poured drops of it in the crack of Z's back; without any hesitation Z arched his back as the puddle of wine cascaded down his spine of his back. JJ slowly pulled himself out of Z's mouth and, before a drop of wine could hit the Persian rug in front of the fireplace, he licked it off of Z's back. He began to push his entire tongue into Z's rectum and Z moaned with pleasure. He knew he'd kick JJ out in a heart beat but he would have to leave the dick and the tongue. Z was now begging for Jeremy to fuck him. He pulled the lubrication and condoms from underneath the couch and slid them both to JJ. JJ was anticipating fucking Z hard and long tonight, maybe even trying to punish him for wanting to kick him out. He didn't know whether to use the cocaine or just make love to Z without the little powdered substance. He decided to fuck with the powder; it was a stimulant and he needed it to keep up with Z. He pulled a little plastic bag from underneath the Persian rug as he continued to eat Z's ass. Without skipping a beat, JJ managed to put cocaine on his dick, with lubrication and also a condom. He started to sprinkle a little 'caine in the crack of Z's ass, but decided against it. He wanted Z to feel every inch of his eleven inch pipe; he wanted Z to bleed and feel the pain. He wanted Z to beg him to stop; then he would determine whether he would choke Z to death or break the wine glass over his head and cut his throat.

After one hour of straight fucking, Jeremy started giving Z deep, sensual tongue kisses. He massaged Z's back as he started making love to him. While giving long and passionate strokes, he positioned Z on top of him, but now he was in complete control. Z threw his head back and Jeremy gripped his hips and controlled the up and down motion. Tears rolled down Z's face as he dug his nails into Jeremy's shoulder. He begged for JJ to go deeper, harder and faster, but JJ refused. He wanted to see the pain and pleasure on Z's face. If JJ knew he was about to come he could slow his pace and last another thirty minutes; he knew this would drive Z crazy because he was sore now and JJ knew it. Z shouted, "Fuck me now,

Jeremy! Fuck me harder!" Instead, Jeremy started kissing him, only to shut him up. Z could be so loud at times. He then started licking Z's nipples, as Z continued to sit on his dick. Z started to shoot cum all over JJ's stomach; it seemed as though the fluid would never stop. Afterward, Z seemed lifeless as he just sat there. semen started to drip off JJ's stomach, onto his side and now onto the leather couch. Z grabbed his shirt from the floor and wiped the semen from his stomach and the couch. He held Z and they both fell asleep. It felt so good as he felt his dick deflate inside of Z's poor little sore rectum. Jeremy smiled as he heard Z started to snore.

CHAPTER 25

I Ain't Gay

Tré answered the phone, "Speak!"

"What up, baby," the male voice said.

"Who the fuck is this?" Tré shouted.

"This is your favorite baseball player."

"What up, nigga!" Tré answered.

"Tre, where are you? I want to see you, man," begged Lincoln.

"Sorry, man, I can't; 'bout to jet."

"Well, when are you coming back?" asked Lincoln.

"I'll be back on Sunday night. Why?"

"I want to see you. I miss being held by you."

Tré cut him off. "Well, man, I don't know when that will happen again. I don't usually get down like that. I'm going through some shit and that night set me back, yo."

"Well, my wife is having a birthday party for me next Saturday. I want you to be there; it would mean a lot to me. Your name is the first name on the list and if you don't come then I won't be there either. By the way, where are you flying off to?" asked Lincoln.

"Well, first, I'll be in San Juan; I have a 12 hour lay over and then I will be in Hawaii with a 24 hour layover. Why all the questions?" Tré asked very abrasively.

"I just want to see you again; man; just one more time and I promise I won't bother you again if that's what you want. Promise."

"Okay, man, I will call you once we land in San Juan," replied Tré.

“That’s all I’m asking. Hope to see you soon. One,” Lincoln quickly responded. The phone went dead. Tré stared into space for a moment to gather his thoughts. “Damn, my shit is still banging; he’s already sprung,” he thought as he walked out the door, smirking.

CHAPTER 26

Forgive me for I have sinned

Malia had fallen asleep in the study downstairs. She was completely drained from today's alarming events. She didn't even hear Drayton come in with dinner. She woke up with the smell of shrimp egg foo yung filling her kitchen. Drayton knocked on the open door to the study. "Baby, dinner is served," he said.

"Oh, Drayton, I'm not hungry. I think I need to take a hot bubble bath and sleep the night away. I have a very demanding day tomorrow," replied Malia. "Did you hear about Nikko capturing the suspect in Nikki's murder? I know tomorrow is going to be grueling and confusing; the media is going to have a field day with this." Drayton told Malia to follow him upstairs to get into the bath he'd drawn for her. Malia oozed into the bubbling luke warm water, thinking of nothing but heavenly bliss. When the water started getting a little cold, Drayton was right there pouring in vanilla scented bath beads and running more hot water. After an hour of soaking and looking like a prune, Drayton dried her off, kissing her body ever so gently. Malia just stood there like a three year old baby, blushing yet very tired. After five minutes of passionate kisses, Drayton urged her to relax. "Come over here, Malia and take the towel off," he ordered. "I just want to look at you for a second. Baby, you look tense. Let me give you a deep spiritual massage. Let me explore your soul and captivate your heart; I want to feel the essence of your existence." Malia chuckled. "It sounds corny," Drayton replied. "Okay, how 'bout you let me take you to a land of ecstasy. I'm gonna make you climax uncontrollably. I want to give you a tongue massage; I need to glide my tongue from the end of your earlobes to the crack of your ass. I want to lick you, baby, from the tip of your pussy. Let me lick those feet." Malia was quivering and trying to pull away, only wishing Drayton would stop. She felt her eyes roll in the back of her head, her toes curling as she lay there in the middle of the bed, motionless. "That's right, baby," Drayton whispered. "Let nature take its course." Malia started to wriggle away, trying to escape from the pleasure that her body so desired. Drayton pulled the coconut oil from the night stand. Malia just lay there, lifeless, as she fell into oblivion. She was in a faint sleep as the twinkle of the candles hypnotized her and her body was now under Drayton's spell. Wrapped in Malia's thighs; he continued to whisper, "I want my tongue to move down your body like melting ice. Don't shiver or shake; just let me do my job. No screams or moans can save you now. I want to go deeper inside of you, making you explode with spiritual ecstasy. I don't want to see the tears of satisfaction; I only want to see the drippings of your essence fill my mouth. I want to take my sex and touch your soul. Your body will react to my voice. I want you to get moist and your nipples to get hard at the sound of my name. I want to take you to a place of heavenly bliss. I want a smile to cross your face, knowing that I want to make love to you endlessly. You are my soul mate, Malia, and I'm your slave. I'm your prisoner for life. Only let me out to satisfy your desires; I don't mind, boo. Chain me up and take away the key to my heart. My fate has been served; I'm summoned to love, cherish, protect, and honor you forever. After an hour of passion and love-making and multiple orgasms, Malia fell back into a conscious state. "Baby, let me dry your sweaty limbs. You did well tonight; just lay here for a moment while you catch your breath and compose yourself. Let me feed you the chocolate strawberries and wine I prepared; you need your strength for later on," Drayton said.

Tré finally made it to his destination, checked into his room and began his routine schedule of preparing for tomorrow's activities. He was very tired; the flight over had been very drama filled, with uppity (bitches) wanting and needing everything under the motherfucking sun. He hated working in first class. He preferred working in coach, where the real people where, and they could laugh and talk and have a good ol' time, but today was over and now he needed to rest. As he dried off from a long hot shower and after calling to see how Junior and Keisha were doing, he started thinking about Lincoln and how good it was touching, kissing, licking, sucking and freaking with him. After he slipped into the hotel bed, nude, he jumped out of bed and kneeled on the floor beside the bed to say his prayers. "My heavenly father, my(nigga), my friend, please forgive me for I have sinned. I know I come short of your glory and blessings, but God, I need guidance. I need you to show me the right way for my life. The urges and feelings I have for a man are not right. Please help me to find the right way. Why am I suffering from flesh and spirit? God, why do I lust for another man? I don't want to be bisexual or gay or catch AIDS. God,, I'm tired of fighting my sexual desires: I don't want to hate faggots, but they got me like this; all of them. God, please help me, please. In your son's name Jesus Christ, amen".

It was 2 o'clock in the morning; Malia had just enough strength to answer the phone on the third ring. She hesitated as she answered, hoping it was not an emergency from Lake or Nikko. It was Z. "Gurrrrrl, he's back," Z whispered.

"Who?" Malia asked.

"Girl, I was about to kick that mother fucking big dick out the door, oh yes I was, but girl, after he laid the pipe… girl I just opened my legs and let him do his business. Child, the dope was a misunderstanding. He uses the cocaine for sex," and Z just kept rambling and whispering. Malia slipped out of the bedroom where Drayton was snoring lightly, with the towel still wrapped around her rejuvenated body, she ran across the hall to the upstairs office. Z continued. "Bitch, and then he fucked me right. He sure did, and the motherfucker made me come, Malia, without me even touching my clit." Malia almost tripped on the rug after she heard Z called his dick a clit. She was now laughing like a hyena. She begged Z to repeat himself, but he just kept right on talking. "Well, girl, I gotta go. JJ is still on the couch in the living room. I'm gonna let the motherfucker stay there until the morning. I think I'll go get a towel and cover up his dick; wouldn't want the dick to get a cold. Smooches!" Z hung up the phone.

Z just lay there for a moment, looking at the flicker of the lights from the bedroom candles. Tears started to fall from his eyes. He was moved to get on his knees and pray. "God, I hope you hear me. I don't pray much, but you are always in my heart. God, you know faggots like me know how to pray and we know your word. I'm not a bad person; I just don't like to be punked out. I know I go off on people, but I have to, because if I don't then who will? God have mercy on my soul. God, I have a confession; I love dick, I love big dicks. I love the dick that is sleeping in my living room right now. To me, it's a sin, it's a disease. I need that desire to be taken from my body; I don't want to get weak for the flesh. God help me with these feelings. Also, have mercy on my best friends, Nikko, Lake, Malia and my cousin Tré. Please watch over them, please help all of us get closure on Nikki's death. I know she's up their helping the angels walk the cat walk. Oh, God, please help me; please control my life and make me a better person. I am your child, a child of God, and I will always be. In your son's name I pray, Amen."

Malia headed for the master bedroom where Drayton was snoring but made a quick U-turn. She started for the guest bedroom and before she could start her prayers, the tears started rolling down her face. She fell to her knees. "My God, my heavenly Father, My Savior, I come to you in prayer for forgiveness, guidance and strength. I come to repent for my sins. I come to you, oh Jehovah, to bestow your holy spirit on my soul. I have disobeyed your word, God. I will not allow heavenly flesh to rule my heart. I know Drayton is a married man, and I must let him go. I know I will find comfort in your word and if I continue to live in this earthly sin then my fate will be hard and unforgiving. I ask you my father just to give me strength. Your faith will endure, and I know what I must do. God you have been so good to me and you bless me immeasurably, but my patience is growing thin when it comes to my family of friends. Nikko is suffering. God I know you're not going to put on him more than he can bare, and I must be supportive, but God, I need a special prayer for my earthly brother and friend; he needs to know in this time of despair that you're carrying him and he should never fear, and God, please continue to bless Lake, Kennedy, Tré, Drayton, and definitely Z; they need to know that you are the most high and through your blessings all things are possible. Through your power and your glory, and your son, Jesus Christ, Amen."

"Cameron, how long do I have to stay in this fucking place? They already have my statements; I'm tired and frustrated," Nikko complained.

"I understand, Nikko; just a little while longer. I'm sure the commander will let you go soon; it's just a long process, baby," Lake explained... Nikko grabbed Lake around the neck and Nikko's voice started to crack, "Lake, I feel like I'm losing it. I can't take it anymore. Why is God punishing me like this? I have faith and I believe in God's Holy Spirit, Lake, just tell me why. Why?" Nikko asked soberly. Lake squeezed Nikko, begging him to be strong. "God is not punishing us, baby; he's carrying us and testing our love and faith for him and for each other. I promise I will not let anything else happen to you. I'm sorry I wasn't there for you. I will never let anything ever happen to you or Kennedy." Nikko's tears started to come again.

"Lake, I just need to go home. I just want to go home." Lake heard voices outside the door. The commander walked in and told Nikko that he could leave but they may have more questions. Nikko and Lake wanted to know the status of the suspect. "He's in stable condition. You put him in a lot of pain, but he has confessed that he did have sexual intercourse with your sister and that it was consensual, but we know that is a lie. The suspect is schizophrenic and suffers from hallucinations. The psychologist will be doing an assessment with him on Monday and then we can better understand who we are dealing with and also what direction we are going to take. We are still working on a full confession and should have it definitely before Monday. We are looking for the death penalty on this one; the only confusing part is that we have no known leads on the other suspect. Mr. Jamal Wright refuses to divulge the other intruder's identity; he's convinced that he did the deadly deed alone. So much for that, Mr. Grey; you are free to go. I must warn you, though; the media is ready for you, so I suggest you be escorted through the back entrance. It is strictly up to you," the commander mentioned respectfully. Nikko ran directly for the back stair case where the back entrance was located. Lake was close behind, not saying a word. They disappeared into the shadow of the police vehicles, motorcycles and trucks. After entering the Navigator, Nikko wanted to call Kennedy but realized it was very late and she would have been asleep. Lake had called earlier to inform Ms. Aldridge to not allow Kennedy to watch any news bulletins, but the girls were so busy telling ghost stories and eating popcorn and ice creams they never missed the sound of the television, mainly due to the ebullient laughter and giggles. There was a long silence between Nikko and Lake and Nikko decided to break the ice. Nikko solemnly explained to Lake his visit to the doctors, the packet he'd received from Chaston pertaining to the custody of Kennedy. "The fact that I'm HIV positive makes him feel he has a good case. Also, Z is having a get-together next Friday, and guess what the theme is; 'The Black Chair'. It is his way of us putting closure to Nikki's passing and all the other shit we have endured. So how was your day, Lake?" Nikko solemnly asked. Lake almost drove off the embankment when he heard about Chaston's actions. Lake pulled to the side of the road and stopped the SUV. He looked directly into Nikko's eyes. "I will take care of Chaston, Nicholas. I promise." He started the Navigator and didn't say another word until they pulled into the driveway. "Nikko, I'm going to walk the dogs. You go upstairs and get some rest. I will be up there shortly." Lake exited to the backyard where Sasha and Sebastian were eagerly waiting in their kennels. Nikko walked upstairs, exhausted and puzzled over Lake's sudden behavior. He fell to the bed and was fast asleep when Lake slipped into the bedroom. Nikko was still wearing his clothes. Lake pulled off his shoes, socks, jeans and shirt. He tucked Nikko under the burgundy duvet and just watched him sleep. Lake's heart began to ache as he could only imagine what Nikko must be going through. He wanted so desperately to feel Nikko's pain, to erase it somehow.

CHAPTER 27

Monday Blues

It was a glorious Monday morning in the neighborhood for Z. He had just finished giving JJ his tenth blow job for the weekend, cooked breakfast, put the dishes in the dishwasher, called several rental shops for the party for this Friday night and invited thirty of his closest gay, straight and bisexual friends. He wanted this party to be kind of subtle and spiritual; it needed to be full of emotional bliss. It would be centered around Nikko and Lake; the theme would be the subject of closure and rebirth, hopefully. Z tried to call his cousin, Trés sister to see if her or her boyfriend needed anything before he started his errands. The landlord from the duplex answered the phone on the first ring. She informed Z that they both had been driven to jail. Z was astonished to learn that his cousin and her boyfriend had a physical fight at Trés apartment. They had completely demolished the apartment; they'd trashed the dining room table, broken one of the arms off the leather couch, several paintings were broken and there was broken glass everywhere. Cynthia had started the argument with her boyfriend when he didn't come home until 6 o'clock that Monday morning. They had fought for six straight hours and both were now in jail due to a domestic disagreement; both were bloody, tired and drunk. The bail had not been set and probably wouldn't be set until they went to pretrial. The landlord said, "I'm afraid to inform you that Trés lease is now null and void. He will have to move immediately." Z tried to explain to the manager that Tré was not at fault. "He's not even in the country; he's not scheduled to arrive back until sometime this evening." The Landlord abruptly cut him off and hung up the phone. Z looked at the phone. "Oh I know that bitch did not hang up in my face." Now he was pissed as hell.

Z hurriedly (douched), showered, and dressed, knowing he had to get to work, but before that, he had to pay his car note. "So off to see Ms. Connie from the finance company," he said. Z grabbed his trusty whistle from the counter as he whisked out the back door. He continued to make his calls from his cell, calling Nikko, Malia, JJ and the caterer for next Friday night. The trip to the finance company only seemed to take seconds. He asked to speak to Ms. Connie and refused to speak to anyone else. He threw the whistle around his neck as Ms. Connie walked from around the corner with a big patch over her right ear. "Good afternoon, Ms. Connie. I'm Zarius Washington; I believe I'm supposed to give you my payment for my Lexus," Z said shamefully. After realizing who he was, the lady just walked away. Z thought she was going to come back with a gun or the police, but she came back with the manager. He took the payment from Z and told him to have a good afternoon. Z was about to blast his stereo in the car when the cell rung, "(Chello) Do you mean "Hello"??," said Z. "What the hell is going on?!" screamed Tré.

"Who the fuck is this??" Z screamed back.

"What the hell is going on? I just talked to the leasing agent at my apartment and they told me that my lease had been revoked," Tré continued to yell.

"What the fuck you want me to do? I didn't fuck up your motherfucking house. I begged the landlord not to kick you out, but she wasn't hearing it, her sorry ass." Z's phone went dead. "I know that bitch did not hang up on me." Z was fuming as he swerved into the parking lot of Atlanta General. His cell phone rang again; this time he was ready. "What the fuck do you want?"

Malia asked, "How was your day, precious?"

"Oh girl, I thought you were my sorry ass sissy cousin." Z seemed to have calmed down. "Well, darling, I just wanted you to know that everything is a go for Friday. Call me later, sissy." Malia smiled.

"I will, dyke." Z hung up the cell. The cell rang again. "Now who the hell is this? Oh, what up Ma?"

"Hey boy, what's going on with you and your cousin?"

"What do you mean?" Z said coldly. Z's mother started to explain.

"Tré called and told me that you let Cynthia and her boyfriend trash his apartment. He's been kicked out and may have to live on the streets." Z's mother explained.

"Okay what that gotta do with me? I didn't let no fucking body do anything. I just called over to the apartment and his landlord told me what happened. I was totally unaware, Ma, and that's the God's honest truth," Z sympathetically responded.

"Well, he's blaming you for the whole thing, but that's not why I called. Aunt Betty had to be rushed to the hospital; they don't know exactly what happened, so I wanted you to find out; you know they ain't gonna tell us a damn thing." Z's mother sounded very concerned. "Ma, I will try, but why didn't Tré tell me that? Besides going off like a little punk-ass faggot about his apartment, you would think his mother is more important than his damn apartment, stupid ass bitch." Z became irritated. "Okay, Ma; I'll call you as soon as I find something out. Love ya, girl."

"I love you, too, Zarius." Z's mother hung up.

Malia was just finishing a lengthy conference call with Nikko when, Victoria, buzzed and informed her that Ms. Cecilia Greene, who just happened to be Drayton's wife, was requesting to see her. Without breaking a sweat, Malia asked Victoria to escort Ms. Greene in the office. Malia asked her to have a seat. "How can I help you, Ms. Greene?" Malia asked.

"Malia, I'm going to make this short and sweet. I know you have been fucking my husband. He asked for a divorce and I said yes, but I just want you to know I'm going to drain him dry, due to the fact I have the pictures of you and my fucking husband in a compromising position." Malia interrupted her.

"I'm going to make this shorter and sweeter. First thing's first; I don't want your husband and yes, you are correct; let the record show that we have fucked, made love, sexed, freaked, and every time he left Atlanta, and came home to you in DC, you should have tasted my pussy on his tongue. Ms. Greene I'm not the one to fuck with; just let the record show that I'm pregnant with your husband's child, but I'm going to raise it alone. I don't want you or your husband in my life. Don't be mistaken; I love your husband, but he's your husband not mine. I have taken the liberty to take some photographs of my own: pictures of you and Croix. The male escort that fucked you silly on May 23rd of this year and please lets not us forget your lesbian lover, Stacy Gordon. So, Ms. Greene, I would greatly appreciate if you would get the hell out of my office. I have work to do, and if your husband continues with the divorce after I tell him I don't want him, then, Ms. Greene, you have a problem. It could very well be your tired ass pussy. Ms. Greene I wish we could continue this conversation, but I get paid $200.00 an hour and I really don't believe you're in a position to afford my services. Good day, Ms. Greene," Malia said before turning the leather chair around to face the window, waiting for Ms. Greene to exit her office. Victoria couldn't wait to see what the gossip was; without hesitation Malia questioned Victoria's inquisitive behavior, "I didn't call for you, Victoria, so what's the urgency? Victoria just turned around with your tail between her legs. Still looking out the window, Malia called Drayton in his DC office. "What's up, Mr. Greene?"

He responded, "Nothing, my Princess. How's your Monday morning?"

"It's fine. You know how it is; just have to clean up trash and brush it under the rug, and she snickered. "What time are you coming down on Friday? You know the party starts at 9:00." She added, "You know how Z is; he hates when people are late."

"I will be there that morning. I have a briefing with one of my clients at 8am, so I will see you in the office no later than noon."

"How are Cecilia and the girls?" Malia inquired.

"They're fine. Cecilia drove up to Philly for some trade show or convention at Temple, and the baby is in daycare and the older one is in school. Why you ask, baby?"

"Oh, they were on my mind. I was just wondering how the family was. I gotta go. I have a client in 15 minutes," Malia voice cracked again.

"Oh, okay baby. I'll call you later. I love you, Malia," Drayton affectionally responded.

Z had not been at work thirty minutes and the hospital was already on his nerves, He was working the emergency wing today and it was a fiasco from the beginning, The first patient was a thirty year old black man who was run over by a drunk driver. Patient number two was a 15-year-old black female; she was hemorrhaging from her uterus. She'd stuck a hanger up her vagina in hopes it would abort her six week old fetus. Z's third patient was a seventy year old white female with Alzheimer. She was suffering from accidental third degree burns on her arms and shoulders. She was completely hysterical; she was screaming obscenities at everyone in third ward. Z approached her, begging her to calm down; she was making the other patients irritable. She yelled at Z, demanding he take his (nigger) hands off of her. "Get away from me, you faggot nurse," she blurted. Z clutched his pearls and you could actually see the entire emergency room clearing for cover, but Z kept his composure. He requested a female nurse to come over to this (bitch). "Patient needs to be sedated before any other medical attention be can provided," he said. A couple of hours after the madness had settled down in the emergency room, Z decided to go take a look at his new patient, Ms. Diane Prancer; he snuck in her room while she was coming around from all the medication they had pumped into her. The pain of the burns was slowing dissipating and she was quite calm. She woke in a daze; recognizing Z, she asked the (nigger faggot) who she was. He responded, "Oh masser, you are Diana Prince, Wonder Woman. Your helicopter awaits you outside the window; you need to jump out the window and fly away. You must save all the white people from the (nigga) faggots; you know they are taking over the world!" Z opened the window and exited the room. It was now nine o'clock and he realized he had not taken a break; he was tired as hell. He needed to prop his feet up for a moment. He decided to cruise to the nurse's lounge and talk on the phone. His first call was to Nikko; he had been trying to call him every hour on the hour but didn't get a response, so he decided to give a Lake a call. Lake ran down all the whirlwind events that they were going through then he asked Z to do him a favor. Z asked, "What do you need, Lake?" He asked Z if he could hide a body. Z stood up. "What do you mean 'a body'?" he whispered, his heart beating uncontrollably. Lake continued, "If you can't do that, then I need a secluded room with no windows and it must be pitch black."

Z agreed. "I can pull that one off; there's a hospital room here that I have sex in from time to time."

"Okay," Lake said. We will talk more about it at the party. Thanks, Z, and mums the word; please don't say a word to anyone. That conversation was too much for Z. He worked another eight hours and slept in the lounge until the next morning.

The media ran the entire story about the capture of the suspect every hour on the hour; CNN, Newsweek, People, Time, Jet, BET, Headline News, Larry King, everybody who was anybody knew that Nikko had single handedly captured the suspect who'd raped and murdered his sister. Nikko, along with Lake and Malia, refused to give comments. The chief of police gave his analysis at the press conference, but Nikko refused; instead he drove to the cabin in up state Georgia that Monday afternoon, just he and Kennedy; he wanted her to get away and not be affiliated with all the bullshit that was transpiring. He knew they had to get back on Friday, but if he couldn't, he had hoped that Z and the gang would understand. He needed the water and the peace. He needed to get a grip on reality; he had to deal with the events involving his sister's killer and also Chaston. He finally got the results back from his test, but refused to open the envelope until he had reached the cabin and settled down. Kennedy was melancholy; not talkative at all. Nikko couldn't understand why Kennedy was not inquiring about the drive, and she was not asking why Uncle Lake didn't come with them or why he took her out of school for four days. It was just him, her and the dogs. "Little girl," Nikko asked, "Are you ready for the play? Do you need me to help you with your lines?"

"No, thank you," replied Kennedy.

"Is there anything new you would like to talk about?" he asked as he drove up into the driveway of the little two bedroom cabin. Nikko cut off the car as he waited for an answer from Kennedy.

"Uncle Nikko, I do have one question."

"Yes, baby, what is it?"

"Uncle Nikko, what is a faggot?" asked Kennedy. Nikko's heart stopped.

"Kennedy, why do you want to know about a faggot?"

She replied, "This girl at school named Morgan said that you were a faggot, and I really didn't know what that meant uncle Nikko. I asked my teacher, but Ms. Chapman, just put Morgan in timeout, and told me to just have a seat. So I'm asking you, Uncle Nikko." "Well, I don't know how to answer. I don't think I'm a faggot, but I have been called that in the past. Let me answer your question; the dictionary says that a faggot is a bunch of twigs or sticks; however, mean people who try to hurt others may say that a faggot is a man who acts like a girl or a sissy. It's kind of demeaning; its like if a person were to call a lady a bitch, but a bitch is a female dog. That can be cruel and harmful, so never let anyone call you that name, and if they do, you have the right to punch them in the eye. Never let anyone disrespect you, Kennedy. Another hurtful word that you may hear is nigger or nigga; no matter how it's pronounced, it's degrading and humiliating, so if anyone ever calls you that word, you correct them and tell them you hate that word. So, Kennedy, did I answer your question?"

"I guess so, Uncle Nikko; a faggot is a bundle of sticks," replied Kennedy. Nikko grinned.

"Is there anything else you want to discuss with me?" he asked.

"Well, Uncle, why didn't you tell me that you had caught the guy who killed mommy?" Nikko just started into space. He was silent for a long time, and then he responded. "Kennedy, what are you talking about?" he struggled to respond.

"Uncle Nikko, that's all everyone was talking about at school this morning, before you came to pick me up. They were saying you were a hero except that Morgan I told you about."

"Now, Ms. Lady, I have a question for you."

"Yeah Unkie? What is it?"

"Well if you had a choice to live with me forever or to live with your father, which would you prefer?" Now it was Kennedy's turn to be silent.

"Daddy asked me the same thing, Uncle Nikko, and I told him I love how it is now. When I look at you, Uncle Nikko, I see my mommy, when I talk to you sometimes, I hear my mommy, and when I'm with you and

Uncle Lake and I close my eyes, I feel my mother. I don't want that to change for nothing in the world. Unkie did you know Ms. Oprah gave me this necklace that is in the shape of an angel and she said it was made of diamonds? She also told me when I'm feeling pain and want to cry, I should hold the necklace in my hands and my mother will ease my pain and fill my heart with love. And guess what, Uncle Nikko; it works." Nikko just shook his head in agreement.

"Well, little girl why didn't you tell me about this little necklace Ms. Winfrey gave you," he asked. Kennedy smiled.

"Because she gave it to me, but if you want one I can give her a call. Unkie, can we get out of the Navigator? I gotta pee." Nikko burst out laughing.

"Sure, baby girl. Sure."

Tré was furious as he walked through the door of his apartment; it was in shambles. He could not believe his eyes or the condition of his apartment. No sooner than he dropped his bags, his landlord appeared at the front door. "Hi, Tré," she said sympathetically. He completely ignored her. "I'm sorry to have to be the one to inform you, but your lease agreement, which you signed, boldly states that any damage that is done to your dwelling space may void your lease." Tré interrupted her.

"I have a question; if I can get the apartment completely repaired, could I continue to stay rather then being put on the streets?" Now she interrupted him.

"Well, the damage will be approximately $7500. I checked with the rental insurance company, and they don't pay for domestic violence or negligence, but if you think you can pull it off, I will give you two weeks, Tré. You've been a good tenant for five years, but this is the best I can do. Two weeks."

"Thank you," Tré said, and closed the door. "Where the fuck am I gonna get $3,500?" Tré started pulling off his clothes and checking his messages; he had 17 messages, from the jail, his father, the hospital, his older sister, Lincoln, and also from Junior and Keisha. Lincoln was calling on his cell, "What up, big man?" Lincoln asked.

"What up, Linc? Man, my fucking apartment is fucked up; my sister and her fucking boyfriend demolished my shit, and the fucking landlord is going to charge me $7500 to get the fucking bitch fixed. Where the fuck am I going to get this shit? I need to go get a drink and figure out where the fuck (I'mma) I'm going to get this cash," Tré rambled on. "Well, man, where are you going to get a drink? I just left the car rental place; maybe I can be of help. I got an idea. Meet me at Sparkles; it's a strip bar on the east side," Lincoln begged.

Tré agreed. "Let me call little man, and I'll be there in twenty minutes."

"Cool." Lincoln was thrilled. "Oh man, before I forget, thanks again for my fantasy weekend."

Tré replied, "Anytime, nigga." Tré smiled as he called Junior and Keisha. Keisha answered on the second ring. "Hello!"

"What up, baby girl." Tré sounded thrilled.

"Hi, Tré. We've been worried about you. Your mother is in the hospital and your sister called asking me if I could get Cynthia out of jail. I can't do that and besides I don't have that much money; I believe her bail is $2500 and that's largely because she don't live here, so they need all the money." Tré completely ignored her latter statements pertaining to Cynthia. "What did Cassandra say about my mom?" Tré sounded concerned. Keisha replied, "I think she said she had an aneurism. I tried calling the hospital myself in DC to obtain some information but everybody was tight lipped. I spoke with Zarius and he said he was going to get some answers and relay it to your family and you, once he gets in contact with you," Keisha explained empathically.

"Where's my little man?" Tré asked.

"He went to the store with his uncles," Keisha said. "They should have been back by now."

"Call me as soon as they get back; I want to talk to Junior before he hits the sack." Tré hung up the phone, slipped on some baggy jeans, a Sean John T-shirts, baseball cap and some burgundy Timbs and headed out the door. Once in the car, he called up to New York to speak to his father. His cousin, Shawna, answered the phone on the first ring. "Hello," she said. Shawna was his favorite female cousin; she'd played basketball in high school and didn't take any shit from nobody; she could knock a guy out with a single blow. Now she was fifty pounds heavier and the mother of three. "Is this my favorite cousin?" she asked. He could hear the pain in her voice.

"What's going on, Shawna?"

"Tré, you don't know? Your mom is in the hospital. I think they are saying she had an aneurism. Your Father and Cassandra are at the hospital. Are you flying up, and did you get Cynthia out of jail?" Shawna asked.

"What's the number to the room? I need to talk to Pop." Tré asked. Shawna gave him the number and told him to be strong and everything would be alright. He called the hospital and his father picked up on the first ring. "Pop, how's Mom doing?" Tré asked. "Hi, son. They have her resting now; she had an aneurism and it caused a lot of damage, but they stopped the bleeding and now she's in ICU. So now we just have to wait," his father responded. As Trés tears began to form, he kept saying to himself, "Real men don't cry, real men don't cry." Tré thought back to the arguments he and his mother had about his life; she'd called him worthless and good for nothing, she yelled austerely and screamed about the ungodly nature of his lifestyle and how he would never amount to anything. At times he hated her and really didn't want to show any emotion, but his heart went out for his father; the relationship they had was remarkable and immeasurable. He didn't want his father to feel pain and knew he had to get to Washington, if only to give his father support. "Pop, if you need me to come I will leave tonight," Tré mournfully replied. Tré headed to the nudie bar feeling withdrawn; he knew he did not want to be alone, but he really didn't want to be with the gang, so he was looking forward to seeing Lincoln. Much to his chagrin, Tré was enjoying Lincoln's company; he enjoyed the talks, laughter and the closeness. It was fucking perfect; he didn't worry about whether he would see any of his boys or if they questioned him about fucking pussy, didn't have to worry about, bills, friends, family or life. Is this Tre talking or the writer talking???(Damn, could he be feeling for this nigga?)???The parking lot was full; there were luxury SUV's, Bimmers, Big Benzs, every type of expensive (ass) car, truck or SUV you could imagine. Tré paid his $20, turned his cap to the back and headed to the table where Lincoln was waiting. "What up, man? What you drinking?" Lincoln asked.

"What up, nigga? "I'll have Hennessey on the rocks." The strippers were live as hell; the pussy was floating tonight and all the girls were asking if Tré and Lincoln wanted a table dance. It was like a circus. Nipples were hard, dicks were hard, the money was flowing and the music jelled it all. There were other pro athletes in the club, along with some local celebrities and hard working niggas who would be spending their entire paychecks tonight. Tré thought, "I know there are gonna be a lot of motherfucking niggas in the dog house tomorrow." There was one female who caught Tré's eye; her name was Passion. She was a goddess; big pretty titties, small waist and the prettiest ass this side of the Mississippi, and she was all real: hair, lips, tits and ass. He felt a woody coming on. Lincoln noticed Tré's reaction and asked if he wanted a table dance. Tré replied, "Hell yeah." Lincoln motioned Passion to come over. She began gyrating as she untied her g-string and exposed her pussy. She pulled her lips apart and Tré could have sworn her pussy was actually talking to him and his dick. Tré's head fell back in amazement. "Damn, bitch. Where the hell you learn how to do that?" Five hours later and with Lincoln $3,000 poorer, he and Tré found themselves highly intoxicated in the hotel room with Passion sucking both their dicks. He and Tré kissed each other as Passion was giving one a hand job and the other a head job. Lincoln pulled out some condoms, Ecstasy pills and some lube from the night stand. Lincoln started fucking Passion in the ass as Tré started fucking her in the front. The threesome made love for over three hours. They where completely exhausted when the sun finally peeped through the blinds. Passion rolled from between the dynamic duo to take a quick shower and once completely dressed she demanded her $1,500 from Lincoln, bidding him a farewell until they met up again. Lincoln pushed her out the door and he jumped back in bed as he and Tré slept in each other's arms until 3 p.m. the next day. They showered, ordered room service and ordered box tickets to the Atlanta Braves seven game series. They became inseparable that day. Lincoln took Tré in the locker room to meet the entire Braves team. Once they were back at the hotel room, Tré talked to Junior about not calling back the other night. He also called to check on his father and to see the condition of his mother and finally to check to see whether Z had gotten his sister out of jail, because Tré refused. He and Z exchanged words as usual, and they made arrangements for the social on Friday night at Malia's house. Tré invited Lincoln to be his guest and gave Lincoln the address, time and date; Lincoln, in exchange, invited Tré to fly up to attend his surprise birthday party on Saturday night. Tré needed to go home; he hadn't been home since that night he came back from his flight and he was scheduled for another flight the following morning. He knew he needed to prepare himself for the grueling schedule. Lincoln didn't want him to leave, but he didn't want to seem selfish. Tré felt good about the days he spent with Lincoln, laughing, smoking, freaking and eating. He couldn't help but think about that night he'd spent with Lincoln and that whore who came to the room. Tré smiled as he thought, "Being a celebrity does have its perks." Tré was not ready to face the unexpected. Tré unlocked the door to his apartment and to his amazement fell to the floor. The entire apartment had been redecorated with a new living room and dining room suits. There were new pictures on the walls, new carpet, new paint, new drapes, new light fixtures and a brand new 56- inch plasma TV. There was a card on the table. Tré opened it with great anticipation.

I want to say thank you. It's been wonderful having you in my life. The first time I saw you I knew I needed you to complete me; I was not going to let you slip away. I knew you were the one; it felt so real and natural. I want you in my life however you want to be. I'm here. This is the least I could do for the person I…

After reading the card, he just fell onto the new soft Italian leather sofa. He noticed there was another piece of paper in the envelope; it was a statement indicating that the entire bill of $7,500 was paid in full. Tré's phone rang; it was his boys, Q, Jazz and Head. "What up, nigga?" they yelled through the speaker phone.

"What's up with you, ladies?"

"Nigga, we ain't seen you in a fucking minute. You must get some new pussy you ain't letting us know about, nigga."

"Man, my mom's been in the hospital and you know I travel, motherfucker," Tré added. "You motherfucking' niggas, what y'all doing; sucking each other dicks?" laughed Tré. "Man, we need to get our spades game going on. You know tonight is Wednesday, yo, and Bernie Mac is on the tube. What time you coming through," asked Q.

"Man, I gotta get ready to fly out in the morning."

"What time, faggot?" asked Jazz.

"Okay, bitches. I'll be there in thirty minutes, and I'll bring my shit over there and leave from your crib, Jazz; is that cool? Hold on; I got a call coming in." Tré clicked over. It was Lincoln. "Did you get the present I sent?" Lincoln asked.

"Man, I don't know what to say, but thank you. You planned this entire shit, man. You kept me from the apartment and had all this shit done while I was gone. You are fucking amazing." Tré smiled. "Are you coming back to the hotel? I'm missing you, man," Lincoln begged.

"Damn, B, I made plans; my boys called me and wanted to hang out? I haven't seen them chumps in a minute," Tré replied. Lincoln's attitude changed.

"So you'd rather be with your fucking boys than hang out with me," Lincoln shouted. "Who the fuck are you yelling at, nigga," Tré shouted back.

"I just thought maybe we could watch a DVD, especially after all the shit I've done for you," Lincoln retaliated.

"You can come get this shit; material shit don't impress me man. Besides, I thought you did the shit from the heart." Tré slammed the phone down. "That bitch," he yelled. The phone immediately rung back, Tré yelled again. "What the fuck do you want now, nigga??" Tré's boys said, "Damn man! Who were you talking to?"

"Oh shit, my bad. I forgot I had you girls on the other line."

"Damn, yo. Whoever you were rapping with got your panties in a knot." Everybody laughed, except Tré.

"Okay, fellas, I'll be over there in a minute." The home phone started ringing again, and then the cell. Instead of answering, Tré turned the ringer off on both phones. He packed his bags and headed out the door. He began thinking of all the reasons he hated faggots, sissies, and gay men in general; give them a little time and they think they own your ass. "Damn. I thought B was different; he's a man with no feminine ways and he's obnoxious as hell. Plus, the motherfucker is a challenge. I like that shit, but the punk-ass thinks he can buy me. I could only dream that I could find somebody like my boys to hang and kick it with; damn I wish at least one of my own got down, but my boys are too hard for that shit. Lincoln gets on my fucking nerves. Shit, I considered even giving up the ass for that punk. Stupid bitch-ass motherfucking nigga," he thought as he pulled into Jazz's driveway. "Yo, what's up playa?" Q screamed as he opened the door for his spades partner. "What took you so damn long, man? I need my dick sucked," yelled Head from the kitchen.

"Don't start no shit, man. If Q and I win, tonight you and punk-ass partner, Jazz, will be sucking me and my partner's dicks."

Jazz screamed back, "Man, you too late your partner already gave us some courtesy head, and I came in his mouth."

"Man, shut up and get ready to take your ass beating like a man," was Tré's rebuttal. After five hands of card playing and more shit talking, Jazz and Head won, three to two. "Man, its 3 o'clock. I gotta get some sleep; I gotta get up at 7." Tré ran in the guest bathroom, took a quick shower and crashed. The terrible threesome was still up, talking shit. It was about 4:20 a.m. when something woke Tré up; he could have sworn he heard a man's voice, fucking or getting fucked. He laid back down, too tired to be curious, and just assumed Jazz had one of his freaks over and was fucking her down. "You go boy," he thought as he fell back to sleep. Tré almost threw the alarm clock against the wall when it went off at 7 o'clock. He got dressed in forty-five minutes and was ready to head out the door. He went in to tell Jazz to come lock the door when Q came out of Jazz's bathroom, and Jazz was butt ass naked in the bed, dead to the world.

"Good morning, nigga. I thought you went home," Tré said.

"Naw man, I ended up sleeping on the couch; too damn drunk to go home, but I gotta get out here; gotta be at work in an hour," Q tried to explain.

"Well, man, I gotta jet. I'll be back in town tomorrow night. I'll catch you cats later. I'm out."

CHAPTER 28

The Social

Z and Malia had prepared everything to perfection; the house, the food, the decorations, the music; everything was completed to a science. It was 7 o'clock and no one had heard from Nikko or Lake. Tré called and said he and Keisha would be there no later than 9. Malia had some very good news for Nikko and Lake, but some very bad news for Drayton; she had toyed with her decision for four days. Malia knew what she had to do; her love for God was much greater then her love for Drayton. She knew the future would be bleak after his absence from her bed, but she knew what she had to do. This party would definitely put closure on her life with Drayton and reopen her life with spiritual completeness. The guests were starting to arrive; first to arrive was Charles and his wife, Pamela, a couple from the law firm. Darren and his new boyfriend arrived shortly after. Lawrence and his girlfriend, Karenna, dropped by unannounced. Z hesitated to let them in, but eventually accepted their presence. Z informed them that this was more of a closure party for everyone who was invited. It's called "The Black Chair" party. The house filled up quickly. Tré finally got there at nine-thirty, and Lake and Nikko finally arrived at ten. Z served wine and champagne along with various liquors, but the specialty drink of the evening was a sour apple martini. Malia hired five servants, three servers and two waiters. The food was indescribably delicious; Malia and Z had outdone themselves. The table spread was simply a work of art. Nikko seemed to be enjoying himself, laughing and giggling with the guests, cracking jokes and smiling uncontrollably. Lake didn't know how to accept his behavior; he could only imagine the time he and Kennedy spent together was much needed. Nikko's disposition was fresh and renewed; he agreed to go on one local talk show in the near future and even talked to Ms. Oprah and agreed to go on her show next month. Lake was in a daze when Z asked him if he want an apple martini. Lake thought the party was remarkable. He nudged Z and asked him to follow him to the basement. "Z," Lake started, "I need to kidnap and torment somebody for a couple of hours." Z became immediately frightened. "Who?" Z asked with hesitation. "It's Chaston. I need to teach him a lesson; one he won't forget. He's trying to take Kennedy and the money Nikki put away for Kennedy's trust fund. I will not let that happen; I will die first," Lake explained. "I could have him killed but that would seem very strange since he filed a lawsuit against Nikko asking for custody, so I need to hide him for a couple of hours in the hospital in a dark room. He's upstairs now, but I need to drug him. I asked Malia to invite him, just to show there are no hard feelings from me or Nikko, but I need you to put this drug in his drink, and then, after everyone leaves, we can drop him off at the hospital for about twelve hours. If this don't work then I will shoot him," Lake whispered, pressing the vial into Z's hand.

"Okay. I will do it as long as I can undress him; I want to see what the bitch is working with." Z smirked as he ran back upstairs. JJ had finally arrived and there was a mystery guest; Lincoln had finally made it after getting lost twice. Lincoln spotted Tré, but didn't know how to confront him. "What up, my Nigga?" Tré greeted him first. "Yo, man this is my girl Keisha, Keisha this is my boy I told you about."

"Nice meeting you," Keisha smiled. Lincoln was astonished; he responded, but didn't know why. "Yo, man, can I get you a drink?" Tré asked.

"Yeah, man. That will be great. I'll have a rum and Coke," replied Lincoln. The guys had gathered in the entertainment room and were discussing baseball and the NFL. Lincoln had relaxed a lot more and was in the middle of the discussion and bragging how his team would win the series next year because he would be fully recovered. It was getting late; the majority of the guests were leaving, giving their regards and talking about how much they'd enjoyed themselves. Darren, Drayton, JJ, Lincoln, Malia, Z, Lake, Nikko, Tré, Katie, Chaston and Victoria were still there, just laughing and talking. They didn't have anyplace to go and didn't want to leave. Z started asking individuals about dreams and what they really meant, and then the conversation switched to reality and how the two compared. Z started off once again about how he wished he could be in a meaningful and unconditional relationship with someone he could call his own. He wished he could be accepted just for his internal being as opposed to his flamboyant exterior. "I wish society would accept me for my gift of being a nurse compared to being a nigga or a faggot. I've been called that all my life and I had to grow a tough skin. I don't feel I'm different; I bleed and breath just like the next man, but what really hurts me is when my family and friends don't accept me when God accepts me. I wish I my dream was tangible and not impossible." There was complete silence when Lincoln felt the need to take a seat in "The Black Chair". I'm Lincoln Buchanan. I play major league baseball and I've been married for ten years to my loving wife, Annemarie. I have a seven year old daughter and I make a lot of money, but I feel my life is incomplete. I feel like my soul mate is still out there. I feel empty at times and lonely the other times. I can't believe I'm confessing this to complete strangers, but it hurts my heart to know my love is out there in the world; someone to complete me and someone who can accept me for my obnoxious, egotistical, pompous ways. God has accepted my search for true love, so I hope my love will someday be complete." Now it was Chaston's turn. He started by saying, "I'm Chaston, Kennedy's father, and I was married to Nikki for two of the most wonderful years of my life. I'm here tonight to ask for forgiveness from my ex brother-in-law. I fell in love with Nikki the first time I saw her on a cover and I searched until I found her. I begged her for about six months to marry me. I was so jealous of her I didn't even want her to breathe without me being present. I smothered her. I wanted her to quit her job and when she didn't, I became furious and physical. I struck her once and that was it; she filed for divorce that next day. I never got the opportunity to apologize for my wrong doing and when Kennedy was born, Nikki never mentioned that night I hit her. I feel God has punished me, my life and my career for striking one of his angels, so tonight I hope she hears me and accepts my apology. Since Nikki is not here, I want to ask her brother Nikko to forgive me. I will drop the petition for custody of my daughter; there is no one I'd rather raise my daughter than you, Nikko. You have the same blood flowing through you body as Nikki did, and that means your heart is good and pure. Tonight, I hope my impossible dream has come true, and that's forgiveness." There was complete silence. Z handed Chaston a drink and said, "I forgive you, my brother. I know that was very hard to admit. Drink up; this will make you feel a little better". Now it was Darren's turn. He was a lawyer who'd helped Malia on several of her cases from time to time. "I'm Darren Harper, and I'm a distant relative of the gang. I wish I could find a woman who could accept me for me. I meet women of every nationality, but there is nothing more beautiful than a black woman. I just wish they would let their guard down and accept a good brother for a good brother. It seems as though every sister wants a thug; someone to beat, ridicule, shame and belittle them. I'm looking for true women, powerful women by spirit who aren't measured by the fruits that lay between her legs. I wish God would bless me with a woman like my mother, who is true, sophisticated, simple, loving, compassionate and full of spirit." Lake wanted to share his impossible dream. "As you may or may not know, my impossible dream came true seven years ago; that's when I met Nikko. Before Nikko, I was completely heterosexual. I'd never even looked at another man before in my life, but when I first saw him, I had to have him. I didn't fight the feelings, I didn't curse God for giving me these feelings for another man; my manhood had not changed. I still hang out with the fellas, leave the toilet seat up and sometimes leave my drawers in the middle of the bathroom floor. So it doesn't offend me when I hear someone yell out faggot, punk or sissy because, for some reason, I refuse to accept that from anyone. I hear it and don't hear it. I don't fight for gay rights because my rights have been protected. I found the person, the man, the soul mate of my life. I will kill or die for my man; he has given me life and liberation. I need him beside me to breathe. I will protect him and my niece from any harm and anyone who crosses our path. He is the only man on this earth who can slap, spit, and kick or stab me and my love will not dissipate. I can't explain my feelings; I can only explain my heart. I never really knew my mother or father; they were killed when I was six, and I had been swapped and given to different people who accepted me in their lives. I had a very difficult childhood; so unbearable, I refuse to mention. Nikko is my life, my past, my present and my future. If anything ever happened to him, you can say it happened to me as well; I refuse to live without him." No one said anything after Lake's speech of closure. Nikko and Lake just hugged each other. Z blurted out finally, "Hey, you guys want to meet us at the gym tomorrow?"

"That will work; me and JJ got a score to settle," said Lake. "We'll meet you guys at nine in the morning at Run 'N' Shoot."

"Good. Nikko, I need you to help me in the weight room. Afterward we can get some lunch before I go to work," whispered Z. Malia wanted to discuss something with Nikko and Lake. Z decided to thank everyone for coming out to the Party of Closure. JJ insisted on helping Z with the usual task of cleaning and restoring the house to normal. JJ confronted Z in the kitchen, eager to ask him about his speech about having him as his lover and friend. JJ whispered, "Z your words were touching and heartfelt, but I thought we were kicking it and I thought this could be something long lasting." Z cut him off.

"I wish it could be, but I feel its only sex and comforting. J, I don't know where you work; I don't even know where you are half the time and I don't really care. I only see you at night, so I feel the only thing you want from me is my ass and my mouth. We don't go anywhere in public together; you make me feel you're ashamed of me, just like the others. As long as I'm cooking, washing and giving up the ass, life is great, but I need mental and emotional stimulation; a movie and a walk in the park once in awhile. I have feelings for you, J, but are you willing to sacrifice a little for me?" JJ was speechless and was not ready for the bomb that Z dropped on him. JJ's come back was, "I do care about you, man, but I must be honest; I have never fucked around with a guy that is effeminate and flamboyant as you."

Z interrupted. "Okay, sweetie; you knew this from the very start, J. I am what I am and this is all that I am. I don't have stripes, and they don't magically change in public. I don't become this super trade-acting motherfucker, trying to please the public and trying to convince the world that I don't like dick up my ass. I'm sorry; I have never been that way and never will be that way."

J interrupted him for the last time. "Can we talk about this at home?" Z just looked at him, and thought to say, "Home? Motherfucker, you ain't got no home." Instead he said, "Sure."

Lake, Nikko, JJ and Z arrived at Run 'N' Shoot at the same time. Lake and JJ immediately got on the basketball court, while Nikko was left with Z. Z wore some short shorts and a cut off tank top. He entered the weight room all wide eyed and bushy-tailed as if to say, "I'm here," but his bubble was burst when he saw there was no one in the weight room; at least no one to whom he was attracted. Nikko felt exuberant, as if a weight had been lifted off his shoulders. He was very energetic and he seemed to be glowing. Z noticed Nikko's new attitude but didn't want to inquire; not yet, anyway. Nikko started Z off at the bench press machine. "Z," Nikko instructed, "put the twenty-five pound weight on that side of the bar." Z could barely lift it.

"Damn, Nikko how much this girl weighs?" Nikko started to blush.

"Man, its only twenty-five pounds," Nikko laughed. "Okay. Get up under the bar and I will spot you on the weight. I want you to lift the bar off your chest and lower it without letting it touch your chest." Z bounced onto the bench, evened his hands with the bar and struggled to lift the bar. He grunted, and blew but could not lift the bar. "Damn!" he yelled. "This machine is broken." Nikko turned his head so Z wouldn't see him laughing. "Maybe it is; let's try to lessen the weight. I will demonstrate how to use it. Look at my form and then you can try it. Z! Z!" Nikko yelled, trying to get Z's attention. Z was busy looking in the mirror, playing with his hair and tank top. He yelled back, "I gotcha, sweetie. I got it." Z started chewing and popping his chewing gum as he got back on the bench and tried to lift the twenty pound bar. He lifted the weight with no problems; he finished about twenty reps, and then summoned Nikko; it was time to go. He whispered to Nikko, "I bet you thought I couldn't lift it, huh?" Nikko just smiled and said, "Let's go watch our men play ball." Z couldn't wait to watch JJ play. Lake was playing power forward and J was playing shooting guard. They had a pretty good game going when one of the players on the other team accidentally elbowed JJ in the chin; JJ hit the court hard, busting his lip. Without hesitation, Z ran on the court and punched the guy in the eye. It was a melee; the owner had to come and stop the game, ordering Z off the premises. It was a complete fiasco. Totally embarrassed and ashamed, no one said anything as the four of them shamefully walked out of the gym. Z never apologized; he was pissed off because he'd left his knife in the car. Z told Nikko and Lake he would call them later; he had to get ready for work.

Tré, Junior and Keisha were running late. Tré decided to fly Keisha and Junior up to New York to the birthday party, only to spite Lincoln; he knew it would piss Lincoln off and this was his way of getting back. They had spoken the night before and he promised he would come to the party and they would spend some time together. Lincoln had met Keisha before; he'd made a nasty comment to Tré, insinuating that they could both have sex with her just like they had with that whore from the strip club. Tré was outraged but didn't let Lincoln see it. He knew he was going to pay him back for that remark. Tré was in Keisha's living room, begging her to hurry up when his phone rang. "Hello?" he answered. It was his father. "Good morning, son. You still coming up here today?" he asked. "It will definitely be tomorrow, Dad. I'm bringing, junior and Keisha with me. Junior wanted to see you and mom; by the way, how is she?" Tré asked. She's doing much better. She's not out the woods yet, but it looks very promising. Tré was happy to hear that. Well, Pop, can't wait to see you and mom, and I'll call you once I get up there." Tré was so busy rushing Keisha to come out of the bedroom that he accidentally left his cell phone on the coffee table. They made it to the airport in the nick of time. They were flying stand-by but he wanted to make sure they got to New York on time. After arriving in the city, he noticed that he'd left his phone. He called back to Atlanta to ask Keisha's next door neighbor to lock it up, but there was no answer. One of Tré's friends had booked them in the Marriott at a complimentary rate, so they had the entire day to spend shopping and touring. Junior had never been to the Empire State Building or Rockefeller Center; they took a ferry across the Hudson, visiting the garment district, the zoo and finally went to Ground Zero where the city of New York was busy reconstructing the entire (WTC-World Trade Center Site)financial district. Keisha noticed that it was already six o'clock; the limo would be ready to pick them up at eight. Tré didn't even think about calling Lincoln to let him know he had gotten to New York or whether he was still coming; he wanted him to suffer a little and thought, "Boy, how is he gonna feel when I come with Keisha and Junior?" They got back to the hotel room at 6:45 and there were five messages on the hotel room voice mail. It was Lincoln asking where he was and giving details about the party. "The surprise party will start approximately at nine; it will take the limo forty-five minutes to get to upstate New York, so I will probably be there no later than 10 p.m. The servants will accommodate you in any capacity and there will be a lot of celebrities and athletes there as well, but they're mostly normal folk, ghetto and country."

Malia had slept for only three hours after the lengthy conversation she and Drayton had endured for four hours straight. Her decision to proceed with an immediate separation was very unsettling for him. It was bittersweet, but she had to do what she had to do. Drayton cried and begged Malia not to leave him and told her he would truly kill himself if she did. Malia tried her best to console him from a distance. She refused to give in to her carnal desires. She convinced him of the love she had for him and the responsibilities he had as a father. Malia dare not tell him of her pregnancy; it would definitely put a damper on her decision. Instead she went on to tell him about her aunt who dated a married man for over thirty years. "They spent every waking moment together; Christmas, Thanksgiving, and even birthdays, but when he suddenly became ill and died three months later, she had nothing; she couldn't even attend the funeral. She couldn't even say her last goodbyes." Malia expressed her feelings to Drayton, and she refused to be that distraught over someone else's husband. "My aunt was so devastated; she lived and breathed that man and he just up and died on her." She had to leave her home for months; she couldn't bear to stay home by herself. I could never fathom the thought of how he maneuvered or how you maneuver Drayton; every time I need you, you're here, but your family needs you more. Go to your wife, Drayton, and your children, you have a good family, please make it work, please don't put your children thought unnecessary grief and cause them to hate you," Malia begged. Drayton refused to understand her viewpoints, so he just slammed the door. Malia did not run behind him and beg him to stay; instead she headed to the office. Malia had become so enthralled with Nikki's life insurance policy that she continued to research the possibility of suing the alarm company on that night of Nikki's death. During her struggle she had pressed the panic button that horrible night. Investigators found her blood all over it, but it didn't signal the center or the police. "I want justice served," she mumbled. As the treadmill hit the two hour mark, Malia was drenched in sweat. She decided to look at the contract for the security system while still strolling on the treadmill. "I wonder if I can get them to pay $10 million for wrongful death. She decided to bury herself in the research of suing everyone who'd contributed to Nikki's death. Malia became so involved in her thoughts that she accidentally fell off the treadmill onto her stomach. Malia, not realizing that she could have harmed her unborn child, decided to lie on the burgundy leather couch to take a long and much needed nap.

The house was quiet and scented with the smell of crème vanilla candles. Lake and Nikko finally finished grocery shopping, mowing the lawn, dusting, mopping, cleaning windows and cutting the hedges. They'd covered the pool, taken the dogs to the vet, washed, folded and put away the laundry. They were exhausted by five o'clock and were trying to decide what to eat for dinner. As they lay across the bed, Nikko suddenly started to open up his heart to Lake. "Baby, I have a confession. I feel no more pain; the knife is no longer in my heart and my back. I want to live, Lake. I talked to Nikki when I went to the mountains last week and she spoke to me. I needed solitude and the mountains were my sanctuary. One night, it was about four o'clock in the morning, the cabin window in the bedroom flew open; it startled me at first, because I thought the killer had broken out of jail and was coming to kill us; it was crazy and scary. After I calmed down, a white feather flew in the window; it actually floated for about a minute, I swear. I felt Nikki's presence; I thought I even saw her in the corner of the cabin. I lay back as the feather landed on my bed. I feel fast asleep and started to dream of wonderful memories Nikki and I shared; when we were small, when we graduated college. Those were happy times. I dreamed of the time she first got her first million dollar contract. As I sleep, Lake, I felt her touch my face; it felt so real. That next morning, something was lifted; all the pain, the anguish, the emotions I endured was gone. I knew everything would be alright; first it was my brother, then my parents and now my twin sister." The goose bumps came and the tears stared to roll, "I'm not crying; these are happy tears, tears of joy." Lake and Nikko smiled, hugged and endured a long and succulent French kiss.

Keisha, Tré and Lil man were tired from the wondrous and fun filled surprise party. Overall, the party was a complete success; Lincoln introduced Tré and Keisha to everyone at the party. Tré finally met Catherine, Lincoln's daughter, and Annemarie, Lincoln's wife of ten years. They met so many exciting and unusual people; celebrities, athletes, entertainers, and a host of media and sports affiliated guests. This was the second time in a couple of months Tré was outdone; unfortunately, the first was at Nikki's funeral. At the party, Tré had the urge to call his father to inform him that he would not be able to make it to the hospital to see his mom; he had an emergency flight to California. Tré knew he needed the money and it was an easy flight. He decided to fly back to Atlanta and come back during the middle of the week. He figured nothing would happen before then. They were so tired they could barely drag themselves to the hotel; surprisingly, they made it upstairs to the room. It was four in the morning when they finally got to the hotel, and they slept in their clothes; none of them had enough strength to change to their bed clothes. At six a.m., Tré was nudging Keisha and telling her to follow him to the living room; she hesitated as she eased out of bed, leaving Junior in the bed snoring. They ended up on the balcony on the thirty-sixth floor. The sun was coming as the city was still dark with fog. Tré slowly pulled down his pants and pulled up Keisha's dress. He slowly eased his dick inside her from behind. They both needed each other at that moment for different reasons. Keisha needed some release of the pleasurable kind; she needed to be felt and desired by Tré. Their lovemaking was rare because of the inconsistent schedule that Tré created. Tré needed some pussy, some familiar pussy that would be his and would always be. Once the pains of having Tré enter her passed, the pleasure began. They started their usual sexual escapades. They started on the balcony, then the wall of the living room, then on the sink of the suite; they ended up on the couch where they both reached their climax. Their energy was catapulting from a level of high ecstasy to a level of complete exhaustion.

The alarm went off at 10 o'clock that Sunday morning. Junior was so tired; he just wanted to sleep in the big California king size bed with his mother and father. Keisha begged him to get up, but he refused to get up. He snuggled under his father's arm. "Mommy, do we have to go? I want to stay here with you and Daddy," Junior complained. "Stop talking back to your mother. We gotta get out of here and head back home, little man." Tré ordered. "We'll come back next weekend to see grandma, okay man?"

"Okay, Daddy." Junior jumped out of bed and followed his mother to the bathroom. Just as Tré was about to get up, the hotel phone rang. "Hello," Tré grunted.

"What up, nigga? This is Brey. Just checking to see if everything is alright," Lincoln asked.

"Yeah, man, fo' sho'. It was real cool; we had a great time, but we gotta head back to the south, yo."

Lincoln asked, "So am I gonna see you tonight? I'm really missing the fuck out of you, G."

Tré responded, "Yeah, man. That'll work. I was trying to go see my mom but I come back either Wednesday or next weekend. Mom is still not doing well." Lincoln asked if there was anything he could do. Tré completely ignored his request. "So, B, what time you heading down?" Tré asked.

"I don't know, man. I need to take a stand by flight 'cause I got some shit to take care of before I head back to the ATL."

"Cool, man. Just call me once you get there." Tré lay back on the bed and started thinking about how it would be nice to hook up with Lincoln on a regular tip. He even contemplated how he would finally tell Keisha about his attraction to men. "Nah, I ain't ready to accept that shit myself; I ain't no faggot," Tré whispered to himself. He really wanted to visit his mom, but he still had a lot of emotional resentment against her, she was a bitch, always nagging him about not being successful, about being on drugs in college, dropping out of college, getting Keisha pregnant, not marrying her and just being a fucking thug. She hated him and he resented her; at times he had hoped she would die. He hoped that his father would remarry and both their lives would be easier. Keisha yelled, "You'd better stop daydreaming, man, and come on and get dressed. We're going to miss our flight."

CHAPTER 29

Death Rings Again

Z was at work on a lazy Sunday afternoon reading Elle, when his cousin called to inform him that his aunt had died and they needed to tell Tré. Tré's sister, Cynthia, was out of jail and was staying at a hotel with her new boyfriend whom she had just met. She was too embarrassed to call Tré and knew that Z would cuss her out for not going back to New York immediately to check on her mother. She was crying and begging for forgiveness. Z tried to console her as best he could; he told her he would be right over and for her to pack her shit because he was going to drive her back to New York. He immediately called his mom and she was also heartbroken over the bad news. There were family, friends and also one of the deacons there with his trusty bible, reading scriptures of encouragement. He told his mom to hang in there and he would come to South Carolina to pick her up since he was driving up north. Afterwards, he tried calling Tré but his cell was going straight to voice mail. He left a message and begged him to call immediately. Z called JJ, Lake and Malia, to tell them what had happened; he really didn't want to tell Nikko in the event it may trigger some old emotions. Tré could not be found; he really didn't know what time he was coming back from NY, but he thought that Tré should have been there in NY, due to the fact he was supposed to go see his mother. Z informed his superior of what had happened, and then flew out the door. He rushed to go pick up Cynthia. She was devastated, crying, hollering, and screaming to the stop of her lungs; she was completely hysterical. She was begging God to let her die and be with her mother and telling Z how sorry she was. He immediately took her to his house to get her together; she was a nervous wreck. JJ was already at the house when Z arrived. He asked, "Baby, is there anything I can do?" Z responded, "No thanks. I'm going to New York. I don't know when the funeral will be, but I'm going to pick up my mom and brother and head there in the morning. He was thinking that if she died today then the funeral would probably be Wednesday or Thursday; that would give him enough time to pick up his mother from Columbia and drive to New York. "I should get there by tomorrow night."

JJ repeated, "Well, baby, if there's anything I can do, let me know." Z completely ignored him. "I need to find Tré. He's not picking up his cell phone or home number, fucking bastard," Z thought out loud. Cyn, you need to go upstairs, take a long hot bath and try to get some sleep. We have a long day ahead of us and I really need to find your sorry ass brother. Maybe he can at least get you a buddy pass to fly back; then we won't be so uncomfortable driving. Cynthia nodded and slowly walked upstairs. Z rushed to call every number he knew that pertained to his cousin: his job, his boys he hung out with, and then he remembered he had Lincoln's number, so he decided to call him. Lincoln answered on the first ring, "Hello?" he asked.

"Hello, Lincoln this is Zarius, Tré's cousin. Have you seen or talked to Tré?" Z asked. "Nah, man, not lately. He said they were late for their flight and he would be back in Atlanta no later than seven."

"Well, there's been a death in our family and I need to get in contact with him," Z said. "I'm sorry to hear that. Is it his mother?" Lincoln asked. Z purposely ignored him.

"Well, if you see him, he needs to call me; and could you please not tell him anything other than to call his cousin? Any additional information will alarm him," Z, pleaded. "Will do, man. Hey, I just got back to Atlanta; I flew in with my team to try to surprise him. I'm staying at the JW suite number 2405. I know he said he wanted to swing by once he got in, so if you want you could meet him here."

"Okay, I may do that; and thanks again, Lincoln." Z was puzzled. Z asked JJ if he would stay with Cyn, until he got back; he needed to go look for his cousin. JJ agreed. Z first went to Keisha's apartment where there was no answer. Her bad ass brothers were at the neighbor's apartment, but Z didn't know which neighbor. He was about to leave when he heard someone say, "Faggot, what the fuck you doing around here?" Z immediately turned around and started to perch; he could feel the hair on his back starting to stand up. It was Keisha's oldest brother, Damian. He was eighteen now and looking finer then ever. Z yelled, "Motherfucker, who the fuck you think you talking to like that? I'll lay you cross my lap and suck your..." Z trailed off. "Has your sister come back from New York? There's been an accident, and now I'm worried about Keisha and Tré, he asked.

"Nah, man, they haven't come back yet. They should have been back hours ago. Tré left his cell here, but now it's dead. I didn't have a charger to charge the bitch back up." Z asked, "You got the cell phone? I can charge it up and hopefully he will call it." Damian threw the phone to Z from his back pocket, trying to hit Z in the face. Z caught it with one hand. "Thanks faggot," Z yelled. Damian ran up to Z and whispered in his ear. "Yo, punk-ass bitch, when you gonna suck my dick?" Damian asked. Z put his hands down Damian's baggy jeans and grabbed his dick and whispered in Damian's ear, "Listen here, little boy, and I do mean little, I ain't got time for no games. I got a crisis I got to deal with and you got some growing to do. Now when you grow five more inches, maybe I will suck your dick until your eyes roll back, your toes curl and the Black disappears from behind your fucking ears. Holler back at me. I'm out." Z got in the car and started the engine. Damian just looked in amazement. Z immediately put the cell phone on the car charger and then called Malia; she was still in bed.

"Hey, girl. Have you seen or heard from my cousin?" Z asked. Malia seemed out of it.

"No, Z. I thought he was still..." Malia lost her train of thought. Z asked, Malia what was wrong. "Nothing," she said, "I was just dreaming and the phone startled me." Are you alright? You don't sound right," Z said.

"I'm okay, just tired." She purposely did not tell Z of her accident, knowing he had so much on his mind already. "I will call you if I hear from Tré. I broke it off with Drayton yesterday and its taking a toll on me. I will give you a call later," Malia said, and hung up the phone. Z said to himself, "Something ain't right with that girl. I will call her back later or maybe I will drop by if I have time." Z detoured to the JW. When he arrived, Z went straight up to Lincoln's room, and, without even knocking, he turned the door knob. Lucky for Lincoln, it was locked, so he decided to knock loudly. It was about three minutes later when Lincoln finally opened the door. Z was convinced that he and Tré were having sex. Z just walked right in. Lincoln said, "Well just come in, Z."

"Well don't mind if I do," Z said, already headed toward the bedroom. "I came to talk to my cousin."

"Well, he ain't here. I thought he would have called by now, but he hasn't." Z didn't even notice that Lincoln was completely naked. Lincoln, clearing his throat, said, "Z, Tré is not here, man. Can I get you anything? Z wasn't sure about Lincoln's clothing and refused to turn around; he was starting to blush with embarrassment. Still facing the bedroom, he said, "Lincoln, please tell me you have on a flesh-tone body suit." Lincoln just stood there, still waiting for Z to turn around and see his dick stiff as a board. Z, totally embarrassed, decided to turn around and face the music. Closing his eyes as he spoke, he said, "Lincoln, I'm very sorry. I was so focused on finding my cousin, I didn't notice you were naked, but damn, I don't know how I missed that," apologized Z, opening his eyes and looking down at Lincoln's dick as he spoke. The phone suddenly rang, breaking up the tension that was quickly developing in the room. The thickness of sex was growing every second. Lincoln answered the phone on the second ring and Z dropped to his knees as he began to salivate over Lincoln's pulsating dick. Z could not help himself; he was in a sudden daydream as he began to swallow the huge vessel. He swallowed the dick in a single gulp. Lincoln was amazed and embarrassed. Lincoln could barely confirm the room service attendant's request. "Yes, I ordered lobster and salmon, with mashed potatoes, no gravy, string beans, roll, butter and a pitcher of tea." Lincoln sunk deeper in the chaise lounge in the living room and his eyes started to roll backward as Z sucked, kissed, massaged and licked his dick.

Tré rushed to the hotel door in hopes that he would beat Lincoln to the room; he had some good news about his wanting to commit to Lincoln; he'd finally admitted that he was really feeling him and wanted to take it further. As Tré picked up the house phone, he hoped that Lincoln did not make it to the hotel first. He tried calling the room and the phone went straight to voice mail. "I'll be damned," Tré thought. He noticed one of the Z's gay friends working at the desk. "How you doing, Tré," Keith asked effeminately. "What up, man?" Tré boyishly replied.

"Your cousin, Ms. Z, was looking for you. I think he went upstairs to meet your other cousin."

"What cousin?" Tré was getting touchy.

"You know the famous baseball player. I asked him one time if you were cousins after I saw you all together with that dancer and he said you guys were. You know his entire team is here. I'm waiting around until it gets late and maybe I can get lucky with one of them."

"Man, you're crazy," Tré said as he abruptly cut him off. "Yo, Keith, I lost my key to room 2405. Do you think I could get another?" Tré asked. As Keith was making a duplicate key, he asked Tré, "I know you're not gay, Tré, but, man, your cousin is so fine. Do you know if he gets down or not? He's always staring at me." Tré abruptly interrupted him.

"Nah man. My cousin is married, happily married," he said as he snatched the key from Keith. "That's Lincoln, but I can always put a good word in for Z," Tré said as he started to laugh. "Child, please. What can two girls do together besides rub pocket books together?" Keith snickered as he answered the phone. "Good evening, JW Marriot. Keith speaking at the front desk; how may I assist your call?" Tré disappeared through the opening doors of the elevator. He was wondering why Z would be in the hotel looking for him and he didn't understand why Z didn't answer his cell phone when he called. As the elevator doors opened to the twenty-fourth floor, he thought, "I'm gonna kick his ass." The room service attendant was about to knock on Lincoln's door when Tré stopped him. Tré yelled, "Hey, man, I'll take that. Thanks for bringing it up." He gave the attendant a five dollar bill. Tré slowly opened the door in hopes of surprising the daylights out of Lincoln. The hotel suite was dark and there was noise from the TV blasting from the bedroom and the only light was from the television. Tré continued to creep in the bedroom. To his astonishment, Z was deep throating Lincoln's dick like his life depended on it, not noticing Trés presence. Tré stood there for a minute in shame and disgust. He had visions of him cutting Z's throat and slashing Lincoln's dick. He switched on the lights and pulled Z by the back of the neck from Lincoln's dick. Before either realized what had happened, Tré punched Z in the left eye, and blood started pouring everywhere. A shocked Lincoln jumped up, his log still swollen from the previous encounter. He didn't know what to do; he just stared at Tré in humiliation. Tré was petrified; he just stared at Lincoln and tried to rush out of the hotel room. Lincoln caught him in the hallway, still completely naked. Z had grabbed a towel as blood continued to gush from his eyebrow. Lincoln and Tré started fighting in the hallway. Lincoln was begging him not to leave, to stay and talk about it. The veins in Trés temple were pulsating harder and harder, his nostrils were flaring and he had started to cry. "Fuck you, you motherfucking bastard! Get off me you sick ass nigger! I hate your punk-ass!" He broke away from Lincoln's grasp as he made it to the elevator. The other guests, including some of the baseball players, ran out into the hallway to see what all the commotion was about. They were staring at Lincoln's nakedness, Z's bleeding eye and Tré face; he was crushed and speechless. Z made it to the elevator with Tré. "Tré, please don't leave," Z pleaded as he began to cry. "Your mother passed away today; I was coming to tell you." Tré screamed, "Fuck you, fuck that punk-ass nigger and fuck my momma!" as he pushed Z out of the elevator back into the hallway. "Sick-ass bitch," Tré repeated. When he got off the elevator, he got in his car and rushed to Keisha's house.

CHAPTER 30

The Truth

It was 3 o'clock in the morning when Lake hesitantly answered the phone. "Hello?" he sluggishly asked, "Detective Lake, this is Lieutenant Andrews; I just wanted to be the first to inform you that, Jamal Wright, Nikki's assailant, committed suicide this morning shortly after one o'clock this morning. I don't know whether this will be devastating to you and Mr. Grey, but I felt you should know." Lake became immediately agitated, "How did he commit suicide? I thought he was on suicide watch."

"It happened during a shift change. Unfortunately, a melee broke out in the C pod. Mr. Wright grabbed one of the officer's guns and shot himself. We found a handwritten letter stating that he was going to kill himself sooner or later." Lake was now standing in the bathroom with the light off, trying not to disturb Nikko.

"I need a copy of the report and a copy of the suicide letter on my desk, Lt. Andrews. Is that possible? I'm on my way in," Lake whispered. Nikko was standing at the bedroom door when Lake entered the bedroom.

"Lake! What was that phone call about?" Nikko asked.

"It was Lieutenant Andrews informing me I need to get down to the precinct."

"Is it pertaining to Nikki's murderer?" Nikko asked.

"I'm afraid so, baby," Lake started to apologize.

"Well, I think you need to hurry up, Lake. Do you need me to fix some breakfast for you, since I'm already up?" Lake looked at Nikko, puzzled and also amazed, as if he was relieved of the circumstances that were forthcoming.

"No baby. That won't be necessary. I'll grab some donuts and coffee from Krispy Kreme."

"Okay, well, let me know. Since I'm up I guess I'll do some paper work. I need to put the finishing touches on the revised campaign for Nikki's Revlon ad. I don't know if I told you this, boo, but I really didn't want to go to court. I didn't want to have this trial dragged out for the media to turn it into a circus. I didn't want to rehash that horrible night and I definitely didn't want to have you and Kennedy go through bullshit on top of bullshit. I just hope the media will be kind and have mercy on our lives. I have asked God for forgiveness and strength and he has granted me both." Lake grabbed Nikko and kissed him on the forehead. "Baby, if there is anything that happens to you; know that I feel the pain first. I have watched you almost give up on life, but I also knew that you couldn't because you wanted to live for Kennedy and me. I know about the results of the HIV test. As long as you don't get stressed, exercise, eat right and get plenty of love, we'll both live to be a hundred and five," Lake snickered. "Nikko, you're the spirit of my existence and I'm not ready to breathe without you; I'm not ready to live my life without the essence of my soul. Men and women search the world over to find their soul mate and once they find that person, their future is cut short. Together, Nikko, we have created true, unconditional love. We have cultivated, nourished, mentally breast fed, clothed, cuddled and communicated to a powerful being something that no man or being could ever take away. It's so powerful that it sometimes it consumes me. Sometimes, baby, I just cry because I love you so much. I thank God every night for giving me the gift of love. You have planted a seed of love so powerful and deep in my soul that it burns continuously and eternally. It's not a flicker or a flame, it's like a barn fire, and it's so uncontrollable, it could never be contained. Nikko, I just want to say I love you with every part of my being and as long as blood flows through my body, so does the love I have for you. Nikko, you're the piece of the puzzle that completes me." A knock on the door from Kennedy broke the emotional trance.

"Unkie Nikko, I can't sleep. I'm getting nervous about the play."

"Come here, little girl," Lake murmured. "Let's go downstairs and I'll make you some warm milk; it will help put those butterflies to sleep." Nikko smiled as he watched Lake carry Kennedy downstairs. It was a little after three and he knew he was up for the remainder of the morning. Nikko decided to put the finishing touches on Kennedy's costume. He was about to turn on the PC when the phone rang again. "Good morning!" shouted Nikko.

"Nikko, this is Tré. I need to talk to you. Man, there's some shit that went down, and you're the only person I can talk to."

"What's wrong, Tré?" Nikko asked.

"Can I come over? I've been driving around for hours, and you sound like you're up," Tré asked.

"Yeah, I'm up. We're all up," Nikko said.

"I'll be over in a few, man."

"Who was that?" Lake was yelling from downstairs.

"It's Tré. He's on his way over." Nikko decided to go downstairs since he wouldn't be getting anymore sleep tonight. Lake was making breakfast: turkey bacon, grits, scrambled egg whites, and wheat toast. Kennedy was trying to make it through little sips of the warm milk. She began nodding off at the breakfast table. Lake decided to carry her upstairs while Nikko opened the front door for Tré. Tré was a mess; it was evident that he had been drinking, crying and a little drunk. Nikko invited him in and immediately asked him if he wanted some coffee. Tré agreed without hesitation. "Nikko, I don't understand why motherfuckers are fucked up; once you let your fucking walls down, the bitches just fuck up. I'm tired of this bullshit. DL faggots are the worst; they get married to cover their fucking craving for dick. Trifling' ass punks don't know if they want a man or a woman. I'm tired," Tré groaned. "Man, I don't understand; am I being punished by God because I'm attracted to men; is this my curse? Is God punishing me because I left Keisha at the altar or because I'm not being a good father to Junior?" Tré began to weep... "Nikko, I caught my faggot-ass cousin sucking Lincoln's dick in the hotel room. I couldn't believe my eyes; I couldn't breathe; I felt faint. My punk-ass cousin was on his knees, deep throating Lincoln's dick like a newborn baby sucking on a pacifier. Nikko, I fell for the bastard; I have never fallen for a motherfucker that fast before. I got a confession." Nikko refused to respond; he just wanted to listen. "Nikko, I have always been in love with you. I was too afraid to admit or confess it. I really didn't understand it; I only realized it once I met Lake and I knew I had lost any chances of us having a future together. Now I have no one to love me but my God and my son."

Lake entered the kitchen, having overheard the entire conversation but completely ignoring it. "Tré, are you okay man?" Lake asked.

"Lake, man, I know you know a real nigga like me, a real soldier don't suppose to go through bullshit from nobody, but man I hurt. I hurt bad," Tré replied. The tears started to roll down Trés face as Nikko grabbed his hand and told him everything would be all right. "God will prevail; the pain is there, but it will lessen."

Lake interrupted, "Man, sometimes God puts people in our life for the good, the bad and the indifferent. The good is to teach us a lesson, the bad is to learn a lesson, and the indifferent is to be a lesson. What you have to determine is which Lincoln is and which is Z. Zarius is a good-hearted person; a little twisted, but genuine in heart. Please don't let a piece of meat come between you and your cousin.

"Baby, I gotta go; I'm going to be late for work. Tré, continue to pray and everything will be all right. Call me if you need someone to talk to," Lake said as he kissed Nikko on the forehead. "I'll call you once I get to work. Precious is supposed to be upstairs getting ready for school, but I think she went back to sleep." Lake slowly closed the door behind him and he exited through the garage door. Tré looked into space; he was worried that Lake may have heard the conversation. He decided to break the silence by asking Nikko how he and Lake sustained a meaningful relationship. Nikko gave a sigh of relief and began, "During the weeks you were gone for training, he spent a couple of nights with me, talking about his car and how he wished he could talk to me more about modeling and photography. I started taking photos of him. He didn't want to be a model, but he wanted to be a stunt man; someone who could make a lot of money without the hoopla behind it. I submitted his comp card to a couple of agencies I did business with and they loved him. Lake modeled for me and for some agencies and made a lot of money. The more he modeled, the more we saw each other. He never really told me about his sexual orientation and I didn't ask. I knew that he would go on dates with females, but every night he would crawl into his bed alone. I remember one night, when he was dating Victoria, they had a nasty fight; he never told me what the fight was about but he wanted to talk about it. I asked him to come over, but he wanted me to come to his place; he said he would cook breakfast, scrambled egg whites, wheat toast, turkey bacon and grapefruit. That persuaded me to head over. It was three o'clock in the morning and I was tired as hell. It was a Friday night and I really had nothing to do the following morning. I couldn't understand why he wanted me to come over; he had a lot of boys he hung with. I figured he must have been very upset. He knew about my sexuality but we never really talked about it. When I got there, he had candles lit and a Maxwell CD playing. He was wearing boxers when he answered the door. His mood was subtle and sexy as hell. He'd prepared the table, but he wanted to know if I wanted to eat in the bedroom instead; he was watching some music videos and didn't want to miss any of them. As we began to eat, Lake started talking about how females were so demanding, how Victoria, in particular, wanted everything her way and he obliged because he didn't like arguing or fighting. He said she was a demanding bitch, and she complained about everything; it was her way or nothing. He shared the fact that he wanted more; he really wanted to know how it felt to be with a man, someone who knows what a man feels, how to really touch a man, physically, sexually and emotionally. He wanted to be touched, kissed, held, caressed, and felt. I almost fell off the bed! My heart skipped a beat and I became feverish. I was nervous, but only for a second. I knew I wanted to be with him as much as he wanted to be with me. I wanted to share the deepest, most emotional and sensual lovemaking, ever. I immediately kissed him; Lake did not hesitate. He rolled over on top of me, undressing me as he licked my neck and my nipples. He continued to lick and caress my navel, pulling off my jeans. He felt so natural, so perfect, and so good. He was devoured in his scent and his touch.

We finally made love and I mean love it was the most sensational moments I shared with anyone. I allowed him to make love to me, it was a gentle rhythm, and I couldn't believe he knew exactly what to do, it was effortless, and we made love until the birds started to chirp. That entire weekend, we explored, we freaked, fucked, and did everything under the sun. We ordered pizza, Chinese food, we cut off the phones, pagers, television, we listened to real music, Minnie Ripperton, Sarah Vaughn, Ella Fitzgerald. Mahaiah Jackson, Billie Holliday, Nina Simone, Marvin Gaye, Donnie Hathaway, Tammie Terrell, Smokey Robinson, and the Van dells. The more they sang the more we reminisced and the more we made love. When Sunday night finally came he didn't want me to leave, he followed me home and we've been together ever since. Lake was offered a modeling job in Europe for more than $100,000 but he decided against it. He didn't even tell me I accidentally found out about it almost a month later, from one of the agents. Our relationship has been based on truth, honesty, open communication and love, very simplistic, but long lasting, other than Nikki, you, Z and Malia, Lake is my best friend. We share a love that no one can define or compare. A perpetual love affair that has truly endured the test of time. Our love for each other is somewhat a pious bond. We have touched each other in a way that is very much indescribable; most people can't understand it including our friends and family. Tré I don't know if you know this or not, but I'm HIV positive. I was diagnosed when I was trying to give blood to my sister."

Tré held his head down in shame; he always talked about faggots carrying the AIDS virus, but never knew it was this close to home. Tré shamefully said, "Nikko, I'm so sorry. I didn't know."

Nikko looked Tré straight in his eyes and said, "I know you didn't, Tré. I know you didn't."

"What can I do? How did you get it?" Tré asked.

"Honestly, I don't know. I have always been faithful and Lake and I always used condoms; I just don't know and I really don't care."

Tré looked at Nikko in disbelief. "Why is it that motherfucking faggots can sleep with every Tom, Dick and Harry and come up clean, but loving people are cursed with this virus? It don't make sense."

"Tré, AIDS is a blind disease that attacks people in lust and confusion, not using protection, sharing needles, is just a sense of irresponsibility or addiction, but I don't hold that against them or anyone they may come in contact with the virus. I have always admired you for being yourself; I know you struggle with your sexual orientation, but sometimes you gotta let it go, regardless of what the stigma is, regardless of what society bestows upon you. You deserve to be happy with whomever."

Tré replied, "I don't want to be labeled as a faggot or punk. I know what comes with that acceptance. Nikko, you're the first man I have ever publicly expressed my feelings for. I thought Lincoln would be the nigga I could kick it with; he was married and got a kid, so I thought it would be easy to hang with the motherfucker."

"Tré, you have to be truthful and honest to yourself; that's the only way you will accept anyone into your life. Being homosexual or bisexual is hard for any man to accept. I accepted my sexual orientation long time ago at the age of ten, and luckily I had a very understanding family and a twin to confide in. I think they sensed my sexuality before I did. We spoke openly about the hardship that I might be confronted with and the pain I would suffer. They gave me a level of strength and power that I used to my advantage. As a teenager, Nikki would bring boys home in hopes that I had this magical power to sense whether they were gay or straight. We used to call it gaydar. I don't think I ever possessed that power, but I know a lot of her boyfriends tried to hit on me. I started trying to deny my homosexuality by dating girls and playing all sports, but the fact remained I was gay. I love looking at beautiful women, the hair, the curves, the smell and the touch, but I never made love to one. I discovered I had a natural gift for sports; I started playing sports in junior high. I was the pitcher on the baseball team, the quarterback on the football team; I played power forward on the basketball team and also ran track. I was all American, but I never was fulfilled. Sports and females never gave me any gratification at any level. One day in particular, I was taking a shower in the school gym after basketball practice, trying to hurry up so I could go see Nikki in her first modeling competition. There were two players who were in the showers acting crazy. We were all fooling around, seeing who had the biggest piece and talking about what popular girls we'd had intercourse with. As they continued to talk, their logs got hard, and without uttering a sound they started jerking off in the shower. My dick got so hard just seeing them stroking their muscles that I had to participate. I orgasm first; I was embarrassed and ashamed. I immediately walked out of the shower. I could hear them still moaning and groaning until they both climaxed with excitement and ultimate satisfaction. I had finally come face to face with my demons; at least I thought I had. In actuality, they weren't demons, just confused emotions that I needed to deal with and cultivate. I prayed to God a lot and asked for forgiveness. He gave me his blessings and I became spiritually grounded with his wisdom and courage. I asked God not to send me to Hell. I realized that churchgoers will crucify you and leave you for dead once they find out you are openly different, whether you're gay, straight, addicted to drugs, adulterous, a fornicator, a murderer, you name it, they hate it. I have only been to one church that accepted your spirit and not your flesh here in Atlanta. I was at an age in my life where I had to accept myself as being gay, but I refused to let it rule my life. Being gay was only ten percent of my life; the rest of my life would be consumed with, love, education, and intelligence, and compassion for my family and work. I knew I had to work harder, to be the best in what I pursued. I had to overcome very difficult emotional roller coasters in my life and I'm waiting for the day when we can all be accepted for our character and not the love we have for the same sex. Look at me, man. I'm just rambling on and on about Lake and me. This conversation should have been about you. Look at the time; I need to get this little girl ready for school. How 'bout your hang out with me," Nikko sighed.

"Thanks, man, but I'd better get some rest and face my problems. I'm glad we had this talk together; we really haven't had a one on one in a while, Nikko, and I truly miss those talks, man." Tré kissed Nikko on the lips as he shrugged to stand on his feet. Tré walked out the front door, never looking back to receive Nikko's reaction.

CHAPTER 31

You Bitch!!

Zarius worked a sixteen hour shift at work he really didn't want to go home feeling the way he did. He eventually rushed home in hopes that he could call Tré once more and ask forgiveness. When Zarius got home, he didn't find JJ in the bed like he expected. He assumed he had gone out, but Z could not imagine where he could have been at seven o'clock in the morning. He knew Cynthia was in the bedroom; he went to wake her, hoping she knew of JJ's whereabouts. He knocked on the guest bedroom door, slightly at first. When there was no answer, he just barged in. There were JJ and Cynthia, entwined in each other's arms, snoring. The room smelled of stale sex; there were condom wrappers on the floor, a used condom on the bed, there were beer and liquor bottles on the dresser and nightstand. Z closed the door gently and went downstairs. He started making breakfast as he called his mom. "Girl, what time you gonna be ready? I think I'm gonna pack up and I should be leaving here in an hour." His mother responded, "So where's Cynthia?"

"Oh, the bitch is upstairs just fucking my man," Z said calmly.

"What you say, boy?" His mother was hoping she hadn't heard him correctly. She asked again.

"Mom, you heard me the first time. I will tell you all about it later. Oh! Got some other shit to tell you, too; me and Tré had a fight, and don't ask me anymore questions. I will tell you all about it once I get there, Mom. Love you. Bye." Zarius hung up in his mom's ear. "God, forgive me for I am about to sin," Z whispered. He called a twenty-four hour locksmith and demanded he have his locks changed. He'd originally wanted the keys to be delivered to Nikko's address, but he decided against that. He called

Lake on his cell phone to see if he could get JJ arrested for a felony; maybe drug charges. He was trying to figure out a fucked up way of getting rid of Jeremy; this was the last fucking straw and payback was his middle name. He suddenly heard footsteps upstairs, running from the guest bedroom to the master bedroom. Zarius didn't utter a sound; he continued to prepare breakfast for the three of them. Cynthia came downstairs first, "Oh, cousin, I didn't here you come in," she yawned.

"Girl I came here and started breakfast; we got a long trip of head of us. How you feel?" Z asked.

"Z, I'm ready to get home. I've been crying all night over the loss of my mom. I don't know what I'm going to do without her."

"I know, Cyn, I know. Is there anything I can get you? You know we didn't have a chance to talk last night; I was too busy looking for your trifling ass brother," Z exaggerated. He started to place the breakfast on the table.

"What's wrong with your eye, Z?" Cynthia yelled; it was still puffy from last night. "The same thing that's about to be wrong with yours for fucking my man. Do you want some turkey bacon, Cyn?"

"What are you talking about, Z?" Z was getting ready to hit Cynthia with the sizzling hot frying pan. The same frying pan he had just finished frying the sausage when the ringing of the phone broke his concentration. Cynthia ducked and ran outside wearing nothing but an oversized T-shirt and shorts. "Hello!" Z screamed.

"This is your mother. Boy, don't you ever hang up on me again. Zarius Kenard Washington, don't make me take you out the same way I brought you in," Z's mother yelled in the phone. Z started apologizing as he ran and locked his front door.

"Momma, I don't want to be rude, but I need to take out the trash. Can I call you right back? It won't take but a minute," Z asked.

"NO!" his mother sounded off. "I can tell you're up to no good. Put Cynthia on the phone," Z's mother demanded.

"Momma, that's the trash I need to take out. That (bitch) is a fucking, stinking (whore)," Z sharply rebutted.

"Put her on the phone now. I don't have time for this bullshit from you, Zarius."

Z went outside and yelled, "Cynthia your aunt wants to talk to you." As Cynthia watched him from across the street, Zarius threw the phone across the street as hard as he could, trying to hit her; luckily, the phone landed in the shrubbery. JJ was watching the whole episode from the upstairs bedroom. Zarius rushed back into the house, picked up his cell phone, and called 911. "What's your emergency?" the operator asked.

"I got some shit in my house and if you don't send someone to come get it, I will stab it to death," Z shouted and hung up the phone. "Get your punk-ass down here and get the fuck out my house, (motherfucking hoe)." Jeremy came downstairs with an oversized duffle bag on his shoulder and, without saying a word, walked out the front door. JJ never looked back; trying to explain would be useless. He knew it seemed as if he and Cynthia had been fucking, so, without hesitation, he left. Zarius would never believe that Cynthia's boyfriend had come to the house. They'd had sex and then started fighting. Jeremy had to defend Cynthia and protect Z's house. He went in her room to comfort her through her mother's loss and the fucked feelings she had for that good for nothing motherfucker. Cynthia walked straight up to Z, who was still holding the knife in his hand. "Z, your mother wants to talk to you," she said.

"Yes?" Z asked.

"Zarius, for God's sake, please don't do this; we are going through so much right now. Please talk to Cynthia to find out what really happened; I need you to understand what she is going through, what we all are going through, what you are going through. Life is too short for ignorance, and I raised you better than that. Baby boy, I need you in my life; you are my center, the reason I breathe. I need you to come get me, baby. I feel so low right now after losing my sister and I need a hug from you and not this childish behavior, so, whatever the situation is, please forgive her and move on. Zarius, I'll be waiting for you. I'll see you in three hours and remember; Momma loves you, baby."

"Yes, Momma," Z replied sympathetically.

CHAPTER 32

Lord Give me Strength

Malia really didn't want to be bothered with the world today; she cut off the phones, television, radio, and computer, lit her candles, turned on her aromatherapy ocean, laid in the bed, and prayed.

Oh, heavenly father I don't know what tomorrow will bring for me, but, whatever it is, I know it will be covered in a blessing. I have sinned and sinned some more, but I'm a sinner who will continue to get up and walk right. I know this child inside of me is not moving, I know I must get up and face my reality, Lord, but right here and now I want to be drowned in the goodness of your love; I want to be suffocated in your spirit. God, Almighty, have mercy on my soul. Give me the strength, serenity and wisdom to continue to walk in your faith, forever more, Amen.

Nikko called his favorite seamstress to put the finishing touches on Kennedy's costume. Nikko tried his best to finish the costume, but he gave up after the seams kept unraveling. Katie was at the house with her husband, Charles. Katie and Nikko were trying to settle the Revlon campaign with the representatives for the commercial. They decided that the commercial would run during the NBA playoffs. It would be unique and hopefully not controversial. They had just wrapped up the conference call when Nikko's cell phone rang; it was Malia.

"Hello, Nikko. I just wanted to tell you I lost the baby."

Nikko was immediately stunned.

"What do you mean you lost the baby?" he shouted. "I didn't even know you were pregnant!"

She candidly responded, "So Z can keep a secret. Yeah, Nikko, I was pregnant, but now I'm not. I'm here in the Atlanta Metro Hospital. I fell the other day when I was getting off my treadmill; I accidentally slipped on the conveyor. I was only three months, but I really didn't want to tell anyone; especially you, because you were going through so much at the time. I felt there was no need. Zarius found out by mistake, as he usually does. I just wanted to let you know I want to see Kennedy, either today or tomorrow, to apologize to her personally for not attending her play. I know she's very excited about it. Nikko, please don't tell anyone, not even Lake or Zarius, when I come out of here. I want it to be a memory, not a conversation," Malia asked.

"I promise," Nikko agreed. "I will get there as soon as I finish up here. Love you, baby girl."

"Love you, too, Nikko."

The phone rang as soon as Nikko put it on the cradle it was Z.

"Girl, have you seen Malia?" asked Z.

Nikko hesitated, thinking this was a trick question.

"No," said Nikko. "I haven't seen Malia. How are you doing, Z?"

"I'm blessed and highly favored," Z replied snidely. "I'm sorry, girl. How are you doing? How's Lake and Kennedy?"

"We all are doing fine," Nikko responded.

"Back to more important things; I was wondering if you've seen Tré. You know we are on the way to New York. I have mom, Cynthia and my brother, Luke. We're in Virginia and should be in the Rotten Apple by night fall. So I asked a question; have you seen my cousin?"

Nikko could not get a word in edgewise.

"Girl, I meant to tell you; I had to put JJ out. Child, I'll tell you the full story later, honey. Can't really talk right now," Z whispered. Nikko heard Zarius' mother ordering him to hand her the phone.

"Hi, baby, this is your aunt Anna. I didn't get a chance to tell you how sorry I was about Nikki's passing, but you know, baby, God don't put no more on us than we can handle. I want you to hang in there and know that God's gonna make it alright. We know we're faced with the same situation; my sister-in-law passed and I don't know how the family is gonna handle it. That woman was like a sister to me, God bless her soul." Z's mother started preaching, and Zarius snatched the phone.

"Momma, please." Z Screams. "Nikko ain't got time for all that. He's got enough troubles. Z continued to explain to his mom as he snatches the phone from his mom's ear and yelling to his brother Luke at the same time. "Stay your ass on your fucking side of the road. You almost hit that truck. Jeeze." Z yells to the top of his lungs. Nikko, I'll call you when I get there.

If you could call my cousin, it would be greatly appreciated. Oh, Nikko, please give the little one my love and explain to her why I can not attend her performance tonight."

Katie knew that something was puzzling Nikko and knew she shouldn't pry, so she told her husband that they needed to go and complete the finishing touches on the Revlon campaign. Kennedy ran downstairs, begging Katie and Charles not to forget her debut performance tonight in the play. They all laughed and promised they would be there with bells on. Nikko couldn't wait for Katie and Charles to leave; he knew he had to rush to the hospital with Kennedy to see Malia, making sure he get back before Lake realized he was gone. He also knew he had to convince Tré to go to New York. Besides Malia, Nikko was the only person Tré would listen to. Nikko decided to call back to the hospital to give Malia the update of what was going on with the broken duo. He explained the situation of Tré catching Zarius and Lincoln in the hotel room and the after effects. The good thing about it was that it was not in the paper and it was not reported to the hotel. Malia was very drowsy and wanted to sleep, but she made herself stay up for Kennedy's arrival. As Nikko continued to convey all the grueling details of the last 72-hours of the Tré and Zarius story, he spoke in code, hoping Kennedy would not pick up on any of the gay lingo or sexual terminology. He had always been very cautious of her learning and picking up any unnecessary words or behaviors from the gay lifestyle. Nikko rarely commended himself and Lake for not being a finger popping, wrist breaking, "child", "girl", "bitch", "Ms. Thing", type of household; they were two manly men who were respected more for their masculinity than their homosexuality. Nikko was starting to hate hospitals and doctors. He was beginning to believe that when people go in, they don't come out alive. Tomorrow would be his first day taking the cocktail medication for the virus; he was anticipating the side effects: vomiting, hair thinning, nausea, diarrhea, fatigue, and loss of appetite, discoloration of the skin or none of the above.

He remembered Z telling him how one of his patients stopped taking the medication; he just wanted to die. He hated the fatigue and the nausea. His viral lode multiplied in the thousands and his T-cell count was only twenty. Later, his wife found a note saying that he couldn't take the pain anymore and wanted to share the remainder of his life with his family. It was very heartbreaking and upsetting, Nikko wondered if he would do the same if he was faced with a life change decision. He immediately changed the subject.

"Baby girl, are you nervous about tonight?" asked Nikko.

Kennedy responded, “No, Unkie just can’t wait for mommy to see me on stage.”

Nikko’s cell phone rang and he jumped.

“Hello?”

It was Lake.

“Where are you guys?” Lake asked.

Nikko hated to lie.

“We have some last minute stuff to do. We’ll see you in a little while,” Nikko shamefully replied.

“What are you wearing to the play? Did you take something out? Should I make dinner reservations before the play, or afterward?”

“Could you take out a pair of black slacks and my blue polo shirt? Let me ask Princess what she wants to eat and when.”

Kennedy immediately replied, “Mickey’s D’s, after the play.”

Nikko laughed.

“We’ll just go to the three dollar cafe.”

Lake interjected, “Let’s get something catered when we get home. We can have it delivered about ten minutes after we get home. I’ll call Benji’s. Love you guys,” Lake grinned. See you in a minute.”

Nikko was now in the parking lot of the hospital. He asked Kennedy to get out and she refused.

“What we are doing here again, Uncle Nikko?” she frowned.

Nikko started to explain.

“Aunt Malia wasn’t feeling good so she had to come to the hospital to feel better.” Kennedy cut him off.

“Is she going to die like mommy?” Kennedy asked.

“No, baby, she just wanted to tell you how sad she is that she won’t be coming to your play,” Nikko tried to explain.

“Unkie, I don’t want to go. Please don’t’ make me,” Kennedy begged.

Nikko didn’t force it. He called Malia from the cell phone and gave Kennedy the phone. “Hello, Auntie Malia. I’m scared; if I come to see you, you may die like my mommy. Do you understand? Could you please get better and I will see you later,” Kennedy asked. Malia was so sedated, she could barely understand Kennedy. Kennedy gave the phone to Nikko.

“Hello, Malia.”

The nurse grabbed the phone from Malia.

“Mr. Grey, Ms. Mayerson is very sick. She had a miscarriage, and the fetus has poisoned her system, breaking her placenta. We had to undergo an immediate blood transfusion to save her life.”

Nikko couldn’t believe his ears.

"We're moving her back to intensive care. Her mother and father are on their way. Mr. Grey, are you still there?" the nurse asked.

Nikko tried hard not to show any feelings. He thanked the nurse for the explicit information and he promised he would come back later this evening. The nurse continued to inform him that visiting hours would be over at nine o'clock sharp. Kennedy stared at Nikko and was reading his reactions.

"Please don't tell me Aunt Malia is gonna die like mommy." Kennedy became agitated. "No, of course not, baby girl. She will be alright and she wanted you to promise that you will do your best."

"I promise," Kennedy replied.

Nikko immediately changed the subject.

"Baby girl, I can't wait to hear your solo. Are you ready?" Nikko sounded confused.

"I'm ready. Do you want me to sing it for you now?" she asked.

Kennedy just started belting out the words to Out Here on My Own. When she finished, Nikko did everything but cry. He couldn't believe the range and control his little girl possessed.

"Where in the hell did you learn to sing like that, little girl?" he asked.

"My voice coach Mommy got for me would come to the house and teach me. She would teach me control and how to train my voice with different breathing techniques," she whispered.

Nikko was amazed and astonished; he couldn't wait to tell Lake how wonderful his little girl sounded. Her voice was so mature, it was remarkable.

Z and his family finally made it to the big city later that night. Most of the family was still there. Uncle Kenny was doing fine; he was a robust man who never really showed any emotion. Z had always admired his uncle and was quite fond of him. His presence was deserving of physical admiration. His voice was deep, rich and very proper. He could have been a great orator; he reminded Z of a dark skinned James Earl Jones. His voice was, at times, powerful like Dr. Martin Luther King. He was trying to stay strong, but as soon as he saw his sister and his daughter, Cynthia, he started to cry. The tears were uncontrollable, whether they were for the loss of his beloved wife, seeing his sister and daughter, or the absence of his son, Tré. Everyone at the upstairs brownstone wanted to ask, but were too afraid.

"Where is Tré?" Kenny asked.

Zarius was the first to blurt out, "Tré is still in Atlanta. He's taking this very hard and he didn't want to ride in the car for that many hours. Uncle

Kenny, I think he's bringing Junior and Keisha with him."

The house became very silent when Uncle began to speak.

"I just wanted all my children here; that's all I asked.

Zarius was trying to make his presence known.

He whispered, "Mom, do you want to go to the hotel and get some rest?"

"No baby, I think I need to stay here with Kenneth; I think he needs me," Anna explained. "Zarius take the luggage and come back as soon as you check in. Take your brother with you."

Luke was busy checking out the unfamiliar females who were at the house and asking if they were related or just friends of the family. Luke was trying to figure out how much pussy he could hit during his short stay in New York; he would start with Cynthia and Stephanie's friends. Unbeknownst to them, he was a smooth talking, good for nothing, out of work, father of five children, (baby momma drama having), in and out of jail, wannabe pimp with a big ass dick. Luke stood 6'3", 195 pounds with a deep caramel complexion. He thought he was God's last gift to women; he was only twenty-four, but he was in and out of jail. His face was aged like (stale) garlic meat; he was still very handsome and sexy, but he looked ten years older. Most people mistook him for Z's father instead of his brother. He and Zarius were like night and day; Zarius loved and hated Luke and Luke hated and loved Zarius; their mom was the only reason they didn't kill each other. They used to argue, fuss and fight day in and day out. They were only two years apart and had different fathers and looked nothing alike, but when times got hard, Zarius was there for his brother, and neither one would let outsiders talk about the other. They loved to hate each other, but knew when to pull together; especially when it came to family. Luke started.

"Damn, yo, I can't believe this shit; all this pussy around at the house. Man, I'm gonna have a field day, bruh."

"Luke, we're here to give our love and support to our family, especially our uncle; he just lost his wife and heaven knows how this will damage Uncle Kenny forever." Z explained. "Man, I know but, it's a shame to deprive all these ripe honeys, especially when they're mourning the loss of a loved one," Luke continued to explain.

Z just shook his head.

"It's no use talking to you, man. You're always thinking and talking about pussy, pussy and more pussy."

Luke was becoming frustrated.

"Well, if you got some pussy you probably would stop thinking that you are pussy!" shouted Luke.

Z stopped his car on the Brooklyn Bridge headed towards Manhattan and slapped the shit out of him. Luke immediately returned a punch right over the Z's left eyebrow; the same eyebrow Tré had cut earlier. It started bleeding again.

"I'll be damned, you (fucking bitch!") shouted Zarius.

The people in the cars behind them began honking their horns and swearing. He slowly turned the key to start the car and told his brother to get out the fucking car. Luke did not move.

"Get your boney, druggy, and good for nothing wannabe thug ass out my fucking car, bitch."

Luke just sat there, not uttering a word.

"Okay, motherfucker, that did it."

Zarius slammed on the gas, going sixty miles an hour on the streets of New York.

Luke finally uttered, "I'm sorry, bruh. Please slow down."

He said this as calmly and sincerely as possible. Luke knew how to push Zarius' buttons, but the older they got; the pushing of buttons occurred less but was more intense. Z eased up off the accelerator, blood still dripping down his face. Luke and Zarius didn't say a word for the rest of the ride to the hotel. Zarius checked in at the desk of the hotel while Luke got all the bags and took them upstairs. Z went to the corner drug store to get some alcohol, Neosporin and some bandages for his eye. Zarius got back to the room to find that Luke had put all the clothes away and was waiting for Z in the living room of the suite. It was a beautiful, but cramped, two bedroom suite. Completely ignoring his brother, Z rushed to the bathroom, locked the door, and started running some bath water. Luke wanted to talk, but Z needed some solitude and peace. He needed to communicate with his spirit, to try and understand his actions and come to some conclusion. Luke begged Z to come out so they could talk, but Zarius refused and instead insisted that Luke go back to Uncle Kenny's house and pick up their mother; he would be there when they returned. When the front door of the suite closed, Z looked in the mirror and asked God what was wrong. After tending to his cut and trying to mend it in a way that it would not cause attention and lighting aromatherapy candles, he finally melted in the bath water that was luke warm, soothing and cathartic. Zarius knew he had to let go whatever demons he was holding in. He had to pray and let God do his work.

God, I'm so tired. I'm so tired of life, my life. I thought I was strong and I knew how to persevere, I'm falling into this life I said I would never endure. I live, sleep, eat and breath this gay world; it has corrupted and paralyzed my thoughts and my will. Heavenly Father, give me the strength and the wisdom and the patience to live and survive.

Z suddenly submerges his head under water leaving his feet pressed against the wall of the tub.

The play started at 7:30 sharp. The auditorium was filled with parents, children and camcorders. The children were so excited to doing an updated version of Romeo and Juliet. If Shakespeare could have heard his words being blurted out by seven and eight year olds, he would surely have rolled over in his grave. Kennedy played Juliet and John St. Michaels, the class clown, played Romeo. The rendition of the play was so enchanting and amusing. Nikko was so busy speaking Kennedy's parts that he forgot all about the rest of the parents and other kids begged him to be quiet. Lake had to pinch him twice to quiet him. When it was time for Juliet to sing her solo, the audience was completely silent; you couldn't even hear a pin drop. Her voice echoed every word with every note of the piano; she had perfect pitch. When she finally finished, there was not a dry eye in the entire school. She received a standing ovation and couldn't help but smirk when it was time for her to sip the poison before she made her dramatic death an everlasting one.

After the play, some of the kids were asking Kennedy for her autograph, but she just laughed and said she was too young for autographs. Instead, she gave almost fifty hugs to everyone who wanted one. Lake couldn't wait for his little celebrity to jump in the backseat and become a little girl again. Nikko was in a daze, just smiling and giggling at everything. It was almost sickening to see the huge grin on his face. They stopped at American Roadhouse, a famous restaurant, where they ate and laughed like three little kids on a playground. After dinner, Kennedy was full and tired and she slept all the way back to the house; this gave Lake and Nikko a little time to talk. Nikko asked Lake if he could put an APB out on Tré; he had been missing for over twenty-four hours.

"I'll make a call," Lake suggested. "I'll send a search party out for his car first, and then when we get home, I'll start the procedures for an all points bulletin." Lake asked, "do you think something happened to Tré? Something like foul play?"

"I'm not sure," responded Nikko. "He was pretty broken up when he came to the house the other morning. I gave him some coffee and told him he should go home and get some sleep before he flew to his mother's funeral. I know he has to be broken up over her death; at least he should be."

Lake interrupted, "well you know Tré. He doesn't like to show his emotions and he's dealing with a lot. He's the type of cat who holds a lot in; that could really be devastating to his mental and spiritual level."

Lake started to smirk.

"What's so funny, babe?"

"I never knew Tré had a crush on you. I overheard him that morning when he came over. It blew my mind," Lake admitted.

Nikko stopped him. "It blew my mind, too. He stayed with me for over a year before he became a flight attendant and when Keisha put him out for the last time, he was pretty messed up emotionally. He really didn't talk much about any personal stuff, and I guess he just kept everything inside. Baby, I'm so glad when I fell in love with you it was only you. It was never a decision or contemplation between you and another man or woman, but some brothers are so confused when it comes to their sexuality. Tré and I talk from time to time and my heart really goes out to the brother. He is really, excuse my French, fucked up in the head," Lake whispered.

Nikko continued, "That's why I pray for him constantly and all my friends."

Lake interrupted, "Baby, I need to tell you something pertaining to Nikki's death. The forensic guys are still checking out all the leads, but they recently discovered that the other intruder was a female, according to the investigations. We don't have any leads though and it's driving everybody at the precinct crazy. The assailant had to be a professional, but it doesn't make any sense. The guy who killed himself was not a professional; he was a maintenance man at the Apparel Mart where Nikki did most of your shows during Fashion Week. When we searched his locker and his home, there were pictures of Nikki everywhere. Every magazine she was in and on, he had a copy of it; some in frames, most plastered on the walls. He even had photos in the bathroom, bathtub, and the refrigerator. It's kind of bizarre; he only had a couch, 13-inch TV, a twin bed, and nothing else. He was indeed a stalker and most stalkers work alone, not with someone who doesn't leave fingerprints."

Lake was trying to explain everything as they drove up into the garage. He opened the door as Nikko got the limp and exhausted Kennedy from the back seat. Lake let Sebastian and Sasha out the back door to go run and use the bathroom. The phone rang as Nikko was helping Kennedy get ready to take her bath. Lake thought Nikko was going to answer the phone and Nikko thought Lake had it. The message went straight to voice mail. When Lake finally came upstairs, Nikko was on the phone.

Nikko said, "Baby, I thought you answered the phone."

They played the message back and heard a female's voice.

In a very calm tone, the woman said, "Good evening, my name is Danielle Green."

The background noise was very loud and Nikko and Lake could barely hear her.

Danielle continued, "I regret to inform you that your friend Tre Williamson has been in a bad accident. Lake and Nikko kept listening to the message over and over again but could not decipher the name. Lake immediately hit *69 and they both realized it was Trés cell phone, but no one picked up. Lake started calling his police friends to put an APB out on Tré. The search was on.

Tré had spent over twenty hours in the titty bar and he was pissy drunk. He spent most of his savings and Junior's child support money on titties and ass, big voluptuous titties and ass; he handed out tens, twenties and fifties until he felt fulfilled. He didn't care about the consequences; he wanted to be a normal man again, someone who loved women. Breasts, long legs, the scent, the pink pussy, he wanted nothing but to devour it again, to remain whole; he wanted the lust for men to be eliminated by the presence of pussy. Pussy was the medicine that would take the taste of men, muscle, dick, and ass out of his life. He thought about his son being a faggot like Zarius and the hardships he would endure. He vowed that if he had any indication that Junior had any gay tendencies, he would beat the shit out of him. He would beat his son until he became strong to resist any temptation of faggots, bisexual, DL brothers, trade and especially married confused, bi-curious motherfuckers. He wanted nothing more than to think about his mother, Lincoln, Zarius and the whole gay fucking group. Tré went downstairs in the boom with a stripper named Passion. He wanted a lap dance and that's what she gave him, along with a blow job and a quick fuck, all for a $500 and right in front of everyone who cared to watch. She rode him until he came, and sucked him until he was bone hard again. Tré was not ashamed putting on a show at his son's expense. He managed to waste $3,000 in a 32 hour period. When he finally woke up, he was lying stinking and penniless behind the strip club with the garbage and rats. Standing over him was Lake and two policemen.

"Come on, buddy," Lake commanded. "You've got a lot of explaining to do, so we need to get you showered and shaved."

Tré was stinking so bad they escorted him in the paddy wagon back to Lake and Nikko's house. They hosed him off in the backyard completely naked, with an old loafer sponge and some joy detergent. When he was sober enough to talk, Lake dug into him; he drilled him like a true policeman.

"What the fuck were you thinking, man? You got a child that needs you, your mother just passed for Christ's sake, and you're wasting your life's savings like its water. Nothing can be that bad that you neglect your future for some fucked up situation that happened between you and a man you don't really know and your cousin."

Tré was completely silent as Lake continued to interrogate him. Reality was sinking back into Tré's life; he realized that what had happened was inexcusable and not acceptable in his realm of goals.

"I fucked up again," Tré kept saying over and over. Nikko and Lake couldn't get a word in edgewise. Tré fell asleep before they could really get information from him and let him know about Zarius or about his mother's funeral.

CHAPTER 33

Death Hurts so Bad

Zarius felt someone grab his neck as they pulled him out of the tub.

"Z, what's the fuck's wrong with you?" Luke screamed.

Z looked mortified.

"What are you talking about, Luke?"

Luke was now crying.

"Why are you trying to do drown yourself? Nothing can be that bad, man."

"Man, what are you talking about? I was practicing my breathing exercises under water. I'm doing this for my lifeguard recertification," Z screamed.

Luke felt stupid but didn't believe Z.

"You're my big brother. I don't want anything to happen to you."

Water dripped off both of them. Z was naked as a jay bird and became ashamed and embarrassed having his brother see his nude body.

"Hand me a towel, fool," Zarius was now laughing. "Me? Commit suicide and let all this good pussy go to waste?"

Now both were laughing.

"Go get mom so we can get some rest before the funeral tomorrow," Zarius commanded. "I'm not going nowhere without you. Dry off; we're going together," Luke ordered.

Z just smirked and asked, "Can a queen get some privacy so she can put on her royal threads?"

They both laughed as Luke exited the bathroom.

Cynthia was the most saddened by her mother passing. She knew she needed to be strong for her father, but became overwhelmed with emotion when they entered the Baptist church. There were so many people in the tiny sanctuary. Cynthia suddenly fainted as she caught a glimpse of the closed mahogany casket. Luke was right beside her as he lifted her back to her feet; he literally carried her to the end of the first pew. Unaware of his little girl's emotional distress, Kenneth was teary eyed as his eldest daughter and sister were trying to keep him strong. Kenneth was disappointed in his only son for not showing up. Keisha some how made it to the funeral with Junior; she was disappointed in Tré for disrespecting his family. Keisha still had to thank Tré for keeping her as his companion to fly free whenever and where ever she wanted. Zarius, Keisha, Junior, Stephanie's husband Jerome and their three kids sat on the second pew. Aunts, uncles, cousins and close friends of the family took up the rest of the reserved seating for the family. The rest of the church was filled with church members, which included coworkers from the school. The choir was in the midst of their first song when they heard a loud siren. It sounded like an ambulance was about to run straight into the church. Tré burst through the doors, crying for his mother's forgiveness. His voice shrieks as he belted out a loud cry begging for his mother to come back, begging his mother to accept his apologies. The entire church was in awe. Junior saw his father and he started to cry, along with Kenneth. Cynthia fainted as Tré tried to open the casket. The funeral director, along with the deacons, tried to stop him. Tré literally tried to pull his mother out of the casket, screaming, "Mommy I'm sorry! I'm so sorry! Please forgive me!"

He fainted over her lifeless shell.

Bishop Farmer tried to bring order back to the church by trying to deliver the eulogy. He started reading the Old and New Testaments. Afterward, he asked the choir to sing Amazing Grace, but Tré's commotion was still unsettling. The little church was now filled with moaning, groaning, cries, hollering, speaking in tongues, running and jumping. Kenneth, Anna, Cynthia, Stephanie, Zarius, and Luke were all in a daze; they wanted to know what the hell happened to the funeral. It was now more like a revival, not a celebration of life; but as the Bishop started preaching, and it was a revival of life and of death. The family felt uneasy when the preacher finally stopped preaching and it was time for the viewing of the body. A distinct scent flooded the church; the spirit of Tré's deceased mother filled the air. Kenneth, the beloved husband for over thirty years, had to say good-bye to his loyal and faithful wife; his knees eventually gave way and he was now being supported by three deacons. It was Cynthia and Stephanie's turn to say good-bye to their mother. They were both special daughters to their mother, and she loved them both equally and always displayed that unconditional love. She sacrificed a lot for their growth and maturity; she smothered them with the blanket of affection and wisdom. Cynthia knew that her life would never be the same again; she knew she was Daddy's little girl, but she and her mother shared a special bond. She knew that, in the wake of her mother's passing, she would have to grow up and be the woman her mother reared her to be. She promised her deceased mother, that she would be focused, determined, and strong-willed. She promised her mother she'd stop opening her legs for every Tom, Dick and Rachel that came by. Cynthia sealed this promise with a kiss to her mother's cold forehead. Sister-in-law Anna approached the mahogany coffin, staring at her sister with her blush pink suit on.

"Girlfriend, I'm gonna truly miss you, just the two of us vacationing in Jamaica, leaving the kids with Kenny, us sneaking down to Atlantic City and blowing our tax returns away. Us shopping for the kids, y'all coming down to South Carolina for vacation and all of us going to Myrtle Beach, Hilton Head and Savannah, Disney World, Six Flags and Miami. Girl, I'm gonna miss them times. I know you right there in Heaven earning your wings. Please promise you'll watch over us, 'cause since you ain't here, we gonna need all the help we can get."

It was Luke, Zarius and the kids' turn to approach the casket.

"Auntie, you look good, girl, in the blush pink suit and your accessories are smashing. I see you remember what I told you about accessories. Child, I'm gonna miss them long talks we used to have bout your grown ass children, how you hated that Cynthia didn't want nothing out of life but a piece of dick, how Stephanie married that no good man, and how Tré don't know which hole to stick. Auntie, rest assured your children will be fine; I promise to make sure of that. Soon we will be together again, laughing, talking, crying and praising God."

Luke just looked, stared and touched his aunt's hands as they lay neatly across her heart. The viewing of the body seemed to last forever; afterwards the entire church was now silent, but still mournful. The ride to the cemetery became a complete blur. Everyone was totally oblivious.

CHAPTER 34

Gays and Sports

Malia would have to spend more weeks out of work. Her recuperation level would be very crucial to her health and sanity. Malia spent most of her time at Lake and Nikko's house. Being with Kennedy helped Malia tremendously. She took advantage of this time to mend her soul. The four of them played UNO, Go Fish, Monopoly and Bingo. It was a time of healing and relaxation. Malia eventually revealed to Lake and Nikko the beginning and the end of her and Drayton's relationship. She conveyed to them how she prayed to God to wash her soul of her sins when it came to dealing with a married man. She even told them about her aunt and how she still suffers from the loss of that married man who'd had her heart for over thirty years. As days went by and she got stronger, she felt it was time for her to leave and fly back to her nest. Nikko didn't want Malia to leave; for a very short time, she filled the void left by his sister with the shopping, the endless talks, the cooking, cleaning, the workouts and the secret craving for pineapple sherbet and freshly baked apple pie. By the time she left they all had gained five to ten pounds around the waist. Kennedy was hopeless after realizing that Malia had decided to leave and return to her place of dwelling.

Malia had never been gone from her house such a long period of time; even though it was still in the same city, it was still a thirty minute distance. She lived right off Roswell Road in Dunwoody; there was a guard on duty twenty four hours. She admired her house and realized how much she'd missed it. It was a mansion, and she got it for a steal; it was in foreclosure and due to her quick mind and the best agent in town, she was able to own a $1 million home for less than $300,000. It had five bedrooms, six bathrooms, a mother-in-law carriage in the back, a small lake in front of the house, three car garage, a wrap around driveway and the most beautiful landscaping she had ever seen. It cost her a small fortune to keep running, but it was her sanctuary. When she moved in she already had over half a million dollars in equity. She credited her brilliant mind to her mother; she had always taught all her children how to save, get and keep good credit, and how to invest. Malia snickered, "I got it from my momma." One time she even let a hip hop mogul use her house in their music video, and it was awesome. It was indeed a relief to be in her sanctuary. Her maid had come in and watered the plants, cut fresh flowers, vacuum, mopped, dusted, and even washed windows. As Malia entered the house, she noticed the entire house smelled of peaches. Ripe-scented candles filled the air, she smiled as she dropped her bags and went to every room to grace them with her presence, talking to her plants and asking them if they missed her. The arrival home filled her spirit instantly. "It's great to be back at home," she thought as she fell onto her California king-sized bed and snuggled in her down comforter. The cell phone rang, interrupting her relaxation.

"Hi, my sweetness," Z whispered. "How's my woman doing?"

Malia chuckled, "I'm fine, my evil little step sister."

Z responded, "Well you know I'm having an NBA playoff party and I wanted to know if you were up for it. I'm having all the sports girls over, all my volley ball playing, basketball playing, football watching, and track and field girls over; about twenty five to thirty sissies."

Malia hesitated.

"Um, I think I'll pass; I want to enjoy my self with myself today. I'm going back to work on Monday so I've got a lot of work to do. I have a feeling that, in my absence, they let the dogs out, and I gotta drive them back in," she replied.

"I understand, baby girl, and you probably don't want to be around, shit talking, sports fanatics, beer guzzling, pizza eating, stats knowing sissies. Hey, I don't blame you. I may let them in and come to your house where a diva like me can be diva in a diva's house. We can sit in the theatre downstairs, eat bon bons and watch the game on your theatre screen. Whatever I decide, I promise I will bring you a plate. Always love you," Z closed.

It was a triple header and the guys were coming over in droves. The Hawks were playing the Hornets at 5:00, the Raptors were playing the Sixers at 5:30 and LA was playing San Antonio at 8:00. Zarius had just finished with the lemon pepper wings, barbeque wings and the Mardi gras wings; he made spinach dip, ordered five pizzas and a keg of beer. He put

TV's in every room; the big screen was in the den, and he even had 13 inch TVs in the bathrooms. The game didn't start till 5, but the early birds got there with beer, liquor and chips in hand. Everyone assembled in the den and kitchen. They inquired about JJ but Z shut them up quickly, slashing at them with a knife one by one. They got the hint and changed the subject to the latest city gossip. Brandon started.

"Girl, have you seen the movie The Closet? It's about us, for us."

Everyone agreed that they hadn't but heard it was off the chain. Juston started asking about the new movies from Denzel, Vin Diesel, Will Smith and Shemar.

"Bitch, I'm gonna have front rows seat to all of them. Oohh, child if I could just lie in bed with just one of the motherfuckers, I would be the best little pussy in town," Z chuckled.

"Bitch I heard you was the best little pussy in town," Brandon said.

The entire kitchen and den burst out with laughter. As Z finished making everyone's drinks, they continued to talk about celebrities, working out, the new clubs, the old clubs, the new sissies, the old fems, baseball, football, war, peace, politics and other current events. There were crazy conversations, serious conversations, emotional ones and hilarious ones. An hour later, Lake and Nikko entered the condo bearing gifts: quiche and turkey lasagna.

"Oh shit! Let the eating begin," yelled Brandon.

Everyone got into their zone when the first game started; they knew the players' stats, history, and income. Lake was even impressed with all the knowledge these cats had. Juston, Brandon, Eric and Rod were tearing it down on the Spades table, talking shit and slamming the cards all over the card table. By the end of the night, the Hawks beat the Hornets, Philly beat the Raptors and the Spurs beat the Lakers, but the conversations continued. Brandon and Lake were discussing gays being professional athletes and how they live in the shadow of the work in order not to be outed by their peers.

Brandon was standing up, yelling, "Why is it that we as gay black proud men can not stand up and be proud of our sexuality and be a professional athlete at the same time? That's fucking ridiculous. I can't believe motherfuckers in LaLa land believe that there are no gay athletes; there are so many out there it's pathetic. I remember that one time that cat got on national television, talking about how he had to hide and get a fake girlfriend so his team mates would not be suspicious of his lifestyle. This punk got on TV and lied. The next morning that's all they talked about; you had retired pro athletes talking about how they would have kicked his ass if they'd known he was gay." Brandon continued, "I played football and basketball for college and got drafted for pro football. I wish some motherfucker would talk about kicking my ass 'cause I like men. Some (niggas) forget when you're on a team; it's a brotherhood and a unit that is formed. I saw the biggest dicks, the smallest dicks, the biggest asses and the ugliest asses on my team mates, but they were like brothers. I didn't hide my sexuality when I played ball; I wish a motherfucker would have stepped to me the wrong way.

There were three brothers in the background of the living room playing cards saying in unison, "You go, girl!"

Lake had to interject. "Well, Brandon, why didn't you pursue your career in football or basketball?"

Brandon immediately responded, "Because my senior year in college, I was told I was infected with HIV, so I followed my heart and utilized my degree in Electrical Engineering. Eleven years later, I don't regret my decision."

A thick silence covered the entire space in Z's condo. Z broke the silence.

"I don't understand what difference it makes if you are gay and play professional sports; women do it all the time. I know women personally who play basketball and soccer professionally and they take showers together, hang out together and the ones I know are openly gay; it's just when it comes to stupid ass insecure men that have fucking hang ups that the ladies have a problem. I remember that interview, and the little punk was crying," Z continued. "This man, showered, shaved and shitted with the (stupid ass niggers) and now that he decides to be open with his lifestyle, they want to get upset like he broke the DNA of man's genetic make up. Now if I was on a team, the men would know, 'because I would pull a bench in the shower and stare at dicks all day. I would drop the soap every minute on the minute and when it was time to pick it up, ((I would doing)) a fucking Chinese split and tell them to come get some good boy pussy."

Z made the whole house laugh in harmony again.

Lake concluded, "I take showers at the precinct and at the gym, and most of my close fellow workers know that I'm gay. They don't seem to have any hang-ups because we all have dicks and asses and we are like brothers, so, really, it's no big deal. They've seen my dick and ass and I've seen theirs."

Brandon, Curtis, Billy and Jonathan all stopped Lake.

"Can I have your job?"

Everyone broke out in laughter. The conversation went on for another hour or two when Z realized it was one o'clock.

"Okay, girls, time to go. You ain't got to go home, but you know the rest."

Lake and Nikko decided to stay and help Z clean up. As they put away the dishes in the washer and the furniture back in their respective places, Z felt the urged to talk openly about JJ and how they had not spoken since that day he asked JJ to leave.

"I miss him. I never realized how much; I miss his snoring, dirty drawers, him leaving the toilet seat up, him not taking out the garbage, but I can't ask him to come back nor do I want him to come back. I refuse to allow his absence get the best of me," Z confessed. Nikko interjected, "I got an idea; how 'bout meeting us in church tomorrow before the playoffs start? Church should be over by one o'clock."

Z hesitated at first, and then agreed.

"Church will do me good after all the shit I've been through in the last month."

CHAPTER 35

Is Church for Sinners or the Self-Righteous?

Z entered the doors of the church and was completely blown away by the sight of all the people; they were gay, straight, old, young, ushers, deacons, and the choir. He was in complete awe. The choir was sensational; singing Smokey Norwood's latest song, the congregation sang, danced and said "amen" after each verse. After a long prayer from one of the deacons and a welcome to the newcomers from a church mother, the preacher entered the stage. The preacher was a slim, very attractive man, with a bald head, goatee, and a voice that could shake the heavens. Z was ready to devour the spiritual food from the preacher and the church, he was feeling so good that he decided to join Lake, Kennedy and Nikko for church and they were excited and thrilled that he did show up. Z even stood up when he heard one of his favorite songs lead by a heavy set dark-skinned lady; she was singing the fuck out of Yolanda Adams' song Miracle. The preacher began by saying his heart was heavy today; he wanted the congregation to open their Bibles to Leviticus. He went on to say that he was so tired of men not being men, and women not being women. As he continued, Z's left eyebrow went up. He was curious to find where this sermon was going.

The preacher repeated, "I'm tired of my members and visitors coming to my church on Sunday when less than twelve hours prior they have been with the same sex, lusting and kissing and God knows what else."

Z's right eyebrow went up, and this time Z sat straight up, listening to every word, as Lake and Nikko stared into space. The entire church was amening as the preacher continued to preach the word. The fire was igniting in Z's heart and eyes; he began clearing his throat every time the preacher went to another passage. This time Nikko and Lake looked down; they felt the church move. Z started coughing so loud that it literally drowned out the preacher and everyone in the row behind him and in front of him was now looking. The usher rushed over to ask him if he needed some water or some fresh air. Z completely ignored her, but instead he stood up and looked directly into the eyes of the preacher. The minister felt the gay demons surrounding him and could not bear to look in Z's direction. He started to stumble over his words and lost his place in the Bible. The Christians in the church were puzzled by the behavior of their beloved preacher. After five minutes of intense staring, the preacher asked Z if there was anything he could deliver him from and Z burst.

"Yes, father you can."

Nikko and Lake closed their eyes; they were both wishing they had stayed in bed this morning.

"Father, I have sinned."

Z was pulling him in.

"I have laid down with another man."

The church was in complete silence.

"You see, my father, this man was a man of the cloth; much like yourself. This man was a married man; much like yourself. This man was tall and attractive; much like you. This man had a church very similar to yours, but this man was a loving man of God; he accepted me and my sexuality as a gift, not a sin. Mr. Minister, may I ask you a question?" Z asked. "Have you ever a homosexual thought?"

The entire church turned their heads to the front of the church in unison. The sweat was now pouring from Nikko's, Lake's and the preacher's foreheads. Z was feeling quite angelic.

"I know I have sinned, father, but so have we all. Does this make me damned to hell? Because I lust for men, am I wrong to come visit the church to have my sins washed away or am I ridiculed for being here? I see your congregation whispering and staring at me, but if I can't come worship in your company for my savior, Jesus Christ, where do you prefer I go? I am still a child of God, am I not? Let the church say Amen," Z shouted loudly.

People in the back rows, and the balcony started standing and applauding. All the sissies stood and gave praise; one sissy started speaking in tongues. He was feeling the Holy Ghost; he started running up and down the aisle while people everywhere were crying and begging for forgiveness. Z sat down for a moment, got his composure, looked around, and stood up again as to say, "My work here is done," and waltzed out of the church. Sinners and saints everywhere were running up to the pulpit to be saved. Lake and Nikko just looked in amazement as the Holy Ghost was truly present today.

Malia lay in bed as she prayed and begged God for guidance and more faith.

There were several times when she wanted to pick up the phone and call Drayton, to call the one person who could make her feel whole again, but she didn't. All of a sudden she jumped to her feet and ran to the bathroom; she needed to be cleansed, to feel refreshed. As she ran the bath water, she got on the phone and called her masseurs, her manicurist and pedicurist, her Neiman Marcus stylist and her personal trainer. She needed to lift some weights; it always relieved her of stress. As she hung up from her trainer, Malia started thinking about how fine he was. He was all man; muscular and masculine from head to toe. His voice, his hands, his fingers, his touch, his back, his abs, his shoulders, his skin, his eyes, his complexion, his height, his legs, his walk, his smell, his tongue, his dick. As she knelt down to feel the warmth of the bath water, she started fantasizing about her trainer being inside of her, giving her much needed pleasure. She day dreamed that he would follow her in the ladies locker room while it was completely empty and lay her on the bench and have his way with her; every stroke would burn off more and more calories, she would be covered in his sweat and her lust. Just as she was about to reach her climax, the door bell rang. Malia fell out of her trance, completely naked in her Jacuzzi tub and realizing she was fantasizing about another married man. The bell rang again along with the house phone. Malia answered the phone on the third ring, standing in her bedroom covered with bubbles from shoulder to toe.

"Hello?" she asked.

"Good afternoon, sugar. This is Sunday Sunshine. Open the door; I'm bearing cheesecake, girl," Z's voice was gleaming as he screamed how he was bearing gifts.

Malia just smiled as this is truly what she needed.

"I'll be right down, boy."

Malia leapt downstairs as Z was on his cell phone running his mouth about how he delivered the sermon today and how he ripped into the preacher. He kissed Malia on both sides of her cheeks as he continued his conversation. He was yelling and screaming about how Lake and Nikko would probably disown him but he had to do what he had to do. As he continued to gossip over the phone, he noticed Malia's lips trembling; she was crying. Z immediately hung up the phone without even saying goodbye. Z's voice changed. "What's wrong baby girl?"

Malia just broke down. Z consoled her, telling her that it would be alright. Z started to cry because his precious sister was in pain and he didn't know why. Malia felt so alone, so empty that she just wanted to sleep become comatose. Malia belted out a scream that shook the entire house; she fell to her knees carrying Z with her. Z was in shock; he had never seen Malia in this state. He didn't know what to do besides hold her. Lake and Nikko were knocking at the door, but neither Malia nor Z could hear it; they both were separated from reality. Nikko finally used the spare key after hearing the screams from within the house. Both he and Lake rushed to Malia's side, helping her and Z from their knees. Lake picked Malia up with one swoop and laid her on the couch and Nikko rushed to the down stairs bathroom to get a hot cloth for her forehead. Z regained his composure and started checking Malia's pulse, trying to determine what type of attack she was having. Malia started to shake uncontrollably. Lake and Z had to restrain her until the trembling stopped.

CHAPTER 36

The Mile High Club

Tré was about to board flight 656 just as his cell phone rang. Tré answered, "Speak." \The voice on the other end said, "Tré, I need to see you, man," Lincoln begged.

"Can I call you back? I'm bout to board my flight," Tré responded before hanging up the phone as he boarded the 747.

As Tré prepared himself for the flights to Chicago, LA, back to Chicago and finally back to Atlanta, he fell into a whirlwind of memories of Lincoln. The sex, the laughter, the jokes, the good times and the bad, he started to smile as the passengers started to board. Tré was relieved that he had to service first class; it was a rarity but he really wanted to stay as busy as possible, not wanting to think about family, friends or loved ones. The plane was filled to capacity when the stand-bys started loading the plane. There was only one seat left in first class and about five in coach class. Tré was busy taking drink orders for his passengers when he felt someone press against him. Trying to avoid the obvious, he completely ignored the passenger until he noticed the passenger resting his body in the first class section. To his amazement, Tré noticed it was Lincoln, who was wearing a smile that could make Mona Lisa blush. Tré started to smirk as he strolled over to Lincoln, trying to stay calm and professional at the same time.

"Sir, would you like a drink?" Tré asked.

Lincoln whispered, "Your cum."

Trés dick instantly got hard. His heart started to soar. Lincoln smelled so good and looked even finer. Tré started speaking so loud that he was sure his passengers heard him.

"Damn, that motherfucking nigger is fine as fuck." Tré whispered.

The plane landed in Chicago and people started to exit the craft. Lincoln stayed behind, trying to get Tré's attention, but he was nowhere to be found. He finally went to the back lavatory where Tré pulled him into the tiny bathroom. They started kissing profusely, and within five minutes, Lincoln was performing oral sex on Tré; as his muscles began to cramp, Lincoln was determined to make Tré climax in his mouth. After five minutes of tonguing, sucking, kissing and deep throating, Tré tried to push Lincoln's head away as he began to orgasm. Lincoln was determined to taste the essence of Tré's existence; he swallowed the entire load. They resumed their tongue kisses until the clean up crew knocked on the lavatory door.

Tré yelled, 'I'll be out in just a minute!"

They started kissing again. Lincoln flew with Tré for the rest of the day; both were anticipating their return to Atlanta.

Z realized that Malia was having combination of a panic attack and a diabetic seizure. No one knew that Malia was diabetic; she kept it a secret and kept it under control. Z decided that he didn't want Malia to stay alone, so he volunteered to stay with her as long as she wanted. When Malia finally came to, she asked Z to call Victoria; she wanted her to stay a couple of days because she was so far behind in her work. She knew Victoria was up on her work and knew what she needed.

Z reluctantly agreed, adding, "But if that (bitch) gets in my way I will decapitate her and bury the body in the backyard beneath the rose bushes."

After telling Victoria the situation and also the ground rules, Victoria agreed. Victoria hated Z, Nikko, Nikki and especially Malia, but she was loyal to her, and when the time came she would destroy them all, especially Lake, for what they'd done to her and her family. She felt that this was an opportune time, to kill Malia, and set her house on fire. Victoria had a million thoughts of how she would get rid of the fag hag of the century, but now she had to assist in getting her health up to par.

CHAPTER 37

I love Him

Lake and Nikko finally got home with Kennedy in arms. It was almost two in the morning and they were dead tired. Lake had to be at work in six hours and he could barely keep his eyes open as he jumped in the shower. Nikko was wrestling with Kennedy, trying to get her bed clothes on as she laid comatose on her day bed, Sasha and Sebastian just looked in amazement. Nikko finally got Precious in bed, tucked Lake in, put away the church clothes, put away the breakfast dishes, dusted, mopped the kitchen floor, vacuumed downstairs, and took the dogs out for an early morning walk. He finally got ready for bed at 3:15, when he knelt on his knees to begin his prayers.

My heavenly Father, I realized how much I love you. God, as the days go longer, you have indeed shown me your strength and your power; when I wanted to give up on life you guided me through the storm. Almighty God, you have lead me to the light and out of the darkness, now please help my family, my Lake, my Kennedy, my Malia, my Tré and definitely my crazy Z and crazy auntie. God, I don't need much because you have blessed me with so much in my life and I am forever grateful. I realized when Nikki was taken from me that my life is still blessed and my dreams are not impossible; they are here with family and you, regardless. This life could not be better, thank you, oh Jehovah, for being my God. In your son's name Jesus Christ, Amen.

Lake didn't say a word as he heard Nikko's entire prayer; the tears just rolled uncontrollably down his cheeks as Nikko got into bed, his back against Lake's chest. Lake kissed on the back of his head and whispered, "Baby boy, I love you so much." Nikko thought Lake had been sleeping the entire time.

He responded, "I love you too, Lake. More than you will ever know."

Lake's dick began to pulsate. He rolled on top of Nikko and the caressing began, then the groans of satisfaction; it was something they both desperately needed. Lake massaged Nikko's body with his tongue, starting from the back of his neck down to the crack of his back. His tongue slid deep inside his rectum, and Nikko cried with the ultimate pleasure. He lay motionless on his stomach while his ass became moist from Lakés tongue. Lake continued to the thighs, the backs of the knees, down to the ankles and started massaging Nikko's feet and sucking softly on his toes. Nikko screamed into the pillows. Without hesitation, Lake eased his member up into Nikko's rectum. Nikko stopped him, asking him to get a condom. Lake ignored his request as he was overwhelmed with desire. Nikko's insides became lubricated naturally with every thrust of Lake's log. The pleasure he was feeling was indescribable; they had never made love without a condom through their entire six years together. He wanted to make Lake stop but the pleasure would not allow him. His HIV status lingered in the back of his mind as he took every inch of his lover's dick; he felt so good, so right and so natural without a condom. Lake had tears in his eyes, as he slowly and intensely made love to his lover. Lake knew the consequence of unprotected sex, but Nikko was his lover and that was all that mattered; he didn't care about being infected because his love for Nikko was stronger then any disease could ever be. The love making lasted for hours; the sun was peeping through the bedroom blinds when they realized it was six-thirty. Lake and Nikko were both exhausted and definitely pleased with the satisfaction they'd both experienced. Lake slowly dragged himself to the bathroom to have a quick shower. Nikko just lay there, puzzled and confused; this was the first time they'd ever had sex unprotected, but it seemed so natural, so right and so normal. Nikko allowed Lake to come inside of him without any hesitation. His mind was in a complete state of shock and confusion. Lake rushed into the bedroom trying to prepare for work, without a minute to lose. Nikko stopped him dead in his tracks and asked," Why?"

"Why what?" Lake responded. Lake continued, "Baby, we are one. I belong to you and you belong to me, regardless to what the situation is. Husband and wife make love, and it's normal. Why can't we? Besides, I'm not worried about you getting pregnant," he laughed as he rushed back into the bathroom with a big grin on his face.

Nikko just stood there, mouth open and more complacent then ever. Just as he was about to prolong the conversation, he heard the patter of little feet running down the hall way; it was Kennedy waking up for her morning ritual, giving hugs and kisses to her two favorite men in the world. Lake rushed out of the bedroom once again, fully dressed, while Nikko was still standing in the middle of the bedroom mortified.

"Baby, I got this. Go get yourself together while I get Kennedy ready for school. We'll see you downstairs in a second. Hurry up; I know you have much cleaning up to do," Lake said, grinning.

Nikko finally snapped out of it. He ran into the bathroom, took care of his necessities and flew downstairs to see his favorite two people in the world. Kennedy was still tired from the previous night. As she sat at the kitchen table eating her breakfast, she muttered to Nikko, "Good morning, Uncle Daddy."

Nikko's eyes got as big as fifty cent pieces.

"Good morning, my little daughter-niece," Nikko said in amazement.

Lake just winked as he urged Kennedy to hurry up, he was going to drop her off today at school. Nikko decided to take the dogs on a long walk to clear his head; today was the first day for him to start his medication. He decided to take the ten mile nature trail. At the last minute he decided to ride his bike instead of walking; he needed to have a long talk with God. He had uncontrollable energy and the need to exert it in any capacity. Rolling the bike out of the garage, he heard the phone ringing from the kitchen. He made an immediate U-turn to see who was calling this early in the morning. It was Malia apologizing from yesterday's fiasco.

"I don't know what happened," she explained. "I'm usually very much in control of my diabetes; combined with my anxiety attacks, I just lost it. Nevertheless, Nikko, I've decided to adopt a child. I need to be complete and I know a child who is deserving of my love will do just that."

Nikko just listened until Malia was finishing confessing.

"I think that would be great. No one is more deserving of your love then a wanting baby." Malia interrupted, "I decided to adopt a little girl; someone around the same age as Kennedy. I feel a newborn baby would be too much of a responsibility and raising someone old enough to go to the bathroom would be very rewarding to me," Malia grinned.

Nikko shared in her laughter; he felt her heart being truly blessed.

"Well, I just wanted to tell you that, I feel today is gonna be a good day. I have so much work to do for home and the office," Malia blurted out.

"How was it last night with Victoria staying over? Nikko curiously asked.

"It was fine. We laughed and talked about work; she brought me up to speed with the latest gossip. "Victoria is a lovely girl despite what everyone says about her; she's the best assistant I've had in a long time,"

Malia added.

"Well, baby girl, be very careful. I just don't trust her. There's something about her; I don't know if it's the way she looks at me or if it's just my intuition. I really can't put my finger on it, but I smell evil when she's present. I'm sorry, Malia, I'm acting like my aunt again. It's probably nothing. Maybe she is a lovely girl, maybe it's just me. I don't think she ever really got over the situation with Lake or the fashion show, but I have a gut feeling, she has always been up to no good," Nikko continued.

Malia heard a faint click on the phone and abruptly asked him to hold on. She ran downstairs to see what Victoria was doing; she heard the back door open and saw Victoria coming in with a beautiful bouquet of freshly cut pink roses. Malia was shocked. "Hi, Ms. Lady, how are you?" Victoria greeted.

"I'm fine. How was your morning?" Malia asked.

"It was fine. I felt the need to got brighten your day with some sweet smelling roses; every woman needs a rose in her life sometimes," Victoria added.

Malia, still slightly shocked and trying to catch her breath on the sly, said, "Thanks, Victoria, but you didn't have to do that. I'm doing much better today. I feel I just had so much pressure on me these last couple of weeks. I just needed some rest and prayer." Victoria cut her off. "If you would like I can prepare some breakfast; turkey bacon, egg whites, fresh orange juice, wheat pancakes and some coffee, if you would like," Victoria offered.

"That would be great. I'm going to take a hot shower. I'll be back in a sec," Malia responded.

Running back up stairs, she realized she had completely forgotten Nikko was on the phone. When she picked up the phone, all she heard was a dial tone.

"Oh, shit! Nikko!" She whispered. She dialed his number, while she undressed and turned on the shower. Nikko had already started his ten mile ride; he was calling her on his cell phone, with his trusty earpiece in tact.

"Malia what happened?" Nikko asked.

"Oh, nothing. I thought someone was listening to our conversation, but I guess it was just my imagination. Nikko, where are you?" she asked.

"I'm on my bike; I decided to take a morning ride with the dogs," Nikko explained. "Well call me later; I have something I need to ask you," Malia continued to whisper.

Lake's spirit was great, but his body was tired as hell. He slumped over his desk, trying to stay alive with some black coffee and a bagel. He had work up to his neck; he had a pile of murders, kidnappings, robberies, killings, the list was endless. He decided to take a break even though he'd only been at work for forty-five minutes. Lake decided to take a ten minute break just as his office phone rang.

"Officer Lake, here; how may I help you?"

"Officer Lake, this is Tonya in the crime lab. I got something that may be beneficial to the Nikki Grey case."

"I'll be down there in a minute," Lake answered.

Lake was in such a rush that he took the stairs instead of waiting for the elevator. He pushed open the door to the crime lab and went straight to Tonya's desk.

"What you got for me, T?" Tonya just laughed.

"Well, L," she giggled. "The blood samples came back and it seems as though there were more than two intruders as we originally thought. We've done forensics on all the fiber at the crime scene, and it's very puzzling. Unfortunately some of the cops that got the call fucked up some of the evidence. They trampled over a lot of useful evidence, not to mention all the blood that was compromised," Tonya continued as Lake's facial expression suddenly changed. "But I do have some good news; the skin that we found under Ms. Grey's nails proved to be the DNA of a female. I even analyzed the blood and now we have to send that back to the lab for more testing. These results prove that there was definitely someone assisting in murdering your sister-in-law. Who ever the assailant was, she watched as Ms. Grey got raped and, from the looks of the evidence, she held Ms. Grey down while the primary assailant did the act."

Lake became furious at every word Tonya uttered. Lake's entire demeanor changed; he would never have thought a woman had assisted in murdering Nikki. He wondered if he should tell Nikko or keep it to himself. Tonya's voice faded as Lake thought about the last time he saw Nikki alive. She was so beautiful, with her hair, lips, eyes, skin, nose, lips, and her overall spirit. He started thinking of Kennedy and how she has adjusted to being without her mother. It was just amazing how the ordeal had not altered her behavior or her mental capacity. He drifted back to this morning and thought about how unbelievable the love making was with Nikko; it was so natural and surreal. He loved his family and wouldn't change it for the world, but he knew he had to find Nikki's murderer and bring closure to the nightmare.

"Lake! Lake!"

Tonya shook his left shoulder.

"Wake Up!"

Lake stood up with an enormous hard on. Realizing it immediately, he put some papers in front of his blue casual slacks.

"Whoa!" Tonya blurted. Tonya's eyes were as big as silver dollars. Her phone rang and she answered on the first ring with a big smile.

"Atlanta Police Department Crime Lab, Tonya speaking; how may I help you?"

Lake felt this was his golden opportunity to escape any further embarrassment. He was blushing as he tried to walk briskly up the stairwell, his soldier finally going down.

Tré slept in Lincoln's arms for the entire night. Wiping the gunk from his eyes, he just lay there motionless, waiting for his limp body to revive from last night's insatiable evening of fantasy. Tré slowly drifted back to sleep and heard his mother in his dream. She was shaking her head, crying.

She repeatedly cried, "Please, Tré, don't be a faggot. I want more out of you. Marry Keisha. She's a lovely girl; she's the mother of your child, for God's sake."

Tré started to jerk in his sleep; his body was becoming agitated by the sudden nightmares about his mother. She didn't let up. She persisted with her annoying voice, demanding him to straighten up and stop being a punk like his cousin, Z. Tré began to talk in his sleep and tried his best to wake up, but she wouldn't let him; she had a hold on his life that he couldn't shake. Even from her grave she controlled his conscience and now his life.

Tré screamed, "Shut the fuck up!"

Tré jumped up out Lincoln arms and out of the bed. Upon realizing where he was, he became very embarrassed and ashamed. Lincoln was totally oblivious to what was happening. After both realized it was a terrible nightmare, they both got back in the bed nestled like the last honeymooners.

"What's wrong, baby?" Lincoln asked.

"B, this is wrong, two men having sex, kissing, caressing, holding each other; God is not pleased with this, man. And you're married; we are going straight to hell." Tré continued to ramble, ("Nigga,) I can't do this. I got mad feelings for you but I got to marry a woman and live happily ever after; it's the normal thing to do. I promised my mom and dad I was going to get married and live my life for my wife and kids. If I continue being a fucking faggot, I'm destined to be a destroyed man; with my luck, the next flight I take, the plane will fall out the fucking sky or I may die of AIDS, or worse, everybody I know will find out about me and I will be considered less than a man. Shit, man, I'm a soldier, a pimp from the streets; we ain't supposed to get down like this, with another man. I feel faggots are less than a trick on the street. (B) you don't know what I go through; the nightmares, the anxiety, the shit I have to endure, I'm cursed. I'm never ever gonna find true love because I'm attracted to dick and pussy."

Tré began to get angry, humiliated that he let a grown man see a side of him that no one is privileged enough to see. Lincoln stood there for what seemed like an eternity. Finally he spoke.

"Do you think you're the only motherfucker who goes through this shit? There's a million brothers who feel like they are Dr. Jekyll and Mr. Hyde; two fucked up personalities. Every night I pray to God to take this craving I have for men away from my flesh. I'm at home in bed with my wife plenty of nights lusting for you, Tré. I used to make love with my wife every single night when I was home and I loved it, but recently I haven't been making love to her, but fucking her, because I want to bust a nut and go to sleep so I can dream about your sorry ass. I'm sexing her, thinking about you; how fucked is that? And you stand here complaining about your fucked up sexuality? What about me? What about all us motherfuckers? I grew up believing (niggas) like me with big dicks should fuck as much pussy as our dicks can handle, but secretly they want to fuck a man in the ass or get fucked my a man. Tré, you don't know half the shit we have to put up with. There are places you can go if you wanted to and talk about your situation, but where in the hell can a pro athlete can go and tell? There ain't no fucking support group for this shit. I would be burned at the fucking stake. Motherfuckers in the league will have a price on my head if I come out and say I'd rather be with a man than woman. The psychological bullshit I have to endure and most pro athletes have to endure is devastating. And don't talk about the homo demons on your back, telling you to confess my sins to my wife, my team mates, my manager, my agent, my coaches, my family, my friends, to the league, to my daughter."

Suddenly, Lincoln broke. He fell back on the bed and balled up like a fetus and started to cry out loud.

He belted, "Man this shit hurts! It hurt so bad I want to die; I want to kill myself and then the pain will leave. I won't have to live this double life, the humiliation. People just don't know how this shit really feels."

Tré just stood there, helpless. He didn't know what to do. He was in complete shock. He tried to move toward the bed to comfort his… at that moment, Tré didn't know what Lincoln was to him; a friend, a lover, a fuck buddy, or someone who would fuck him over in the long run.

Tré suddenly leaped toward Lincoln, begging him, "Baby, don't cry. I love you, man, I loved you from the first day I saw you on the plane."

Lincoln looked up with his tears still flowing.

"I love you, too, Tré."

Both started to cry, not knowing the repercussions of saying those three little words they never said to one. After the cries of liberation filled the luxury hotel room, after the whimpering slowed down, they felt awkward and distant. Tré and Lincoln reached a point in their lives where they had someone to count on, someone who shared the same fears and humiliation. Tré was a street wise, confused DL brother who was a masculine, muscular, flight attendant, who wore Timbs and jeans to cover up his sexuality, and Lincoln was a million dollar athlete who wanted to be free with a man and live his life happily ever after with a wife and a child on the side. After an hour and a half of more love making and confessing their love for one another, they both realized that they needed to get up and start a new lease on life; Tré and Lincoln, both shit, showered, shaved and exchanged pleasantries along the way. Lincoln was catching a flight back to New York to be with his wife and daughter by dinner time and Tré had to take care of his errands, scheduling, and to check on his much needed friends by answering all the emails and voice messages they left on his PC and voice mail on both his home and cell phones. Tré dropped Lincoln off at the Hartsfield-Jackson Airport, hoping to go unnoticed in fear of one of his employees questioning his presence at the airport on his off day. Lincoln winked at Tré while giving him a firm handshake, leaving a crisp one hundred dollar bill in his hands. Tré became immediately puzzled.

"What's this for?"

Lincoln responded, "Because I love you and you need to go get your hair and nails done." Tré smirked.

"Yo, pimp, don't play me like that, dawg," he said as he sped away.

Lincoln stood there, laughing his ass off before entering the corridor for ticketing. Lincoln was unknowingly being watched by two private detectives; one was taking pictures with a high powered digital camera and the other with a video camera from across the parking lot of the airport.

Tré was tough, hard, and emotionless. He once ran with the cut throat drug dealers and street thugs. He never wanted to be a part of that lifestyle again. He never forgot how he would not bathe for days, eating out of garbage cans, and robbing little old women at his leisure. He just gave praise to God for how he'd changed his life of destruction on the streets of New York, how his family disowned him and threw him to the wolves when he dropped out of college in Atlanta and moved back to New York. He had to give so much love to Nikko, Nikki, Malia and his dear gay cousin, Z. They saved him from the streets of Brooklyn one late fall night ten years ago, Z drove eighteen hours, found his cousin on the streets, cleaned him up, and put him in rehab. Nikko and Nikki groomed him, gave him clothes, and a new look at his future compared to his dark past. Malia created a flawless resume for him and assisted him in learning interviewing techniques. She had to cash in some of her favors in order to assure him an interview with some of the major Atlanta companies. She got him over ten interviews from some top notch companies. Tré knew he was blessed with a circle of friends that really came to his side, even though he rarely admitted it. Everyone was surprised and relieved when he landed a job with Destiny Airlines. He was determined to work hard and finally recapture his long lost dreams. The family was back together again, from the yesteryears when they all were in college, when they all struggled with exams, tuition, midterms, social events, boyfriends and girlfriends. The first years of college were good for everyone; Tré had a full four year scholarship to play baseball, Malia and Nikki were going to school for law, Z was going to be the first black gay doctor with an attitude, and Nikko was the only one who was financially stable enough to support everyone's needs. He had his photography gig and made excellent money by being one of the local newspaper's photo editors. Nikko was responsible for buying meal tickets for Malia and Z. Nikki started modeling for the local department stores and was now making more good money like her brother. Times were good in college; they were memories that Tré hoped would last forever, with the exception of that fateful night when he was caught robbing the book store in the student center. His world, as he knew it, came to an end. He was never convicted, but the humiliation led to his immediate expulsion from college and his new adventure with the streets in New York. His circle of friends cried for his immediate return upon graduation, but Tré refused. Embarrassed and ashamed, he chose a life of crime and despair.

Tré made it back to his little sanctuary of a loft in record time; he couldn't wait to get his day started right. After three hours of cleaning, folding, vacuuming, he decided to apologize to Z. Tré felt the apology for Z was much needed and long overdue. He knew life was too short to continue to act like an asshole, but before heading to Z's he had to drop by Keisha's to pick up Little Man.

CHAPTER 38

Upgrade Me

Z, too, was busy cleaning, washing, dusting, dancing and listening to music. He had just finished listening to his favorite artist of all time, Little Kim. Now he was listening to Beyonce's upgrade me and J. Z. latest single.

"That diva can sing," Z muttered as he feather dusted the chandelier in the dinner room. He was wearing his favorite clean up outfit: A pair of cut off jeans too sizes to short, a tie dye pink tank top, black combat boots with pink laces and yellow dish washing gloves. The door bell rang, breaking him from his trance. Z headed to the door with a toilet brush in his hands, using it as a microphone. "All the boys in the yard want a taste of my milkshake," he screamed as he slung the door open.

It was JJ, holding a dozen roses and a bottle of Chadon. Z slammed the door back without skipping a beat. JJ knocked on the door again. This time, becoming instantly frustrated, Z opened the door and shouted, "What the hell do you want, motherfucker?"

"I want to talk and I'm not leaving until we talk," JJ responded.

Z whispered, "Talk about what, Jeremy?"

"Talk about us," JJ whispered.

"Well, start talking," Z demanded.

"Can I come inside?" JJ asked.

"Why can't you talk from outside? I'm listening," Z attacked.

JJ became frustrated.

"I'm tired of this shit."

He pushed Z in the door and slammed and locked it behind him.

"Listen, motherfucker you're gonna listen to me if it's the last thing you do, even if I have to glue your fucking smart ass mouth shut; you talk to damn much," JJ shouted.

Z just stared, but didn't utter a sound.

"Zarius, I love you, man, with your sarcastic remarks, your nonchalant attitude and your feminine ways. I love you from the tip of your shiny head to your size twelve feet. I know at first it was a sex thing man, but I'm feeling you and I felt this way for a long time. I want us to be together and I'm not gonna stop trying man until you say yes."

JJ continued to rave on for about an hour with Z looking out into the distance, not hearing a single word. JJ was confessing his undying love for Z.

"Now, what will it be?" JJ finally asked.

There was a long silence in the house; Z raised his hands as if asking permission to speak. Z simply replied, "NO! JJ, you are a drug addict, you have fucked my feelings with your lies and deceit, you have sold your dick and your ass for money to use drugs, and you planted drugs in my house. For all I know, you could have been selling them out of my house. I may be a lot of things, but I don't do drugs and I don't deal with motherfuckers who do; that's one thing I do not tolerate, Jeremy,"

JJ leaped at Z's throat. Z, known for his quickness, escaped his grasp by jumping on the dinning room table. Z ran to the kitchen, grabbed a knife and launched back at JJ. JJ stopped dead in his tracks. A thick mist of hate filled the condo. They stood in the kitchen for what seemed like hours. Suddenly, the door bell rang, but neither of them moved. Then someone began to knock on the door. Z heard the voice of his little cousin.

"Cousin Z, open up; it's me, Junior and daddy," yelled little Tré.

Z screamed, "Come in, the door is open." But it wasn't; it was locked. Tré sensed something was dreadfully wrong and looked for the spare key that was hidden underneath the porch in a little key case. He opened the door and, to his amazement, he saw Z's 145 pound frame with a knife pressed against JJ's throat.

Z screamed again, "You better come get this motherfucker before I slice him into little pieces."

Tré tried to blind Little Man from seeing what was going down; he never wanted to have his child be a witness of the shit that could transpire when it comes to bullshit with (psychotic niggas).

"Call 911," Z said in a calm voice. "This motherfucker was trespassing and breaking and entering, and now I'm gonna lock his sorry ass up. How you doing, junior? Cousin Z is just blowing off a little steam. I'll be with you in a minute. I'll take you to get some ice cream as soon as Atlanta's finest come and lock this man up," he calmly said to Junior as he dug the knife a little deeper into JJ's neck. Tré grabbed the knife from Z and persuaded both of them to sit down and talk about their problem in a civil manner. Both did calm down and realized that the romance and sex was over. Z was adamant about pressing charges on JJ if he were to ever pull a stunt like that again. Z gave him the last bit of clothing that he was saving for him, pictures that they had taken together and a bunch of cards and letters he'd decided not to throw away. He stuffed it all in a duffle bag and handed it to JJ.

He whispered in JJ's ear, "I will always love you, but right now I need more in my life." He reluctantly left with his tail between his legs, hoping that he could maneuver back into Z's life and recover the key load of cocaine he'd hidden in Z's attic. His plan A had fallen through, now it was time for plan B, the final plan. After much needed apologies, Tré and Z made up and took Little man out for some ice cream as promised. Tré revealed to him his feelings for Lincoln, and how he had mixed emotions due to the fact he had never found any solace when dealing with a man and their emotions. In that instant, Z decided to have a BBQ to celebrate his cousin's liberation from all the societal bullshit.

"Let's have a small gathering; we really haven't been together in while, just the gang." Tré reluctantly agreed. Watching the cousins from a store front window were the same two detectives who had earlier taken pictures of Lincoln when he departed from Atlanta.

Z got on the cell and immediately called Nikko, Malia, and Lake. He informed them that a BBQ was much needed this afternoon and declining would be completely unacceptable. They needed to catch up on each other's lives and juicy gossip, he explained. Within a matter of minutes, Z had organized a fabulous outing with toppings to boot. He was able to invite his dearest friends, and the best dessert caterer his money could buy. It had been a while since they'd all sat down and caught up on all the latest since his aunt died and the anxiety attacks Malia suffered. The evening was warm and humid; perfect weather for a BBQ. Z prepared a wonderful array of dishes: A cucumber salad, tossed salad, corn on the cob, Swedish meatballs made of ground turkey with his secret ingredient, Lipton's onion soup mix and baked beans. Tré and Junior handled the grilled chicken, Jamaican grilled fish, and honey barbeque steaks and shrimp shish kabob. Z needed to stay occupied, trying his best not to think about JJ and how much he really missed him, but he knew he had to cut him off and stop the bleeding. He missed the conversation, the lovemaking, the company of a man; someone who had taken the empty space in his lonely bed. The time he spent with JJ was therapeutic. He thought JJ would pass the tests he gave to anyone that dared to be with him; he had secretly given JJ an AIDS test which he passed, but the drugs and deceit were things that Z could and would never tolerate.

He remembered the effects drugs had in his house while growing up; his father stayed drunk and high more (than) he was a father and husband. Z hated his father for all the right reasons: neglect, infidelity, betrayal and disapproval of his lifestyle. Z often resented his mother even more for staying with the deadbeat motherfucker. The physical and mental abuse was too much for anyone to bear, but his mom stayed and prayed, prayed and stayed until one day, sclerosis of the liver took his father away. Everyone was sad except him and his mother, who seem to be most proud. Z had mixed feelings about his father's death, but his mother seemed to be glowing during the entire time of his father's bereavement. It seemed as if her prayers were finally answered; that, in some bizarre way, her impossible dreams were realized. The fifty thousand dollar insurance settlement that was left was willed to his girlfriend and children, but his mother did not blink an eye or shed a tear; she was finally liberated to live her life for her self and her children. She was elated to know the abuse had stopped for her and Z. There were times when Z grew older, he'd attempted to poison, suffocate, stab and slice his father's throat, but his mother stopped him on every occasion. It was as though she felt his spirit and knew when he was on the verge of getting rid of his father for good. They shared secrets and sometimes their souls; they were the best of friends. She always knew her oldest child was special and different. For some strange reason, she felt God gave gay children special gifts; the gift to be themselves, to be free, to be creative and to live life, where most straight people hesitate when being themselves and are afraid of the unknown. When she first sensed Z's differences, she prayed that he would grow out of it. She introduced him to trucks, cars, and sports, but Z always wanted to read and play with dresses and wigs. After accepting the inevitable, she knew she had to make him strong in his spirit. She started reading the bible to him every night, telling him not to let anyone disrespect him ever. She instilled in him the responsibility of a man; that he had to stand up for this right, regardless of what the outcome might bring. She didn't encourage his feminine ways, but she didn't discourage it either. She made both her boys be proud of their heritage, and their culture. Z's mother and father fought constantly over Z's sexuality. At the age of six, Z's father broke his arm with a beating when he caught Z playing in his mother's makeup. There had been more life threatening incidents, but after that, the only abuse he displayed to his son was verbal. Eventually, he gave up and accepted the fact that his son was gonna be a faggot. He made Z's mother pay for the guilt he suffered about his son's sexuality. He tried his best to beat the faggot ass behavior out of Z vicariously through Z's mother. She didn't mind taken the beating from him just to save her son's life and her family unity. On the day they pronounced her husband's death, in the back of her mind she had always believed that Z had finally escaped her love and poisoned his father. Z had persuaded his father's mistress to give his mother as least half of the insurance money, but his mother would not accept it. She didn't want anything to do with her dead husband or his money; her peace of mind of satisfaction were enough, but Z took the money, put half in a mutual fund for his mom and gave the other half to his brother; who spent it all in a matter of months. Z's brother never talked about their father's life or death because they were the best of friends. They did everything together when his father was sober; his father taught him how to play sports, shoot a gun, have sex, and gave him his first drink. Luke adored his father and was more devastated over his death then his sibling and his mother. He accepted his father's infidelities and abusive behavior towards his mother. Luke refused to take his father's passing lightly; he couldn't understand how a man that was so fucked up with one brother could treat the other like a best friend. Luke and Z argued on every occasion when it came to their differences with their mother and father. Luke never tried to console his mother, even though he would hear and see his father beating the shit out of her. It was always Z running to get the knife and threatening his father to leave his mother alone and leave their home. His father would be gone weeks, sometimes months at a time until he felt the coast was clear. Z would often go to his father's girlfriend's house and beat his father, his girlfriend and the three teenage boys she had. This situation created a great deal of tension in the high school; the three boys often tried to triple team Z, but his friends, who were mostly female, were not having it. Eventually the three teenagers had to attend summer school due to the fact of missing an enormous amount of days from school due to an abundance of suspensions. This settled the dust until the day his father died. Z reluctantly buried the hatchet with his no good father and even went to bed with the youngest son just to show there were no hard feelings or animosity from him or his mother.

It was around seven in the evening when Malia, Lake, Nikko, Kennedy and two other friends of Z's showed up. They devoured the food in a matter of minutes. Good food, good music and good friends; they couldn't beat it. Lake started the conversation about the new findings at work pertaining to Nikki's assailant; he continued to elaborate on the findings while watching Nikko's reaction. He felt it was necessary to mention the investigation in the company of others rather than Nikko having to face the news alone. He knew that Nikko had started his medication today and he didn't want to upset him even more. Nikko took the news well; he didn't even comment on the conversation, but he did excuse himself immediately afterwards. He rushed to the bathroom to vomit. Lake was two steps behind him, sensing something was wrong. He rushed in the bathroom behind Nikko.

"What's the matter, baby?" Lake asked, looking very concerned.

Nikko responded, "It's the meds, Lake. I think my body is rejecting them. I've been throwing up all day. I thought it would be better after I ate, but now it's getting worse. Lake, I've taken eight pills already and had to take an additional four more. I don't think I can do this for the rest of my life."

Lake's eyes began to fill with water. Nikko stopped his conversation and stared at Lake. "What's wrong?" Nikko asked.

"I refuse to lose you, Nikko, or allow you to give up on life, or give up on me or Kennedy; you have so much to live for, so whatever it takes, we will get through this. Baby, let's go home," Lake ordered.

They said their good byes to their clan and rounded up Kennedy, who didn't want to leave the company of Junior, whom she rarely played with. The ride home seemed endless. There wasn't a sound from anyone, just the humming of the engine and the light snore of Kennedy who was once again asleep in a matter of seconds.

Back at the ranch, Z, Malia and Tré started their ritual of exchanging stories of their life. Tré started first.

"Guys, I think I'm ready to accept the inevitable. I think I'm ready to fall in love with a (nigga)."

Z and Malia hesitated. Z couldn't hold it in any longer.

"Since you're out of the closet, in the morning you're gonna grow a tail and wear a big 'F' across your chest for 'Faggot'."

Malia busted out laughing, drawing an imaginary 'F' on Tré's AkaDemic sweat shirt.

Tré shouted, "I don't have to put up with this bullshit from you motherfuckas!"

"Well, honey child, if you think we're gonna give you a hard time wait till the world finds out you're fucking with the same sex; you ain't seen bullshit till you hear motherfuckers calling you punk, faggot, girl, sissy, bitch, baddi boy, antiman, blood clot; you ain't heard name calling till someone call you a faggoty blood clot," Z said with authority.

"Stop it man, you know Junior is upstairs sleep. I don't want him to hear that shit," demanded Tré.

Z and Malia stopped in mid laugh.

Z cleared his throat and preceded to whisper, "K, life is not easy when accepting this lifestyle. It's a painful cycle of continuous heartbreak, sadness, rejection, loneliness, games, drama, bullshit, humiliation, and there are the happy moments, which only come in sports. I constantly ask myself why anyone wants to live this lifestyle; you love to talk about how you hate faggots and punks. Tré, child, aint it funny how the tables turn," blurted Z.

"It's time for me to go," Tré responded exasperatedly.

He rushed upstairs to wake up Junior and in a matter of seconds they were downstairs, out the door and in the car before he realized he didn't even say good-bye. He just held Junior, who was still fast asleep. The emotional roller coaster started to overwhelm his ability to think reasonably. He wanted to puke at just the thought of being called a faggot or girl. He was a man, a real man, for Christ's sake. Trés cell phone went off as he was carrying Junior into Keisha's apartment. He realized it was scheduling to ask him if he would be interested in doing a red eye from New York to California back to Atlanta. He agreed to do it in hopes that he might get a chance to see Lincoln, if not only for a second. He only took an hour and a half to get home, shower, shave, pack and head off to the airport.

Z and Malia were still cracking jokes when the phone rang. It was Nina; a friend of Z's who was an interior decorator. She wanted to know if she could come over and leave some swatches for Z to look at. He was interested in redecorating his living room and also the family room. Nina was a long, lean and sexy specimen of a woman. She met Z at a slumber party at which they were bidding on the same dildo and scented lubrication. Nina was a sex goddess and she used it to her advantage. She could make men pulsate with an erection just by her conversation alone. She got a lot of business from hard up men who wanted to tap a piece of that round ass of hers, but Nina was strictly dickless. She loved pussy and wasn't afraid to admit it. This made men drool even more. Her eyes were light hazel; she had perfect white teeth, short curly sandy hair, one dimple on the right side and a beautiful pecan tan complexion. Nina was slightly bow legged, and fitted on her 5'10" frame was a perfect one 125 pounds. She played basketball, volleyball and softball in high school and college. Her presence, and even her voice, demanded attention; it was very raspy yet sexy with a New York accent. Z screamed when he opened the door.

"Hi, bitch!"

She replied, "Hey, ho'! Just needed to drop over these swatches you requested. I hope its not too late; I have to catch a flight early in the morning, so I wanted you to go over them while I'm gone and when I get back maybe you're be ready to start with the family room."

Malia was shocked by this woman's sex appeal. She was wearing some hip-hugger jeans, a cropped red top with dome sleeves and matching pumps, accessorized with diamond earrings, a tennis bracelet and a diamond pendant. She wore a 2 carat gold ring on her middle finger. It resembled a man's wedding band. Nina never really acknowledged Malia, and Malia was slightly amazed and appalled. Malia interrupted the conversation between Z and Nina's cackling.

"Hi, I'm Somalia. If you don't mind, I'm interested in redoing my master bedroom. Do you have a card and maybe you could come over to see what I can do? I need someone with a very distinctive, but creative eye."

Nina, without hesitation or eye contact with Malia, pulled out a gold business card with red lettering and gave it to her. Z and Nina were too busy looking at swatches; they didn't even hear Malia mutter under her breath, "Bitch!" Malia just sat there until the two cheesy cats stopped cackling with each other. Afterward, she turned to Malia and looked deep into her eyes.

"Somalia, if it's not too terribly late, I would love to come over and look at your bedroom, and afterwards I could email you some swatches and ideas; I would love to redecorate your master bedroom for you," Nina said.

Malia was elated after realizing that she was paying attention and Nina remembered her name.

Malia replied, "I would be honored."

Z stood up and demanded, "Bitch you ain't going nowhere until you help me clean up this shit," pointing his finger at Malia.

Nina rushed to her defense.

"I will help you guys but it's gonna cost you that dildo," she whispered to Z.

The three began laughing and cutting each other up until they all were drenched with tears. Across the street was a black sedan containing a person covered in black from head to toe. They were studying the movement of all the innocent bystanders. The car drove off with a shriek instantaneously when the barking of a dog startled the person. The threesome was so engulfed in laughter and tears that they were unaware that someone was watching them from afar.

The routine was the same at Nikko and Lake's house; putting Kennedy to bed was becoming a chore for Nikko day after day. He had to muster the strength to prepare her meals, prepare her bath water, get her ready for bed, read a bedtime story and take those horrible pills. He became weaker and more perplexed as the days went by. Lake tried his best to help whenever the opportunity presented itself, but Nikko insisted on doing the majority of caring for Kennedy himself. Lake had an emergency meeting after getting comfortable in bed and really didn't want to leave his family, but it was an emergency so the decision was not his. He kissed Nikko on the forehead and promised he would be home shortly; Nikko was so disillusioned that he didn't remember Lake leaving the house. In his haste, Lake forgot to lock the top lock or put on the alarm. The same black sedan, with an onlooker, watched Lake back out of the drive way and off into the night. The onlooker noticed there were no lights on in the house and decided to check the doors. The trespasser was still covered in black, with matching skull cap, gloves and shoes. The dogs suddenly started barking, startling the trespasser. Nikko drowsily approached the bedroom window to get a glimpse of a black sedan speeding down the street. At first Nikko thought he was dreaming but reality set in when Sasha and Sebastian continuously barked until they were satisfied and the neighborhood was now clear. Nikko lazily headed back to bed; his stomach was so upset from the medication that he needed to sleep and pray that the pain didn't get any worse.

Malia and Nina entered the house within thirty minutes of leaving Z's condo. Still cracking jokes, Malia gave Nina a tour of the finished basement, the main level with living room, formal dinning, room, two bathrooms, family room, oversized kitchen, wrap around balcony and patio and a sitting room. They almost tripped upstairs from laughing so hard. Nina was telling a sexual joke about her escapades with two men at the same time. Malia gave Nina a tour of the three upstairs bedrooms. After entering into the master bedroom, Malia turned around to find Nina planting a kiss on her lips; Malia just froze, unable to move or speak. Nina continued down Malia's top caressing and massaging her now erect nipples. Malia continued to be frozen in time. Nina's movement was slow and sensual; there was the succulent sound of lips touching breasts and nipples. Nina slowly moved her way down to Malia's navel. She kissed and licked until she had unfastened Malia's pants. Nina stopped in mid-caress. She looked up at Malia as she stared into space.

"You're not gay, are you?" Nina asked.

"No, I'm not, so could you please fasten my pants back?" Malia demanded.

Without hesitation, Nina fastened up Malia slacks, stood up and started to apologize profusely. She was not embarrassed, but she excused herself and didn't stop until she got to the front door. Malia accepted her apologies and told her it was alright. She encouraged her to come back to finish the conversation and also to send her the swatches as requested. Malia moved in slow motion as she cut off the lights, set the alarm, and started to fill the tub with warm water. This was her sanctuary; the water was symbolic for washing away her tears, sins and nightmares. She lit her aromatherapy candles and started to pray as she soaked for about an hour. As she was about to get out of now the chilling water, her phone rang. It was none other than Z.

"Hello?" she asked.

"Girrrrrrrrrrrrrl, I heard you got your pussy eaten by some real pussy," Z burst out laughing.

Malia was not laughing and she became suddenly numb again.

"Hey, Lesbo, you there?" Z asked.

"I don't think that's very funny, Zarius," she said in her nonchalant voice.

"I'm sorry, Miss Thing. Nina called me apologizing, and getting mad at me because I didn't tell her that you were not gay."

"Gay!" Malia shouted. "Do I look gay??"

Z interrupted, "What is that supposed to mean, Somalia?"

"It means, do I look gay?" she replied.

"What the fuck is that supposed to mean? How is a gay person supposed to look?" Z sounded agitated.

"Let's change the subject before someone regrets something they may or may not say," she demanded.

"Yeah, let's," Z agreed.

"Z, you know I'm going to sign papers tomorrow to be a foster parent."

Malia's voice had gone from frustrated to excited. She continued to explain the good news to Z, but he had no response.

Z started to speak.

"Malia, do you think that's a good idea?"

"What do you mean?" she snapped.

"I mean, you just got over Drayton and you haven't had time to heal spiritually, and now you're ready to take on the responsibility of a rug rat. I don't think you're ready, Malia," Z said sympathetically. He continued, "Malia, do you remember when I wanted to adopt a child because I felt this would complete me—"

Malia interrupted, "That's different, Z; you're gay!"

The air suddenly became hot.

"Okay, bitch! What the fuck is that supposed to mean?"

"What I mean, bitch, is that you are a whore. You don't have time for children, because you prefer sucking dick to raising a child and if you did try to raise a child it would probably grow up to be a child molester. Don't go there with me, Z; you wouldn't like me when I become a tired old drag queen; I will read you till your hoes get home."

"Hold up," Z demanded, "Wait a minute, you little itty bitty titty bitch. I hope you do adopt a child and I hope it is a male because that's the only male who can bear to look at your crusty pussy, you hermaphrodite."

"I know you not talking about a hermaphrodite. The next time you want to buy some dick, try to work some overtime; I'm tired of loaning you money for the male prostitutes you pick up on Cypress and the next time you try selling that leaky discharge ass of yours, make sure you take a penicillin shot. You work for a hospital, bitch. Get checked before selling that shit on the streets."

"No this skank didn't, you no-winning lawyer; girl, you haven't won a case since you represented Jesus and you know what happened to him. You couldn't buy a case if your pussy depended on it. Oh, girl, I forgot your pussy is depending on it. Let me tell you something, you Beyonce wannabe; you look more like Ms. Cellie in drag with a taste of She-nana. You look more like the monster from the Black Lagoon. I heard about the threesome you had with fuckin' Freddy Kruger and Jason, you halitosis-having' Gila monster."

"All jokes aside, Z, I need someone, something in my life. I won't be able to have children ever so I need something to call my own, to be complete."

"Malia, a child is good, wonderful, maybe the best thing in anyone's life, but if you are spiritually broken, a child can hinder your outlook on life. I hear and see so many women and men talk about how they want kids and after having them they wish they would have waited. I'm not saying you don't need a child; what I'm saying is that you should wait a while until the time is right."

Malia began to cry silently, but when will it be the right time? The only man I have ever loved was married to someone else, and other men are so intimidated that they're scared to approach me. I'm a successful, black woman with a heart of gold, willing to share my life with a good man."

Z interrupted, "Malia, what's your definition of a good man? What are the qualities he needs to possess?"

Malia thought for a while.

"I want a man who is sensitive, funny, honest, trustworthy, loyal, responsible and most of all spiritual."

Z interrupted, "Does this man have to be tall, dark and handsome?"

Malia continued, "Hopefully, but not necessarily. He has to make me laugh, someone like Lake. He's a real man, strong and loveable."

Z asked, "Have you ever met a man who met those qualifications?"

"There are a lot of men at the firm, but I don't want to go that route again, and I think it's wrong to attend church just to look for a man. Z, I'm ready to love again. I'm ready to share my life with someone who wants me for me."

"Malia, I feel your pain. That's why I feel you're not ready to adopt a child."

"Z, I know you mean well, but when talking to my God, I asked him if I was ready to love and he said it was time for me to love someone."

"Wait a second, when God talked to you, Malia, did he say he wanted you to adopt a child or did he say he wanted you to love again?"

Malia solemnly replied, "He said I was ready to love."

"Well there you have it; now you're ready to allow true love into your heart, by all means. I'm not saying you shouldn't continue with the adoption procedures, but don't close your heart to true to re-enter into your life, because if you do you will resent that child for the rest of its life. Malia, you are indeed one of my best friends, and I wouldn't tell you anything wrong. I love your too much to allow you to make such a grave mistake. There's someone out there for you; I feel it in my bones, and I said my bones, not my rectum."

Malia replied sniffing, "Thank you, Ms. Z. I love you, too. Now I have to get some sleep; I have a big day tomorrow."

"Okay, girl, do your thing. Momma gotta run to make; gotta go see a man about a horse." Z went online for some dick, first checking on the gay sex sites, then the gay sex phone lines. He found nothing, just a bunch of lonely as faggots using fakes pictures and fake ass stats.

"Oh, here's one; Bisexual, discreet, 6'3", 205, muscular, 45 inch chest, 32 waist, 10.5 inch dick thick and a top, this bitch is lying; he's probably a fat ass motherfucker, little dick with a 38 inch waist. Girl, get real."

Z headed out the door, not knowing whether he would do a club or the strip; he just knew he needed some and didn't know which would be quicker. Should he go to the club, be social and pick up or take his chances on the strip with all the other lonely motherfuckers. He decided he would take his chances at the club. "Maybe I will check the names in my little black book just for a backup," he thought. Z was still taking precautions when it came to JJ. He was hoping things would have been better between them, but he couldn't cry over spilled milk. It was still early, around one o'clock in the morning when he finally got to the club. It was crowded for a Thursday night, but the pickings were slim; every one was fat, old, a druggy, a sissy, a club queen or a drag queen.

"Damn, what's a girl to do?" Z whispered to himself. "I need some dick. I'm 'bout to go crazy. Damn, I need dick up in me."

Z was so deep in thought he didn't hear his cell phone ring. On the third ring he answered the phone.

"Hello, who is this?"

"This is Keith."

"Keith who?"

Z pretended not to know, but he knew his prayers had been answered. Keith was tall, thin, and dark and about nine inches and thick; just what Z needed. He was a professional brother by day but a freak at night. He was manager for a computer repair store; Z met him when he needed some more memory for his pc. Z had no idea about Keith's sexual orientation; he thought he was too nerdy to be a queer and to geeky to be a homo.

Z told him, "I want you; I was thinking maybe you needed some company."

Keith answered, "No, I don't. I'm cool."

Z barked, "Are you serious? No massage, no toe sucking none of the above?"

Z was begging now.

"How about some Haagen-Dazs ice cream? I got a taste for some ice cream," Z demanded.

"That's cool. I'll be over in twenty," Keith said, sounding rejuvenated.

"Make it thirty minutes; I need to take care of a little something something" Z purred as he started the engine.

"Bitch gonna get some good dick tonight."

He started singing, "Freak in the morning, Freak in the evening."

Z was home in 15 minutes flat. He jumped out the car, not noticing JJ was at his front porch ready to attack. Z was startled and didn't see JJ's right fist knock him across his left chin. The blow knocked Z to the ground. Within a split second, JJ was ready to attack again, this time with a switch blade.

He yelled, "You punk ass bitch!"

Z's first reaction was to play the game. "JJ, what are you doing? You know I still love you."

This gave Z enough time to gather his composure. He kicked JJ in the nuts, bringing him to his knees. JJ managed to cut Z on the thigh, ripping his jeans. Now they both were struggling for the ownership of the knife. JJ was bigger, but Z was quicker. He managed to bend JJ's wrist back, causing the knife to fly out of his hand. Z got on his feet first. Not realizing he was cut, he kicked JJ in the chin, hoping this would paralyze him enough to get the knife and get in the house or run back to the car. Z decided to fight one on one. His 5'8"frame was small but he was street smart.

"Come on, you crack head motherfucker, fight me like the punk that you are!"

JJ stood up and lunged at Z, causing them both to fall to the ground. JJ punched him in the jaw and tried to get up to get the knife.

Z yelled, that's all you got, you stupid bitch?"

Z grabbed him by the ankle and twisted it, making JJ fall to the ground again. A neighbor heard the screaming and called 911. Z continued to fight; he started boxing the shit out of JJ like a prize fighter. The fight was a sight to see; Z was dodging and ducking like Jill on Charlie's Angels. It became humorous after awhile; Z had beaten JJ to a pulp. The cops and Keith drove up at the same time. After detailed questioning from neighbors and Z, JJ was hauled away in handcuffs. Keith was more than willing to assist Z up the stairs and into the bedroom. He kept apologizing for not getting to the house sooner. Z kept insisting that things were fine; he'd just broken a nail. All he wanted was to be massaged, lubricated and laid. Keith pleased Z's every desire, always careful not to touch the face and the slightly damaged thigh. They fucked, they slept, they made love, they rested, they freaked, they caressed. Z got about four hours of sleep before it was time to hit the time clock. The sex with Keith was much needed; he was a sweet, normal guy, with a nice job and nice dick to boot. He was someone Z could mold into a hip hop wannabe. He was very intelligent, cultured and a homebody.

"Maybe this would work," Z fantasized.

"Hey man, I get off at 11:30. Feel like getting a bite to eat?" Z asked

"I would love to, Z, but I gotta pick up my girl from the airport at 10:30 and drop her off at home."

It was as if someone had just let the air out of Z's heart. He rebounded quickly.

"Okay, that's cool. Whenever you're ready to get down again, just holla at me."

Z was embarrassed, but he couldn't allow Keith see that part of him.

Z couldn't resist asking, "Why are you over here, man? To fuck my brains out or to get your dick sucked; which is it?"

Keith thought long and hard and then suddenly spoke.

"Because I've been digging you for over a year and you never gave me a chance. Ever since I fixed your pc a year ago, I've tried to get to you, but you put up a wall. Yeah we have good sex, but that's all you want from me, at least that's the impression you gave me."

"I was just testing you, and it takes time for me to get to know you. I didn't want to rush into anything," Z explained.

"That's perfectly understandable man, but I tried to get with you for over a year and all you wanted was sex, sex and more sex; that's the impression you gave me. So now you're saying you want more?" Keith asked.

"NO!" Z was now perplexed. "I want things the way they are, but if you have any extra time, we could spend it together. I know you have a lot on your plate."

"Actually, I don't," Keith explained.

"Well what about your girl?" Z interrupted.

"What about her?" Keith smirked.

"Never mind, it's all good. Hit me up tonight if you get some time."

Z was becoming agitated. His phone rang, breaking up the thick tension that was about to develop between him and Keith.

"Hello," Z demanded.

"Good afternoon, Z. This is Danielle. I need to talk to you about a pressing situation."

Z became immediately concern, ignoring Keith by turning his back on him.

Danielle continued, "What time are you going to work? I can take a late lunch, but I need to talk to you as soon as possible," she pleaded.

"I'm scheduled to be at work at 3:00. I really don't know where I'm going to be, but I'm quite sure I can get away, at least for a moment."

Danielle and Z shared several secrets and whenever she called, Z would drop everything just to listen and give her advice. He was the only male friend she trusted. Danielle, who preferred to be called Dani, was simply a beautiful woman with striking features, fair skin, long hair, keen nose, wonderful dimples and a perfect size 6 frame. Dani had secrets that only Z could understand or would even accept.

"I need some fertility pills but my doctor will not prescribe them to me," she began to explained.

Z stopped her.

"Don't say another word. I will see you in about an hour."

Z rushed Keith out the door and silently hoped that they would see each later on tonight. As Z backed out of the drive way his cell phone starting ringing.

"Who the fuck is this?" he asked himself.

He didn't recognize the number.

"Yeah?" he asked.

"May I speak to Mr. Zarius Washington?" a female voice asked.

"Sorry, Mr. Washington is in Zimbabwe. Can I help you with

something?" he responded sharply.

"When do you expect him back?" the voice continued.

"Neverary, the 32nd of 2008. If you give me your address I will have him send you a postcard," Z grunted.

The voice began to ask another question. Z cut her off again.

"I'll be damned; Mr. Washington is on the other line calling me now; if you hold I will let him know you're on the other line."

The female voice responded, "Okay."

Z powered the cell phone completely off as he sped down interstate 85.

"Wait on it, bitch!" Z laughed. There was so much Z was thinking about on his way to work; he felt something was not quite right today, his spirit was telling him something bad was going to happen to one of his dear friends or his cousin. He turned the cell phone back on and started calling his peeps. He started with Malia, casually asking her if everything was alright. She said it was. Malia was also feeling funny today, as if the world was complete filled with evil spirits. They decided to call Nikko together, but there was not answer at the house, cell phone or even at the office. They decided to call Lake and there was still no answer. They both began to worry. Malia decided to call Katie, and she, too, had been trying to call Nikko all day, but there was no answer. Malia immediately chose to head to the house. She informed Victoria to hold all calls until further notice. Z had to report to work for two reasons; he was the head nurse today and also to be there for Danielle. Malia promised she would call him as soon as she found something out.

Nikko was in severe pain; he had taken his 4 pills that morning right before his 10 mile bike ride. Anticipating a big lunch, he neglected to eat a good, balanced meal. The medication started to have a devastating effect on Nikko. The nausea began and was joined with fever, diarrhea, cold sweats, stomach pains and dry lips. These were just some of the side effects that Nikko would endure on a daily basis until his body could adjust to the cocktail drug. Lake found Nikko in the bed covered in vomit with a 103 degree fever. Lake was overwhelmed by the sight of Nikko in the bed. He immediately picked him up and tried to revive him. Nikko was weak and slightly disillusioned. Lake immediately started crying, but was determine to be strong for his lover. He grabbed some towels and started wiping up the vomit that covered the Duvet and sheets. Nikko tried to explain to him how his body was rejecting the medication. He felt nauseous after riding ten miles today. He tried to eat something but that's when the room started to spin and he had to crawl upstairs to the bedroom. He knew he needed to lie down, hoping that he would feel better. Lake did not want to hear anymore. He finally picked him up and carried him to the bathroom, then downstairs, then finally to the Navigator and off to the hospital. Sasha and Sebastian started barking because they didn't understand what was happening. Lake called Tevona to ask her if she could pick Kennedy up from school. He then called the school to inform them that the babysitter would be picking up Kennedy. Lake finally called Nikko's doctor to inform him of Nikko's current symptoms and status. Nikko's doctor was shocked; he couldn't understand why Nikko was having such severe side effects with the drugs that were prescribed. He was puzzled, but advised Lake he would notify the hospital of Nikko's arrival and also the symptoms; hopefully they would be able to see him immediately. Lake was thinking, "Here we go again." Lake was so frustrated with all the problems he and Nikko had to deal with. Sometimes Lake wanted to curse God and be done with his life. Lake knew God knew his heart. God knew his heart was genuine and pure. He had always been a God fearing man, a man who loved his God and had faith, despite his sexual orientation. His life was filled with love. But recently, he felt God has turned his back on him and his family; Nikki, Nikko's HIV status, Tré mom dying, Malia losing her baby, and now Nikko with his sickness. "How much am I supposed to bear," Lake thought. As his eyes began to fill up with tears, Lake started to recite certain scriptures that had always kept him strong and focused: Isaiah 40:29 and Psalms 59:17. As he continued to recite these scriptures, an overwhelming sense of soundness filled his soul. He suddenly became uncomfortable when Nikko asked him why he was crying.

Lake immediately responded, "I'm not crying baby, just got something in my eye. How do you feel?" he asked, changing the subject.

Nikko shrugged, "I'm better now, baby. I just need to know what's wrong with me."

"I called your doctor. He informed that he will call the hospital, so we shouldn't have a problem once we get there," Lake replied.

"Lake, I know you don't want to hear this but, if anything happens to me now or in the near future, I would want you to find someone else to continue to love you like I do; I wouldn't want you not to love again," Nikko whispered.

Lake responded, "We're here," completely ignoring Nikko's request. Lake jumped out of the SUV, grabbed a wheelchair and placed Nikko in the chair. Fortunately, there was a nurse and two attendants to expedite Nikko's admission, leaving Lake in the tiny waiting area to fill out paperwork. He refused to fill out certain paperwork especially the Advance Director's form. Lake started calling Z, Malia, Katie, Tevona, and his supervisor to inform them of the current situation.

Nikko was suddenly, poked, stuck, punched and yanked as he began to have series of tests. The doctors were determined to find out why his body was rejecting the medication after the first regiment. Nikko being anemic didn't help in diagnosing his current status. Nikko was drowsy and sluggish; he fell into deep thought, ignoring the screaming and yelling from across the hallway. The hectic surroundings made Nikko fall into a deep sleep where he had sweet dreams of this family; his father, mother, Nikki and his only brother, Gramyko. Gramyko had been in and out the insane asylum ever since their parents were murdered. Visions of the family moments filled his spirit. The family gatherings were so heartfelt, when they all were together, sharing the birthdays, Thanksgivings, Christmas, family reunions, fun days in the park, family trips, family cruises and school dances. Nikko always felt that Gramyko's, who was three years younger than Nikki and he was their mother's favorite. Gramyko, Nikki and their mother would be in the bedroom laughing and talking about heavens knows what. Sometimes, Gramyko would have Nikki and their mother trying on clothes or making homemade dresses for them. He had always wanted to be a famous designer from his early years. He even started making dresses for most of the debutantes in high school. Sometimes this would frustrate Nikko because he wanted his little brother to be more athletic like he and his father were. Nikko played baseball and basketball in high school, Gramyko was in drama and homemaker class. Nikko was the junior year class president and school president his senior year. Gramyko was focused on dance and fashion. Gramyko designed Nikki's prom dress and also her homecoming queen gown. Nikko resented him so much because he could see how upset it mad their father. Mr. Grey was the principal for the high school and his mother was a paralegal. It was difficult at the time for Mr. Grey to discipline his son at school and at home because Gramyko was always in a fight over someone calling him a faggot.

On that one fateful day, when Nikko and Nikki arrived home to find their parents murdered, Gramyko was there, hidden in the basement covered with blood. He gripped the scissors that held his mother and father's blood. Gramyko stopped talking that same day; he hasn't uttered a word since. Nikko tried his best not to think about his brother or his existence. Nikki, on occasion, would go visit and take Kennedy with her. Nikko knew that Nikki never blamed her youngest brother of the death of their parents but Nikko did. After they sentenced Gramyko to life in the asylum, his two siblings decided to transfer to a college here in Atlanta, Georgia. Nikko decided to be transferred Morehouse and Nikki decided on Morris Brown but later attended Spelman. This is where they found the new friends who would take their problems away from the tragedy of Poukeepsie, New York.

Lake had been shaking Nikko for about thirty seconds when he realized that he was in a recovery room. Lake told him it was time to go; the tests had come back and everything looked fine. They both were relieved and were ready to go home. When they entered the waiting room, they saw Malia, Katie, Kennedy and Tevona. Kennedy ran up to her uncle. Seeing him wheeled out in the wheelchair had puzzled her, but she didn't care; she hadn't seen her uncle in over twenty-four hours. He was whisked away to the homecoming celebration; Z had prepared another fabulous welcoming party with hats, whistles paper Mache and confetti. Z had managed to recreate Nikko and Lake's home into the scene from the Lion King. It was like something from the Wizard of Oz with a little touch of Queer Eye for the Straight Guy. Nikko was surprised to find that Malia had asked Victoria to surprise him with two welcome home baskets; one with aroma therapy candles, soap, cologne, lotions, incense and Janet Jackson's new CD and Beyonce's sophomore CD. The other basket was full of exotic fruit. Everything was simple and wonderful. Friends had come to visit; even Keisha and Tré had dropped over. Nikko felt fine, but Lake insisted that Nikko needed to get some rest and everyone agreed. Lake wanted to make sure his two favorite people were upstairs and resting properly. Lake took the responsibility of having to dress Kennedy to bed, while Nikko took a quick shower. Entering the master bedroom at the same time, Nikko from the bathroom and Lake from the hallway, they both grabbed each other with saying a word and hugged for dear life. Lake once again broke the timeless moment by suggesting to give Nikko a quick massage. Nikko hesitated at first but eventually gave in to Lake's request. Nikko burst open the welcome home basket with it assorted lotions and fragrances. Lake opened the seal of the bottle of lotion and began rubbing it all over Nikko's body. Nikko felt squeamish as Lake rubbed the unusual smelling lotion all over his body. He secretly knew the touch of his body would generate sudden erections for him and Lake. He could faintly hear Z downstairs chewing bubble gum and telling lies.

He finally whispered to Lake, "Please don't try anything; we have a house full of guests downstairs."

Lake retaliated jokingly, "We've done it before. Can't we do a quickie? I need it."

Nikko responded, "Stop, Lake before we get caught in our own house."

"Okay, but you owe me one," Lake laughed. "Oh shit, I forgot the dogs; they're still at the kennel. I guess I can pick them up in the morning," Lake added.

Suddenly Nikko felt at ease; the massage was overwhelming and totally relaxing. Lake finished with his deep tissue massage, and then tucked Nikko neatly in bed. Nikko suddenly became very drowsy and lifeless again. Lake kissed him on his forehead and cut off the lamp on the nightstand.

It was getting late, but Z was not ready to leave; however, Malia started cleaning up, hoping Z would get the hint. Z was in the living room loudly talking to some of the neighbors who decided to pay a visit at the last minute.

"I don't think my lifestyle is different from anyone else's," Z was now yelling. "I've been attracted to men ever since I could remember; I've been sleeping with men ever since I was twelve. I believe we all have gay genes and I feel those genes stay dormant until they are triggered. That's why some motherfuckers don't start experimenting until they are in college, married or on social security," Z yelled again.

Z continued, "Some gays, particularly men, emulate a female role model; others emulate the lifestyle. For example, I emulated my mother, and when I got older I adored the famous drag queens Lady Monroe, Machon Black and La Toya St. James. I studied their walk, their talk and the way they dressed and I felt my calling in life was to be a famous drag queen. Somehow I got caught up with helping people; my life is doomed. I could have been the most famous drag queen, even better than that tall bitch, RuPaul, but instead I became the best nurse on this side of the Mississippi."

Everett had to get his two cents in.

"Girl, that's right. I knew I was Donna Summers when I was growing up."

"More like Eartha Kitt, you butch bunny bitch," Z called out. Malia felt this was her moment to ask her gay friend a question she'd wanted to ask for years.

"Z, how do you think God feels about homosexuality?"

Z answered, "He don't like it. All of us sitting here are his children, but we all sin; me having sex with guys is a sin, and I sincerely do believe that, despite what some evangelists may have you believe. It's in the Bible and I do read and believe in the Bible. I do pray, but I'm wise enough to pray for forgiveness. Me getting fucked in my ass is no different from you getting fucked in your pussy; it's all a sin. Next question," Z demanded.

"I have a question," a voice from the back sounded. "Why does size matter to gay men?" Z cleared his thoughts before saying, "Why does it matter to women? We all are built differently inside and out. My rectum is a little deeper then most men and in order to be satisfied I must come with the tools so I can feel it. Some women, like men, don't and can't take a big dick, but that's them not me and I'm not ashamed of my actions or my desires. Next!"

Tré broke his silence, "Do you consider yourself a whore?"

Without turning to face his cousin, Z proceeded to answer his question.

"I don't consider myself anything; do you consider me a whore? I love sex, I love sex with men, I love men fucking me, but I always decide when and how I want it. A straight man loves women. He loves fucking women and women love to be fucked by him. He tells them that he may or may not have more then one woman; is he a whore? He's honest, direct and loves women. Is he a whore?"

Z answered the question without looking at his cousin.

He continued, "I'm not fake, confused, disillusioned, sexually insecure or fucked up in the head, unlike a lot of men I have come across."

Katie needed to break the sudden tension.

"Z," she asked. "Can a woman tell whether a guy is bisexual?"

"You ask him while looking straight into his eyes; be stern and direct and don't only ask him that question, ask him a series of questions; how's the relationship with his mom, is he dating someone, does he have any kids, is he gay, is he bisexual; things like that."

"I have a question for you," sounded a voice from across the room. "There was a big ordeal when a female caller called the radio station and indicated that her husband was gay because he allowed her to stick a dildo up his rectum and it was obvious that he truly enjoyed it."

Z couldn't wait to answer this question being that he was heated when he heard the same statement on the radio.

"Common sense," he answered. "Your rectum has nerve endings; if you massage those nerve endings they become sensitive and soothing. Apparently she eases it up his ass, widening his rectum, by doing this he was able to relax and take the dildo. Most men don't like anyone playing with their ass due to the fact that it's the dookey shoot. It is meant for shit come out, and nothing to go in, and most heterosexuals don't even like to clean their asses properly. I'm glad I'm not a straight man, they are nasty; no offense to the straight men in the room," Z started to snicker.

"Okay class, that's all for homo sex 101. Class is over," Malia blurted.

Lake seconded that.

"I have to go back to the precinct, fellas. Now, unless you cats wanna take care of my angels while I work, you're welcome to go," Lake commanded.

Z started giving orders as everyone proceeded to the foyer.

"If anyone care for more sour apple martinis we can head over to Malia's house for a nightcap," Z sounded.

Malia murmured, "You bitch."

Everyone could hear Z singing, "I know you are but what am I?"

Everyone was headed to their cars when Victoria informed Lake that she accidentally left her purse on the kitchen table. Lake and Victoria rushed back into the house. Victoria ran to the kitchen, unlocked the back door and picked up her purse. Lake thought that was strange but didn't have time to ponder it. He was in a rush to get to work knowing that Tonya had some new disturbing evidence pertaining to Nikki's death. He purposely didn't want to annoy Nikko with the information; his goal was to make Nikko as comfortable as possible. Lake contemplated going to get his HIV test and couldn't imagine what the results would be.

Lake finally got to the precinct and once again he headed down to the lab where Tonya was busy discovering evidence in support of her theory about Nikki's death. Tonya's theory was right on point.

"There was a female intruder who entered the house after the original assailant," she explained to Lake. "The fibers from the hair samples were a real and faux. The hair samples indicate that the hair was fused together. I called my local hair stylish tonight and she told me that hair fusion is very expensive; that indicated that this person spent about three thousand dollars. The hair looks very real and convincing. There was skin under Nikki's fingernails, and it was from a female. What is very strange is that the DNA from the male and female assailants indicated that they were related even siblings."

This information was overwhelming for Lake, but he continued to listen with intensity, taking mental notes.

Tonya continued, "I can only assume that this person knew the layout of Nikki's house. They didn't take, touch, or break anything in the house; it looks like this was a premeditated rape or intrusion that suddenly became violent."

Lake excused himself and stumble back up to the fifth floor, he decided to take the stairs instead of the elevator; he needed to be alone. He finally got to his desk and started running over his mental notes of all Tonya had conveyed. He needed to research more, going back over the evidence with a fine-toothed comb. He remembered the day he last saw Nikki alive and well. She was all decked out in her brother's baseball cap, oversized tee shirt and jeans, 1 carat earrings and custom made bracelet. Lake began to look puzzled; he looked in the database for information pertaining to Nikki's clothes and jewelry, but there was no mention of her bracelet. He suddenly became overwhelmed with anxiety; there was no evidence of a bracelet filed. He called down to the third floor to have the clerk research the crime information again; he needed to know did they found a bracelet of any kind in the report. He scratched his scalp. He reluctantly called Nikko. The phone rang once before Lake decided to hang it up, hoping this matter could wait until morning; he didn't want to alarm Nikko any further.

Z got a call from Keith, begging to see him tonight. Z reluctantly agreed.

"What do you want to see me for?" Z became very defensive.

Keith began his speech.

"I really don't know; you're obnoxious, irritating, bitchy, flamboyant, rude, and very annoying. You want things your way, man. You don't want to compromise for any reason and all you want is sex. I feel you need someone to love you, and love you right. I'm not talking about having a big dick and fucking you until you come. I'm talking about movies, dinners, spending quality spiritual time together, taking trips, sharing your heart with someone, opening up with your deepest fears and explaining your regrets. I know you act this way because you feel you have to. You have a lot of anger inside, playa. You don't know how to love because no one has ever loved you. They may have fucked you real good, but other than that, they used you. You're the type of brother who gets booty calls late at night because your sex and tricks are the bomb, but those brothers ain't trying to fall in love with you nor do they want you to fall in love with them. They just want a good nut and you're the person who's most available. What I'm asking of you, Zarius Washington, is to allow me to love you, man. That's all I'm asking."

There was silence on the phone; that meant Z was listening.

"The first thing I want is to drive you up to Château Élan tonight, get up in the morning and drive to Savannah and spend a couple of days together. I want it to be just me and you; no phone, no friends, no job, no distractions, just you and me. I don't want you to pack anything but a toothbrush, deodorant and some mouthwash." Keith started to grin. "I don't like kissing a brother with bad breath or smelling a brother's arms. What's it gonna be, little man? I'm your knight in shining armor; let me take you into the sunset and be your man," Keith asked slowly.

There was a long silence before Z finally responded. "I have to think about it and call you later. Z hung up the phone. Keith, instantly broken hearted, was going to continue his travel to Chateau Élan, with or without Z; he was determined to have an evening of bliss.

CHAPTER 39

The Confusion

Tré decided to take Keisha to Centennial Park. There was something that was aching at his heart that needed to share with her. Keisha had always anticipated a re-engagement of some sort with Tré, but as Junior got older those hopes seemed to fade painfully. They arrived at Centennial Park. The moon, the stars and the sound of endless laughter were joined by beautiful colors of water shooting from the underground fountain. They had managed to take Junior home, put him to bed and leave without any flack from Keisha's younger brothers. Tré and Keisha sat on one of the benches for hours until Keisha reminded Tré that she had to get up early in the morning to take the boys to school. Tré put his hands around Keisha's waist as they stood up.

"Keisha, I have to tell you something that has been on my heart for years. I wanted to apologize for not being the father you wanted me to be for Little Man. I want to apologize for not providing you with all the dreams you deserve. I want to apologize for getting cold feet when the word marriage came around. I'm a man now, not a fucked up (nigga) who don't have any direction in life. I'm secure enough now baby to understand that my life is short and I gotta be the real (nigga) I'm supposed to be. I think someone was watching over me when I was selling drugs, hanging in a gang, getting in street fights and robbing faggots for pleasure. Keisha, I was running from insecurities, my demons that continued to haunt me ever since childhood."

Tré looked deep into Keisha's eyes and said, "Keisha, I'm bisexual."

Tears started to pour from Trés face; the pain pierced his heart, but his soul was uplifted. "Keisha, this is the hardest thing I ever had to do; I'm confused and ashamed of being a fuck up. It's something I've hated all my life and something I tried to deny. You have always been in my life and my heart. Baby, there were times when I wanted to shoot the pain in my heart; I wanted to kill the feeling by killing myself. I cried almost every night begging God to take this taste out of my heart."

Tré's tears became heavier as Keisha held his face and kissed his tears.

"Tré, you will always be the father of my child, you will always be my first love, you will be the man of my dreams; no one could or would take your place in my life and in my heart. I feel our spirits are meant to be together, and deep in my heart I felt your pain; I felt you wanted to be with me but something was holding you back. Tré, I know you so well; I knew something was there, but until the trip to New York for Lincoln, I hadn't put the puzzle together. I saw the sparkle in his eyes when he saw you. His heart just lifted with joy. It was at that time I knew you loved him, because that's the way you make me feel every time I look at you. This is the way I will continue to feel about you because true love never dies, so stop crying; the worst is over and the best is yet to come." Keisha ended.

Z called Malia on the cell phone.

"Girl, I gotta go. I gotta go see a man about a horse," Z cried with laughter.

"What do you mean, Zarius?" she replied.

"I think Keith just proposed to me girl. He told me to clean up my act or else; that's how we propose in Homoville," Z continued.

Malia shouted, "What am I suppose to do with a dozen people coming to my house for martinis, Z?"

"Girl do what I would do; ditch them girls. Don't go home; make a detour. They will understand, they always do," Z suggested.

Malia was so furious she hung up the cell and cut it off. She murmured, "I'll get you, my little pretty. Oh shit, I'm using gay lingo." She smiled as she decided to head to the liquor store before it closed.

Seven minutes later, she was at the corner liquor store trying to hurry and purchase some more gin, rum and vodka for her unwanted guests. Rushing to get the much needed items, she didn't even realize a gorgeous hunk standing behind her in line. Malia's presence took his breath away. He was admiring her stature, legs, lips, hair and especially her smell. It was drawing him straight to her. Malia's total of Goose gin, Bacardi rum and Sky vodka came up to $92.00. Malia realized she left her purse in the car and told the clerk she would be right back. The handsome man waiting in line thought this would be his golden opportunity; he purchased her liquor without a second to spare when Malia rushed back in the store with her credit card. The clerk smiled as the man handed Malia the bags containing her new purchased items. Malia looked dumbfounded. The man introduced himself.

"I'm Edward Jackson. I didn't mean any disrespect, but I couldn't resist myself. I was enthralled by your presence and had to do something to get your attention."

"Thank you so much. I'm Somalia, but everyone calls me Malia," she blushed.

Ed was tall, 6'2", 215 pounds, light brown complexion, salt and pepper hair on his side burns and the most beautiful eyes you could see on a man. They were sparkling orange-colored eyes and his lips were the ripest lips Malia had ever seen on a man. They both stood there in the entrance of the liquor store for about thirty seconds without uttering a sound. Ed started the conversation.

"If I'm not being too forward, will I ever get the chance to be invited to your party?" Malia was taken with his voice; she immediately fell into a trance.

"Oh, I'm sorry; I was just taken with your voice. Where are you from?" she asked.

He answered, "I lived in Belize until I was fourteen then my family moved to upper state New York."

"Then what's brings you here to little town of Dunwoody?" she asked.

"Well, my wife passed about two years ago and I felt it was time for me and my daughter to get a new lease on life. There were so many memories in New York, all good of course, but change is good; and besides, my daughter is six and I wanted her to have a southern upbringing, not one by the hustle and fast pace living in New York. I just moved here about three months ago and so far the scenery has been more than remarkable. I'm an investment banker. I asked for a transfer about nine months ago and I finally got it. I think I'm gonna love it here." He smiled and winked as he finished his summation.

"Oh, I'm sorry, I don't have any cash, but I need to pay you back for purchasing my items. I need to hurry home; I have some guests coming over and I hear my phone buzzing in my purse," she explained.

"Well, if you invite me over we can call it even; I would love a night cap," he suggested. "I would love to, but I don't allow strangers in my home and besides, don't you have to get back home to your daughter?" Malia questioned.

Ed took out his driver's license and dropped it in Malia's bag.

"Now I'm not a stranger. I just gave you my license; what stranger would do that? You got all the information you would ever need to know about me and I'm positive the rest is yet to come," Ed explained as he gave Malia the biggest smile, showing his pearly whites and one dimple.

Malia just melted.

"Okay, you pulled my finger. Follow me and try to keep up; I drive fast."

Z called Keith back.

"Where are you?" Z asked.

"I'm at the Élan willing and waiting to be with you and you're not around. Is this how you gonna start our honeymoon?"

"I'll be there in 15 minutes, baby."

Keith smiled. Z hung up the phone again and dialed Nikko's number. The phone rang four times before Nikko finally picked up.

"Hey, hoe!" Z snickered.

"Who is this?" Nikko asked, still drowsy from the new medication and the earlier massage.

"This is your friendly neighborhood Spider Girl. I didn't want anything just wanted to tell you that I'm going on my honeymoon. I'm on my way to Château Élan to consummate my marriage to Keith what's his name… Oh shit, I don't know the motherfuckers last name! Damn, that means I don't know my last name; what's a girl to do?" Z screamed. "What time is it?" Nikko asked.

"Sissy, I just called to tell you that. I'll bet we will get married before you and Lake. Smooches, I love you," Z blurted.

"I love you, too," Nikko murmured.

It was 12:45 when Nikko's phone rang again. This time it was Malia.

"Hellllllo," Nikko whispered.

Malia was elated. "Nikko, I'm sorry. I thought I was calling Lake on his cell. I didn't mean to wake you, baby boy. Nikko, I met a man. He is gorgeous; he's following me now to the house for a cocktail with the rest of the crew. I need to call Lake and ask him to run his I.D. Nikko, he really is fine. I love you. See you tomorrow."

"Good bye, Malia."

Twenty minutes later the phone rung again, it was Lake.

"Hey baby, you up?" Lake asked.

"Yeah, baby, I'm up. I'm so tired, Lake, but every time I get comfortable, the phone rings. Z called about getting married to Keith and Malia called telling me about a man she just met." Nikko explained.

Lake apologized for also calling late, but he informed Nikko they needed to talk once he got home. He continued to tell Nikko it was about Nikki. Lake went on to say who he thought the other killer was and how they were going to arrest her. I'll be home in about two hours; gotta make sure that we have an arrest warrant. Baby, lock all the doors and I'll see you shortly. I love you, baby," Lake ended.

"Love you, too, big head. See you soon," Nikko responded.

CHAPTER 40

The Nightmare

Nikko lazily dragged himself to the bathroom to take sleeping pills; he just needed to sleep. Nikko checked on Kennedy before heading back to bed. He forgot all about checking the doors. He just wanted to snuggle in his bed and fall into a deep sleep.

Nikko fell into a deep dream. His vision was blurred but he managed to see all his loves one downstairs in the living room. Z was there with Keith, Malia with Ed, Tré with Lincoln, Keisha and Junior and there was an older looking Kennedy. She was taller and her hair was longer with beautiful long locks. Kennedy even had breasts; she appeared to have been twelve or thirteen. They all were sitting around talking about something he really couldn't figure out. Z was in rare form; he was non-animated and seemed to be serious. He talked about finally living his dream, finding a man who loves him for him, how he really started loving himself and not what he thought he should be. Z talked about the marriage with Keith; how they got married in San Francisco and how it was the best thing he had ever done in his life. He now was complete. Z ended his conversation by saying how his dreams did come true, whether he wanted them or not. "Dreams are snippets of reality and us giving up the opportunity to manipulate our fears in order to captivate our reality." Z suddenly started to cry.

Then it was Malia's turn. "I always thought my dreams were impossible to achieve. I'm a black woman who always wanted to be loved. I've sacrificed a lot to be independent. I fell in love with a married man and I disrespected the love that God had for me. I cursed Drayton for making me bitter and spiritually dead. I had to find love and peace with God before he would bless me with a man of my dreams, a step-daughter and a beautiful daughter."

Malia's daughter was the spitting image of her mother, but she had father's eyes and his one dimple. Nikko's dream was so real; it became less blurry and more realistic. Tré stood up as he started to explain his sexual freedom. He had never felt better about himself; the cries of self hatred were no more. The thoughts of suicide had finally faded. The tears that were shed in darkness were now tears of joy and happiness. Tré explained that he was still a man, a devoted father, a street wise thug and not afraid of life and what it had to offer. He had once dreamed of ending his life because of his confused state of sexual unrest. Now his dreams are possible to share, to hold and to live.

Nikko started to wake up from the dream; it had become too painful to see his friends. He couldn't understand why he wasn't there, and he was wondering why everyone seemed despondent and upset. Nikko thought to himself that something was dreadfully wrong with this dream, but he refused to wake up when Kennedy started to speak.

"Dreams are your unconscious voices that talk to your spirit," she began. "Growing up without a mother is not a dream, but a nightmare. Having someone to take the place of my mother was a dream. Living my life without really knowing my mother is a cruel trick God has played on my life, but understanding that God is a God of love made me love him even more. I don't know why my mother was raped and murdered, but her life continues to grow inside of me as I continue to live my life inside of her. I know that impossible dreams are a never ending cycle of confusion and despair, but if I live and love long enough, I'll understand love is full of dreams and dreams are possible to achieve, not impossible to live."

Nikko's dream flashed into another time and place; a place where Lake was standing over a hospital bed. He stood looking at someone who was sickly and covered with sores. At first the person was indescribable, but as the dream became clearer, he realized he was looking at himself. His hair was thin, his eyes were sunken, and the bones were visible in his face. Lake was cussing God for allowing Nikko to suffer. He cursed himself for having a one night stand and having it unprotected. He was cursing the world and himself for being a (fucking) coward and not coming forth to tell Nikko in the beginning that he had picked up a male prostitute one night for a well-needed -(oral sex job). He hated his life and at that moment, wished he could trade places with Nikko. The suffering was ending with tears and despair. Nikko was actually crying for his dreams, crying about knowing the truth of contracting the AIDS virus and crying because Lake was not honest and faithful. It was time to wake up from this nightmare, but someone had closed the doors of reality. He couldn't wake up; he just lay there as flashes of his life came and went. Pictures of his family, his mother, father, brother and Nikki rushed through his imagination. Memories of the first time he met Tré, Z and Malia, his first kiss, his first time with a man and the only time with a woman and the first time he held his niece. Nikko started to scream, but his cries were suffocated by the nightmare of flashes that were yet to come. He was now looking at the first and only time he made love to Tré, how it just happened. The dark room in the men's dorm was scented with the stale aroma of a man's musk; the touching, feeling, the pulsating of bodies rubbing together. Tré just lay there as Nikko performed most unforgettable fellatio on Tré. The curiosity that had plagued Tré was no longer. He couldn't believe he was getting a blow job from a man; it felt so good and so right. Nikko tried his best to forget that moment until it rushed into his dreams. Nikko felt his life was running out of time; he heard Nikki calling his name, begging for him to join her. He heard Lake whispering in his ear to wake up. The sound of Nikki's voice was now accompanied by his parents and younger brothers. The voices were now overshadowed by Lake, Kennedy, Zarius, Malia, Tré, and someone saying, "Wake up, Nikko! It's only a dream." Lake was shaking Nikko for dear life. Finally, Nikko came back to civilization, gasping for air; one of the pills was lodged in his windpipe, stopping his breathing. Nikko was flushed from the lack of oxygen. Kennedy was rubbing the back of her uncle's hand and trying to give him some water. Nikko slowly sipped the water. He could taste the chalky residue of the pills in his mouth and throat. Lake was all teary eyed with smiles.

"It's gonna be alright," Lake whispered.

Nikko finally smiled and said, "I know."

CHAPTER 41

The Beginning of the End

Z didn't want the weekend to end. He didn't know whether he would have a job or not once he got back from his sultry weekend with Keith. They played tennis, went horseback riding, 5 mile hiking and even mountain climbing. Z was exhausted and all he wanted was some rest and a cocktail; Jack Daniels would have done just fine, if only Keith hadn't drunk it all. Z noticed that Keith would drink a fifth of rum, vodka, gin, whisky and even brandy all in one night, then afterwards his lazy drunk ass would not want to fuck, just sleep his tired drunk ass away. The tell-tale signs were becoming more evident as the weekend went by. Tonight was different, though; as Keith finished the last of Jack, he told Z to go take a shower while he got everything ready for the night. Z was so happy he was finally gonna get him some. Z needed some dick; he'd been craving for some since he saw the dick that was on the horse he was riding earlier. He ran to the bathroom, turned on the shower and jumped in, singing "pussy don't let me down tonight" at the top of his lungs over and over again as he pulled out his little waterproof bag with his douche bottle. Z proceeded with his regiment until he was fresh and clean and finished up his shower as he whistled the song Luck be a Lady Tonight. Keith finally slipped back in the room with a small gold-colored ring box. Keith was obviously drunk when he presented the box to Z.

"Zarius, I know we haven't been together for long, but I fell in love with you the first time I met you, and finally I get a chance to prove it. Z this is a token of how much I love you and want to be with you."

Keith eventually opened the box displaying the one carat diamond ring with three stones clustered in white gold. Z was mesmerized as he slipped the ring on his finger.

"It's gorgeous," Z said. He continued the conversation for about five minutes when he heard snoring. "I'll be damned. Tired as motherfucker went to sleep on my ass again."

Z picked up the phone, called the operator of the hotel and asked, "What's the closest gay bar in the city of Savannah?"

The clerk did not respond. Instead she transferred Z to the front desk.

"J W Savannah, how may I assist your call?"

Z blurted out, "I need to know where the nearest black gay club is in this city."

"One moment, please."

The clerk immediately put him on hold and Z became instantly furious. He hung up the phone, took the elevator to the main lobby and rushed up to the front desk in his pink bedroom slippers, do-rag on his head and a Wonder Woman bath robe which he made himself. The clerks at the front desk saw him coming and tried to escape like trapped mice in a cage.

There were about fifty guests in the lobby when Z shouted, "Somebody better tell where the nearest black gay club is in this city, where there are big dicks men who cheat on their fucking wives!"

The entire lobby was completely silent as the front desk manager, along with a hotel security guard, was now approaching Z. They were professional, conservative and had looks of urgency on their faces.

"Sir, could you follow us in concierge's office please?"

Z was about to go off again until he noticed the security guard winked at him. The entire lobby was silent until the door to the concierge's office slammed shut. The manager began first.

"Mr. Washington," he started, "Miss Thing, girl you got a mouth on you child." He and the guard started laughing, leaving Z more confused then ever.

"Child, the club don't start jumping until midnight; we're going as soon as we can get out these monkey clothes," the guard said.

The manager interrupted, "I need to shit, shower and change and I'm off to the club, bitch. I gotta get my drink on."

"Bitch, where you get that fucking rock from, hoe?" the security guard asked, his eyes growing bigger.

"My drunk-ass husband just proposed to me tonight and the motherfucker got drunk and passed out. I'm going to the club and find me some dick; fuck that motherfucker."

"Girl, don't fret none. You can hang with us. Here's my card. Call me at 11:30; we should be ready by then." Z grabbed the card and gave his smooches as he walked out the door. Some guests were still in the lobby staring at Z as he pushed the button for the elevator. Z couldn't wait to get the night started. He felt like eleven thirty was not going to come soon enough. Z realized he didn't have anything to wear; he needed something to make a bold statement. Something to say, "I'm here!" Z decided on the low rider jeans with the faux fur on the buttocks and the inseams of the jeans and a navy blue low cropped summer sweater that showed his navel ring. He accessorized the get up with diamond-studded ear rings, accompanied with a choker with a fake diamond-studded heart. "Perfect!" he murmured as Keith laid butt-ass naked on the floor, holding his dick and scratching his nuts. Z stepped over him and hesitated, thinking about stepping on Keith's dick. "I'll see you later, darling. Going to the market to get some milk," Z whispered.

Z met his party downstairs in the employee's parking lot as planned. Charles, the security guard, was still winking at Z and Alex, the front desk manager, was enthralled by Z's attire.

Alex screamed, "Bitch, you better work! Where in the fuck did you get those jeans, ho?" Z replied, "I had them made by a designer in Atlanta. I can give you his number; if you give him the jeans he will design the fur anyway you want. He don't believe in real fur so he only uses fake shit, but the boy is bad as hell."

Charles interrupted, "Man, you look good enough to eat."

"Well, you may get a toothache 'because this pussy is sweet; too sweet for you."

Z was saved by the ringing of his cell phone. It displayed Nikko's name.

Z answered, "What's up?"

"Z, this is Lake. When are you coming back to Atlanta?"

"I'll be back tomorrow night. Why?"

"Well you know Revlon is giving a sneak preview of Nikki's commercial, and Nikko wants everyone to be there. It will be at 3:00 tomorrow," Lake explained.

Z interrupted, "Say no more, I'll be there. By the way, how's Nikko doing? I've been thinking and praying for him."

Lake interrupted him. "We'll talk about that tomorrow once you get here; can't talk about it right now."

Z picked up on his hesitation. "Gotcha. We'll talk tomorrow. Smooches! Give Nikko and K a kiss for me," Z asked.

"Will do; see you tomorrow," Lake replied.

Z thought about Nikko for a minute before he realized that they were in front of this hole in the wall bar. There were plenty of cars outside but it was no Lyon's Den or Tracks. Z became instantly disgusted and was about to cuss his new found friends out until he got a glimpse of two fine, beautiful, dark, handsome men who were parking their cars. Z murmured, "I'm 'bout to go get my freak on."

Once in the club, to Z's amazement, it was wall to wall mother fucking men: tall ones, shorts ones, fat ones, light ones, dark ones, it was a meat buffet. Z also noticed the beautiful women. There were straight women, gay women, butch women, feminine women; Z thought, "This club is the One."

Z asked Charles, "What are they having tonight? Why are there so many fish here?" "There's a 30 minute drag show, then a male strip show and then they open the dance floor."

Z screamed, "A drag show? Why didn't you tell me? I always keep a wig in my bag!" Charles burst out laughing. Z retaliated by spilling his cocktail in Charles' lap.

"Sorry, sweetie. Here, take this twenty and go get us another cocktail," Z said apologetically. This gave Z the opportunity to escape and mingle. His mouth became moist as he looked at every man in the club. He noticed there were a lot of military men; he started wondering how military men performed in bed. Suddenly Z's mouth flew open; he noticed a familiar face tonguing someone he didn't recognize.

"What the hell is this?" Z commanded. It was Keisha in the corner kissing a tall, light skinned, broad shouldered woman with short cropped jet black hair. Without hesitation, Keisha introduced Gina to Z. Z grabbed his heart and held on to the wall as he knees began to buckle.

"Bitch! I didn't know," Z whispered.

Keisha grinned at Gina.

"I guess he didn't know."

They both burst out laughing at Z's reaction.

Malia and her new beau, Ed, were lying in front of the fireplace, listening to music and drinking Merlot. They were spending a quiet evening together after running with Ed's friends from work. They'd had a good time at his corporate picnic playing tug of war, three legged race, potato sack race and a game of horseshoes. It was indeed a blessing to lie on the floor after a day of soreness and pain. Ed mustered up enough strength to give a Malia a much needed massage. The deep muscle massage came with a very interesting conversation. Ed wanted to know Malia's views on marriage, God, spirituality, children, politics, poverty, taxes, divorce, infidelity, honesty, loyalty, trust, dreams, goals, death and love. Malia and Ed seemed to have a lot in common. They talked as if they were old friends or old lovers. Malia threw a monkey wrench in their conversation when she asked Ed have if he'd ever had a same sex experience. His response was typical but his summation was all but typical. Ed admitted that he'd had two same sex encounters: The first when he was in college with another football player; it started with the guys just hanging out at the crib after football practice. Someone put on a sex video with some black guys banging the hell out of this white woman. The men in the video had huge horse dicks, but the woman was taking it all; one in the pussy, one in the rectum and one in the mouth. All three men had to have at least ten inches of mouth watering dick. Ed continued telling the story while Malia listened in amazement.

"There were about five of us and the video made us hot and horny very fast. One of the guys went to the bathroom, I guess to bust a nut, and the other two guys somehow ended up in the bedroom, so me and Dre watched the flick until I had to pull my dick out and stroke it. The porno made me so horny; I had to bust a nut. Malia, excuse me for my vulgar language," Ed apologized. He continued, "I closed my eyes and lay back as the stroking sent me to another place and time. Suddenly I felt a warm mouth swallow my dick. I was shocked that it was Dre, blowing me off with no shame. Malia, I will not lie, that was the best blow job I have ever had. For some reason I didn't push him off or kick his ass. I just sat in the chair, dumbfounded and embarrassed, hoping that the other guys wouldn't come in the room and catch us in the act. After about ten minutes of straight sucking, I nervously moaned and told him I was coming and tried to push his head and mouth from my dick, but he was like a human suction cup; he did not let up. He held me down in the chair and made me come in his mouth. I was so embarrassed. He sucked and licked me dry. He then went back to the chair he was sitting in, finished his beer, rolled over and went to sleep. I just sat there limp and confused."

Malia listened to his every word. "What was your other encounter?" she asked.

Ed hesitated at first, and then said, "This is very embarrassing, but here goes. I met this girl, a beautiful girl from New York. She was tall, fair skinned, had long flowing brown hair, simply gorgeous. I was working in the bank, doing an internship, I believe, and I think I was opening a checking account. She had some difficulty with her ID and social security numbers; they didn't pan out with Equifax Identification Verification System, but I didn't care. I was so smitten with her looks that I had to ask her out. I reluctantly opened the account just to get her number and address. We went out a couple of times for dinner, movies, plays, walks in the park and then finally one night on top of the roof of my building with a blanket, candles and wine. I started licking her breast, her navel and was almost to her vagina, when she stopped me. She whispered, 'Please be gentle, I'm a virgin,' (so I was)?. We made love for hours; to me, it was so special and very natural. Afterwards she whispered again, 'I got something to tell you.'

I blurted, 'what you're a man?'

She replied, 'Yes. I'm just kidding. I just want you to know I like you a lot E and I hope you like me, too. I really don't get down until I'm sure the man is feeling and loving me.' I kissed her on her forehead and told her that I would never disappoint her. We kicked it for about another month when one morning at work security called me to discuss a particular account I had opened. I looked at the paper work and saw my girl's face, but a man's name was on the paper work. I was devastated, but couldn't show my emotions. Luckily, she never wanted to come to my bank or even have lunch with me, so fortunately no one knew we were dating. Once I got a chance I called her and explained what had just transpired. She was completely silent. She keeps saying it had to be a mistake and she would call or stop by to take care of this misunderstanding. That was the last time I ever heard from her. I felt used, betrayed, and disgusted. I kept visualizing having sex with a transsexual; I felt nasty, because I was having feelings for her, him, shim. It took a while for me to accept and understand her situation. That was the truth, the whole truth, so help me your honor."

Malia was in complete aw after Ed's story. She didn't have anymore question; she just lay there in silence listening to Maxwell's CD and singing the moments away. Ed whispered her name twice, but Malia never responded, she was motionless, refusing to speak. The ringing of the phone broke the thick silence that covered the room. It was Lake on the phone inviting her and Ed to the screening of the Nikki's Revlon commercial. Malia stared at Ed as she continued to speak to Lake on the phone. She asked Lake to hold on while she whispered the invitation to Ed; he immediately agreed. After the phone conversation, Malia motioned Ed to kiss her, and he did without any hesitation.

"Edward, I am so in love with you. I know it's too soon to utter these words but I have to be honest with you and myself. If this offends you or runs you off, I understand. I don't want an answer or a comment. I just want you to hold me."

Tré and Junior were lying in the bed watching Finding Nemo when the phone rang. It was Lake.

"Sup, pimp?" Tré asked.

"Sup with you, man?" Lake responded. "I'm calling to invite you and Keisha to come to Nikki's Revlon commercial premier tomorrow," Lake continued.

"What time you talking?" Tré asked.

"The reception starts at 6:30, but the actual viewing is not until 8:00. Halle Barry, Julianne Moore and Catherine Zeta-Jones will also be in attendance. They are also in the commercial."

"Cool, man, I'll do that. I got a flight tomorrow night but I wouldn't miss this for the world. How's Nikko and Kennedy?" Tré asked.

"They're hanging in there. Nikko is still having problems, but he's getting better one day at a time," Lake replied.

"Man, if I can do anything let me know. You know you cats are like brothers to me. Yo, Lake, I don't know about Keisha; she went out of town with the girls. They went to Charleston to do some sister bonding or some shit they call it."

Junior looked up and whispered, "Daddy, you said a bad word!"

Tré ignored Junior. "I was supposed to hang out with the fellas this weekend, but I had to be with the little one," Tré smirked.

Tré's phone beeped; it was Lincoln.

"Hold on a sec, Lake. Got another call—"

Lake interrupted, "I gotta go anyway, man. I'll see you tomorrow, bruh, be cool. One." Tré clicked over, "Sup, dawg!" Tré asked.

"Missing you, pimp. What it be like?"

"The same here. I'm here with the little one, chilling watching Finding Nemo," Tré replied.

Lincoln snickered. "When am I gonna see you, man? I'm in your city," Lincoln asked. "You can swing by now. I gotta talk to you to about some pressing shit," Tré concluded. Junior yelled, "Daddy!"

Lincoln was confused. "You want me to come over now while Junior is there?"

Tré replied. "Yeah, (nigga)."

Junior put his hands over his ears. Tré smiled.

"Okay, man, I will be there in a few." Lincoln reluctantly responded. "Want me to bring anything, G?" Lincoln asked.

"Naw, man, I'm cool," Tré said.

Tré hung up the phone and started tickling Junior until he started crying with laughter. "Daddy, please stop!" Junior begged.

"Okay, Little Man, I'll stop; don't want you to pee on me. You alright, Little Man, come on get yourself together; I got something to show you," Tré said.

Tré rolled to the head of the bed and pulled out a little blue box from the nightstand. Junior strained to see what could be in the tiny little blue box.

"Daddy, what is it?" Junior asked.

"It's for your mother," Tré answered.

Tré opened the box to display a marquise yellow 2 carat diamond ring. It was beautiful, sparkling with color. Junior asked if it was for her birthday.

Tré responded, "Naw, Little Man, I'm going to ask your mother to marry me. I want us to live together and be a family."

"You mean like Ian and his mommy and daddy? They all live together," Junior explained.

"Yeah, like Ian and his family."

Junior started jumping on the bed with excitement.

"Cool down, Little Man; we don't know what she will say. She may say she don't want a family. Junior, this is our secret; you can't tell anyone, not your mother, uncles or Ian. Do you promise to keep this our little secret?" Tré asked.

Junior nodded, "Yes, Daddy, I promise," with a big smile of happiness.

There was a knock at the door; it was Lincoln.

"Come on in man. Were you at the corner, dawg?" Tré asked.

"Kinda, bruh. I got some brew, man; I thought we might need it afterwards."

Tré completely ignored Lincoln's last sentence.

"Yo, little man, here's your boy, Mr. Lincoln," Tré shouted.

"How you doing today Mr. Lincoln? Where's your daughter?" Junior asked.

"Oh, Katherine's at home with her mom," Lincoln replied.

"Wow, you mean you all are a family?" Junior bashfully asked.

"Yeah," Lincoln responded.

Tré interrupted, "Get in the room and finish watching Finding Nemo," Tré ordered. "What was that all about, man?" Lincoln asked.

"Junior was about to tell you that I'm going to ask Keisha to marry me," Tré replied. The mention of the words 'married' and 'Keisha' made Lincoln's eyes fill with instant tears.

"What do you mean, man? I thought we were feeling each other."

Lincoln grunted as he covered his tears with his hands. He felt the knife piercing his heart, he felt his life collapsing, he felt his throat beginning to dry and his knees began to buckle. Tré invited him to come outside on the porch, away from Junior and his bionic ears.

"Yo, B, man, I'm digging you, but I gotta do what I gotta do. I need substance in my life. I need stability, man; you can't provide that shit to me. You got a fucking family. You don't get lonely at night; if you want to make love, you got your wife right there; I got a fucking pillow, man. I want my son to be proud of me, not ashamed that his ole man fucks around with niggas. I don't hang out with the fellas anymore; I'm always around Nikko and Lake, but I like blunting up, drinking with the niggas and talking shit. It ain't the same, yo. I'm suffocating, man, but you wouldn't understand, B; you got all you need, the money, the career, the family, the success. I need a piece of that. I may not ever be a millionaire, but I can be proud of my son being proud of me. Nigga, you ain't ever gonna understand this shit. I gotta do me, I gotta."

Lincoln just got wiped away his tears and walked to his car. Tré wanted to run behind him but his legs were frozen and his arms were heavy. He wanted Lincoln to stop and turn around, but he didn't he just kept walking, got in his car and drove off. Tré stood there for at least ten minutes before Junior came falling out of the front door. "Daddy, where did Mr. Lincoln go?" Junior asked.

"He had to leave, little man. He just stopped by to say good-bye," Tré replied.

"Is he coming back, Daddy?" Junior asked.

"I don't know, Junior. I don't know."

There was a black car in the distance with two white men who were busy taking pictures of Lincoln and Tré on the front porch. The car was totally undetected in the small neighborhood of Trés complex.

Lights, Camera and Z

Nikko, Lake and Kennedy were having breakfast in the sunroom. They were all excited about the viewing of the commercial, but it was filled with bitter sweet feelings. Everyone was calling from the mayor to the head of National Security giving their warm wishes. It was already a busy day from the phone ringing to flowers being delivered. Malia was the first to arrive at the house around ten that morning, giving her much needed congratulations speech and giving a helping hand with Kennedy, helping her choose a dress to wear for this glorious occasion. Lake and Nikko were full of smiles, thanking everyone who called and everyone who took the time out to hand deliver flowers. Z got back in record time from Savannah; he didn't want to miss a moment of this day that would go down in history for his friends. He didn't even get a chance to sleep; he drove fours hours non stop. He was about to burst from his need to tell someone about the adventure he had in Savannah. Keith was still drunk or tired from the night before. He slept the entire way; Z purposely stepped on the brakes a couple of times just to get a laugh out of seeing Keith drool and hit his head on the dashboard. He dropped Keith off, put him to bed and whisked away in Keith's 2005 Acura.

"That will show that motherfucker. I'll make sure he can't go anywhere, especially to go get some fucking liquor," Z whispered.

Z called Malia and Nikko to see if there was anything he needed to bring even though the viewing was not until that evening. Nikko reassured Z that everything was okay and he really didn't need to come over until later on that afternoon. Z had a splendid idea; he would treat Malia to a manicure and pedicure. This would give them enough time to catch up on this past weekend, and also for him to get the 411 on her new beau. Malia agreed to meet him after giving much needed kisses to Nikko, Lake and Kennedy. Malia was already soaking her feet and hands when Z showed up ten minutes late. He started going off about how motherfuckers can't drive in Atlanta and how people rubber neck so fucking much. The employees all started to giggle as Z sashayed to the seat next to Malia, waiting for an elderly lady to move while he stood there patting his feet. The Chinese nail shop was not busy at all and there were several seats Z could have occupied. Two Chinese ladies started gossiping in Chinese about Z's flamboyancy. Z started his normal conversation with Malia, telling her minute by minute details about Savannah and all its glory. He could over hear the whispers of the two ladies who would bust out laughing after each sentence.

Z whispered with an arched eyebrow, "I think those Chinese bitches are talking about me."

Malia laughed. "How can you tell?"

"Bitch, I understand Japanese," Z interrupted.

Malia burst out laughing again. Z rolled his eyes as he changed his conversation and started talking about dicks, one of his favorite subjects. He was going to get the last laugh if it caused the nail shop to lose customers.

"Girl, I love big dicks, black dicks, fat dicks, dicks with veins running through them; I take them, black, brown, caramel, light, but not white or pink."

The entire shop was silent, but Z kept on going.

"I love, sucking dick, licking dick, swallowing dick and even burping them."

Malia turned reddish blue, but Z was on a roll. The Chinese women were rolling their eyes at Z and he rolled his eyes back as he continued his conversation, primarily talking to himself. Malia reluctantly joined in.

"Drayton had a fat dick with a pretty red head on it." She couldn't believe she had gotten sucked into Z's game. (Z winked his ?– eyes as he told Malia how big Keith's dick was.

"Chow ding dong, Keith's dick was big and fat with lots of wrinkles. I used to have to use a lot of Crisco oil to get it in, and it took me twenty minutes just to put the head in," Z said, looking directly at the two Chinese ladies; they were now embarrassed and running out the door, apron and all. Z giggled as one of them tripped while running out the door. He turned back to Malia and gave her a high five. Now Malia was embarrassed.

"I can't believe I did that."

The employees were stunned; the shop was completely silent until Z and Malia finally left the shop. Malia stood by her CL 55 and stared at Z for a moment and then slowly she asked, "How do you know when you are in love with someone?"

Z stared at her for a moment. "What are you asking me, Ms. Somalia girl?"

"How do I know if I'm ready to love again? I miss Drayton, his smell, his touch, and his voice, everything about him. I find myself thinking about him now more then ever. When I see him at work my heart skips a beat, the lumps gather in my throat and my knees become weak. I adore Edward, but I don't know if my heart is ready to love again. I don't know if I can go through life and not be fully loved or even married. Ed had two sexual experiences with men and I don't know if I can deal with knowing that."

Z was in complete silence as Malia continued.

"It happened almost twenty years ago and he was completely honest, so I should believe him, but—"

Z cut her off. "Malia, if you have a man who is open about his sexuality, that's a good man. I wish every man could be open about their gay sexual experience. So many brothers repress their experiences; it haunts them every day. I have talked to so many confused brothers who are scared to be open about their sexuality. They hate faggots because they are afraid of becoming one when, in actuality, they are one. So many straight-acting, DL brothers want me to stick my thing in them and some even unprotected. Girl, I know I'm going on and on, but if a straight man tells you about his same sex experiences, that means he hides nothing. I gotta meet him, girl."

Malia was in tears; the feeling of relief was overwhelming for her.

"Girl, and if I told you once, I told you twice, you got the power of the pussy. I don't care how many confused motherfuckers out there like boy pussy and girl pussy. Girl pussy will win every time. Men love the way real pussy smells, how real pussy tastes and the way it makes them feel. Now, don't get me wrong, I know a lot of motherfuckers that like the taste of some good clean ass on a man, but it don't compare to the taste of some good clean pussy. Girl pussy is powerful; that's where babies come from. Now I'll be the first to tell you, if men could have babies out their ass, there would be a lot of us bare foot and pregnant, there would be more of us on welfare, but since we can't get pregnant, we'll have to settle for the occasional jelly babies."

Z and Malia laugh hysterically.

"Now work that pussy on your boy and if he even thinks about pussy from anywhere else, his dick will shrivel up and fall off. Malia, you know how I taught you to work that shit with Drayton that's how he got whipped. Girl, I gotta find me a fierce outfit for tonight. What are you going to do until this evening? You could leave your car and tag along with me; I saw some nice come fuck me pumps I'm just dying for you to buy."

CHAPTER 42

Boys in the Hood

Tré was blowing up Keisha's cell phone, trying to find out when she would be back in the city. She finally called him back and was nervous when he answered the phone. "What's wrong, Tré? Is something wrong with Junior?"

"Naw, baby, just wanted to know when you were coming back because Lake called and wanted to invite us to the private screening of Nikki's Revlon commercial this evening," Tré explained.

Keisha said she would be honored and wanted to know if there was anything she needed to bring. Tré said he didn't think so, but he continued by informing Keisha that he had some good news in wanted to share with her. Keisha became immediately suspicious of Tré's actions but couldn't let Gina know anything was out the ordinary.

"Yo, Keish, I got a beep. I'll be over 'bout five o'clock."

"Yo sup Q?" Tré said when he clicked over.

"Hey, man, what the fuck's been up, man?"

"Nothing dawg just hanging out with little man 'til later." "What's popping?" Tre asked.

"Me and the niggas are in your 'hood, man. We coming through, yo; aint talked to yo' punk ass in a minute, nigga."

Q hung up the phone less then five minutes later. Q, Zeus and Shadow were walking through the door with beer and smokes in hand.

"Sup, nigga," they all shouted.

"Sup playas," Tré replied.

"Man, where the fuck you been, yo? I know you ain't working that damn hard, being a fucking waiter in the sky," Zeus giggled.

Shadow was opening a beer while putting his feet on Tré's coffee table. Junior heard the men and ran in the living room, running straight to his daddy.

Zeus shouted, "What's up my nigga? Damn, you're getting big, little man. You gonna be bigger than your ole man in a couple of years."

Shadow was busy rolling a blunt and totally ignoring Junior's presence.

"Yo, go in the bedroom and watch TV. I'll fix you some lunch," Tré ordered. "Close the door!" Tré yelled.

Tré walked right up to Shadow and snatched the blunt out of his mouth.

"Motherfucker, don't' you ever do that shit in front of my son, nigga." Tré was furious. Shadow replied, "Be cool, nigga, my bad, dawg."

Q broke the tension by asking Tré "What's been up man?"

"I've been around, man, just been working overtime; I need to save some money," Tré replied.

Zeus asked, "Man when you get this new furniture? I ain't seen this shit last time I was over; this shit is expensive as fuck. Who did you have to fuck to get this shit?"

Tré completely ignored him as he went in the kitchen to prepare Junior's lunch.

"You motherfuckers need a glass or a coaster?"

They all looked at each other and whispered, "Coasters?"

The phone rang and as Tré was about to get it, Shadow answered the phone.

"Who dis?" he asked.

"This is Lincoln. Is Tré there?"

Shadow continued, "Lincoln Buchanan?" "Lincoln Buchanan the baseball player?"

Tré snatched the phone. "Nigga, you pushing it," he yelled at Shadow.

"Yo, man, can't talk right now. I'll call you later man. One." Tré hung up the phone and stood there, fuming.

"Yo, KS, we got some shit going down and wanted to know if you wanted in," Q asked. "We got some boys on the west coast trying to deliver some white girls to the east coast and we thought maybe you wanted in. It pays a lot, man."

Tré continued to hover over his boys.

Q continued, "We just need you to put it on the plane and then we will pick it up from the airport. It'll pay you between ten and fifty thousand dollars for five trips. I know you hard up for money, man, and this could get you what you need."

Tré walked to the door and opened it.

"Get the fuck out my house," Tré commanded.

CHAPTER 43

The Commercial

The Rialto was crowded with cameras, lights, reporters, celebrities and mostly people who did their best to look important. Nikko, Lake, Kennedy, and Z were in one limo, Malia, Edward and his daughter, Paige, Tré, Keisha and Junior were in another. They all arrived thirty minutes early to avoid the paparazzi. The limo pulled in the front where a beautiful red carpet awaited his entourage. They whisked in without uttering a word to anyone. They found their respective reserved seats before even talking to anyone, including the Revlon producer and director. This commercial was extremely important to the Revlon Company because they never had anyone to die prior to the debut of a featured commercial. Halle was the first to run up to Nikko, hugging him and thanking him for the still photos he took of her for the campaign. She also wanted to give her condolences once again in person. Halle was one of the first actresses to start a fund raiser in Nikki's honor. Halle, Nikko and Kennedy stepped away from the rest of the group for some privacy and good wishes. Afterwards everyone started to congregate with other celebrities and dignitaries; this lasted for about forty-five minutes until the president of Revlon begged for everyone's attention and asked everyone to take their seats. For some odd reason, Nikko felt wonderful. He didn't have any headaches or side effects after taking the new drugs. The nightmares that he experienced that night still haunted him, but didn't think much about it anymore. He was simply thrilled by the overwhelming support he received from the Revlon corporations. He fell back to reality when the curtains of the Rialto Theatre opened and the lights went dim and the projector began to roll. Everyone got instant goose bumps.

The commercial started with, Nikki, Halle, Julianne and Catherine were all getting into an elevator and going to the penthouse for a party located at the Trump Tower. Suddenly, the lights went out and the elevator stopped. The women didn't panic, and suddenly the announcer began to speak.

The announcer asked the question. "What does every woman want?"

As the lights came up slightly, Halle said "A good man," Julianne said "Diamond and Pearls," Catherine said "Cold Cash, and lots of it," but Nikki never said anything. The elevator started to move up to the penthouse floor and suddenly the elevator door stopped on the twenty second floor and all four walls of the elevator folded down and there were gorgeous men, of every nationality. Halle stepped down off the elevator and disappears into the crowd of men. Z started to fan his face as he winked to Halle in the next aisle. "That's what I'm talking about, girl," he whispered to himself. Suddenly the elevator became a platform and started to move. The bell of the platform rang and stopped again on the fiftieth floor. This time, diamonds and pearls were everywhere. Julianne ran off the platform. Catherine became anxious and the platform began to move upward, suddenly, the platform stopped on the seventieth floor to overlook piles and piles of cash. Catherine leaped off the platform as she looked back at Nikki and whispered in her sexiest English voice, "I couldn't be happier", as she disappeared in the sea of cold hard cash. The platform of the elevator started to move upward again, past the penthouse of the Trump Tower and stopped on the roof top. Suddenly, Nikki began to speak, looking directly in the camera; she is simply mesmerizing. Every woman dreams of looking and feeling beautiful at every given moment. The platform stopped to reveal a bottle of perfume. Nikki stepped off the platform and walked toward the perfume bottle; it was entitled "Dreams".

The commercial lasted only forty seconds, but seemed like a lifetime. It indeed sent a message and everyone was pleased. Nikko was only concerned about the effect it would have on Kennedy. Chili and T-boz of TLC would call Kennedy from time to time and send warm wishes. Oprah continued her commitment to Kennedy, calling, sending telegrams and presents; she had accepted Kennedy as her little niece along with the many children she had already accepted in her life. Nikko and Lake were pleased with her efforts because they knew how important it was for Kennedy to live as healthy and normal a life as possible. They didn't want her to be depressed by the absence of her mother, but in actuality it was Nikko who was suffering more. Children have the ability to accept the lost of a parent better than a sibling. He looked at Kennedy and her strength and her willingness to accept the reality better then he or Lake could ever imagine. He sometimes didn't understand that children are not compromised by the reality of death.

Nikko became astounded when the president summoned him and Kennedy to come to the stage. Nikko was presented with his sister's Lifetime achievement award. Kennedy was overwhelmed with enthusiasm. This was the happiest Nikko had been since Nikki's death.

CHAPTER 44

The Proposal

The reception was wonderful; there was champagne, caviar, salmon, escargot and the finest lobster money could buy. Revlon did not hold back when it came to the private showing. Everyone continued to party, but Malia and Tré needed to depart for their own selfish reasons. Without a second to spare, they were whisked away in the first limo. The driver dropped off Malia and Ed first, and then afterwards Tré asked the driver to drop off Junior. This would be Tré's golden moment. The driver started driving the limo in the westward direction on I-20. The driver exited on a ramp that gave beautiful scenery of Atlanta's sky line. Keisha became a little suspicious but didn't let on; she was kind of tipsy from all the champagne she had consumed earlier at the viewing. Tré began his proposal of telling Keisha how beautiful she was and how much he'd missed her this weekend. Keisha's eyes were sparkling and the evening gown she wore was simply elegant. She wore a knock off Valentino that was a deep moon light blue halter gown, with a low back that displayed the tattoo on her lower back. She wore tear drop diamond studs, a matching choker that was a present from Gina and her hair was pulled back in a long pony tail. Tré suddenly became nervous and didn't know how he should propose to Keisha; he kept fidgeting with the ring in his pocket. Without thought he burst out, "Keisha will you marry me?"

Keisha's eyes grew big as fifty cent pieces; she was just startled and caught off guard. Keisha sat erect and Tré pulled out the ring and held it in his hands. Her heart began to beat faster as she tried to regain her composure. Tears began to flow and she tried to speak, but nothing would come out. She was choking with words when she uttered that she had a secret. Tré's heart beat slowed down until it was beating a mile an hour.

"Tré, I love you with all my heart but I would be less of a woman if I didn't tell you that I've been seeing someone who I truly have feelings for," Keisha murmured.

Tré felt his heart stopping as Keisha continued.

"I've been waiting for this moment again for us to be together, to be a family. As I continued to love you, Tré, I fell in love with a person who makes me feel true love." Tré interrupted, "Who is the motherfucker, Keisha?"

She continued, "I met someone who has touched my soul and lifted me to unrecognizable heights in my life. I've been so lonely in my life and feeling that there's no hope to live for tomorrow, especially after you got cold feet the first time and didn't marry me. I have struggled with raising Junior and my brothers, but I never felt the love I needed until recently. The only love I knew was yours until I met Gina."

"Gina?!" Tré yelled at her. "You're choosing some fucking dyke over me? Keisha, you lying; Gina is not a dyke."

Keisha continued, "She made me feel whole again. She listened to my heart and she wanted to be a part of my dreams. Gina made something deep inside of me live again and blew life into my being. I felt that making love to you, but Gina is different; her love making is spiritual, Tré. I wish you could understand; she filled that void that I so needed in my life. She's like a sister, someone I can talk to in the middle of the night. She would stop what she is doing to listen to me and doesn't judge me for any reason. Gina is like a sister I never had and also the mother I desperately needed."

Tré was now silent with his head held down.

"Tré, you are the father of my son and should have been my husband."

Tré was sulking, contemplating that fact that he was losing Keisha to some pussy eating dyke. The disgust started running through his head, imagining Keisha getting her pussy eaten and licked by some bull dagger with a flat chest and flat ass. Gina has hung out with them on several occasions, always whispering in Keisha's ear. He imagined Gina poking Keisha with a strap on dildo and his son sleeping in the other room. He refrained from slapping her and kicking her out of the limo.

"Tré, I love you and I will marry you if you will have me," Keisha responded.

Keisha kissed Tré on the cheeks, pushed the button to let down the window that divided them from the driver. She asked the driver to take her home as Tré stared out the window in a daze. Tears rolled down his face and he now stared at Keisha and pulled her to him.

"Keisha, I can not lose you to anyone. I will fight for your love and your heart. We were meant to be together, for the good and the bad times, the ups and the downs. I want to live the rest of my life making you happy. If I have to work ten jobs to make you happy, so be it. Keisha, you complete me and without you, I'm a nobody with nothing to live for. You have always been my beacon of light and I will die if you're not my wife." He slipped the engagement ring on Keisha's finger and she let the tears flow. They kissed and hugged all the way to his apartment.

They slipped off their clothes at the front door; Tré was butt ass naked when he lifted Keisha off her feet. He began to lick her from her earlobes to her toes. She smelled scrumptious, good enough to eat. She had rubbed some of the Dream perfume on her neck before leaving the Rialto. She was becoming moist as he nibbled on her neck He was giving Keisha his best performance. He grabbed some ice from the fridge and rubbed the ice all over Keisha's body with his teeth. He sucked her nipples and sometimes iced them up. This drove Keisha wild; the chills went from the back of her neck down to her toes. He gently pushed ice into her vagina, making her shiver with ecstasy. Keisha moaned with pleasure, asking for more, but begging him to stop. Tré was on a mission to stop Keisha from ever thinking about making love to a dyke and convincing himself that he never wanted to think about sleeping with a man again. Keisha started to scream softly as Tré sucked her toes with the ice, sending sensations of her first climax. This made Tré suddenly erect with anticipated pleasure. On most occasions it took Keisha time to adjust to Tré's perfect nine inch dick with a six inch girth, but this time was different; her body was begging for him to enter. He eased in as he continued to kiss her, drowning her moans and cries. She was now on the little breakfast table as he gently stroked her hair and sucked on her neck. Keisha was not minding the hickey that he was trying to brand her with. Keisha came again as Tré pulled off her fake pony tail and threw it in the sink.

"Keisha, I love you, baby. Don't leave me; be my wife," Tré repeated over and over again.

Keisha couldn't hold back. "Fuck me, Tré. Fuck me now."

Tré continued to kiss her and repeated, "Keisha I want to make love to you all night long, baby, my future wife." The lovemaking started in the kitchen, in the living room, and the bedroom and lasted for forty-five minutes and ended up in the shower when Tré started to scream uncontrollably, "Keisha, I'm coming! Keisha, Keisha, damn Keisha." She tried to pull Tré away, but he deliberately held her close and ejaculated inside of her. Tré did not want to move or pull away from Keisha. They were both exhausted as they limped out of the shower. Tré started drying Keisha off as she faced the mirror in the bedroom and he was standing behind her. They suddenly looked in the dresser mirror where they were admiring their nakedness.

"We belong together; look how beautiful we look together, Keisha," Tré smiled.

Keisha returned the smiles as she whispered, tomorrow we both have to tell Gina, and then tell our family and our friends."

Tré agreed. "But now my dick is getting hard again; its time for some more Keisha."

She was completely sore but couldn't resist Tré or his dick.

She laughed. "Anything you say, Mr. Keisha LaShan Washington."

"I got your Keisha LaShan Adams," he said as he started licking her nipples and rubbing her pussy at the same time.

Z was on the internet trying to find some good dick on the sex sites. He was talking to five different guys who wanted to swing by or have him come over. He wanted to have someone come over and satisfy his sexual needs while Keith was in the other bedroom. Z was horny and needed some dick, regardless whether Keith was in the other room drunk or dead. He found empty liquor bottles in the garbage underneath the rest of the trash. It was repulsive to believe this motherfucker would rather drink than have sex. Z was becoming frustrated by the games that the motherfuckers on the site were playing. They were all asking him fucked up questions about, his stats, was he feminine, did he live alone... "Fuck all y'all fake-ass punks," Z was yelling at the computer screen. As he was about to log off, someone instant messaged him. It was someone with the screen name "CueDawg11inches".

"Hmm, sounds interesting," Z thought.

"Sup G?" Z asked, giving the DL jargon.

"Sup with u pimp?" CueDawg11inches replied.

"What's the jump off tonite yo?" Z continued.

"I can't call it yo. At the crib bout to beat my meat, wanna help me?" Cuedawg11inches responded.

"I can beat it, suck it and whip it, but what you gonna do for me yo?" Z wrote. "Are you down for trading pix and shit? If so here's my addy," Z added.

Cuedawg11inches responded. I don't trade pix, I don't eat ass, I don't suck dick, I want you to suck my dick and I want to fuck you."

Z looked at the ceiling, sucked his teeth and finally responded, "Here's my digits dawg, and I'm out, one."

There was a long silence then Cuedawg11inches wrote, "If you're fucked in the face nigga, I ain't fucking you in the ass."

Z screamed, "I got you, you stupid bitch."

Z cut off the computer and called Malia.

"Girl, I'm off to the see a wizard, a wonderful wizard of dick." Malia chuckled as Z continued, "I hate the fucking internet, but it's the easiest way to get some good dick. They don't ask for a last name, health status or cash; they just wanna fuck."

Malia became silent, then slowly asked, "Z, is it safe? I had a case once where a guy was killed because he used the internet to get straight men to come to his house. He would pose as a woman on the phone or the internet and once the guys came over he would try to seduce them with weed, liquor and ecstasy pills. One came in and actually tied him up and killed him by strangling him to death and robbed him. The jury sentenced him to life in prison, but the price the poor innocent victim played in order to have sex..."

Z couldn't take any more. "Girl, what that gonna do with me?" Not a damn thing. Get off my phone; you just pissed me the fuck off. I'm bout to a long hot shower and play with Keith's drunk dick until I get tired." Suddenly the phone beeped from an unknown caller. "Ms. Malia, girl, hold on."

Z changed his voice to sound deeper and masculine. "Who dis?" Z asked.

"This is Cue, nigga, what's the deal man? You swinging through, nigga?" Cue asked.

Z's voice got deeper. "When, man?"

"Tonight, pimp. Here's my address, yo. 213 Maple Way Drive.1."

When Z clicked backed over, Malia was singing, "A hoe is a hoe is a hoe".

Z interrupted, "Your momma. Girl, this is the address: 213 Maple Tree Way; write it down. If I don't call you by tomorrow, call Lake."

Malia agreed and muttered, "Stupid bitch" before hanging up the phone.

Z was reluctant about heading to the unknown caller's house, but convinced himself that everything would be alright. Driving to the house, Z kept thinking about Keith and his problem. He really didn't know the best way to handle it. He did like Keith, but only when he was sober and coherent. "The motherfucker continues to lie about his addiction, saying that he's only a social drinker," Z thought. "Tomorrow is a new day," he thought as he realized he was in the middle of the 'hood off Bankhead

Hwy. Z always kept his switch blade in his shoe, but decided to have some back up and put his pepper spray in his sock. He decided to throw his car keys in the bushes by the porch and would use the emergency key he hid under the left side bumper. Z's attired was hilarious; he had his baseball cap turned backwards, his oversized throw back jersey on and his only pair of loose baggy jeans. They were hanging down below his ass and his only pair of Timberland boots. He accessorized his attire with a long fake platinum chain with a silver plated medallion and a black and mild behind his ear. Z stood at the door and thought how much of a fake bitch he was; he's constantly bragging about how true he was to the game of the gay lifestyle and now he was fucking with his own integrity. He agreed this would be his only time compromising his integrity.

Z heard heavy foot steps approaching the door.

"Who dis?" The voice of the other side of the door asked.

"Zarius!" Z answered in his normal voice. The door slowly opened and their eyes met. The face looked familiar but Z couldn't place where he had seen this thug before. They both stood there for a moment sizing each other up.

"Come in nigga," the stranger ordered.

Z sashayed in with his normal stride.

"Have a seat," the stranger ordered as he disappeared in another room.

Z heard voices; his gay senses told him to leave, but when he was about to, the man reappeared with another stranger, both stared at Z for a moment then the first stranger asked him, "Man, you down for sucking both our dicks?"

Z mouth started watering as he anticipated sucking eleven inches of dick. Z finally looked up and realized he definitely knew the other stranger who was now hovering over him.

"I know you, man; you hang out with my cousin, Tré," Z said as he stood up. Both guys were over six feet tall; one was about a hundred eighty pounds and the other was two hundred pounds.

"Naw, you don't know me, nigga."

Z ordered, "Show me what you're working with."

The guys looked dumbfounded at this little faggot motherfucker giving them orders. They pulled down their jeans to their knees; Z held one of the soft dicks in his hand while he started to massage the other with his mouth. Suddenly it started to grow and without any hesitation, he started sucking the other, both men were amazed and excited. Z became disgusted; this little piggy went to market with a seven inch dick and this little piggy was confused between an eleven inch dick and a skinny eight inch dick. Z stood upright and was about to exit when the first guy asked him where the fucked he was going.

"I'm out, dawg," Z said without hesitation.

One guy pushed Z up against the bedroom door and told him he was not going anywhere. "We gonna fuck you, you little faggot bitch." Both guys were now, approaching him. Z slowly backed up in the bedroom and was thinking about how he was going to kill them both. Z asked who wanted to fuck him first. The first guy went to the bathroom to get some lube and make a call on his cell phone, while the other guy ordered Z to undress. Z pulled out his switchblade and pressed the knife against the guy's throat within a split second. Z whispered, "Tell your boy the party's over."

Suddenly the stranger overpowered the Z and snatched the knife from him, knocking Z on the floor near an ironing board. The stranger in the bathroom heard the commotion and started toward Z. Without hesitation Z pulled out the pepper spray, blinding both guys. Z left them screaming in pain. He snatched his faithful knife which was now lying on the bed. He ran out the door as the men ran around in a daze trying to find him. He grabbed his keys out the bushes and was off in his car in five seconds flat. Z prayed all the way home, asking God for forgiveness and saying he was through with sex hook ups and sex sites. Finally arriving home, he sat outside his house for about thirty minutes and was thankful he was alive to know that he needed to change his ways and alter his devious behavior.

CHAPTER 45

The Morning After

Nikko was in heavenly bliss as he slept, resting after an evening of overwhelming memories of his sister's commercial. Suddenly the phone rung, it was six thirty in the morning. Nikko hesitated to reach for the phone, asking himself who could be calling him this early in the morning.

"Hello," Nikko mustered.

"Nikko, this is Tré," he whispered.

"What's up man, what time is it?"

"It's a little after six. I have a flight at eight thirty, but I wanted you to be the first to know that I'm getting married. I asked Keisha to marry me. We want a quick wedding, maybe in two to three months," Tré said.

Still groggy, Nikko responded, "I guess congratulations are in order."

Tré continued, "I want you to direct the wedding. I know you haven't done it in a long time, but there is no one I would want to direct the wedding other than you."

Nikko replied, "I would be honored, man; anything for you. I would have to call my old buddy K. Allen from Columbia, but I'm quite sure he will clear his schedule for an old friend."

"Nikko, don't worry about the cost; it don't matter. I just want it to be a storybook wedding," Tré closed.

Nikko stopped him. "Tré, I couldn't charge you; this would be one of my gifts to you and Keisha'."

"Two more things before I hang up; I would love nothing more than if Kennedy could be in the wedding," Tré asked.

"Cool, Tré, I can arrange that. What's the other thing?" Nikko eagerly asked.

"I want you to know that you're the only man, I ever loved and that night in the dorm room changed my life forever; I realized at that moment that I desired men as well as women. I have tried to fight this feeling for over ten years, but it's inside of me. I tried to curse it out of me, but I couldn't. That night I realized my desire is physical and sexual. I desire to be with a man because it feels good. The warmth of another man's body became a disease for me; the touch became an addiction and the sex an everlasting craving. Nikko, I can't explain it; I thought it would be something that would disappear and I could live my life as a normal man. I have cried in the dark plenty of nights, after having a complete stranger suck my dick in a fucking book store. Then I turn around and beat the shit out of him for liking it. I hate faggots, feminine motherfuckers, the entire fucking lifestyle, but I hate it because I'm a part of it. I can't let the craving of sex with men go, the desire lives with me, it wakes me up in the morning. I fooled myself into thinking that men suck dick better then women and that's my reason for fucking with them. I convinced myself that getting sex with men is easier; this allows me to justify my actions. I am convinced that there are brothers out there who are ashamed of being on the DL; the fact that they need, not want, to be with a man. I know this marriage with Keisha will not cure my desire, but it may ease my pain. A female has a level of security that men like me need. Some women gotta know their men are sleeping with other men, but somehow they imagine they don't. Nikko, I can't tell you that I won't sleep with a man again, but I can say that my first priority is to be faithful to my wife and my family, so I want you to know, I'm putting closure on my secret love for you. I have slept with over a hundred men trying to recapture that moment I shared with you in our dorm room over ten years ago."

Nikko was flabbergasted after the final words of Tré, he tried to muster up some words of wisdom, but he couldn't. "Tré, if you ever want to talk about anything, please don't hesitate to call; call me before you do something you regret, before you make a decision you will regret for the rest of your life. Tré, you have my blessing and I know your relationship with Keisha will be filled with dreams of happiness and overwhelming possibilities."

There was silence one the phone for moments, when Tré finally said, "Nikko, I love you and I always will. Take care and God bless my nigga."

Lake finally rolled over, asking who was calling this time of morning. Nikko smile and said, "Tré and Keisha are getting married."

Lake grinned, "I thought they were already married. And are they getting married this morning?" Lake asked.

"Naw, he wants me to direct the wedding and also wants Kennedy to be in the wedding and he wants this in about three months."

"Whoa, baby, you got your work cut out for you."

Nikko interrupted, "I'm sorry, sir, but we got our work cut out for us."

"How so, sir?" Lake asked.

"We have a lot to do in preparations for this wedding, so get some sleep; you're gonna need it."

"Nikko, parts of me can sleep, but parts of me need some attention. Can you give us some assistance?"

"I can do that and you can give parts of me some assistance." Nikko crawled under the sheets and started performing oral sex to his lover while Lake reciprocated.

Tré was floating on air as he sipped his last drip of coffee and thought how wonderful the day would be. He grabbed his jacket to his uniform and was locking the door when he saw a familiar figure standing by his car. It was Lincoln leaning against his car with a folded newspaper in his arms.

"'Sup, nigga!" Tré greeted.

Tré I can't take this any more, man This shit is killing me; I need you in my life," Lincoln begged.

"Yo, B, I can't really talk about this shit; I gotta get to work. I'm already late," Tré responded.

"Fuck your job, bitch! Get in the fucking car!" Lincoln ordered. He was now pointing the newspaper in Tré's face; peeking out was a nine millimeter.

"B, I ain't got time for this shit, man. If you think a gun is going to scare me, you got me fucked up. I'm a fucking thug; what I care bout dying or getting shot? Pull the motherfucking trigger, B," Tré yelled.

Lincoln dropped the newspaper.

"I'm sorry, man. Tré, baby, I love you. I can't eat, sleep, or concentrate on anything. I told my wife about us and told her I will give her a divorce and she could have everything, if you would take me back. Tré, let's leave now. I have five million dollars; we could leave now, go to an island and live off my money. If you say no, I'm going to kill us both right here, right now, I swear."

Tré was about to lose it. His instinct to take the gun and shooting Lincoln was flicking on and off like a switch. He suddenly remembered in his training how he should continue to talk to the assailant, making him surrender his intentions.

"B, I love you, too, man, but I have committed myself to Keisha; I am going to get married to her. Your threats won't deter that, B. Let me do this and maybe things will be better for us. My plans were for me to get married, and then we all could go on trips during your off season; me, you, Keisha, Ann-Marie and the kids. B, I gotta go to work, man. What you gonna do?" Tré asked. Lincoln was now crying and shaking. "This grown-ass faggot, a professional baseball player, worth millions, got everything he could ever want, and he's crying like a fucking baby; it's pathetic," Tré thought.

"Tré, call me when you get back, man," Lincoln begged. "I'm late for my therapy."

"I'm out, B; I'll call you when I return." As Tré got in his car and sped away, Lincoln had second thoughts about how to get Tré back.

CHAPTER 46

The Confrontation

Z left a message on Keith's cell phone. "Keith when you get from work, we need to talk." He then called Malia at work. "I need to speak to Malia," Z ordered. Malia had a new administrative assistant; Victoria had taken an extended leave of absence, and she was still dealing with her parents in California. Z was happy the ugly bitch hadn't come back; he was hoping she was running from the cops. The new assistant responded, "I'll put you right through, Zarius. One moment please."

"Hey, bitch," Z started giggling.

"Hey, whore," Malia said, smiling. "Why do you insist on calling me at my place of business, harassing me," Malia asked.

Z retaliated, "I got bigger fish to fry, girl. Malia, I'm going to have a heart to heart talk with Keith; I honestly must say girl, I like him, I don't love him, but there are things about him that makes me feel good. (I want him to get some help for (?him) and I have a list of agencies that he can get help from. What do you think, girl?" Z asked.

"I think that's a good idea. Why have you waited so long to make this decision?" she asked.

"I had to make sure. I'm not getting older, only better and also, I never give anyone a real chance; you know my motto; once things start to go wrong, cut it off and stop the bleeding, but with Keith, I'm willing to give him a chance. He's a good guy; he's sincere, patient, compassionate and has a great sense of humor," Z said.

"I'm proud of you Z. This is indeed a revelation, and I know that you and Keith will work it out; just don't give up on him that easily," Malia insisted. "Z, guess what?" Malia waited for Z to say, "What". There was silence for a moment.

"Girl, what?" Z shouted.

"I think I'm pregnant," Malia whispered.

"Girl, you are lying to me." Z became excited.

"No, I took an EPT test and it was positive and I missed my period this month."

"Girl, when did all this happen?" Z anxiously asked.

"The night before the commercial viewing, we made love. Z, it was so good, and you could not imagine how beautiful it was. When he was coming, the condom accidentally broke but, he was pulling out at the same time, so I really didn't think anything of it."

"So what are we gonna do?" Z asked.

"I really don't know," Malia replied.

"Are you gonna tell Ed?" Z asked.

"Not yet; I need to see if it's just my body or if I'm really pregnant," Malia explained. "Girl, come see me at hospital after you get off; I can have one of my doctor friends give you an examination," Z insisted.

"I can do that; that way I can be more prepared to confront Ed with this," Malia agreed. "Bitch, what are we gonna do about this wedding with Tré and Keisha?" Z asked.

"I don't know. I told Tré I insisted on paying for the reception. I told him not to spare any expenses," Malia said proudly.

"Bitch, are you crazy? It's gonna cost at least five thousand dollars," Z shouted.

"And?" Malia interrupted. "Tré is just like a brother and Keisha is a beautiful girl; they didn't get married the last time, I feel they deserve a story book wedding and reception," Malia explained.

"Girl I just don't know. I hope they go through with it; Nikko is working his ass off. I'm kinda glad, and this wedding has put him back in reality mode. He and K. Allen are doing the damn thing. They are going to make a five thousand dollar wedding look like a Bobby and Whitney Wedding."

"Z, you are so damn funny, you know they didn't get a divorce, girl."

"I know and I hope Tré and Keisha don't follow in their foot steps." Z started laughing. "Come on, Z, it's not funny. I wish we all could find love and live happily ever after.'

Z interrupted, "Keep dreaming, girl. That's fiction; we're living in fact. How in the hell are they going to find true happiness when both of them are gay?"

Malia cut him off. "Z, stop it now. So what if they are?"

"Girl, both of them like dick—oh, wait a minute, he likes dick, and she likes pussy." Z started laughing. "That was a good one."

Malia's attitude changed. "I thought you told me you had a conversation with God and you promised to change your attitude."

Z settled down after hearing the G word. "Malia, I did, but it's true; we all know Tré is on the DL. I know because he's my cousin and we run in very similar circles and when I was in Savannah, Keisha was there with one of her friends, and I mean one of her pussy eating friends. But it's all good; I love my cousin and you know I love Keisha, but I'm just saying they are going to have problems, because I don't care how much pussy you fuck or eat, once a DL man, always a DL man. Now with Keisha, it's different; she loves Tré's shitty draws. She always did and always will. I think the reason why she was doing it with another female because being a female and making love with another female is not the same as a male; it's a fantasy, not a sin."

Malia stopped him. "Sex is sex, Z."

"Malia, girl, wake up; I know that and you know that, but people like Keisha and Tré don't believe or understand that, so that's why they are confused and they will always be confused when it comes to their sexual orientation."

Malia stopped him again. "How do you know so much?"

"Malia, Malia, Malia, come to the light Carol Ann. I've lived my life as a gay man, sissy, and faggot whatever you want to call me these days. I have had sex with DL brothers, bisexual men, confused motherfuckers, doctors, lawyers, athletes, policemen, drug dealers, hip hop motherfuckers, dancers, strippers, firemen, preachers, deacons, teachers, principals, atheists, mortician, magicians, veterinarians and politicians and they all say they are not GAY, let me repeat myself; they all say they are not GAY. Now, being that you are a brilliant lawyer of Atlanta, Georgia, what do you call it?"

Malia was speechless as Z continued. "I'm a believer in if it fucks like a duck then it's a duck. People may call me a hoe; bitch, faggot, sissy, but they won't call me a stupid whore. I know what I am; I'm not confused about my sexuality or my lifestyle. I feel sorry for men out there pretending they don't get down with brothers like me, but I'm the one in control. Yes, we may fuck, and afterwards, I'm not ashamed of what I have done, they are. I learned in my psychology class in college that homosexuality that is abnormal is when you don't accept the fact that you are. Malia, girlfriend, I met a lot of motherfuckers who don't know what they are. My cousin is confused, and I feel sorry for him and his DL brothers. He and a lot of men look down on me, but I look down on them, too. I laugh at them because my people got something that their people want and that is another MAN.

They run around talking about they want a DL brother, they don't want a fem, fat, flamboyant sissy, but what I don't understand sometimes is that if all they want is sex from a man, does it matter who it comes from? Now tell me, who is confused?" Z ended his speech, leaving Malia speechless again.

She rebutted, "Okay, hoe, get off the soapbox. What are you going to give them for their wedding present; another speech?" she asked.

"I haven't decided yet. I want to help with their honeymoon or buy them some fake Louis Vuitton; a five piece set should be enough," Z smiled.

"Boy, you are so crazy. I don't care what no body says; you were raised by wolves," Malia continued.

"Girl, half my life I was raised by female wolves and the other half was by male wolves. You know what? I'm going to write Oprah a letter. I need to be on her show or ask her to give me a show. If she can give Dr. Phil a show, I'm quite sure the world can not wait to get a load of me," Z chuckled.

Malia laughed, "Yeah, Z, I can't wait. What will the title of the show be?" Malia reluctantly asked.

"The Gay mouth from the South Talk Show, guaranteed to satisfy your every need," Z burst out laughing again, patting himself on the back. "Girl let me let you go. I'm too much for you or me today; smooches."

"Bye boy, I'll see you later around six o'clock," Malia hung up the phone, laughing uncontrollably.

CHAPTER 47

The Meeting of the Minds

Nikko, Keisha, Tré, K. Allen and Katie were sitting down at Nikko's house going over the second stage of the wedding arrangements. They had sent all two-hundred and fifty invitations. The wedding was to take place at the Tabernacle in Midtown, since that was Keisha's church, and the pastor had already started the marriage counseling. The flowers, soloist, ushers, bride maids, maid of honor, the groomsmen, the food, decorations, song selection had just been finalized. When Z showed up unexpectedly, he rushed in the house, yelling, "I'm here!" He sat down, grabbed some snacks and listened intently, without saying a word. K. Allen, a very good friend of Nikko's, had emailed him the entire list of wedding gowns and tuxedos from all the well known boutiques in Atlanta. He insisted that it be an evening wedding with candles and crystal bells to ring in the bride to be. He also thought it would be fabulous to have a horse drawn carriage to bring in the bride. All agreed except Keisha.

"How much will all this cost?" she asked.

"Don't worry about it. I made one about a year ago that I keep in storage. I will have it shipped here and I'll pay for the shipping."

Keisha started to cry. "How I can ever repay for all you are doing for me?" Tré grabbed her hand and pulled her closer to him.

Nikko interrupted, "We told you it was going to be a Cinderella wedding and we weren't joking. If you're crying now wait one moment."

K. Allen, Nikko and Katie disappeared and reappeared with five wedding dresses. Keisha started crying again. "They are all so beautiful."

Tré spoke. "How in the hell did you guys get these damn dresses?"

Nikko responded, "My man, K. Allen got connections all over the world. He just called up one of his contacts and told them that he needed them."

Keisha was shaking as she touched the dresses, how much do they cost?" she asked. "These are Vera Wang's samples, but I can get the originals at cost; they are usually priced at seventy-five hundred to twelve thousand dollars," K. Allen replied.

Tré looked at Keisha. "Which one do you want, baby?" he asked.

"Tré, we can't afford it. The ring alone has put you back. I can get a two-hundred dollar dress from the outlet," she explained.

Z jumped up and said, "I'll pay for it." Everyone looked at Z in amazement.

"Naw, Cuz, I can't let you do that, man, it's up to the groomsman to buy the dress," Tré said.

"No, that's wrong; it's up to the family to buy the dress, to take care of the wedding, to make sure that this is the happiest day in your life, and we all are family, case closed. Now Keisha pick out the one you want and someone tell me who I make this check out to."

K. Allen cleared his throat. "Ms. Thing, I know you, I need a cashier check or cash." Everyone in the room started laughing, but Z, just rolled his eyes and smiled.

Gina was knocking so hard on Tré's front door that it was shaking the vases and candles in the living room. Tré ran to the door thinking something definitely had to be wrong. He swung the door open and to his surprise, it was Gina.

"We need to talk!" she demanded.

Tré thought, "This has not been my month."

"Go for it," he shrugged.

"You took something I had and you didn't want and I want it back," Gina commanded. "Gina, are you talking about a piece of property or are you talking about my future wife?" Tré retaliated.

"I'm talking about the one I saved; I helped her grow into the woman you were too scared to marry the first time and now because you think you're not the scared little punk ass bitch you used to be, you think you're man enough to go through a wedding and marriage," Gina growled. "You are a faggot-ass punk. I've done my investigation; I know you love dick and ass and not Keisha," Gina growled again.

Tré felt his temperature rising and his temper getting shorter.

"Gina, you dyke, I'm not going to fight you over something I got and you want. I will never hit a woman; I only do that to men, but if you make another remark like the previous one, I'm going to take it as if it's coming from a man and break your jaw. Gina, you have two choices; you can get out my front door and go away or I will make you so fucking angry and provoke you to hit me. I'll blow your fucking head off, call my friend, Lake who's a (private)?? detective and tell him you tried to break in my house and kill me. Gina the Dyke, the choice is yours." Tré stated.

Gina stepped back and said, "Ms. Tré, this is not over. I will have the last laugh. I will make your life a living hell."

This time, Tré growled, "If you try to hurt me, you'll be hurting Keisha and Junior. I am determined to make my marriage work and to prove this, I am extended you an invitation to the wedding and reception. Now, my nigga, I must bid you good-bye and you have less than five seconds to get off my fucking porch. One thousand one, one thousand two, one thousand three..."

Gina backed up and walked away, rolling her eyes as she got in the car.

Tré suddenly had a headache and decided to take an aspirin and go over his list of things he needed to do before he headed to Keisha's. He grabbed a beer and started to watch the tube. He was dozing off, when the phone rang, it was Angie. A girl in the neighborhood he used to kick it with when he and Keisha were having problems.

"Hello," he said.

"Sup, you," Angie asked. She had the sexiest voice around. "I heard you were getting married and I hate that it isn't me." She explained, "I thought we had something special, Kobra," she continued.

"What's up, girl, now you know I got feelings for you, but you also know Keisha has always been the love of my life and the mother of my son." Tré found himself explaining again, while rubbing his forehead.

"Kobra, you've been out of sight for awhile, hanging with the high society motherfuckers like that female black lawyer and that supermodel's twin brother, the model that was killed. Kobra, I missed that one-eyed monster that I used to deep throat. You know you miss my tongue, throat, pussy and those long talks we used to share on the roof top of my building. Tell me you don't miss it," Angie challenged.

"Angie I can't tell you that, man, 'cause I would be lying, but like I said before, my heart is with Nik, I mean Keisha."

"Did you say 'Nikko'?" Angie asked.

"I was trying to tell you the name of the brother of the supermodel that died. His name is Nicholas Grey."

Angie completely ignored him. "Kobra, can I see you one last time?" She was now begging.

"Angie as much as I want to, I can't; I must stay focused on my future wife; if I sleep with you, I'm gonna slip up. Please forgive me, Angie, but I can't. I hope you understand." Tré tried his best to explain.

Angie just hung up the phone. Tré had drifted off to sleep in a matter of minutes, dropping the bottle of beer on the floor. Tré immediately started dreaming of his wedding day; he saw himself standing at the church waiting for Keisha to come through the door in her magnificent wedding dress. As he waited he noticed all the beautiful faces that were cheering him on. There was Nikko, Lake and Malia. Z was dressed in a bride's maid gown; he felt this was odd, but realized it was a dream. Junior was the ring bearer and Kennedy was the flower girl. Jerome, his best friend from childhood, was his best man. He noticed his father and sisters there, smiling with anticipation. His aunts, uncles, nieces, nephews, friends, co-workers and supervisors, all stood there waiting for the bride to appear. Suddenly he noticed Angie, Gina and Lincoln in the corner laughing and pointing at him. The three of them started chanting, "She aint coming, she ain't coming, then one by one everyone started chanting, "She aint coming, she aint coming." Tré realized everyone in the church was singing, "She ain't coming, she ain't coming," even the preacher, soloist, and the pianist. Junior was even singing, "Mommy aint coming, mommy ain't coming." The chanting and singing was getting faster and louder. Tré saw himself sweating and now crying, trying his best to wake up from an afternoon nightmare. The ringing of the phone broke his trance.

"Hello, Hello!" he screamed into the phone.

"Daddy, what's wrong?" Junior screamed.

Tré composed himself and said nothing after realizing it was Junior on the other end of the phone. Wiping his face, he asked, "What's the deal little man?"

"Daddy, mommy wanted to know what time you were coming over," LIL MAN asked.

"I'll be there in a minute, I just over slept," he explained.

"Okay, Daddy," Junior hung up the phone.

Tré arrived at Keisha's in a matter of minutes. Junior was outside on the stoop waiting on his father.

"Sup, little man?" Tré greeted as he jumped out the car.

"Hey, Daddy, what took you so long? We've been waiting for hours," Junior complained.

"I'm sorry, little man. I promise it won't happen again," Tré apologized.

Keisha walked out the door with attitude. "About time," she murmured and, without hesitation, gave Tré a kiss on the cheek.

"Daddy, are we going to see our new house?" Junior asked.

"Who told you that, boy?" Tré asked.

"I heard mommy, Eric and Paul talking about us moving into a big house," Junior said. "Shut up boy, you talk too much. Here; listen to Barney on your CD recorder," Keisha shouted.

Keisha decided to break the ice. "Do you know how to get to the house?" she asked Tré. "Yeah, it's not too far; it's down 85 south," Tré said. "Did you have a chance to go over our budget and how we can afford the down payment and the rest of the bills after the marriage?" Tré asked.

Keisha pulled out her organizer. "After the wedding our total bills will be about eighteen hundred a month; that's counting entertainment, clothes, gas and miscellaneous expenses. However, we still could have five hundred a month if we budget on point. In a year we could save $6,000, not counting interest. At seven percent compound interest daily, we could have approximately $6,420. We could do that with an option to buy this house if we like it."

Tré was pleased with Keisha's financial knowledge. He remembered she had to do it most of her life, trying to figure out whether to buy food for her household or keep the electricity on. That's one more thing he loved about her. Regardless of how hard it was for her financially, she never tried to sue him or take him to court for nonpayment of child support. He always tried to give her at least four hundred a month when he was hustling but had to decrease the amount once he started working a legitimate job. Now and again he would do a return for his boys or drop a package off from one part of town to another or sometimes he would allow a delivery to be sent to his crib. Every time he indulged in any illegal activities and profited, he would give the money to Keisha and she never asked any questions. Today Tré handed Keisha a cashier's check for $3500.00; this was most of his 401K, and he was penalized for an early withdrawal.

"Baby, this is money for Junior's tuxedo and also your brothers. The remaining will be for the furniture that we talked about. We can pick up the day after we officially move in, provided we like it. I have the money for the first and last month's rent, if we like the H O U S E," he whispered to Keisha.

"Daddy, that spells house," LIL MAN smiled. They both laughed at his intense nosiness.

"I hope we like it; you know this is the last one on the list and if it's no good, then we gotta move into an apartment," Tré said.

"We will like it baby; think positive," Keisha said optimistically.

They arrived in a nice and pleasant neighborhood with a nice schools and a park in the Riverdale area. This was perfect for Tré since the airport was just a hop away. Keisha would have to commute by train or drive to work, somehow she didn't care. She also suggested to Tré that if the traded in his car and got a newer used car, they could have a bigger car that could seat the five of them comfortably and was more reliable. The car he had was an old Sentra and hers was a 1995 Honda accord. It was something someone gave her as a trade off when she sat with an elderly lady at night. As a trade off she decided to negotiate the car for pay instead of money from the elderly ladies children, they agreed.

They arrived twenty-five minutes late and this didn't sit well with their future landlords. Upon entering the house, they noticed the trees, the others houses and the children outside playing. Outside the house, they were amused by the two car garage, the big front yard and the front porch. Entering the house was pleasant, with lots of windows and space. It was a three bedroom house upstairs. The master bedroom was nice with a master bedroom and walk in closet, there were French doors that led to a deck the landlord informed them that this was something she wanted so she had it built only two years ago. Tré thought about all the lovemaking he and Keisha would enjoy out on the deck. The other two bedrooms were adequately sized and had character; they were suitable for the boys and the hall bathroom was spacious with two sinks. Junior fell in love with that, claiming one of the sinks as his own. The living room was rectangular and the dinning room would be nice for the five of them. The kitchen was oval shaped with lots of cabinets and a new fridge and stove. The basement was converted into a huge den with a fireplace and a built in fish tank. This room would be awesome for the boys and over night guests. Keisha thought of ways to add the two sofa beds that they would definitely use the week of the wedding. They were sold on the house after seeing the basement/den with a huge backyard. The carpet needed deep cleaning, but other than that the house was well kept and they loved it. Keisha was already wondering how she could make drapery for the living room and curtains for the other rooms. They signed the needed contracts and gave the landlord first and last month's rent. They also informed their future landlord that they would be moving in next week. They needed to move in prior to having all the out of town relatives and friends, because they needed a place to stay. The landlord agreed and promised she would have the carpet replaced along with a new coat of paint for the entire house.

They were excited as they drove down the street. Keisha was humming as she asked Tré when his next flight was.

He answered, “I have a flight tonight, then tomorrow I’m off.”

“Don’t forget, we’re scheduled to take our AIDS tests tomorrow at noon,” she reminded Tré.

Tré suddenly started sweating and he jokingly said, “Oh, I almost forgot,” and immediately tried to change the subject.

Junior overheard the conversation and asked his mother, “Mommy, what is AIDS?”

“Tré Jr., why do you ask so many questions?”

Tré came to his son’s defense. “It’s Acquired Immune Deficiency Syndrome,” Tré explained.

Keisha continued, “It’s a virus, baby, that breaks down your immune system, making you unable to get well from any illness, like a cold.”

Junior sat back in the seat and said, “Oh, I see,” as he started to look-out the back window of the car, admiring the scenery of the big airplanes flying overhead

CHAPTER 48

Surprise Surprise

"Ed, I'm pregnant. Ed, I think I'm pregnant. Ed, what would you do if I told you I was pregnant?" Malia had been rehearsing what to say to Ed all evening as she prepared dinner. She had invited him over for dinner to tell him the news, good, bad or indifferent. She really didn't care what he would say; she was definitely going to keep this baby. The only hardship would be to tell her parents. Her parents would probably hang their heads in shame. They were an astute family with wholesome values and impeccable morals that should never be blemished. Malia tried to provide a wonderful life for her family, spoiling them with the latest in technology. She installed a kitchen with Dutch ovens because she knew how much her mother loved to bake. She loved to shower them with gifts during holidays or any day she felt she needed to, but she was no longer the little girl who recited Dr. Martin Luther King's speech when she was eight. She was not the teenager who wrote articles for the city newspaper at the age of fourteen. And she was not the little girl who hadn't yet been married at the age of thirty and desired the company of a male companion. "I don't need my parent approval for this unborn child," Malia thought. "Then why in the hell am I so scared to call and tell them?" Her phone rang, snapping her out of her trance.

"Ms Mayerson, this is Mr. Edward Jackson. Could you please buzz me in, please?" Ed asked. Malia was nervous and anxious when she answered the phone, hesitating when she heard Ed's voice. As he buzzed him in, she stared in the mirror to make sure everything was in place and she was looking exceptionally sexy. "Here goes nothing," she murmured as she opened the door and waited for Ed to walk through.

Nikko and Lake were lying in the den. Nikko was busy trying to reorganize Tré and Keisha's wedding, while Lake was busy opening the mail and watching the news when Kennedy burst in holding a map of Hawaii.

"Uncle Nikko is this where I was born?" she asked, shoving the map in his face.

"Yes, little girl, you know where you were born. What do you have up your sleeve?" he asked.

"Well, since you asked, summer is right around the corner and I was thinking that maybe we could take a vacation, just the three of us."

Nikko sat up. "And who's paying for this vacation?" he asked.

Lake just lay there, ignoring there entire conversation; he was too busy watching the news and what was still happening in Baghdad.

"My mom had promised me that if I made straight A's in school, she would take me to my birth place. I think it would be good for us to get away, it's been a very hectic nine months for us all," she explained.

Nikko was amazed by her maturity level.

"Okay, I'm listening, and again, who is going to pay for this?" Nikko asked again, smiling at Kennedy.

"I saved over a hundred dollars in my piggy bank and Ms. Oprah told me if I ever needed anything to just give her a call." Kennedy was on a roll.

Nikko interrupted, "Ms Oprah doesn't have money to be sending us on a vacation." Lake looked at Nikko, smiling, while opening an envelope from Nikki's attorney's office. There was a certified check in the envelope for the amount of $10 million. Lake was speechless; it was attached to a letter from Nikki's attorney, informing them that this was the first check that Nikki's insurance had left. Lake handed the check to Nikko, and finally acknowledged Kennedy.

"Baby, I think we can go where ever you want to go in the world. Go pack your bags; we're leaving tonight. Lake smiled. Nikko's eyes grew bigger than fifty cent pieces. Kennedy, didn't know what was going on; her uncles where acting silly and childish. Nikko cleared his throat. "Okay, princess after Tré's wedding we can go to Hawaii, but it's our secret; you can't tell anyone, not even Sebastian and Sasha." Both dogs looked up after hearing their names. Kennedy burst out in laughter.

"Thank you so much. I love you, Uncle Nikko. I love you, Uncle Lake. I love you, too Sebastian and Sasha." She exited the den, running upstairs with Sebastian and Sasha close behind. Nikko was speechless.

"I'm at a loss. How in the world? I thought Nikki's estate had to stay in probate for a minimum of two years. What are you going to do with the money?" Lake asked.

"I definitely want to continue Nikki's foundation and Kennedy's schooling, but other than that, what do we need?" Nikko asked.

"I really don't know, baby. We are so blessed and we have everything we want," Lake added.

"There's one thing for sure," Nikko continued. "We are going to take Kennedy to Hawaii and afterwards we have some investing to do."

"That's right; maybe we can build you a bigger office," Lake added.

"Baby, I got a question for you," Nikko asked.

"What is that, big head?" Lake responded.

"Have you ever cheated on me?" Nikko asked.

"Where in the hell did that come from?" Lake stood straight up.

"It's just a question that requires a yes or no answer," Nikko explained.

"I'm not going to answer that bullshit question. How dare you ask me some fucked up shit like that? You know I love you more than life itself." Lake's temper began to flair. "Sorry I asked you that question, but you just gave me my answer." Nikko stood up, exited the den and headed toward the kitchen. Lake ran behind him.

"What the fuck you mean you know the answer?" Lake was now screaming. Nikko looked straight in his eyes.

"I don't stutter, man. You heard exactly what I said and keep your voice down; remember Kennedy is upstairs."

Lake yelled louder, "This is my fucking house! I'll yell as loud as I want!"

"Well do that; I'm leaving if you continue to yell and scream."

Lake, trying to keep his composure, asked, "Nikko, what do you mean you already know the answer to the question?"

Nikko told Lake calmly, "I asked you if you've ever cheated on me and you did not answer the question. Are your ready for this, Lake? I hope you can handle it. Do you remember that night when I thought I was dying and when I finally woke up?" Lake nodded. "During that time I couldn't wake up, I had several nightmares; one was with my parents and Nikki begging me to follow them, another one was everyone was having Thanksgiving dinner, everyone except me and the other was I was in a hospital bed dying, looking like a skeleton, literally on my death bed. You confessed to allowing an infected person that was in your custody in your police car to suck your dick, giving you the virus and you passing on to me. Lake, you have never even said you were going to get tested and after seven years of safe sex, we now have unprotected sex. The dream didn't make any sense and neither does the fact that we are not having safe sex." Lake started to say something, but Nikko cut him off. "All I want to know if the dream had some kind of validity. I love you, I will always love you. We have never lied to each other and we have always prided our relationship on open communication."

Tears of guilt started to roll down Lake's face. Feeling he was against a wall; he grabbed his keys and walked out the kitchen door. Nikko didn't run behind him; instead he cut off the lights in the kitchen and den and went upstairs to give Kennedy her bath.

Nikko didn't sleep the entire night; he was tossing, turning and feeling the other side of the bed, looking for Lake's warm body. He woke up several times thinking he heard a car driving up. He was upset he mentioned it, but he knew he had to. He wanted to call Lake on the cell phone, but decided against it every time he picked up the phone. Nikko lay in the bed and thought how his family was $10 million richer and still had problems. He grunted as he thought, "Money don't buy happiness." He finally fell back to sleep only to be awaken by the touch of someone's hands grabbing his neck. It was Lake kissing him on the lips and begging for his forgiveness.

"Nikko, please let me speak," Lake asked. "My love for you is more pure now than it's ever been before. There have been more occasions ((())) where men and women have thrown sex at me, and every time I have rejected it. I won't lie; there are times when I thought about it but never acted on it. We know I'm willing to take a bullet for you, to die for you and to live for you."

Nikko responded, "In my life right now baby, I don't care what has happened, I only care about what is going to happen. We, together, have a little girl to raise. She needs a lot of love and support. We have witnessed disease; I will have bad days and good days and I don't know what tomorrow may bring only what today holds. It holds for us to be here on earth together as one. I could never imagine life without you."

Lake stopped him, "Nikko that first time we made love without protection, I purposely wanted your pain, and if you were to suffer then I felt I deserved to suffer. We have shared good times and with Nikki passing, bad times as well. In marriage it says we have to live through sickness and health and I'm willing to live through our sickness and our health together until death. Baby what will I do if I hurt you, what will I do if I lose you? We are all that we have. I'm sorry I hurt you, I'm sorry I disappointed you and I'm sorry I yelled. Do you forgive me?" Lake begged.

"All is forgiven," Nikko nodded.

"Nikko, we are not going to wear condoms anymore despite what you may think or say. I need to feel the inside of you, the warmth the wetness and the love you share."

Keith was enjoying a glass of Jack Daniels when Z walked in. Without hesitation, Z knocked the glass out of Keith's hand. Keith just sat there in shock.

Z demanded, "I need you to make a choice either; me or your liquor."

"What are you talking about?"

Keith, you have a problem with liquor and I love you and can not live with the fact that you may be an alcoholic. Listen here, motherfucker, if I didn't care about you, I would have left you in Savannah that weekend when you got pissy drunk. Keith, I went out and had a good time with the front desk manager and the security guard, while you lay your tired ass in the hotel room. I want to be with you, but I refuse to deal with the problem you have; you hide liquors bottles throughout my house and yours. You always smell like fucking liquor. I can't and won't take this shit from you, Keith," Z angrily responded. "Are you finished, Z?" Keith asked. "I'm fucking dying, Z; I've been waiting for the results from the doctor. I have colon cancer and it's at a stage where there's nothing the doctors can or will do." Z fell to his knees right in front of Keith. "Z, if you remember when we first start kicking it, I only drank on occasion. But you're right, I've been wallowing in my sorrow and liquor seems like it's my only true friend and lover. Z, I am crazy about you; I just needed you in my life in any capacity. I didn't care whether you had sex with someone else in Savannah, while I laid in the bed drunk or you go on the internet and make hooks up while I'm in the other room. If you remember, we chatted on the net before you came to where I worked. It was no accident that I called you about your computer; you had given me your number before. I met you on a sex site and my handle was trekkydicky. Z, you hit me up and we started chatting, you gave me your number with a picture. I was too afraid to call you then, but when you came into the store to get your pc fixed, I saw it as my golden opportunity. I fell in love with you the first time I saw your picture. I started loving you the first time we made love. And don't think I'm not familiar with your track record: the men, the fights, the confrontations, the haters and the games you have played with people and their feelings. I just wanted to spend some quality time with someone who could be my companion while I was still living. Z, you are sincere, understanding and compassionate. I understand the reason you put on the tough demeanor, but underneath you is a kind person, despite what the public may say." Keith mustered up a smile. Z's ice cold heart finally was pierced with an arrow of sadness.

"Keith, I didn't know. How can you ever forgive me?" he asked.

"I have to go to the doctor in two days to see whether the cancer has spread and if so, I can find out if radiation might be a final way of treating the cancer. Z, I want you to go with me and if it turns out to be the worst, I want us to start planning my funeral and any other necessary arrangements that may be needed."

Z stood up. "I won't; I won't let you think like that," he commanded.

Keith interrupted, "I have no family and very little friends. I admire how you and your friends get along; you guys are like a family, a family I wish I had or could be a part of. Z, don't get me wrong; I don't want to stop you from running around or doing what you're doing, but I just want to continue to spend quality time with you. Just having you in my presence is all I need, and if you want me to stop drinking, I will. At first I wanted to drink myself to death; I felt it would be easier to deteriorate my liver then to face dying of colon cancer," Keith explained. Z just stood there motionless in the living room. He couldn't move or utter a sound. He just started crying about how much of a bitch he was for always thinking about himself. Keith finally stood up, held him in his arms and kissed Z's tears away.

"Don't cry for me, don't be shedding any tears," he said. Z's legs just gave way and Keith just held his lifeless body in his arms until Z regained his composure. His tears were uncontrollable.

"Men ain't supposed to cry," Keith whispered as he laid Z on the living room couch. "So, what will it be? Will you hang with a brother dying of cancer and who sometimes doesn't have the urge to have sex, but just wants to be in your presence?"

For once in his life, Z was speechless, only nodding in approval. Z's cell phone rang and vibrated in his pocket holster.

"Are you going to answer that?" Keith asked.

"No; if it's important, they will leave a message."

"It's after midnight, so who ever it was knows that you get off eleven-thirty, so you better answer it," Keith encouraged.

Z reluctantly answered the phone. "Hello?"

"What's up, Z, we need to talk. It was Malia, I really can't talk right now Malia, he said. But its important Z, I need to talk to you about Ed," Malia asked.

"Could you call me later, Malia?" Z suggested.

"What's wrong, Z? You sound like you've been crying?" Malia asked.

Z started crying again and Keith took the phone. "Hi, Malia, this is Keith. Z just heard some very bad news and didn't know how to handle it. If you would like to come over to my place, I'll be more then happy to have you. He may need you to be with him."

"What's your address, Keith? I'll be right over."

After giving Malia the address, Keith hung up the phone.

"See what I'm talking about? Within a split second, one of your friends is coming over to see about you. When I found out about my cancer, I had no one to call; no mother, father, sister, brother or friend, but, I'm a strong black man and can take any bad news; I just allowed liquor to be an outlet, but not any more."

Within a matter of minutes, Malia was knocking on Keith's apartment door. Z was still lying on the couch with his back to the world. Malia and Keith gave silent salutations as she walked directly to Z's side, smelling the scent of alcohol in the air.

"What's the deal, baby boy?" Malia asked sounding very concerned. Z looked at Keith, his eyes asking permission to reveal Keith's secret. Keith approved by looking directly a Z.

"It's Keith; he has cancer and I've been acting like an asshole, and there's nothing I can do about it."

Malia was puzzled. "You can't do anything about Keith's dying or your being an asshole?" Malia thought some dry humor would moisten the stale air of sadness and sorrow. They all laughed as she tried desperately to console Z.

Malia asked, "What can I do to help?"

Keith said, "You can draw up my will; I want to leave everything I own to him."

Z screamed, "Shut the fuck up! I don't have time to listen to this shit."

Without hesitation, Malia instructed, "We need to pray."

Z and Keith both looked at her as if she was crazy.

"We need to bring peace and order to this situation. There is no better way to do that, than to pray," she ordered.

The three of them faced the living room couch, knelt down and folded their hands.

"Close your eyes," she told Keith. "Heavenly Father, we come to you in unison. The fate of this house will lay in your hands, God. There is turmoil in the world and this house. We come to you take this disease from our lives. You are a merciful God and a forgiving God; please forgive us for we know have sinned. Give us the strength to endure all the obstacles we may have to face. God, we need your guidance and your vision in hopes that it will help with the pain we are feeling and to understand it won't last forever. We ask for them in loving memory of your son, Jesus Christ. Amen."

Both Z and Keith said "Amen" with tears in their eyes.

It was three weeks before the wedding and it was the talk of the town. Everyone was raving about this wedding. Keisha's co-workers were planning a bridal shower; to be organized by Z. Lake elected to give Tré a bachelor party. He wanted to include the thrills of strippers and all. There were guys from the precinct begging to come. Tré's co-workers wanted to pay to come and most of Tré's road dawgs couldn't wait to hang out at the party. Everybody had RSVP'd the invites over a week ago. Nikko and K. Allen could not believe the responses of people dying to come this wedding, partly because of who was directing it. K. Allen was a renowned wedding director who lived in Columbia; he has traveled all over the world to direct weddings or to be a guest. He is called the original Wedding Planner.

Nikko was trying to put the finishing touches on the wedding and also the vacation for Kennedy; he definitely wanted to take to her birthplace back in Hawaii. He also felt the time away would do him some good. He was excited about the wedding, but it had indeed taken a toll on him; the sleepless nights, the stressful days and trying to maintain a household and also a business was sometimes unbearable. His business had picked up after the news got around that he was back on the block doing better then ever. Katie, the trooper, was doing her best to run the office and the new contracts, but she knew she had to hire some help and it had to be the best help around. She needed more photographers, graphic designers, writers and five more assistants. Nikko corresponded with Katie as much as possible; he told her to hire as many people as she needed, but now the office was getting crowded. Everyone was sitting on each other, begging for space, but overall business was good and prospering.

Malia was greeted at the door by Nikko; they needed to discuss the reception and the overall expenses. Nikko wanted to maintain a sensible level of spending; he really did not want the dinner to be outrageous. Everyone had been so busy with their own lives; it was good to see each other and to share each other's company. They went over the budget and put the final touches on the reception; now it was time to come up to speed with everyone's life. Malia started first. She was pregnant and she and the baby were doing fine. Ed asked her to marry him, but she told him she had to think about it. Victoria was no longer working as her assistant; her leave of absence had expired and all her letters were now being returned to the office. Lake served coffee to them as they were busy chatting, gossiping and catching up on time lost. Malia continued her story of how her parents were furious after learning of her pregnancy; she would give them enough time to cool off by not calling them for a while. She had started Lamaze classes, looking at baby clothes and redecorating one of her many bedrooms. She'd recently started researching different religions and felt she knew she would be cleansed spiritually by practicing Buddhism.

Z knocked on the door after ringing the bell once; Lake greeted him by asking him if he wanted some tea. He accepted as he sat down beside Malia, rubbing her stomach.

"Girl, I can't believe you gonna have a bundle of joy before me. What you girls talking about? Not that damn wedding again; you would think Janet Jackson and Jermaine Dupri was getting married, the way y'all been acting." Z Shrugged.

"Nope, Ms. Mighty Mouth, we are talking about you," Nikko laughed. "What have you been up to? I haven't seen you in a minute," Nikko asked.

"Well I've been spending a lot of time with Keith. He definitely has cancer, and it has spread. He started chemo and we hope that will help; we are still being optimistic. I must admit, I never really knew how much I cared for him, his wittiness, his will and determination. We are planning to take a vacation after the wedding; I think it will do us some good. He's getting weaker now but he's still determined to work. Other than that and work, I've just been the homo homemaker, trying to pay for that damn dress. I told Keisha after she takes that bitch off, I'm going to wear it to work, gym, and church and to the grocery store, and I'mma get my money's worth out of that girl," Z nodded.

"Where you guys going for a vacation?" Nikko asked.

"We are thinking about Paris or Cancun; you know it's for lovers."

"That's funny, Ed and I are thinking about going to South Africa. He won a trip with his company and if he doesn't use the voucher, it will expire. We are going to take a fourteen-day tour of Senegal, the Ivory Coast, Johannesburg and some more cities," Malia said.

"You guys got to be lying! Lake and I are taking Kennedy to Hawaii for our vacation. She wants to go back there because this is her birthplace and Nikki had promised her. I don't believe this," Nikko yelled to Lake. "Theses two are taking a vacation the same time we are; the day after Tré and Keisha's wedding."

"Come on now; I don't believe you guys," Lake added. "Hey we got something else to tell you guys; especially you, Malia. We received a cashier check from probate court, but I thought it should have taken longer. It really depends; if someone pushed the paper work along, it could have very well been expedited."

"Bitch, you been holding back. How much was the check, hoe?" Z asked.

Nikko responded nonchalantly, "It was ten million."

Z screamed, "Bitch, you mean to tell me you got a check for ten million dollars and you didn't tell your Judy Judy girlfriend?"

"We didn't know whether it was a mistake or not, and I'm telling you now," Nikko grunted.

Lake changed the subject. "Z, are you coming to the bachelor party?"

"No, child, I'm going to the Bachlorette party; we're having male strippers."

"We're having female strippers," Lake said, looking at Nikko for approval.

"Yeah, we've having three female strippers and guys are coming from, the gym, Tré's job and from Lake's job," Nikko added.

"See, I can't do that heterosexual shit; I got to go with the girls this time. I got see some dick; pussy makes me regurgitate, and no pun intended, Malia," Z acknowledged. Everyone looked at Z and just nodded their heads.

Reality Check

Tré was getting butterflies by the minute. He tried his best to hide his nervousness, but it was apparent he was having cold feet. He was thinking more and more of Lincoln and how much he was missing his presence. He chose not to call, but was wishing that Lincoln would call him. That day outside his apartment, he lied to Lincoln to temporary settle his heart. As the wedding day came closer, Tré was hoping he'd made the right the decision, or if he should have waited instead of marrying too soon. He loved Keisha; he certainly didn't want anyone else to have her, especially a woman, but was he being selfish by wanting her without thinking of the consequences that would be involved?

Tré was deep in thought when the phone rang.

"Hello?" he asked.

"Hey boy, how's everything going down there in Hotlanta?" Tré's father asked.

"Hey, ole man, how have been Pop?" Tré asked.

"You know, boy, I have my good days and bad days. Still missing your momma; can't believe she's gone sometimes," Kenneth said. "Enough about me; how you been doing, boy? You been on my mind lately you know the wedding is only two weeks away," Kenneth added.

"I'm doing fine. Cant' wait 'til this thing is over. I didn't know it took so much of your time and money. I gotta say that I got some good friends; they are paying for the wedding, the reception, and can you believe Z is paying for Keisha's wedding dress?" Tré mentioned.

"Now that's a hoot; stingy ass Z, with all his bills and the collection people harassing him," Kenneth laughed. "Now after all we been through,

Tré Lamar, I know when something is wrong; you been in my spirit and my dreams lately," Kenneth relayed with that James Earl Jones' voice.

"Pop, I'm scared, man. I want to marry Keisha," Tré said.

"I sense a 'but'. Boy, spit it out" Kenneth demanded.

"Pop, I'm.........scared," he said.

"Tré, are you scared or afraid? Boy, don't have me to come through this phone. Now tell me and stop stalling," Kenneth commanded.

Tré felt this was the hardest thing he had to do; he had to admit to his father his sexual experimentation with a man.

"Pop, I have had niggas suck my dick. I have had sex with niggas, and I'm the kind of man that they talk about being on the down low," Tré whispered nervously.

"Boy, you on the DL. I know what that is; I watch Oprah. Son, let me tell you a story." Tré thought he would die if his dad told him he was living a double life on the DL.

"I don't think you remember my step brother, your uncle Phil, the one who committed suicide. Well, you know, uncle was bisexual. We don't talk about it much in the family 'cause it's one of those secrets we keep in the closet. Phil's father was Jamaican, and when Phil told his daddy he was attracted to boys at an early age, he sent him to live with us, for fear that if the Jamaicans found out that Phil was gay, or a sissy, they would catch him and stone him to death. He came to live with us, me, your uncle Isaiah and your aunt Ruth. We had to adjust our lives, because he was 15 and we were much younger, but we learned to love him; even my father started treating Phil as his own son. Well as the years went by and black people became more homophobic, Phil got married to this beautiful girl named Eliza. They married and moved back to Jamaica; his father needed him to come back and run the business because his father was getting up in age and it was Phil's responsibility to take over the business. When Phil moved back to Jamaica, I used to visit a lot and Phil and I became very close. He used to confide in me his sexual desires for other men, and how they would haunt him. Even though these feelings were repressed the entire time he lived with us in New York, they resurfaced when he moved back to the islands. As the years went by, Eliza had three babies; these are your second cousins. You don't know them because they won't visit. After the third child, Phil secretly started seeing the male doctor who'd delivered his children. They spent an awful a lot of time together. Sometimes Phil would even spend the night away from home, leaving Eliza alone with the kids. Well one night in the neighborhood park, Phil was having sex in the park with this doctor. They got caught in a very compromising position. The village was horrified; people stopped going to the hospital where the doctor worked, and they both started receiving death threats. On several occasions, people tried to burn down Phil's house and this made life difficult for Eliza and the children. They were ridiculed where ever they went, the market, the church, the school. They were completely ostracized. Phil couldn't take it no more. One summer night when Eliza took the kids to a revival, your uncle Phil purchased a gallon of gas in a can and literally poured it all over his body. He sat in the car and lit a match; he lit himself on fire. Later that year, I received a letter from him which was postmarked a month after his suicide. I opened it and read it out loud one night while sitting on the stoop; it took me a week to get enough strength to open it. It read:

My dearest brother, forgive me for what I have done to my family. I have shamed my father and his name. I have shamed my wife and my beloved children. The life I chose was not the life I wanted to live. I wanted to be free to love without any prejudice or repercussions. In life, God has given us a heart, feeling and the desire to be loved. I was born to love a man, and I knew I was a man. I hate myself for being an anti-man. Life is free, but it wasn't for me, I was a slave of society and prejudice, but now I'm free; the pain has gone and now I my spirit can live, because I couldn't live my life as a man on Earth. I love you my little brother, please give my love to everyone who deserves it. Until we meet again, God bless you."

Kenneth finished his story as the air became thick.

"Son, are you there?" Kenneth asked. Tré was totally silent and his heart was heavy with tears. Tré was imaging the pain his uncle went through, emotionally and physically. "Dad, how did you feel after realizing Uncle Phil was a faggot?" Tré asked.

"My brother was not a faggot and I don't want you to ever say that again. My brother was a bisexual man. It was different; in those days we didn't have a name for men who didn't act like sissies. It was very undercover and people just ignored it; now a days, y'all got all kinds of names: gay, lesbian, down low, bisexual, homosexual, it reminds me of when we was colored, negro, African Americans and now black. Today things aren't the same; we as black people are so damn homophobic and we don't embrace brotherhood as we used to. We all talk about black power but we continue to hate each other. When King was living, we didn't hate; we didn't have black on black crime cause we stood together. Martin had people believing that they should judge by the content of their character and not by their sexual orientation. One of Martin's advisors was gay and they were best friends; Martin didn't hide what he had for that man, but today brothers gotta hide and be ashamed their love. Tré, you can say what you want about that damn Z, but Z is real; he's feisty and flamboyant, but the boy don't bite his tongue and hés not ashamed of who he is. Son, do you love this man?" Kenneth asked.

Tré was startled by what his father had just asked him.

"Pop, I never said there was a man involved," Tré explained.

"Boy, you wouldn't be having second thoughts about marriage if there wasn't a third party involved."

"Dad, this guy is a professional ball player. The nigga is married and got money. We spent a lot of quality time together; we even shared a stripper together, a female stripper. Before I made the decision to marry Keisha, I had to break off the friendship, but now I miss his crazy ass. The nigga was cool. Sometimes we just chilled, watched sports, played pool, took shots of gin and worked out together, but I had to let him go."

"Tré, y'all been wearing protection when y'all be doing IT?" Kenneth asked.

"Man, what kinda question is that, Dad?" Tré sounded frustrated.

"It's one you better answer, boy, and be honest about it," Kenneth instructed.

"Yeah, Pop; Keisha and I took all I tests and they came back negative."

"Another question, son; do you dream about this man? Remember, dreams are the spiritual guide to our souls; dreams can tell you what you need to know, good, bad, or indifferent."

Tré was deep in thought when he answered his father.

"I have dreamed of him, but lately I have been dreaming of Keisha, Junior, and the three of us. Dad, why do I feel like you're interrogating me?" Tré asked.

"I'm not interrogating you, son. I just want to make sure you make the best decision for yourself and not society. There are a lot of men who are married with children and live secret lives. They wish they could have done it differently. It would have saved a lot of anguish, heartache and tears. I notice when people talk about a brother who's on the DL, they don't understand why he hides the fact that he has sex with men. Now, I asked you son, why do you hide?" Kenneth caught Tré off guard. Tré cleared his throat.

"Dad, if a man sleeps with another man, it's dirty and disgusting; hés less than a man. Pop, when I first let a man suck my dick, I felt nasty, but superior. As time went on, I realized that sex is sex and it's no onés business if I decide to get my dick sucked by a man or woman."

"Boy," Kenneth shouted, "we been on this phone for almost two hours.

You know I got to take my pressure pills. Tré, before I hang up son, I want you to know that when you went to jail, I loved you. When you were strung out, I loved you. When you was gang banging and robbing folks, you were still was my son and I love you more now than ever before because today you have proven to me that you're the man I raised. Whatever your decision is, I love you and your mother loves you too," Kenneth ended.

"I love you, too, Pop," Tré said, as he hung up.

Tré closed his eyes and envisioned his mother giving him her approval.

Bewitching Hour

The bachelor and Bachlorette parties were minutes away. Z was on the phone calling the stripper to make sure he would be on time. The stripper had assured Z he did have a big dick and he knew how to use it. Keith decided to go to the bachelor party, even though he was feeling a little under the whether after having dialysis earlier that morning. Fifteen girls were already at Malia's house waiting in anticipation as Malia volunteered to go pick up Keisha. She was dead tired after having to pack, move, unpack, decorate and still get ready for the night's festivities. All the way to Malia's, Keisha kept thanking her for all she had done.

"I wish there was a way I could repay you and the rest of the gang," Keisha said.

"I want you to just be happy and understand the true meaning of marriage; it's an institution that takes love, understanding, patience and communication. Malia explained. "Malia you could never imagine how long I've been waiting for his moment; for Tré and I to become one in God's eyes. I couldn't believe that he wanted to help me raise my brothers. There's no one I'd rather be with than Tré. You know, girl, he was the first and only man I ever had sex with," Keisha admitted.

"Girl, you are lying! That's a miracle within itself," Malia added.

"I don't know if you know this or not, but we met when I was in the eighth grade going to the ninth grade. It happened one summer when he was down here visiting from New York. He was here visiting Z; he had gotten in trouble up there and he needed to place to lay low. I was working at the mall, my first summer job, when he and this boy named Trey came in the record store where I was working. His friend started trying throw his Mack on but, I wasn't having it. It was my first job and I was not going to be distracted. Eventually his friend gave up and they walked out of the store. Later on, before closing, Tré came in by himself and asked if he could take me home; I was so naïve, I didn't realize the boy didn't have a car until we started walking to the bus stop. He started laughing and said, 'I didn't ask you if you needed a ride; I asked could I take you home.' He was so adorable and sexy; that boy's legs and the way his jeans fitted, lord have mercy on my soul. That summer, we spent every moment together. He told me about his family and the gang he was in and the people he had to rob so there wouldn't be a hit out for his family, especially his sister Cynthia. She had beaten up one of the gang leader's girlfriends, and in order to spare her life, Tré had to rob certain people. He gave me money to help pay my rent for me and my family; lord only knows where he got the money from. Tré bought all my school clothes that summer and even helped me buy clothes for my brothers. That summer before school started back and before he had to go back to New York, I lost my virginity to him. It was so beautiful; he borrowed on of his friends' cars. I don't' even think he had a license. We drove to this man made beach about an hour away from here. When it was dusk, he lit candles in the woods near the beach; the candles lead straight into the water. He had prepared a wine and cheese basket with imitation champagne for me. He laid down the blanket and fed me strawberries, grapes and pineapples; he started licking my body with strawberries still in his mouth and smoothed them all over my body. He then took some ice and licked me even more; the coldness sent chills to my spine. That summer I had my hair braided, he started to stroke my hair ever so gently as he licked my neck, breast and navel. My body went into orbit; my nipples started getting hard and my vagina was getting wet, girl. And then he did it; he went down on me. I started scratching his back, begging him to not stop and crying at the same time." Malia was no longer listening; she had started thinking about Drayton and their love making as Keisha continued. "He sucked and licked knee caps, toes, feet, the back of my spine, the top of my neck, and once I felt that I couldn't take anymore and was about to orgasm, he stopped me; I had never in my life felt like this. As he told me how beautiful I was, he slipped on a condom and went inside me slowly. Girl, you talking about the heavens opened and I lay with the stars and moon; I was spellbound. I literally left my body and I could see how he was making my body his body with the rhythm of every stroke. The sound of the night filled my soul; the sound of the water touched my spirit. I felt like Eve making love to her Adam; it felt so natural and so good after that night. I vowed to him before he left that I would never sleep with another man again as long as I lived." Keisha began to cry. "I kept my promise and when he told me he was coming down here to go to college, I couldn't believe it. Malia, Tré is my soul mate. I've tried to ignore it, but wéve been through so much together I can deny that hés my destiny."

The ringing of the cell phone startled both her and Keisha had they were entering Malia's subdivision.

"Hello?" she answered.

"Where you hoes at? I can't entertain no twenty women; therés a little too much of me to go around," Z laughed.

"Girl, don't get your panties in a bunch," Malia busted out, smiling.

Z responded, "Malia sometimes you can be the last man." Z hung up the phone. Z had prepared games and party favors; he supplied all the guests with gift bags, and he introduced the Sex Lady, a friend of his who sold sex toys, crèmes, edible under garments and even swings. Keisha was having a wonderful time, laughing, talking and dancing with her friends. There was a knock at the door; they had been anticipating the arrival of the stripper. Keisha rushed to the door, beating Z by a matter of seconds. The stripper came in dressed like a pizza delivery man. He asked Keisha, "Did someone order a pizza?" and before anyone could respond, Z snatched him up, putting dollar bills down his shirt. Everyone in the house started yelling and screaming for more. The door bell rang again; without hesitation, Keisha ran to go open it. It was Gina, asking if she could see her for a moment. Keisha's smiles and laughter came to a sudden halt. She snatched Keisha outside where they could have some privacy. No one noticed the disappearance of Keisha; everyone was busy undressing the stripper.

"You are not going get married to Tré and that's an order," Gina commanded.

"Gina, we have already had this conversation. I'm getting married in two days, whether you can accept that or not."

"I won't let you do it," Gina retaliated.

"Let me know who the fuck you think you are! My mother is in a crack house and my father is dead, so who do you think you are, Gina?"

"I'm the only one who really loves you. I'm the one you talked to when you were having problems with Tré and dealing with the hatred of your mother and your father getting beat to death. Keisha, I was there when you needed money for this or that, I was the one who stayed up with Junior when he was sick and you needed to sleep. I was the stupid bitch who picked up Junior and dropped your brothers off at practice, and now you actually think I'm going to let you marry some punk-ass motherfucker? Hell fucking no," Gina repeated.

Suddenly Malia and Z rushed outside.

Z asked, "What the fuck is going on?"

"Nothing," Keisha said.

Malia asked who Gina was and if she was invited to the party.

"And if she wasn't, why is she on my property?" Malia asked.

Keisha was trying to calm everyone down.

"Malia, this is a friend of mine, Gina. She was about to leave," Keisha explained.

"I'm not going anywhere, and if I do, you're going with me."

"Oh, the dyke is demanding," Z blurted.

"I got your dyke you pint-sized wannabe pussy faggot," Gina struck back.

"And the tongue for dick got a mouth on her, too." Z struck a nerve.

Malia said, "I suggest you get off my property right now, before I call the security guard at the gate."

"Who you think let me in, you stupid bitch."

Z pulled out his switchblade and pressed it into Gina's stomach.

"Now, therés one thing you don't do; you can call me all kinds of names because, I have heard it all, but onc thing you don't do is disrespect my friends. Now you psycho bitch, if you want to live to see tomorrow, you better leave by the count of five. Five." Z pressed the knife harder into Gina's stomach. Gina backed up and started to leave.

She yelled to Keisha, "Baby girl, this ain't over yet! I love you, baby cakes. That's what you used to call me: baby cakes," Gina yelled with tears in her eyes. She slammed her car door and sped off. Keisha started crying while Malia tried to console her. Z broke his silence first. "Stop that damn crying; you have no reason to be crying. The bitch is crazy; let me handle her. I won't hit the bitch but I can make sure she will be paralyzed for life." Malia was still confused. "Who was that?"

Z looked at her and said, "Girl, that baby, is sucking all the air from your brain. That's her girlfriend."

Malia, still looking dumbfounded exclaimed, "Girlfriend!"

"Yeah, girlfriend," Z yelled. "Buy the book Malia, buy the book."

The bachelor party was kind of boring until the strippers burst on the scene. They stirred things up right on time. Tré tried to maintain his composure, but couldn't help himself; he felt the ass of one of the strippers the breasts of the other one. His dick was bone hard, just like every one else including Nikko and Lake. All of Trés boys were there: Shadow, Zeus and even Q. Trés cousins from South Carolina and New York, Luke, Z's brother stole the show by harassing one of the strippers, Luke was a sex addict and couldn't help him self when pussy was staring him in his face. He ended up giving one of the strippers extra just to give him oral sex in the car. The women danced for about two hours, grinding, stripping, gyrating to the beat of the music; it was enough to make a gay man sick. Lake and Nikko were ready to leave after the first hour to have a little party for themselves. K. Allen was ready for everyone to leave; he needed quietness to marinate the thoughts of how to put the wedding finale together. He and Katie were busy, separating, sorting, calling, decorating, fussing, arguing, laughing and joking about how wonderful this wedding would be. The wedding was in two days, but the carriage had not been delivered, neither had the white horse. K. Allen was thinking of a secondary plan. He knew he was not going to sleep until everything was organized to perfection.

Keisha was sleeping when Tré came home. He was trying his best not to wake her or the out of town guests, but she was up waiting for him; she knew that they needed to talk. The first thing he did was kiss her on the forehead, not realizing she was up.

"Hey, baby, what are you doing up?" Tré asked.

"I got in about an hour ago. KS, I had a blast; the girls really know how to throw a party. Oh, don't let me forget Z; he is hilarious. I think your sisters enjoyed themselves, especially Stephanie. Tré, we need to talk," Keisha said.

"What is it, baby?" Tré looked concerned.

Keisha started explaining, "I need to tell you that Gina showed up at the party tonight, uninvited. She tried to cause a scene, but Z ran her off. Baby, I'm scared; I'm afraid that shés going do something to interfere with our wedding."

Tré interrupted her, "Don't worry about Gina or no other nigga. Nobody will stop us from being together." Tré became furious. "Get some sleep, baby cakes. I'm going downstairs to talk to the old man; you know hés up watching the tube." Tré kissed his bride-to-be on the forehead and rushed downstairs to talk to his father.

Kenneth was downstairs in the den where he could give his undivided attention to watching the highlights of the earlier games.

"How was the party, son?" Kenneth asked without looking at Tré.

"It was great, Pop. I really enjoyed myself. I'm still kinda tired, though; those women wore me out. Your nephew, Luke, almost went to jail, trying to rape one of the strippers right in front of everybody. That nigga got a serious problem," Tré added. He went into detail telling his Dad about all the crazy stuff the strippers could do.

Keisha was restless. She didn't know if telling Tré about what happened earlier was the right thing to do. She was afraid that if she didn't, someone would tell him and he would be upset. She decided to go downstairs and get a glass of warm milk. Not really trying to listen, she could overhear Tré and Kenneth laughing and talking like college boys. She was about to run back upstairs when she heard the words, down low, Lincoln's name, homosexuality and calling off the wedding. Keisha couldn't hear the entire conversation, but went into immediate shock from the words she did hear. She started to cry, and prayed to God to not let what happened before happen to her again.

"Not this time. If anyone is going to cut off the wedding it will be me, not anyone else." Keisha cried herself to sleep.

The following morning was a beautiful day; it was a day of wedding rehearsals and heavenly bliss. Keisha woke up in Trés arms, with his chest against her back. She laid there for a while wondering if she should confront him or question his father. She knew Tré had a very short temper and his father would never tell her anything. Keisha felt sick with butterflies and nausea. She began to silently cry as she slowly pulled herself out of his arms. Keisha decided to take a long, hot shower in hopes this would wash some of the tears away from her soul. There was so much running through her head; did she hear what she thought she heard, or was she just tired and sleeping and her mind was playing tricks on her? She decided to cook breakfast for the entire house; this way she could read the faces of Tré and his father.

Keisha ran downstairs and decided to cook a smorgasbord of food. She cooked scrambled eggs, turkey bacon, wheat pancakes, grits, and hash browns and freshly squeezed orange juice. She woke everyone up as she prepared to serve he house guests. Cynthia and Cynthia shared one bedroom. Trevor, Stephanie's husband, their son, Blake and Cynthia's boyfriend shared the other bedroom.

The boys slept in the living room and Kenneth had the entire den and third bathroom to himself.

Everyone smelled the food at the same time and was at the dinning room table in a matter of minutes. Everyone served themselves, except, Tré, Kenneth, Junior and Stephanie's daughter. Cynthia prepared their plates along with Keisha.

"Girl, sit down and take a load off; you seem exhausted. This is your day; you're gonna need your rest," Cynthia smiled. "Stephanie and I will clean up the kitchen and get the kids ready for the noon rehearsal."

Keisha had to maintain her composure; she had to do the final fitting for the wedding dress, get her hair done, pick up her makeup, get a manicure and pedicure, talk to the photographer and talk to the make up artist, gather the bridés maids and give them their gifts. She put on a happy face and gave her thanks to her (hopefully) new in-laws. She rushed upstairs, gathered the necessary belongings, and off she went. It was only nine o'clock but she didn't have a second to spare...

On the way to the hair salon, Keisha picked up the phone to dial Gina's number. She needed someone to talk to, someone who could ease her emotions and erase her pain. She fumbled with the cell phone, hesitating to dial that last digits. Then she thought it would be best to drive by Gina's house; maybe this would be a better choice. As she started in the direction of Gina's neighborhood, she made a quick detour. She decided to talk to the one person who could understand her better then anyone. The one person who would give her the guidance and strength she desired; her God. Keisha decided to head to her sanctuary.

The church was dark and a little spooky; Keisha strolled in and felt the presence of Jesus Christ staring at her from the pulpit. She knelt down and prayed to God for about thirty minutes, feeling the Holy Spirit cover her spirit. Keisha wasn't a very religious person, but shéd learned to love and appreciated God for being in her life. In less the forty-eight hours she would be back at this same church, sharing her vows with her future husband. Suddenly someone touched her on the shoulder and Keisha literally pissed in her jeans. It was the cleaning lady who was cleaning up for today's rehearsal. Good Morning, Keisha," the lady said.

"Good morning to you," Keisha said, still startled and embarrassed.

"Are you ready for special day tomorrow?" The lady asked.

Keisha nodded.

"I know you're going to make a beautiful bride; everyone is talking about it. God will also be happy for you; He feels you and Tré were meant to be together," the lady added. Keisha was becoming puzzled. "Are you coming to the wedding?" Keisha asked.

The lady replied, "I wouldn't miss it for the world. Well you got God's blessing and my blessing, and I know you're going to make a beautiful wife," the lady kept saying as she disappeared behind one of the doors behind the pulpit.

After washing, setting and styling, Keisha was even more radiant than before; her hair was long, but her stylist was able to wrap it for tomorrow's event. Keisha purchased some additional hair pieces to give her hair a fuller look for tomorrow. Her nails were manicured and polish with a French nail acrylic and her feet had been soaked, massaged, scraped and polished with a clear polish that included iridescent colors. Keisha felt new again; the washed hair, the perfect manicure nail and the speckle of sunlight on her toes made her feel like she could handle the world. Her girlfriends finally tracked her down and begged her not to leave the salon. After five minutes of waiting and becoming agitated, she noticed a stretch limo driving up in front of the salon. "Surprise!" her girlfriends screamed. They all started kicking and yelling, acting like high school girls. She jumped in the car and instructed the driver to head to Nikko's where she was to be fitted for her wedding dress. It seemed like only seconds had passed when the limo was driving up into the sub division. Keisha waltzed up to the door where the crew was waiting on her. She stopped in mid step. The first thing she noticed was the dress on the mannequin; it was simply gorgeous. The top part of the dress was a halter bustier encrusted with rhinestones. It tied behind the neck. The entire back was open. The bottom of the dress flowed with the slightest movement. The train was about two to three feet long. All the girls just stood there and marveled the beauty of the dress. Keisha would truly look like Cinderella, even if she didn't feel like her. The dressers rushed in into the guest bathroom where Nikko, K. Allen and the rest of the crew was waiting. Keisha emerged looking like a princess; the dress was indeed a work of art. She looked as if someone had drawn the dress on her. The dressers and the stylist that Nikko hired played in Keisha's hair for about ten minutes; afterwards she emerged again. This time she was even more beautiful. Everyone was in a daze for a moment, until K. Allen yelled, "Chop chop, people. It's almost show time. We need to head down to the church. We can't have people waiting on us. We need to be waiting on them."

Keisha did a quick change in a matter of moments. She really wasn't ready to face Tré, but she knew it was inevitable.

Rehearsal started with a bang; everything was in sync. Junior and Kennedy were awesome; they hit their marks in one take. Keisha had eight bridés maids, with Tiffany as the maid of honor. All the girls needed to be told once or twice the proper way to waltz to the music of the soloist number. The men were even more embarrassing; there were a couple of times where, K. Allen had to put on some pumps and show the men how to march with the women down aisle. After two hours of going over and over the steps, the entrance and the exit with the groom's men, K. Allen screamed with relief, "By George, I think they got it!" Nikko was in the back of the church laughing his ass off.

Keisha tried her best to avoid eye contact with Tré and his family. She talked to the girls, K. Allen and mostly Nikko about nothing. Everyone sensed her unusual behavior, but summed it up as nerves on her wedding day. Even Junior asked her what was the matter. She replied, "This is a big day for all of us, baby; just got some things on my mind." But it was apparent that Keisha was queasy; she just needed to lie down for a moment, but K. Allen would not hear such a thing. He insisted that she should get fitted one last time for the wedding dress, this time making sure the pumps matched to perfection. He also wanted to know how the veil would compliment the dress, since it was designed by one of his contacts who specialized in making head pieces. This would give the surprised guests a chance to rehearse their songs for the wedding.

Malia had been up on her feet since six o'clock that morning in heels and she needed to lie down, if only for a minute. It was a long and exhausting rehearsal. Ed had called her five times, trying to see did if needed or wanted anything. She refused to call him back. She just needed to rest. As soon as she closed her eyes, her new assistant called her; Malia asked her what the problem was; it was Saturday afternoon.

"What could be so important that it couldn't wait until I get back from vacation?"

"I was asked to give you a call about your last assistant, Ms. River," she explained. "Proceed with it," Malia demanded.

"Well therés a warrant for her arrest. Therés an all points bulletin for her arrest. The partners of the law firm told me she had something to do with the murder of Nikki Grey," the assistant continue to explain. Malia was shocked and confused. She immediately called Lake, because the news would have been too much for Nikko.

"Lake, what is going on?" Malia asked.

'It's true, Malia. We have been working on this case intensely, and the evidence shows that the DNA of Victoria matches the DNA that was under Nikki's fingernails. We also discovered that the guy who raped and assaulted Nikki was Victoria's brother. I should have figured that part out, because when I dated Victoria, I remember how she had a step brother who had been convicted of being a stalking and raping a little girl, but got off on a technicality. The only piece that we are not sure of is the time factor and if Victoria was there when the guy was raping Nikki. We just don't know her involvement, but we had enough evidence to get a search warrant to her house. She left in a heated rush, but she also left valuable evidence. She left Nikki's bracelet in her own jewelry box," Lake explained.

Malia's head was now spinning; everything started coming together. Victoria's whole demeanor was very strange after Nikki's death; the mood swings when it came to the sudden death of the assailant and her sudden departure, begging for an emergency leave of absence.

Lake continued, "I know this is an inconvenience, but I will need a sworn statement from you, Malia. Any way you can assist with capturing her, it will truly help the precinct." "Anything you need, I'll be more than happy to help," Malia agreed. "How is Nikko taking all of this?" she asked.

"Very well, if I should say so myself; the wedding and our vacation have taken precedence over everything," Lake explained. "You know him and Z never really liked Victoria. I know why he wasn't fond of her, but Z always said he didn't like her, and didn't know why. I guess it's true what that say: a true diva knows," Lake smirked. Malia chuckled. "Are you coming to the rehearsal dinner? If so I'll give you a statement then; it would save time. This morning sickness is taking a toll on me."

"That will be cool. Get some rest and I'll see you in a few," Lake ordered.

The rehearsal dinner was a smash. The girls from Keisha's job pitched in and made all the food. They were giggling all the way through the rehearsal and the dinner. The entire wedding party ate first; Keisha and Tré were in awe of the dinner and the people that organized the dinner. Trés co workers presented him with a voucher for a honeymoon in Jamaica; his heart sank for two reasons: He wanted a honeymoon, but couldn't afford it, but also he thought about his uncle and how Jamaica impacted his life and his death. Keisha was so graceful, but she didn't know if they would be able to go. They both had a week off from work, but they had planned to spend it cleaning and decorating the house. Kenneth spoke up and insisted that they went. He demanded that they went and he would keep the house and the kids while they enjoyed a honeymoon. He joked about them making some more babies on their honeymoon. Everyone cheered them on with excitement; even Junior was telling his mommy and daddy to go to Jamaica, even though he didn't know where Jamaica was. Tré and Keisha took this time out to give presents to their wedding party; Keisha gave out pearl necklaces, along with charm bracelets. Tré had become very traditional in his decision making; he gave his groomsmen solid gold keys engraved with their individual initials and neck ties. It was almost midnight when Nikko and K. Allen insisted that it was time to close this party.

"We all have a big day tomorrow," they both ordered. The preacher gave a closing prayer and everyone started breaking down for tomorrow's wedding extravaganza. Tré walked Keisha to the limo and wished her a wonderful day tomorrow. Keisha was feeling a little better, but was still uneasy about the conversation shéd overheard earlier. She asked Tré in a humorous tone, if he wanted to call off the wedding, and he responded, "I wouldn't miss this wedding for the world."

Keisha knew that this would be the last time she would see Tré until tomorrow at the wedding. She started to get teary eyed as he leaned up against the limo and gave him a long and juicy kiss. Someone from the wedding party yelled, "Y'all got along lifetime to do all that." Someone else yelled, "Can y'all wait until tomorrow?" Everyone who heard the remarks laughed loudly. Once Keisha got in the limo, her girlfriends were busy talking about the guys in the wedding party; who was fine, the ones who were gay, the ones who worked for IBM (Itty Bitty Meat) and the others who worked for Ball Park Franks or VBD's (Very Big Dicks). They gossiped all the way to Keisha's car, which was still at the hair salon. She insisted on picking it up; it was her old faithful and heavens forbid if someone would have stolen it. The girls were so busy laughing, talking, giggling and singing, they never noticed they were being followed by a black sedan. Keisha jumped out of the limo and bid her girlfriends farewell, but not before all of the kissed her and wish her a wonderful day tomorrow. The limo sped off as Keisha fumbled for her keys, suddenly the black sedan ran up against her car. Keisha heard the car, but could not move in time, the car was inches from her as she jumped on the hood of the car. Startled and frightened, Keisha jumped in the car and started crying. She first thought it had to be Gina, paying her respects for the wedding, but realized Gina would never do such a thing. She gathered her composure and she finally found her keys and drove home looking for the black car to reappear. She started to call Tré, but instead called Nikko. Nikko answered on the first ring.

"I think someone is trying to kill me," she cried.

"What do you mean?" Nikko asked.

"Someone was trying to run me over as I got in my car."

"Where are you now, Keisha?"

"I'm on Orange Blossom and Maple Blvd."

"Hold on." Nikko clicked over, called Lake and had Lake call a police car to escort Keisha home. Within a matter of seconds, a police car was pulling around the corner. The policeman, pulled up beside her, knocked on the window and begged Keisha to roll the window down. Keisha hesitated, but Nikko told her it was alright.

"Look on his badge; it should say Officer Myrick," Keisha nodded.

"Yes, it says that."

"Okay, let me talk to him, Keisha." Lake was on three-way informing the officer what to do. Officer Myrick gave the phone back to Keisha and told her drive home and he would escort her and take a report afterward.

Nikko talked to her all the way home, trying to calm her down. She asked Nikko and Lake not to tell Tré any of this. She didn't want him to worry. They agreed. Keisha did not realize her car had been damaged. It wasn't bad, but it would be costly. The officer took a full report, and then called Lake, to inform him that she was safely at home. Keisha tried to communicate to Kenneth and the kids, but she was too exhausted. Kenneth could tell she had a lot on her mind and told her he would get the kids ready for bed and would bring her up some warm milk. Keisha dragged herself upstairs, took a long hot shower and then decided to take pregnancy test; something was definitely going on, and she wanted to rule out any possibilities. She put the timer on as she started to get dressed for bed. Someone knocked on the door; it was Tré with a cup of warm milk. Keisha was shocked and relieved. Lake had given him the news and within a matter of minutes, he was at the door. (??He'd) He had told his father what had happened and he was not pleased at all. Keisha asked, "What are you doing here?" "Don't I live here?" he asked.

"But Tré, you're not supposed to see me until tomorrow at the wedding," she added. Tré sat her on the bed, and said, "I got something I need to tell you and then you can tell me if there's going to be a wedding. Keisha, I love you with all my heart; you have been my soul mate for life. But, I've been unfaithful to you and myself. I have been living a life of deception. I've been struggling with my sexuality. Now, I ain't no faggot or gay, but I have slept with men, baby."

Keisha's tears were instantly uncontrollable, but Tré didn't stop.

"This has been heavy on my heart. I'm a nigga from the streets; I've been on drugs, in a gang, in jail and now those things are behind me. I fought those demons and I won, but this demon has lived with me since the beginning; in a way I did all those things in order not to face this one. I hated myself for being that way, so I wanted people to hate me." Now, Tré was crying as weight of his heart began to become lighter. "I have had nightmares of waking up and seeing myself as Z. I have to live my life hard and be hard, because I don't want no motherfucker see me on the streets and say, 'Look at the fucking faggot.' I wanted to tell you, but how can you tell the woman you love, that you been fucking around with men. Keisha, there's no easy way, and people are always saying, the man needs to tell, but it ain't no book out there to tell this to anyone, so I hide it. I know there's a lot of (niggers) that's out there that hide it. I hear when people say our society is homophobic, but I don't know. If society embraced DL niggas, would we still stand up and be identified? We have hated faggots, homos, sissies, drag queens all our lives. This is something that we have been taught since birth. We have been taught to ridicule them, to make fun of their lifestyle. But day by day, I noticed I was becoming attracted to men, and then I cursed God for playing this trick on me. The thing I hated most is the thing I was becoming: a lover of a man and woman. So I started to hide my attraction for men by being hard core, being a hip hop nigga, by being a drug dealer, then a drug addict; these are things that I am more proud of the being attracted to a fucking nigga. I feel faggots are the lowest thing you can be in life; less than a man and less than a human. But now I'm no better than them and if I think about it, I'm worse. I'm a fake, a punk, the scum of the earth. I allowed my hatred for niggas to overshadow my love for them. Keisha, I tell you this because, you have to help me. I had to be honest with myself and honest with you. You know I'm clean; I have never done anything unprotected. I don't believe in that shit. Our HIV test came back negative, now I need to know if you still want to marry me." Keisha's face was salty with tears, just as she was about to answer Tré, the alarm for the pregnancy test went off. She jumped up and ran in the bathroom. The result was positive. She felt faint and sat on the edge of the tub. Tré immediately became worried and peeked in the bathroom. She tried to hide the box, but couldn't.

She cried, "Tré, I'm pregnant."

He lifted her and carried her back to the bedroom and laid her on the bed. He touched her stomach as he continued to cry for forgiveness. He kissed her as he took off his pants and underwear.

"Please marry me. Please let me be your husband. Please allow me to make you happy. Please allow me to give you the life you deserve."

Keisha pulled him closer; she needed comfort and she needed to be loved. Tré started kissing her nipples and her thighs and ended up between Keisha's legs. As he performed oral sex on her he looked into her eyes as she stared into the heavens, begging for God to send her a sign. The tears continued to flow as the pleasure of Tré was apparent. They made love until the darkness was becoming light. Unbeknownst to them the black sedan was in the midst of darkness waiting to strike again. Tré slowly eased out of the bed as Keisha radiated from a night of ecstasy.

The Wedding Day

It was eight o'clock and the morning and they crew had been up since dawn. The horse was ready to do his thing; the carriage was waiting to be picked up from K. Allen's contact. The surprise guest was at the Ritz-Carlton, resting until someone called them at twelve noon. Nikko, Lake, K. Allen, Z, Keith, Malia and Ed were having breakfast and going through their final checklist; the one for the wedding and also the one for their separate vacations. As they all sat, eating and drinking mimosas, they presented K. Allen with a new lap top computer along with some new additions to his Louis Vuitton luggage. He also had hidden a check for five thousand dollars that Z had purposely hidden in his attaché case.

Z was the first to say, "I'm going to miss you guys. I expect souvenirs and gifts from where ever you girls are going."

Ed looked up because he really didn't understand the lingo Z was using.

"What time you guys leaving?" Malia asked Lake.

"Our flight will be leaving at seven in the morning; we are going to be dead tired, but the good thing is that we have already packed. We're scheduled to get up at forth-thirty and hopefully be to the airport at five thirty. Lake added. We're scheduled to leave at six in the morning and we have a long flight; it's gonna take up about nineteen hours to get there. Thanks for the statement; we have some leads on Victoria. We do think she's in California. Hopefully by the time I get back she will be in custody."

Z interrupted, "See, I told you that bitch was ruthless. I knew something was wrong with the whore, but no one wanted to listen. I should have cut the bitch with my blade when I had time."

Keith stopped him. "Z, don't take that knife on the plane. We can not be detained or you will be in custody when I get back from Europe." Z rolled his eyes.

"Well I hope they just catch her, because as long as she's on the streets, none of us are really safe," Nikko added.

Malia changed the subject, "Z, when are you and Keith leaving," she asked. We're not leaving until tomorrow night; I gotta make sure mom, Luke and his fifty children are back home after the wedding. That reminds me, I need to get the money for his three hotel rooms. Oh, I meant to tell you bitches, I got a promotion waiting for me once I get back from Europe."

"Congratulations, man." Lake was the first to acknowledge him. "What will you be doing?" he asked.

"I will be head of the janitorial services staff for the hospital," Z chuckled. "No, I'll be one of the administrative nurses for the hospital."

Malia started crying, "I'm going to miss you guys. I really am."

Z stopped her. "Girl, that baby is really fucking up your hormones; them mood swings are coming every 15 seconds."

Z had everyone in the dinning room dying of with laughter.

"We better get a move on we have a lot to do before six o'clock." K.

Allen ordered. They all agreed, as they exited with kisses, hugs and cries.

It was four o'clock and Keisha and Tré's house was a zoo; people from everywhere were trying to get dressed or trying to get Keisha dressed. She had someone, doing her nails, her feet, makeup and hair. The stylist was ordering everyone around; she had come highly recommended and she didn't take kindly to anyone who didn't respect her reputation. She and Cynthia almost got into it twice, but her professionalism overtook her street minded attitude and she decided to pull Cynthia's weave out after the reception. Kenneth was trying to help the kids get dressed; he was busy trying to find socks, T-shirts, underwear and shoe polish. The old man was tired but he wasn't going down without a fight. As it got closer to five o'clock he managed to have all the kids dressed and sitting in the living room like well mannered grand kids.

Keisha was a nervous wreck, still upset over the incident, over Tré and also the pregnancy, she was thinking, "We just got this house and in nine months it's going to be too small." She laughed at the little bundle of joy that growing inside her; this made her feel better. The lovemaking was another episode in her immediate life that took her by storm; it was unbelievable. She had often heard that you could really tell if a man was bisexual or on the DL by the way they made love; they made love. They didn't worry about getting theirs or fucking a girl to death. They concentrated on the spirit, mind, body and soul. She grinned to herself as she thought that some of her girlfriend's men could take some lessons from their male peers.

The stylist pulled her out of her trance. "Keisha, it's time."

The dress was there waiting to be a part of her. She slipped it on and she knew this day was right; everything she wanted in her life was right here waiting for her approval. Last night she couldn't tell Tré yes, because of the hurt and the betrayal. Keisha sat there as the stylist had someone to retouch her hair and makeup. The stylist decided to replace the veil with a tiara and Keisha agreed. It was the icing on the cake. Keisha was flawless; and she had been transformed into something out of a magazine. She didn't look real; everyone was in awe as she waltzed downstairs. Junior got a glimpse of his mom and screamed, "Mommy you look beautiful." Everyone in the house was drooling; she definitely was a work of art. Keisha ran out of the house and looked back as she was rushed into the limo. She saw her family, her son, her brothers and also Tré's family. When she returned that night, they would all be connected, and as she was the knot that would make them one.

The limo drove past the airport, straight down 85 south until they were downtown. This was the check off point where, Keisha would move from the limo to the horse-drawn carriage. For a split second, Keisha thought she had seen the black sedan from the night before. She was afraid but was eager to see the man she would she share her life with. Tré was organized; he got lunch, drove himself from the room of the Ritz-Carlton and in less than thirty minutes he was at the church awaiting his bride to be. Tré finally met the special guests; Chante Moore and Kenny Lattimore. They would be singing at the wedding. It was indeed an indication of what a wedding should be.

CHAPTER 49

The Wedding – The Impossible Dream

Reverend Davens presided over the ceremony; he read scriptures from the old and new testaments of the bible. He encouraged people to pray for this new couple because everyone needed prayers. Everyone in the sanctuary laughed as everyone was trying to settle in and get ready for this harmonious occasion. The ringing of the bells indicated the ceremony of a lifetime was about to begin. The little girls rang the little crystal bells as the little boys carried the candles. Kennedy placed the rose petals strategically down the aisle in array of waves along the side of every pew. Junior looked dapper and all grown up as he strolled down the aisle with the rings on a soft satin pillow. Suddenly, as the wedding party was about to proceed down the aisle, from up above on the second level, Kenny Lattimore voice engulfed the entire church. The guest's heads went up with cheers and amazement. After he finished his signature song, Chante appeared near the front of the church and sang, With You I'm Born Again. The wedding party resumed their march down the aisle. Tré entered from the rear and marched nervously to the altar. Alongside him was his best man, with the ring and the rest of the wedding party. He thought about how he wanted to spend his life with Keisha. He knew there would be good times and hopefully not too many bad ones. He was excited about the fact that he would be a daddy again, and how he would do it right this time. He couldn't wait to see his future wife and forget about all the headaches and tears he'd endured. It was all worth it; last night was uplifting and his desire for men, hopefully, would eventually disappear. The desire for Lincoln or any other man would be no more. His wife would remedy all of this as she was indeed his sanctuary.

"Thank you, God for seeing me through all of this. A nigga couldn't do it without you. Thanks for seeing me through the battles I had to overcome. I love you, man. Thanks for looking out," he prayed, silently.

Finally everyone stood when they heard the wedding march of the bride. Kenneth was elected to walk his future daughter-in-law down the aisle and he was anxiously waiting for the carriage to appear, but it never did. After 10 minutes of waiting, K. Allen became impatient and radioed the driver of the limo, then the driver of the carriage. There was no answer to either. After moments of waiting, Tré thought about his recurring dream of Keisha not showing up. He became nervous and started to sweat heavily. His palms were sweaty as he looked on, first looking at Junior; he also was wondering where his mommy was. K. Allen called Nikko to the outside of the church, giving him the status of the limo driver and the missing carriage. The limo drove up as K. Allen and Nikko gave a sigh of relief, but Keisha was no where in sight. Everyone was getting antsy, even Z, Lake and Malia. The all got up at the same time and exited toward the front of the church. Every one looked confused as to what was going on. Lake called the precinct; he wanted an emergency APB on a horse drawn carriage. The dispatcher wanted him to repeat the last request. He looked at his cell with disgust.

"You heard me the first time."

Tré faintly heard that familiar voice.

"You stupid nigger, she ain't coming."

The voice echoed in his head like a scratched record player. The tears started to roll from Tré's cheeks on to his lapel. Junior, seeing his father cry, began to cry himself, not realizing what was going on; he did feel his father's hurt and also the absence of his mother. Cynthia grabbed Junior's head and forced it close to her heart. She wanted to spare him the humiliation his father was enduring.

Suddenly the doors of the church opened and there stood Keisha, a vision of light. She radiated with so much glow that everyone was blind for a moment; then the spirit of her presence smothered the room. She stood there for a moment awaiting her brother to come and escort her to the man of the hour. Tre couldn't believe his eyes; his heart screamed with anxiety. His heart skipped beats as his tears went from sad to ecstatic. The musician started to play and the guests stood simultaneously. Tre started his prayer to God; he wanted to beg forgiveness.

"My God, I've done a lot of bad things in my life. I know I done a lot of bad things to some good people and I know I done a lot of good things for some bad people. I know I put you through a lot in my life, and never gave you credit for pulling me through. God you know, I've been a drug addict and a drug dealer. I am a thug, a playa, a hood rat, a nigga of the streets, but I'm still your child. I am a child of God. I've been a fucked up father and not a good man when it came to Keisha. God please forgive me; please have mercy on my soul. I know my dream was to be with Keisha, I know I was supposed to be a good father to my son. I know my dream was possible. I know my life's experiences have taught me great lessons to teach my son. God, you touch my soul and captured my heart. You didn't give up on me when the world gave me their ass to kiss. I know I'm not the best, but I'm still your child. Please grant my wish and my dream and I promise I will make you proud of me and proud of my life."

Upcoming novels by Mykle-Kane

1 The sequel to Impossible Dreams...***Dream the Impossible!***

2 ***B. A. G. S. Black American Gigolos*** — The story of five strangers that find themselves entangled in a web of drugs, sex, money, crime and deceit. Lust and power keeps them in the game, but what will it take to get them out? Love, murder or God?

3 ***Fallen Angels***...Homosexuality in the church through the eyes of an eighteen year old preacher's son.

4 ***The Diary of Dannielle Green***...The story of a beautiful young woman that accidentally kills her step father at the age of fourteen for raping her. Now her past has come to meet her present, face to face (with a twist). You will never see it coming.